THE ASSASSIN'S WEAPON

BOOK 1 OF THE SA'NAR CHRONICLES

Nic M DiSalvo

The Assassin's Weapon / Nic M DiSalvo -- 1st ed.
ISBN 979-8-9890732-0-7

Dedicated to the one who helped me craft these characters over too many years and left us too soon.

Acknowledgements

I want to thank everyone who's dealt with my obsessive desire to get this book out into the world. Thanks for putting up with my countless edits, all the times I've been busy with "the story," and for all the encouraging words along the way.

I'd also like to thank the numerous critique partners, beta readers, and editors who've helped polish this into a reality.

As someone who lives a hectic, chaotic life beyond the pages, I appreciate how important a good escape is. I hope you enjoy reading this as much as I enjoyed writing it. Emphasis on writing it. Editing was a bitch.

Content Warning

The Assassin's Weapon is set in a version of our modern-day world and deals with... assassins. You should expect violence, death, a bit of gore, a touch of sex, and all the other fun tidbits that go along with a book focusing on people who kill for a living. Imagine John Wick teaming up with the X-Men to take down Resident Evil's Umbrella Corporation. It's written for adults but doesn't contain anything that should be considered too explicit. Of course, that's relative.

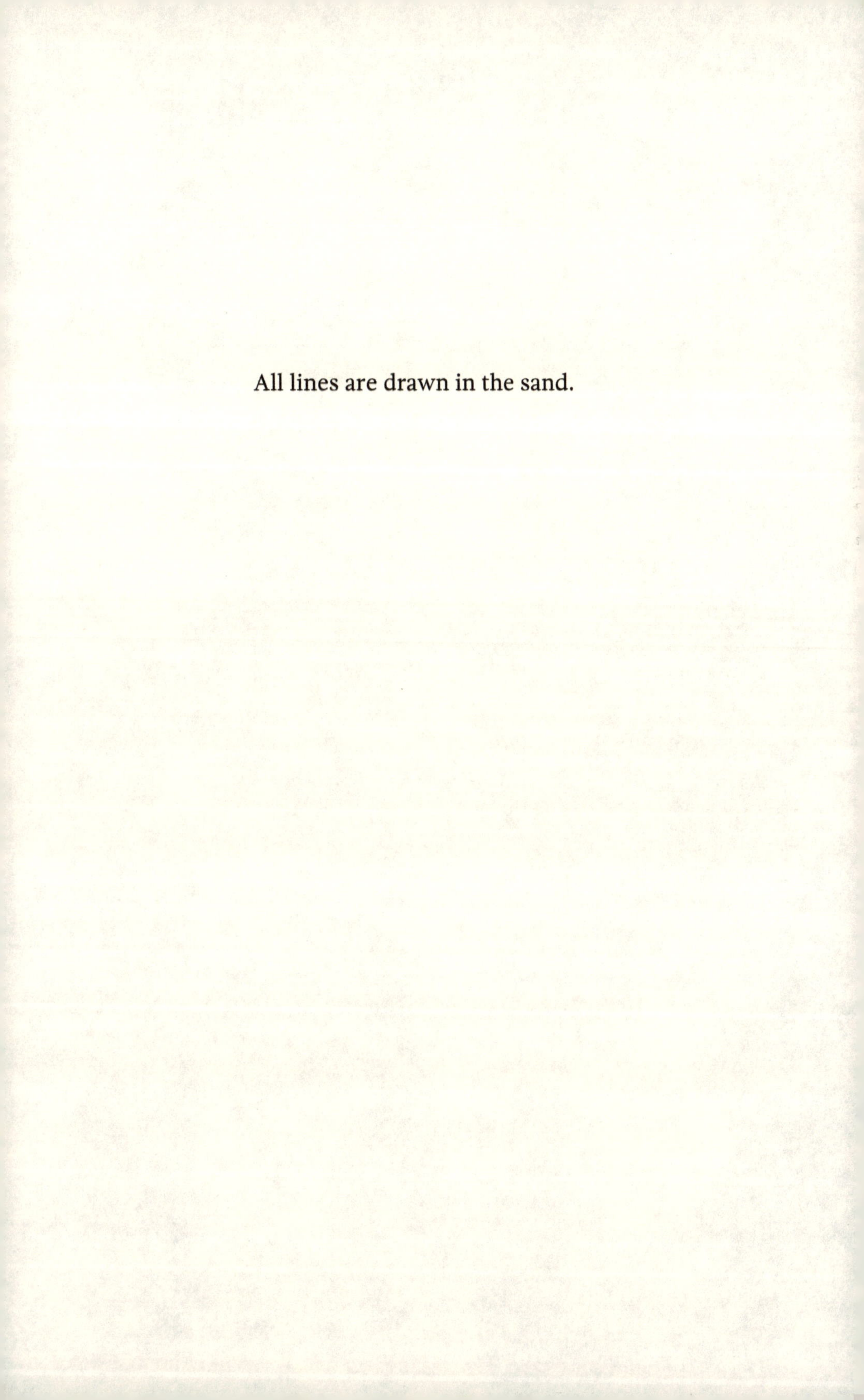

All lines are drawn in the sand.

PART I

CHAPTER 1

Dajah failed to study the life-sized glass maze before him; his eyes kept straying back to his brother. They had Taron restrained to a chair in a room filling with caustic, yellow liquid that bubbled and popped at the surface. A putrid stench reached Dajah's nose as he stood poised to enter. Scientists, embedded behind clipboards and tablets, sat near, observing.

An eternity passed before the light flashed GREEN.

"Hang in there!" he shouted to Taron, squeezing into the maze before the door fully opened.

Hand on the wall, he turned left. Right. Right again. A sizzling noise intensified. Darts flew past mere inches from his face as he dove, rolling back to his feet and continuing down the next corridor. His feet pounded the floor. His heart pounded his chest. Another left had him bracing for impact against the invisible surface. Dead end!

"Damn it," he cursed, pivoting only to find himself face-to-face with a set of serrated teeth. Smoke leaked from a smile. The Babdagoon was a grotesque monstrosity with appendages protruding out at odd angles and a whip-like tail capable of ensnaring prey. Towering over Dajah, its attack distorted spacetime.

Anticipating the strike, he propelled himself forward, flipping onto the creature to find purchase between two vertebral spikes. The

Babdagoon flailed and bucked in attempt to throw him, but his grip held firm even as its dexterous tail caught his leg, slicing through muscle and tendon.

Work faster!

Focusing on the back of its skull, Dajah stabbed with thumb and pointer finger. He dug in, pushing towards the soft, fleshy interior. Found the stringy bits connecting its brain to the rest of its body. The beast gave a desperate screech as he pulled. Cords ruptured like broken piano wires, springing back into wet tissues. With the link severed, the Babdagoon collapsed beneath him. Its death cry gave away his location.

A multitude of turns and quick maneuvering brought him to the center, his brother's cell, but it wasn't over yet. A series of geometric glyphs appeared on the window. An alarm sounded. Lights flashed and the maze walls began lowering. Soon all the creatures would come straight for him.

Sparing a moment to breathe, Dajah watched shapes slide and shift in his mind's eye, revealing the proper sequence. He repeated the movement on the surface, beasts closing in.

TEST COMPLETE, the computerized voice announced. Cages dropped. Thrashing growls declared the monsters' unanimous displeasure, but Dajah kept his eyes on his brother. The liquid drained too slowly. Scents of macerated, blistered flesh revealed Taron's condition before the wounds became visible, his clothing all but disintegrated.

Taron watched Dajah from the other side of the glass, mouthing the words: Knew you could do it. Where's Zayan?

Dajah took a heartbeat to consider their oldest brother's absence. The scientists loved studying them together. If Zayan wasn't in the maze, it meant something worse. Dajah balled his hands into fists, remembering the last time they injected Zayan with Stream radiation. How weak he was. How messed up after. How little he or Taron could do about it.

Movement caught his attention when men entered Taron's cell and checked his vitals. The silent barbarians exchanged head nods. In the blink of an eye, his brother was rolled away still shackled to his seat.

One of the scientists approached Dajah, sliding a tranquilizer gun through a small opening in the glass. "Get on with it," he commanded.

Tears welled in Dajah's eyes from the resulting sting. Seconds later he lost motor function, collapsing on the maze floor. His heart raced with a new kind of fear. Cold steel touched his skin. Weighted cuffs chained him to a sterilized surface. Bright overhead lights painted the room a harsh cream. Despite his body's unresponsiveness from the paralytic, he knew what came next: The needle prick.

A kiss of warmth pulsated through his veins, finding its rhythm in sync with his heart until every nerve blazed agony. Dajah released a blood-curdling wail as the Other breached the surface, pushing him under to drown in the deep recesses of his mind.

From fathomless depths he saw Zayan. Barely standing with the aid of a nearby wall.

"Get out of here! Run!" Dajah called, but no sound left his lips. He tried again. Failed. Willing himself to remain still, his legs betrayed him with each step not of his making.

Why? he demanded of the Other.

The Other lunged at Zayan. Colliding, their bodies crashed to the ground. Fragile bones broke upon impact. Dajah pleaded with the entity controlling him and the corners of his mouth turned up in a sinister expression, reflected on the polished floor.

"Know you can hear me, D," Zayan coughed out.

Tears spilled from Dajah's eyes, blurring the image unfolding. His fingernails pierced soft flesh. Hands squeezed, crushing as warm liquid oozed between his fingers. Choking gurgles. Gasps for air. Silence.

The Other roared in victorious triumph and Dajah drifted to depths unknown, his world shattered.

*

The wonderful aromas assaulting his airways brought reality into harsh focus. Sweet, lingering remains of burnt coffee offset blood and undercurrents of charred wood. Dajah shifted minimally to appreciate the weight of debris pressing against him. *Can't just lie here.*

~Why not? Maybe they'll come back to finish the job.~

He winced at the sound of her voice. Queen had gotten better over the years, but the memory was too fresh. Pain prickled the edges of his consciousness, souring his mood further. Odds were good everyone else was dead. *That's what happens when people get close to me.*

Queen knew better than to comment.

Knowing he had minutes before physical shock wore off, he surged adrenaline, hyper-tuning his senses. His ears picked up the faintest crack of rubble. The scent of a patron's cologne reached his nostrils. Strength increased ten-fold, and dull discomfort replaced all the acute stabbing sensations.

Dajah repositioned himself and gave a firm tug, releasing his arm from the damaged equipment. Skin tore. Aromatic vanilla and char wafted up as the espresso machine clanked into empty space. He stood up, pieces of the display counter peppering his casual attire. Not everything came away willingly.

So much for business as usual. This wasn't entirely unexpected, but he preferred to limit near-death experiences to bi-weekly occurrences. After last week's incident, this bordered on unlucky.

Opposite the mangled remnants of the bar rested one of his earlier guests, the man's neck bent at a bad angle. *Managed to keep hold of that latte, huh?* The biodegradable cup was crushed in his hand, three-quarters full.

~If you were more careful you could have avoided this. Told you to stop asking questions at the packing plant.~

Unhelpful, Queen.

He spared a few minutes to clear rubble from the base of the industrial-strength door and pried it open. Sugar and beans crunched beneath his shoes, but the small room was mostly unscathed. A different type of explosive would have leveled the coffee shop outright.

Was I the target?

Shaking his head, he remembered the low-fat, double shot, caramel macchiato handing him the envelope. *Should've opened it immediately.* He'd been distracted by the new kid hovering over the complimentary cookies. Whether the message was a clue or a warning relating to his current search, he'd never know. It was ash now.

~You were too obsessed over those cookies, Dajah.~

Hey, that was the best batch I'd made so far. Not like you'd understand.

Something heavy and metallic slumped in the front of the shop, causing a cascade of rubble. He yanked a chunk of glass from the muscle in his forearm, ready to launch it at the next fool to step through the door. Blood oozed from the raw wound. Dripped to the floor.

The din settled.

~You're jumpy. They're not going to come back that fast.~

Deep breaths did wonders.

Time for answers, then.

If there was one place in the city with the potential to deliver, it was the Raven.

———◇———

Peering through the telescopic sight, Kiera watched each variable line up with precision. The pad of her index finger brushed the trigger with feather-light pressure. Her target, Evelyn Francis, responsible for the biggest child trafficking ring on the East Coast, was leaving the grocery store with a paper bag in hand.

Every ounce of credible information confirmed the woman was human. The man accompanying her was not. Kitsune were known for their superb strength and speed whether in human, fox, or hybrid form. Having the pleasure and misfortune of knowing a dozen non-humans from her time at OPASA, Kiera kept interactions with them casual – no different from other ethnically diverse humans unless they ended up on the wrong side of her rifle.

Clouds eased across the sky. She adjusted for wind speed and then pulled against the two-stage weighted trigger. *Bye-bye, Evelyn.*

"Too easy," she said to no one, numb to the aftermath as she broke down her SR-25. Unfortunately, the target's mannerisms and appearance poked at old wounds. "Some days I really miss you, Mom, but I think you'd be happy with how things turned out."

The rise of the Organizations changed the face of law and justice forever. They weren't any less corrupt than the former government, but it meant people like her *could* make a difference. This job was flawless. She'd picked the perfect hide site – one floor down was a known government supporter who actively campaigned against the Organizations, wishing things would go back to the way they were. Kiera effectively eliminated two problems.

Sighing, she zipped her rifle case closed and left the roof.

Rad Tattoos catered to all tastes. These days you had humans wanting to appear more animalistic, non-humans wanting to stand out less, and mainstream society ranging from oblivious to accepting of the fact that a difference existed between the two.

The shop's owner and operator, Skullz, waved Kiera over as she made her way to the back. She rested her hand on a cocked hip and studied the clean-shaven, burly man covered in skeletal heads.

"Happy to see we're packed, but aren't you supposed to be closing early tonight?" she asked.

"They know we're closing at seven. Those waiting are here for consultations only. You'll have peace and quiet for the rest of the evening, but invitation's still open if you change your mind."

Kiera smiled. "Doing recon again. Wish your partner happy

birthday for me, though."

"Will do," Skullz said. His toothy grin negated his macho vibe instantly.

She pat him on the arm then continued to the door labeled Private. Once secured inside her loft, a spa-like atmosphere settled around her. She grabbed a bottle of water from the fridge. Being ahead of schedule meant time for a shower and a meal before heading out.

CHAPTER 2

Sipping a watered-down Malibu and Coke, Dajah observed the Raven's occupants. Groups mingled, some laughing, others opting for less crowded corners and more intimate conversations to flaunt their seedy standards. The Raven was the local Organization's attempt to create a neutral zone for anyone registered with them, and some version of it existed in every major city under Organization jurisdiction. Part dive bar, part wannabe cocktail lounge, the rules were simple: No unnecessary violence. Assassination attempts on the premises were expressly prohibited.

Most civilians knew the Raven's reputation. It wasn't uncommon to be solicited by a desperate man, woman, or nonbinary who couldn't afford the Organization's exuberant fees. Unsanctioned assassins and bottom-feeder mercs frequented the underbelly of every city. The difference was that contracts issued through Organization channels were *guaranteed*, and their professionals honored a code of conduct: Loyal to your own.

Registering with the local Organization the week after he arrived was risky, but it meant less interference in the long run. The monthly files allowed Dajah to identify fifteen different patrons within earshot. Information would always be the most valuable currency.

Lots of interesting tidbits for the right set of ears, but nothing on the shop getting blown up this morning.

~You stopped listening for that an hour ago. Who's the woman you keep staring at?~

The question brought the woman feigning intoxication back into focus. Kiera Lin. Muted peach lips sipped a glass of whiskey while she studied a group four tables over. He watched her empty that glass three times and refill it from the bottle she purchased. Several pieces of smooth, dark hair framed her face, the rest tied back. The low-cut white blouse offered a tease of cleavage from a well-proportioned chest. She was beyond attractive physically, but what interested him more was the fact that she seemed oblivious to the man at the bar. The one watching her too closely. The one sending texts.

~It's probably her ex. No one dresses like that to drink alone. Stay out of it.~

Nah, something else is going on.

~Not your business.~

Are you gonna stick around in my head all night?

~Someone has to keep an eye on you. Don't go over there.~

❖

Over the last two weeks, Kiera developed a relationship with the Raven's bartender consisting exclusively of her handing over a Benjamin in exchange for a bottle of JD. If she looked particularly haggard, Pete would throw in a fresh bowl of peanuts with her glass.

No peanuts tonight.

The type the Raven attracted tended to be amusing, but she hadn't been coming for the booze or the company. Two indiscreet men and a woman always sat at the same table. The Employer knew the men were selling information; the woman was the wildcard and potential link to another gang trying to set up shop in their not-so-fair city. All Kiera had to do was discern whom the woman reported to and eliminate both men.

Observation and experience taught her all three marks came armed, capable of protecting themselves, but professionals wouldn't meet in the same location more than once. Amateur hour droned on. She took another sip, wishing the bitter notes of chocolate and orange sliding down her throat had an effect.

Compared to non-humans, her abilities were subpar. Arguably-accelerated healing and a bloodstream that dissolved most foreign substances didn't give her an edge. Hard work and relentless training did that.

I'd still give my favorite rifle for a chance to get tipsy off a fifth.

She giggled at the thought, reinforcing her persona of regular Alcoholic. The crowds and loners usually read her body language and stayed away, but a few always pressed their luck.

The first charmer slid into the booth across from her without even so much as a hello.

Ballsy compared to most. Kiera dropped her right hand to her lap, close to the twin semi-auto SIG .45 ACPs strapped to her hips, and regarded him. "Seat's taken."

"By me now," he said. "No one was sitting here. You're kind of hot and looked lonely, so I thought—"

"You'd keep me company?" she cut him off, eyebrow raised. Head tilted with a faint smile, she gave him the courtesy of a once-over.

Silver hair hung loose, stopping just above his collarbone with choppy pieces framing the contours of a pronounced jawline and clean-shaven face. Most noticeable were his eyes. Vertically slitted pupils took center stage in pools of green that glowed with minuscule movements. Either he was part cat, or he invested in premium lenses to pull off the effect.

This one fits in with the Raven's more eclectic clientele.

Pale, soot-smudged skin gave the impression he made a piss-poor attempt at bathing with a rag. He raised his glass to salute her. Crescents of dirt marred the underside of his short nails. The jacket, jeans, and off-grey shirt were cleaner than he was, lacking any insignias or visible brand labels that suggested affiliations or status.

Starving Rock Musician?

She refrained from looking for a guitar case, but envisioned him on a stool, shredding his Fender in tight black leather pants and nothing else. Musing, she took another swig of whiskey.

"Seemed like a good idea," he said.

"Hate to tell you this, but it's a terrible idea. You should go find someone to keep company, though. What about her?" She sloshed the liquid in her glass, finger pointing to the young prostitute leaning over the bar, tits popping out as she laughed in response to something Pete said.

"Think I'll stay."

Kiera choked on her next sip of whiskey. The woman she was supposed to be watching disappeared, and the men were concluding affairs, preparing to leave.

Not their usual routine.

"Tell you what," she said to her admirer. "Keep this company. I'll be back in a few minutes." She placed the bottle halfway between them and left the booth with her glass.

The next charmer, clearly drunk, knocked her sideways on her way to the door.

"Hey!" she yelled, nearly dropping her glass.

"Fuck you, bitch. Watch where you're walkin'!" He glared as if daring her to say something back. Drawing one of her sleek, Legion Gray-finished beauties would make a statement, but pulling a gun was a surefire way to escalate a nuisance.

He reached for her arm.

"No!" she emphasized, deflecting his hand and delivering a knock-out blow to the temple. The now-unconscious drunk fell backwards, caught by her silver-haired admirer.

"Whoa there, friend," he said, taking the full weight of the man. "Think you had a bit too much. Have a seat." It was tactfully done, propping the man up in the booth as if he passed out there, and not an uncommon scene for the Raven. While he was preoccupied, she set her sights on the exit, set her glass down on the tray of a passing waitress, and slipped out.

"Hey, wait up," the same voice called when she gained the

doorway. "I wanna talk to you."

Kiera turned to face him, noting the .380 pistol resting loosely in his hand. At this range, she could disarm him or end him before he got off a lethal shot, but he didn't look ready to attack. That made him dangerous.

"Aren't you supposed to be watching my bottle?" she asked, playing it off cool.

"Your ass was more appealing."

The corners of her mouth lifted. "Do you have a name?"

"Dajah."

"Ok, Dajah, listen. I don't need a savior or company tonight. Find someone else."

"Your name's Kiera, right? Pretty sure people are trying to kill you."

CHAPTER 3

Crisp evening air stilled. Dajah breathed in the pungent, settling haze of gasoline and liquor outside the Raven. *It's going down any second. The Raven's protection doesn't extend past the front door.*

Kiera's hands found her hips. "People are trying to kill me? You're quickly losing your charm."

"We should go back inside and talk."

"Listen," she started.

Movement came from an unmarked SUV loitering double-parked.

"Might wanna get down," he said, sliding his index finger to the trigger guard of the firearm he lifted from the drunk.

"What?" She turned her head at the same time the first man exited the vehicle. Dajah shoved her into a parked Nissan, aimed, and squeezed off a single round as the gunman raised his weapon. The man took the hit, stumbled back, and regained his footing.

Body armor, huh? Guess I can't be lazy.

Assailants piled out of strategically placed vehicles at once. His next shot bore through the gunman's forehead. Consecutive shots took down two more. Acrid, sour gunpowder permeated the air.

Dajah crouched near Kiera. A staccato percussion of relentless gunfire ensued, pelting concrete. Dinging metal. The Nissan's windows shattered, raining glass down on them. Another bullet ricocheted off the Raven's brick exterior.

That'll set them off.

Like clockwork, the Raven's personal security joined the melee instantly, some firing from the roof, others rushing out the door to defend their establishment.

Whether Kiera realized she was the target or not, she never hesitated in pulling one of her concealed firearms. One assailant grabbed his neck as her bullet pulverized crucial arteries. Another dropped mid-trigger-pull with a hole through the side of his head. The way she sighted, fired, and recovered fascinated Dajah. Everyone carried a gun these days, but watching a true marksman in action was like watching a fish navigate clear waters – effortless.

~On your right!~

Turning at Queen's warning, Dajah felt the one-two punch near his shoulder coming from the wrong direction. Annoyance and rage incited a surge of excess energy from his core. *What the hell was that for?!* He threw his open palm out. A blast of blue-green energy shot forth, sending the shooter flying backwards with a softball-sized rent through his chest.

Queen's silence confirmed he'd made his point. Dajah reined in his emotions, knowing they could kill quicker than the enemy when your ass was on the line. Switching the gun to his right hand, he raised the barrel level with the next target.

The attackers cut their losses. Some piled back into their vehicles and peeled away. Others, trapped in the shootout, fired indiscriminately at anyone that moved. The Raven's security took the brunt of that gunfire, lobbing it back passionately.

"We need to get out of here!" Kiera yelled. Vivid hazel eyes locked onto his. "Come with me." She cleared the space between bumper and fender with another easy shot and took off running.

~Don't go with her, Dajah.~

Fuck off. You got me shot.

◇

Slowing to a jog in the side alley, Kiera scaled the chain-linked fence that partitioned off a block of dilapidated buildings. Heated arguments bellowed from a second-story unit. Music reverberated from another level, punctuated by clouds of weed and incense.

This street should stay deserted tonight in case things get ugly. Cops would respond to the shootout in due time, but they'd take a roundabout way to the Raven. Nu Philly had been under Organization jurisdiction for the last fifteen years. Law enforcement only showed up so taxpayers could keep their illusions of who was in charge.

Kiera knew this section well, slipping inside one of the vacant units. The jammed door presented the perfect opportunity – Dajah kept up.

"Help me with this," she said.

He stepped up to try the door and she leveled her gun at the back of his head. His hand paused midway to the knob and dropped back down by his side as if he sensed it. *Least he's smart enough to stay still.*

"Explaining time," she said. "Better hope I like your answers. You said people were trying to kill me. Are you one of them?"

Dajah sighed without any threatening movements. "No. I've had a shitty day. Saw what was going down, and for God knows what reason thought I should do something about it."

"What are you talking about?"

"The two men with the woman at the center table, four rows from the windows. You were watching them. Someone else was watching you. Happen to be standing right next to him when he sent his texts. Really, you should be thanking me."

Her core tightened. The mere suggestion of a setup raised warning flags all over her last few trips to the Raven. Putting additional pressure on the trigger, she reminded herself to never waste a bullet. "Turn around."

In the dimmer lighting, Dajah's pupils stayed wide until he scowled at her and they constricted back into cat-like slits. "On a different day I might take the contract on you, but I didn't come for that tonight. My shop got blown up with me inside it hours ago. Shoot me or get that damn gun out of my face!"

So much for cheesy pick-up lines.

Lowering her SIG meant nothing, so she humored him. Even took a few steps back. "So you're one of those mercenaries stupid enough to go after the Organization's assassins?" They all had contracts on their heads; Kiera made it a habit *not* to go crazy checking the databases. As long as they stayed in the Organization's good graces, only scumbags tried to cash in on the rare occasion.

"I'm not going after anyone's assassins. I own a coffee shop that was targeted. Went to the Raven hoping for answers." He must have realized how pathetic that sounded because he laughed afterwards. Then winced. "Look, just get out of here. Watch your back."

Kiera considered the man before her. Dark stains spread through his jacket. Only one of the bullet holes went clear through his back. She opened her mouth to comment and shut it when he dropped his pistol.

"Or stand there all night and stare," Dajah said, applying pressure to his wounds. Blood oozed around his fingers.

She'd seen the energy blast, confirming he was non-human. That didn't make him immune from bleeding out. Huffing, she holstered her SIG. "I'm not gonna leave you like this. Might not be happy about it, but you did try to save my life. I've got a car parked two blocks away."

"Gonna drop me off at the hospital?" he laughed.

"No, I'm gonna dig the remaining bullet out of your chest."

"Why?"

"Because if what you say is true, I need to know who sent those men."

"And?"

"And if you were from around here, you'd know most companies use marked ammunition. Some even dip their rounds in poison."

"Great."

◇

Passing out was one of those things Dajah made a habit of doing only when out of immediate danger. He drifted to tires on asphalt and the whoosh of passing cars but clung to consciousness. Too soon forward motion stopped. He cracked an eye and reassessed his body.

Stiff, sore, functional. Not poisoned.

~She was lying.~

You got me shot, remember? Not *Kiera. Go. Away.*

Kiera slammed her door shut then opened his. Somewhere nearby, late-night food vendors fried up greasy indulgences.

"You're not dead yet and I'm not carrying you," she said, grabbing his arms. Before she dragged him across the sidewalk, Dajah sat up and exited the vehicle on his own.

"Why are we at a tattoo parlor?"

She removed a key from her pocket in response.

Inside, Kiera guided him to one of the artist's chairs. He was only a few inches taller than her. The extra support helped now that unbuffered pain made movement unpleasant. She left him to turn on every light at once, evoking another wince and forcing him to shield his eyes.

"Sorry," she said, "but I have to be able to see. Take your jacket and shirt off."

"You know, if I'm taking my clothes off, I expect my partner to do the same."

Not a single drop of humor surfaced in her expression.

"Alright, alright," he said, hands held out in appeasement. Removing the jacket was easy. His shirt had to be peeled off the level of his newest injuries – a sharp reminder that bullets weren't the only things to mar his skin.

One building explosion and a shootout in less than twenty-four hours might be a new record.

Kiera brought over a first aid kit and paused.

"Really like staring at me, huh?" he asked.

Levity edged onto her face. "I'm just impressed. Most people would take better care of themselves *before* going out to try and pick up women."

He assumed she referenced his wounds and not the countless scars. Dajah's body was genetically optimized with all the lean muscles of a martial artist. That wouldn't change, even if he spent every night eating takeout and gorging himself on cookies. *One of the benefits of Caerus's Weapon program.*

~Sit on your ass for a month, eat like that, and see what happens.~

"Was there for information, remember?" he said, easing into the chair while pointedly ignoring Queen.

"Yes, I remember distinct comments about my ass. Not sure how that information was gonna help you."

"Hey, you told me to come with you."

Shaking her head, Kiera angled the nearest light at his chest and picked out a set of hemostats. "Might hurt. Want me to numb this first?"

"No, just get it done."

Seconds into her exploration of the first wound, Dajah's hands clenched the armrests. His pain receptors operated in two modes – on or off – and without a boost of adrenaline to compensate for exhaustion, every tug and twist of instrument triggered micro-reactions in the abused tissues. The mushroomed-out projectile came free with a wet plop. Kiera handed him a wad of gauze and he pressed it into the hole while she studied her prized identifier.

"Happy now?" he asked.

She dropped the bullet on a metal tray. "We're not done. There's more than ammunition in your skin. Give me your arm."

He hadn't bothered to remove all the splinters of glass, wood, and metal still riddling his flesh from the explosion. That kind of work required time, and Dajah didn't want to be there when the police finally did show up.

Kiera took his arm, plucking out the first piece of glass. "What happened to you again?"

"Told you," he said, groaning. A thin piece of shrapnel twinged a nerve on the way out, numbing his fingers. "My shop was blown up. With me inside it."

"Guess that explains some of this." Without asking, she started unraveling the bandage covering his elbow to mid-bicep. Hazel eyes stared, slack-jawed. "Bandages work better when you remove all the shit from your wounds first."

"Yeah, well, I was in a hurry."

"How long you been in the city for?"

"Couple mon— Fuck!" Alcohol saturated the gaping wound, frying every shredded tendon and exposed nerve in agony. His vision swam. Relentless throbs occupied the forefront of his thoughts.

She placed an adhesive pad over the injury. "If you're not more careful, you're not gonna last around here. Take off your pants."

"Huh?"

"Your pants." Kiera motioned to his legs with her hemostats. "Take them off."

"Odd way to get me naked."

"Don't flatter yourself. Keep your underwear on, provided you're wearing any. There's dried blood all over your left calf. From the pattern, I can only assume you did another half-assed job. I didn't come this far to let you bleed to death from stupidity."

He laughed. *Should have seen me after the last city.*

~If you didn't abandon your Beads, you could have healed already.~

Relinquishing magic had its downside, but his body would heal soon enough and he wasn't about to justify anything to Queen.

"If you insist," he said, kicking off his shoes. Waistband unbuttoned, he slid his jeans down. Her eyes followed the movement, widening. Socks matched black boxer briefs, but Kiera's attention was on the colorful bruises trailing down his hip to another bloody bandage.

"Jesus, Dajah, how are you walking on this?"

"Doesn't hurt as bad as it looks."

"If you say so."

I'm sure it's gonna hurt like hell real soon.

He wasn't wrong. Kiera's ministrations seemed to last hours. It was actually a few intense minutes. Afterwards, he observed her work, satisfied with her application of first aid but convinced his body ached worse now than it did after the explosion.

"We keep spare clothes in the back," she said. "I'll get you something that isn't covered in blood. In the meantime, put all this into one of the metal waste bins." She motioned to his discarded clothes and the pile of bloody gauze.

Gathering everything as instructed, Dajah surveyed the empty tattoo parlor. One of the wall pieces – a stylized wolf and forest – made him think of Taron. Fondness followed in the wake of memory, soothing pain.

Those were good times, but it should have been all three of us.

Dajah realized his hands formed fists and relaxed them. *Caerus is here somewhere. I'll find them. They'll pay.*

"Lucas's work," Kiera said, returning with a pair of oversized sweatpants and a loose tee shirt. "Thinking about getting a tattoo?"

He put on a half-smile for show and took the clothes. "Maybe next time."

While he dressed, Kiera snatched a matchbook from the artist's station and lit the entire thing.

"That's gonna smell horrible," he said, anticipating what she'd do with it.

"Don't like leaving things around with blood on them. Need me to call you a cab?" Alcohol accelerated the blaze as soon as the matchbook hit the waste bin, and the scent brought immediate flashbacks of his coffee shop.

"Nah, I can find my way home from here. Thanks for the help."

"Thanks for the bullet."

"You're welcome, though I'm pretty sure you enjoyed digging in my skin and ogling."

"Is that what you're calling saving you from tetanus?"

"Touché," Dajah smirked. "If you find out what asshole's connected to that bullet, stop by my shop and let me know."

"Why?"

"I owe him for interrupting our evening. All the best dancing happens after ten."

He got a smile out of her. Kiera was a nice distraction, even if their interaction was more pain than pleasure, but she had her own problems to deal with.

Offering a farewell wave, Dajah made his way out the door and didn't look back. He had work to do.

CHAPTER 4

Ethan donned the attire of his Sect in preparation for arrival. His hands and fingers traced a series of mudras in the air, and an oval distortion appeared before him. Stepping through the shimmer, he was instantly transported into a dimly lit space.

Alarms sounded.

Three Guardians rushed in, staves raised, guns at their hips. Ethan hadn't seen a firearm in some time. He studied the men brandishing such weapons – young, untested warriors. They didn't know him, but they recognized the gold and blue tunic over black trousers designating him as a Master. Stances relaxing, they bowed their heads in proper greeting.

"Welcome, Master," the youngest said. "Please allow us the honor of escorting you to the receiving room as is customary."

The leather soles of his boots tread silently along smooth tiles leading out of the grotto. It was one of the few locations for hundreds of miles where a portal could be opened. Or so they were taught. The Teachers crafted illusions and proffered half-truths to maintain control with the best of them. He wondered how often anyone still used the grotto.

The receiving room held few comforts. Six high-backed chairs stood as sentinels, representing the Great Teachers who founded their Sect to ensure abominations never threatened the integrity of the realms. In front of those chairs was a round table and stools

– the meeting place of the Teachers. As Ethan and the Guardians entered from one end, doors opened opposite them to admit three elders he knew well.

Accepting their invitation with a two-finger mudra and a bow, Ethan selected an equidistant stool from them. "Thank you, Teachers."

The Guardians stood back. They were neither required to depart nor invited to stay. He imagined curiosity held them steadfast.

"Master Ethan," Teacher Rayur began, "it has been some time since you departed for the Realm of Novusia. We sensed your acquired essence as soon as the portal opened. Share your accomplishments with us."

He pushed up the sleeves of his tunic, ensuring his arms were exposed. Symbols lit up in his flesh. Twelve different colors outlined individual designs – a living reminder of abominations slayed. With each death, many of their abilities became his. Strengthening and enlightening him.

Shocked gasps escaped the mouths of two Guardians. Ethan recalled a time when he was much younger, training hard in preparation for his future. Back then, the record for kills belonged to a woman known as the Preserver. She had sixteen unique colors to her name when most were lucky to count five. Unless something changed while he was gone, that record still held.

He'd break it.

"You honor us with these accomplishments," Teacher Gavin said.

"Have you returned to offer your services as Teacher?" Rayur asked.

"Respectfully, no," Ethan said. "I've been tracking an abomination in Novusia for some time. She found a way into this realm. I'm here to claim her essence."

"You have the full support of the Sect," Teacher Lydia said, eldest and head of all Teachers. "Take as much time as you require adjusting back. Any resources you need will be provided.

We'll inform you at once if the Collective registers any essence spikes."

The Collective – withered and decaying corpses with bulbous skulls maintained in a nutrient-rich liquid. Every Master possessed the ability to pick up energy signatures from the abominations within a certain radius, but the Collective could scan continents. Though powerful, their abilities were limited to this realm. Any confirmed essence spikes were passed to the Teachers. The Teachers then chose who they'd inform.

It wasn't a competition, but it meant anyone trying to break the Preserver's record had to be in the right place at the right time or hunt in one of the other two realms. The number of abominations came far and few between these days.

"Thank you, Teachers," Ethan said. The glow of his symbols faded, dissolving into minimally scarred flesh. Elizabeth's days were numbered. When she showed herself to the Collective, he'd be ready.

CHAPTER 5

Dajah indulged, eating all the whipped cream from his frozen mocha-coffee concoction. Then he requested more to top it off – his reward for a job well done.

Definitely making these once the shop's up and running again.

It'd taken three days for the cops to clear the scene, writing the explosion off as a gang-related incident. Mr. Latte was the intended target, but the hit wasn't an Organization contract. They'd never accept collateral damage – four people died, and Dajah was lucky to get away.

A single vibration encouraged him to check the banking app on his phone. 7:03 a.m. The full payment was transferred. Coincidentally, several café patrons turned their attention to the TV in the corner.

'Breaking News: Tragedy at the Von Arias estate. Multiple deaths reported. Further updates as information becomes available.'

He refused to hide the grin splitting his face.

~That job wasn't a challenge, Dajah. It doesn't take skill to kill people in their sleep.~

No, but it takes foresight to time it appropriately. No one else would have done it that way.

~Because no one else is up scouring those databases all hours of the night. They're doing things they're supposed to be.~

Don't go there, Queen. Money is for the coffee shop.

~So you can go back to baking cookies and mixing syrup in blenders for strangers? Did you forget why we're here?~
    How could I?

He pulled the supply-laden rental truck around the side of his shop and stared at the newest vandalization.

"Downside of choosing a shitty neighborhood."

Pulling down the yellow-black caution tape, Dajah stepped inside and surveyed the damage. Napkins and flour littered the floor. Hints of aerosolized paint lingered. Any equipment not already destroyed was smashed or stolen. He spotted the double oven missing the front door and slammed his fist against the wall. A bottle of cinnamon popped open, pouring out with his patience.

Queen was pleased, though. To her, the shop was an unnecessary distraction. She didn't understand the nuances of Dajah's work. Free Wi-Fi that screened any device linked to the network had provided plenty of useful information.

~If it was so useful, why haven't you found them yet?~

He grit his teeth, preparing for the cleanup.

Once the windows were boarded up properly, Dajah sorted through the rubble, separating trash from anything salvageable. He was in the back when an unlikely sound reached his ears. *Of course the door chime survives.*

"We're closed!" he yelled, carrying his push broom.

"So my savior knows how to sweep," said a familiar voice. Kiera stood in the entrance, smile fleeting. "No one's helping you clean this up?"

"Sweeping keeps me in shape. You here to help?" Compared to his work trousers and long-sleeved shirt, Kiera dressed stylishly. Skinny-leg jeans and a loose, V-neck blouse complimented her physical features. The dual hip holsters obscured by her coat complimented her profession. Open carry was legal as long as you held an Organization ID; Dajah preferred knives and fists to firearms.

"Not exactly. I have some information."

He motioned her into the back and pulled out one of the functional chairs to the break room table. "Have a seat. Bottled water's the only thing I can offer right now."

"Thanks, but I'm good," she said, opting for the chair facing the doorway. "If I ask you a question, will you answer honestly?"

Dajah joined her. "You wanna know if I was involved."

"No, I want to know why you helped."

"Besides the fact that part of me enjoys screwing up someone else's plans?" He smirked. "You looked too good to die."

Kiera stared like she was deciding whether to be flattered or skeptical, but a hint of amusement surfaced in the uptick of her lips. "Since you're invested, I've got a job offer."

"Have you even read my file?"

"Yes. A few nonspecific skills, amateur rating... You won't get access to better contracts until the Organization sees what you're capable of."

"Doesn't sound like much to go off. What makes you think I can help you?"

She gave him a flat, level stare.

"Alright. What's the job?"

"Julius Matthews runs a company called OPASA – Organized Protection and Asset Security Affiliates. I need him dead. Few professionals would accept a contract on him because of his clout in the Organization, so I'm not bothering to make it official."

"You mean you don't want him to know you're gunning for him. He set you up?"

"He issued the new contract. You mentioned it, so I'm sure you're aware I'm wanted *alive*."

"One-point-five million's a lot of money to take someone alive. They're offering half that for your corpse." Kiera wouldn't have her cohorts hunting her, but the Organization wouldn't go out of its way to protect her, either. Even if she was one of their top snipers.

"That contract went out two days before we met. You'll

understand if I'm suspicious. The analysis of the bullet confirmed OPASA's involvement. Julius and I have a history. He knows as well as I do that the fastest way to cancel a contract is to eliminate the one who issued it. He'll expect me to come after him. Or run."

"And you're not a runner," he guessed. "If this guy wants you alive, why were they shooting at you?"

"Think about it, Dajah."

"...they were shooting at me."

She nodded, tracing a spray-painted dick on the table. "Which makes it less likely you're involved."

"So let me get this straight, you wanna hire me to take out OPASA's CEO. A job you've admitted only a fool would take."

"I said only a *few* would take it. OPASA's been in bed with the Organization for years, helped them overthrow the government, but you're a nobody to them. You can get closer to Julius than anyone else."

"How?"

~You're not actually considering this.~

"Employment," Kiera said. "OPASA has code names for select positions. Show up at their front door, drop the right name, and there's a good chance Julius will interview you on the spot."

"And the catch?"

"It's secure. You'd never walk out alive if you attempt anything, and you'll never reach him with any weapons."

Dajah laughed, leaning back in his chair. "This sounds like a terrible job. Why would anyone take it?"

"Because Julius Matthews is a monster, and the world would be a better place without him."

"I'm not here to make the world a better place."

"But you can understand," she countered. "Some of the scars on your body are too precise to be accidents. I know an experiment when I see one. I used to work for OPASA. What they force their employees to endure is inhumane at best. At worst," she trailed off, shaking her head. "Whatever he wants with me now, I won't let him get his hands on me again."

"Now you sound desperate." Unfortunately, he *could* relate.

Her shoulders slumped. "Just limited. If you're not interested, say so and I'll walk away."

~Tell her to walk away.~

Dajah drummed his fingers on the table.

~No.~

We have zero leads.

~This isn't a lead.~

Might be.

"OPASA experiments on their employees? What kind of experiments?" he asked.

Kiera's slouch improved. "Body transformations, genetic enhancements, biological weapons research and development…"

Sounds like Caerus. Not a stretch to assume they supply OPASA. He ceased his drumming and leaned forward. "I'm willing to hear your plan in more detail, but I won't risk my life unnecessarily."

Brow furrowed, Kiera tilted her head. "Didn't you already do that when you followed me out of the Raven?"

~She's got a point, Dajah.~

Are you taking her side now?

"This is business, that was pleasure," he said with a smirk. "I don't make a habit out of risking my life unnecessarily."

"Then we have a deal?"

"Almost. We can work out the logistics later. There's something you need to help me with first."

"What?"

Dajah left the table and grabbed the spare broom, ignoring her hands moving to her lap. "You're helping clean the rest of this up – my starting price for hearing you out. Know how to use this thing?"

Snorting, she stood and snatched the broom from him. "How hard could it be?"

"All depends on how you handle it," he grinned. "Come on."

CHAPTER 6

Julius Matthews studied the naked woman before him. She'd been his guest for over two weeks, and he knew so little. Eyewitness reports claimed she fell out of the sky soaking wet. It didn't take his men long to find her. The mystery lay in the fact that Sasha Bekarda called personally, asking him to investigate. The woman's arrival triggered a Stream spike unlike anything they'd reportedly seen before. Sasha suggested it was related to worsening geological events, but she was giving him the company line. She had no idea a woman was behind the disturbance until he told her.

Delicate symbols scarred the surface of the woman's skin, leading Julius to suspect she belonged to some primitive tribe. The lightly tanned flesh and blonde hair reminded him of a less-toned version of his wife. Like any *thorough* scientist, he ran samples of her blood and tissue through the main database.

"Why are you doing this?" she asked, voice a scratchy whisper. Piercing blue eyes met his.

"We've gone over this, Elizabeth. You don't belong here. Your DNA betrays the lies you've insisted on repeating over and over. We have extensive databases with hundreds of thousands of species on file. The closest you come to matching any is five percent. And that five percent matches a string of junk DNA only found in one other." He moved closer, fingertips tracing the markings up a taut stomach, around a supple breast. "Not one species, mind you, one *individual*."

"Just let me go," she insisted, turning away. She'd gained some strength back since their interlude.

Elizabeth wasn't willing to indulge him sexually, but that didn't stop Julius from interrogating her in a variety of ways. An assortment of vials and bottles lined the counter. However, experimenting without Dr. Ashley present always carried a risk.

"How'd you get here?" he asked, selecting one of the compounded solutions.

"I woke up here," she whispered. "I don't remember anything before that."

The same lies. Julius injected the liquid into the IV port in her arm.

"Please," she pleaded.

He stroked her hair, admiring her abused body. "It's possible you remember nothing since we don't understand the nature of your arrival—"

"It's true!"

"—but I'm not convinced. We'll try again in a few minutes." Setting the empty syringe aside, he applied sensors to key locations on her flesh. Elizabeth closed her eyes. If he couldn't get satisfying answers, he could at least satisfy himself by breaking her.

Julius flipped the switch. A continuous wave of electricity sent her muscles into spasms. Her teeth clenched, jaw locking up in a way that prevented her from screaming.

An eerie satisfaction came from watching her naked body writhe in silence. The monitors indicated a substantially elevated heart rate. Elizabeth's blood pressure continued to rise, as did her core temperature. When she reached the limits of what a normal human could withstand, he allowed the experiment to inch past the threshold then shut off the current.

She deflated, breathless and unresponsive.

"Such a waste." Julius picked up the clipboard to tick off boxes. These experiments garnered minimal intel without Kiera for comparison.

A mewling noise escaped Elizabeth's lips with a trickle of blood. Then a gasp brought her back to life. The markings on her flesh began to glow a faint orange. Julius's eyes widened. He set the clipboard down and brushed his fingertips along a line of symbols on her thigh. They shimmered in response.

"Fascinating!"

◆

The knock came while Ethan was laying out another outfit. After living in the youngest realm of Novusia for so long, where travel was done by foot, horse, or carriage, and fabric was homespun and tailor-made, the middle realm of Aetatisia felt too...commercialized. The Guardians brought him a plethora of clothing appropriate for most situations, but the new fabrics were stiff and scratchy. It'd take days to wear-in even the softest pair of jeans.

He'd grown up here, but a lot had changed in the twenty years he spent hunting abominations in Novusia. Ethan remembered a world run by governments. Now it was run by Organizations and companies with influence. Technology certainly improved – cell phones evolved from bulky nuisances to streamlined pieces of equipment capable of taking pictures, tracking precise GPS locations, and accessing the internet with the push of a button. And *those* features came standard. People used 'gender identifiers.' Racial inequity no longer centered on the color of one's skin, but on whether an individual was a true human or non-human. That was perhaps one of the biggest changes – getting used to non-humans functioning in everyday society when they previously kept to the shadows and everyone else pretended they only existed in fairytales.

Given a choice, Ethan would pick Novusia every single time. The air was cleaner. The skylines weren't disrupted by massive buildings and smog. And the noise... He couldn't imagine someone like Elizabeth surviving in one of the megacities like Nu

New York or Nu Tokyo for more than a day. Everything was so *loud* in Aetatisia.

By contrast, he'd only ventured to the oldest realm, Veterisia, once. It was a tomb, a dead wasteland that served as a potent reminder of what would befall the other two should the Sect of Preservation fail.

The Teachers assured him that their mission remained the same, and that the people of this realm remained clueless to the existence of the Trinity of Realms. Novusians had their legends, but the ability and means to travel between realms was a closely guarded secret. As far as Ethan was aware, only the Sect taught it.

A knock brought his thoughts back to the present. Answering the door, he found a young Guardian waiting.

"Master Ethan, the Teachers have a location for you."

"So soon?"

"Teacher Lydia says it will remain exclusively yours for seventy-two hours."

"Inform the Teachers I'm grateful and will be along shortly."

With a head bow, the Guardian departed.

Ethan perused his clothing choices once more and selected a set of dark wash, relaxed-fit denim that most closely resembled his favorite Novusian trousers. A khaki, long-sleeved Henley would attire his upper half, and the wool pea coat should suffice for outwear in most North American and European cities this time of year. If the Collective sent him somewhere tropical, he'd have to rethink everything.

Teacher Lydia had an envelope in hand when he arrived.

"May your journey be swift and your reward bountiful," she said.

Ethan took the offered envelope with a bow, noting its weight.

"Transportation has been arranged," Lydia added. "Inform Widget when you're ready to depart. She'll drive you to the airport."

"The Teachers are ever gracious. Many thanks."

Having relied on horses and his feet for so long, modern

transportation was a true luxury. Ethan packed his satchel with a few comforts. The memoir, a copy of the original notes given by the First Teacher to the founding Sect, was more talisman than reference or reading material. He'd grown up with the book, gifted to him by Teacher Lydia when he was only an ambitious Guardian, and missed its presence greatly during his time in Novusia. It was said certain materials didn't hold up well to portal crossings. He'd never risk carting it through the realms, but now that he was back, it'd stay by his side indefinitely.

The cell phone supplied in Lydia's envelope and a small carving kit joined the memoir in the satchel, and Ethan made posthaste for the garage. Whatever forced Elizabeth to use her abilities was a boon in disguise, but it did leave him wondering. She knew he could sense her when she flared her powers – it was how he tracked her.

"She must think coming here protects her from us," he said quietly.

"What was that, Master Ethan?" Widget asked.

"Nothing, just thinking out loud."

"What terminal am I dropping you off at?"

Ethan pulled out the phone and held it up to his face, waiting for the screen to light up. After a moment of nothing happening, Widget glanced back. "Master Ethan, the encrypted iPhone 32s require both your handprint *and* an iris scan. You need to hold the back of the phone in your palm when you look at it to unlock it."

"Right," he said, adjusting his grip. The screen clicked on. With few apps loaded on the device, he found the digital flight ticket easily enough. "Domestic. Terminal A."

While Widget drove, he pulled up a general map on the phone. There were five major cities within a few hours' drive from the old JFK International Airport he'd be flying into. Four of them were under Organization jurisdiction. Elizabeth could be in any one of them by the time he arrived. The congestion of a city would make it harder to pinpoint her until he was close enough.

Regardless, he expected a call from the Teachers after landing.

Widget pulled up along the stretch of doors for Departures. "Good luck, Master Ethan."

"Thanks for the ride." He exited the vehicle and allowed himself a moment to marvel at the intricate machinations that both simplified and complicated modern man's life. The airport was organized chaos at its finest. He could use his phone to have a pizza delivered to his exact location within fifteen minutes, but airport security still had people funneled through turnstiles and metal detectors. And they *still* had to take their shoes off.

"As much as things change, they stay the same," he said to himself. His little carving kit would never make it through security, and he wasn't about to risk anyone confiscating it. Like the memoir, it held more than practical value – something he'd picked up during his first venture into Novusia. Ethan found his way to the long-term storage lockers before submitting himself to monotony.

CHAPTER 7

OPASA's high-rise headquarters occupied half a city block, and everything above the third floor required authorized access. For a company that prided itself on security, Dajah was surprised at how easily he acquired a meeting with Julius Matthews.

The path to Matthews's office consisted of two checkpoints with an elevator in between. Dajah's escort, a man who never bothered introducing himself, was dressed in a tailored suit. Obnoxiously polished, gold cufflinks caught the light every time he raised his hand to stroke his well-groomed, bushy hipster beard.

And that makes nine times he's stroked it since the waiting room.

Dajah sported a more professional look at Kiera's suggestion. His matching pants and suit jacket were black, and the heather grey button down stayed untucked, tieless.

A cute brunette manned the desk. Her open jacket and blouse were risqué compared to the bland white-and-red uniforms of the receptionists on the ground floor. *She's armed.*

~So's the man that brought you up here.~

Yeah, but he's lost in his thoughts. It's the happy ones you gotta worry about.

"Mr. Matthews is finishing up a conference call and will be with you shortly," the receptionist said with a cheery smile.

Dajah nodded, taking a seat. Camera placement was obsessive, but he didn't come across anything too difficult to bypass, and the ghost tech secreted in his jacket hadn't set off alarms. It was a point of contention between him and Kiera. She worried OPASA's security would discover the surveillance microtech the instant it tried to broadcast anything back, if not sooner. He assured her the man who created it fooled systems far more advanced than anything OPASA had. Of course, that left her with other questions... like what he was doing here to begin with.

~You shouldn't have told her about Caerus.~

I mentioned the name. She didn't recognize it.

~You did more than mention the name, Dajah.~

She needed a good reason for why I agreed to do this. We are looking for a supplier of biological weapons.

~I don't trust her.~

You don't trust anyone.

A male voice sounded over the intercom. "Gwen, is my next appointment ready?"

Gwen picked up, exposing a flash of holster on her left side. "Yes, Mr. Matthews. Shall I send him in? ...right away, sir." She waved to Dajah.

Stepping through the automatic oak doors, Dajah entered a space appropriate for one of OPASA's higher-ups. Matthews's office sported a wall of windows that towered over most of the surrounding buildings. A few high rises in the distance could be used by an exceptional sniper, but the hallmark refraction in the glass meant the first two shots wouldn't penetrate.

Desk's out of direct line of sight anyway.

A whiff of cedar and grapefruit cologne hit as Dajah approached the ornate furniture and sized up the man behind it. He was an identical match to all the images of Julius Matthews, right down to the faint scar above his left ear. If this were a shapeshifter posing for the real CEO, Dajah'd find out soon enough. Shifters always failed at replicating the nuances of their mimic target.

The man rose from his chair, height and well-muscled

physique on display as he offered a hand. Vibrant red and yellow stones peaked out beneath his opposite jacket sleeve, easily mistaken for common jewelry.

And there's our lead. Caerus loves gifting Earth Beads to their favorite partners.

~Be careful, Dajah.~

Dajah stepped forward, taking the hand in greeting.

"Julius Matthews."

"Dajah," he said, returning a confident shake.

Matthews released first, gesturing to the empty chair. "Have a seat. I hear you're new to the area. Looking for a job?" His own chair creaked as he slid back into it.

Palming the ghost tech, Dajah took the offered seat and ran his hands along the smooth, varnished armrests in appreciation. "Isn't easy establishing yourself in a new city, especially one under Organization rule."

"So, you're interested in working for OPASA," Matthews said.

Dajah shifted his focus from the furniture to the man. "Actually, I'm here for another reason."

The faint tightening around Matthews's eyes ruled out a Shifter's involvement. "Care to elaborate?"

"I'm looking for a supplier of biological weapons. Word on the street is OPASA tests products from outside sources."

"We do on occasion." Matthews laced his fingers on the desk as if to intentionally flash his bracelet. "Are you looking for your makers?"

Dajah's eyes narrowed imperceptibly, or so he thought. The smile spreading on the man before him said plenty. *So we're gonna play it that way.*

Matthews tapped his finger on his temple. "Been a while since I've seen that glow. To my knowledge, only one company produces it. ...unless I'm mistaken."

~Dajah...~

Queen's warning sent a trickle of adrenaline into his bloodstream, boosting his senses. The glow in his eyes was a direct result of the radiation used to splice his genes together and enhance his abilities. Almost everyone in Caerus's Weapon program had the same treatment, but few survived. Statistically speaking, Julius shouldn't know anything about that glow unless he had close dealings with Caerus's elite.

We hit the jackpot with this one!

"You're not mistaken," Dajah said, "and since you're so informed, care to tell me how to reach them?"

Matthews chuckled. "Caerus doesn't take kindly to unexpected visitors."

Notes of his fruity cologne drifted over again, making Dajah want to snort. "How 'bout an invitation, then?"

The chuckle turned to a full-blown laugh. "I admire you, Dajah. Few would stroll into my office under pretense assuming I'm going to give them information for free. But that's appropriate for Caerus, isn't it?"

"Says the man wearing Earth Beads."

"Where's yours?"

Dajah grinned. "Don't need them. What I do need is information. You have it. What do you want for it?"

"Are we negotiating now?" Matthews's expression mirrored Dajah's amusement. "As it happens, there is something I want. You're overqualified for any position we could offer here, so this should be easy."

"I'm listening." Dajah leaned back, using his pinky to inch the ghost tech further down the arm of his chair.

"There's a woman I need brought to me alive. Do whatever you need to capture her, as long as you deliver her in one piece."

Warning bells chimed in Dajah's head, and they weren't of Queen's making. Keeping his posture relaxed, he scoffed with a touch of that snarky confidence Matthews seemed to expect. "You need help getting a woman?"

"Yes, that's a way of looking at it." The CEO's smile didn't reach his eyes. "Do this for me and I'll secure you an audience with the head of Caerus's Eastern Branch. Care to tell me what you want with them?"

"It's personal. A business offer of sorts."

Think any of his men recognized me with her?

~Unlikely. The survivors were too busy dealing with the Raven's security.~

"Far be it from me to get between Caerus and one of their... creations," Matthews said. He broke eye contact and opened one of his drawers. Five clicks and a brown accordion-style folder emerged. "Contained within is all the information you'll want, but it doesn't leave this office. Take as much time as you need to go through it."

Dajah released the band around the folder and pulled out the stack of pages within, not the least bit surprised to find a familiar face on the front. "Kiera Lin. I've seen her Organization file."

~And you know exactly where she's at.~

Dajah flipped through the documents, suppressing a frown at Queen's comment. Kiera's vague mention of experimentation caught his initial interest. Her OPASA file spared none of the details. They were the same age, and similar in more ways than Dajah realized.

Images, labwork, summary reports... *Least she was a consenting adult. Signed with them at eighteen, even if she didn't understand everything she was getting into.* On the outside, Dajah kept his composure. Inside, his skin was crawling and his mind threatened to bring up unhelpful memories. *Caerus turns kids into monsters. These assholes just enhance adults.* There was no question half the compounds in Kiera's file came from Caerus – he knew most of them intimately.

After a few moments of silence, Matthews said, "I'm on a time crunch. Can you deliver her within the week?"

"Provided she hasn't left the country," Dajah said, "absolutely." He closed the file and slid it across the desk. If he looked at it any longer, he was either going to throw up or burn OPASA to the ground right alongside Caerus. They deserved no less.

~Don't forget why you're here. Go get the woman so he gives you

the information we need.~

Are you serious?

~Stop wasting time.~

"Seven days," Matthews said. "If you're late, or someone else brings her first, I'll consider our arrangement null." He pulled off the top sheet from a note stack and wrote down a number. "Call when you have her. You'll receive further instructions."

A glance allowed Dajah's photographic memory to store an image of the number for future reference. He pushed his chair back as he stood, ensuring the dime-sized piece of tech firmly adhered to the furniture.

"A little suggestion," the CEO started.

Dajah waited, eyebrow raised.

"Whatever you're really doing here, tread carefully. And happy hunting."

Offering a half-smile and a nod, Dajah left the office to find Cufflinks stroking his beard again. He stood promptly, ushering Dajah out of the reception room.

Departing was as straightforward as entering. Dajah hailed a cab once outside, instructing the driver to drop him off at a nearby restaurant. The people Matthews sent to follow him, more than obvious in the black, tinted-window SUV, would never spot him leaving.

CHAPTER 8

Kiera paced the hotel room. Routine glances at the clock on the nightstand made time stretch infinitely. The longer Dajah was gone, the deeper paranoia's hooks sank. Trusting people she knew was hard enough.

I'm out of my fucking mind trusting some cat-eyed non-human with this!

The Sheraton was the agreed-upon meeting place after his visit to OPASA. They acquired the room that morning and took separate cabs to their destinations as planned. She'd done what he asked – waited on the roof two blocks down from OPASA, rifle ready in case Julius showed himself. He told her he wouldn't return to the hotel right away, but that was five hours ago.

"Should have agreed upon a contingency plan."

Frustration mounted as two minutes passed like hours.

"This is a terrible plan." Kiera fought down the urge to peek through the curtains every time she made it back to the windows. Their third-floor accommodation offered a decent view of the street, as well as the entrance to the parking garage.

Refusing to leave and unable to wait much longer, she removed the phone from her rifle bag and dialed up Connelly's.

"Is Brenna working?" she asked the mechanic who answered.

An advertisement for Connelly's services played while he transferred her call.

"Brenna Connelly," the familiar voice said. "How may I help

you?"

Tension lessened hearing her friend on the other end of the line. Brenna had analyzed the bullet Kiera pulled from Dajah's shoulder. She confirmed OPASA's involvement, but Kiera never elaborated on how she acquired the bullet in the first place.

"Bren, it's me."

"Kiera? What's wrong? What happened?"

She never changes. Kiera sat on the edge of the bed and explained her current predicament, keeping details vague.

"This was the best plan you could come up with?" Brenna asked, concern thick in her reprimand. "See things through with him or take your chances and run. Did he give you a timeframe? Tell you when he *planned* on meeting back up?"

Take my chances and run. The words echoed in Kiera's mind. She'd built something here. She wasn't any more attached to material things than the next assassin, but the idea of running meant starting over from scratch. She wanted to believe she'd helped make this city a better place one hit at a time. It was home.

"Kiera?" Brenna asked.

"Sorry, yeah. No. Not exactly. I—" A knock sounded, launching her to her feet. She pulled the .45 holstered at her side and aimed at the door. "Gotta go. Talk when I can." Disconnecting the call with her thumb, she tossed the phone on the bed and approached the door from the side.

A second knock followed.

"It's me," Dajah said loudly.

Kiera moved her finger to the trigger guard. Heart pounding a steady fight-or-flight rhythm, she unlocked the door with the deadbolt in place and cracked it open. Dajah stood on the other side with a messenger bag. His posture oozed nonchalance, as if his tardy arrival was planned.

"What the hell took you so long?" she asked, letting him in.

He locked the door behind him and scanned the hotel room before answering. "Had to pick up additional gear."

Kiera folded her arms across her chest, gun in hand. "For five hours?"

"Wasn't close," he shrugged. "Come on. Think you'll find this very interesting."

A thin laptop came out of his messenger bag and Dajah set it up on the table. Kiera moved closer. Her heart continued beating its warning, but Dajah's self-assurance helped assuage some of her anxiety. *He didn't set me up. Just has no concept of common courtesy.*

Kiera holstered her SIG while his program loaded. She recognized the up-and-down peaks as audiowave files, likening Dajah's 'ghost tech' to a glorified microphone. "It worked?"

"Didn't set off any alarms," he said, smirking. He chose a point towards the end of a long string of audio and let it play.

"*...really doing here, tread carefully.*" The sound of Julius's voice had her nails digging into her palms. "*And happy hunting.*"

"What were you talking about?" she asked.

"He wants me to bring you in."

Internal constrictions twisted into knots, and her hand dropped back to the level of her holster. She regarded the man before her warily, but Dajah was too focused on speeding up to the next segment to notice.

The playback resumed with a phone ringing.

"*Yes?*" Julius asked.

"*We've lost him, sir.*" The voice on the other end was male, and the fact that Dajah's tech picked it up would have been impressive if she wasn't waiting for a better explanation from him.

"*Scout the area, but I doubt you'll find anything.*" A distinctive click preceded another stretch of silence.

"Did you listen to this already?" she asked.

"No," Dajah said, "came here as soon as I picked up the computer."

On the recording, Julius was making another phone call.

"*Authorization code,*" an automated voice said.

"*Eight seven echo, four seven delta, thirty-six lima golf.*"

"*Processing authorization code.*" Chirpy, upbeat instrumentals mocked Kiera's apprehension.

"*Julius Matthews,*" said a woman in a straightforward greeting.

"*Madam President. Apologies for calling outside our scheduled time.*"

Kiera never heard Julius sound this respectful to a woman, even when he was pretending. He continued, "*Something's come up that I wanted to address with you directly.*"

"*Don't be cryptic, Julius. Out with it.*"

"*One of your uncle's Weapons strolled into OPASA's headquarters asking about a job. This your way of checking up on me?*"

Dajah stiffened then leaned in towards the computer, brow furrowed.

"*Why would I need to check up on you?*" she asked.

"*There's no need, ma'am, just thought the encounter unusual.*"

"*We don't have all of them accounted for. It's unusual, yes, but not beyond the realm of possibility. Did this one give a name? Any memorable characteristics?*"

"*He called himself Dajah. Silver hair. Green eyes.*"

"*I'll have my people look into it. While I have you on the line, any more intel from that disturbance?*"

"*Just the woman,*" Julius said. "*Eye-witness accounts claim she stepped out of thin air. Our questioning sessions have been... unproductive.*"

Kiera snorted, recalling a dozen of Julius's 'questioning sessions.'

"*Keep me informed of any new developments. A similar disturbance appeared.*"

"*Do you need me to look into it?*"

"*No, the White Team's handling it. Is there anything else, Julius?*"

"*No, President Bekarda. Thank you for your time.*"

The call disconnected with a click. "*How I despise speaking with that cunt,*" Julius said under his breath. Shuffling noises accompanied an electronic beep. The audio went quiet.

"You know who that was?" Kiera asked, eyes laser-focused on

Dajah. She knew he knew – his body language gave away that much – but waited to see if he'd lie.

Dajah released a slow whistle. "Your ex-boss recognized me."

"From the Raven?" she asked.

"No, as one of Caerus's *experiments*. So I asked him to help me get in contact with them. It was obvious he had close dealings with Caerus. He was wearing a set of Earth Beads, and I recognized plenty of the compounds they used on you."

Kiera took a step back from the table. "What do you mean compounds they used on me? What are Earth Beads?"

Feline pupils constricted into slits as he studied her. "I offered to help him with whatever he needed in exchange for the information. He asked me to bring you to him. Showed me your personnel file. I think the woman he spoke with is Sasha Bekarda, Caerus's CEO. If I can locate her through Matthews..."

Kiera didn't hear the rest of his sentence. Shame and anger washed over her, and all she could concentrate on was the pounding in her chest. If Dajah read her OPASA file, he knew everything. Every hideous experiment. Every humiliating task she'd done in her younger years to move up the chain of command. No one could blame a brash eighteen-year-old numb to death and violence. It took her over seven years to realize that, although OPASA honed her skills, they were turning her into the thing she hated most.

And I've spent another five atoning for it.

Suddenly she could smell Julius's putrid cologne. Feel him against her. How many times had he lied? Sent her to kill people under false pretenses? And how many times had she obeyed him despite it, hoping to win his favor?

Kiera's fingers wrapped around the handle of her SIG.

"Uh, Kiera?" Dajah asked, gaze locked on her holster.

"I need Julius dead! Are you helping me or just using me now that you've found what you're looking for?" She didn't release her grip or draw the firearm.

Slitted pupils stared her down. Non-human or experimental

Weapon, Kiera knew the telltale signs of a threatened predator. With her back to the door and Dajah visibly unarmed, she held the advantage.

"Play our cards right and we both come out of this winners," he said calmly. "I know a Shifter a few towns over who'd be willing to be live bait for a price. We choose the location for the exchange, and you take him out the instant he hands over the information I need."

The idea of a Shifter mimicking her was almost as repulsive as the memory of Julius's cologne. Her empty hand curled into a fist. "He won't meet you in person for an exchange, and whatever he's promised you for me, don't count on him delivering."

Dajah stood from his chair. Kiera took another step back, muscles tense.

"Understandably, this is taking a toll on you," he said, voice neutral. "I'll help you get rid of Julius Matthews. I agree the world'll be better without him, but we do it my way. There's too much at stake." Grabbing the spare keycard on the dresser, Dajah strolled past with a wide berth.

"Where are you going?" she asked.

"Lobby bar. I need a drink if we're gonna work together. You don't have to trust me completely, but if you pull that gun on me it's over. I'll be back in an hour. Give you some time to decide what you wanna do." He left the room, closing the door gently.

She wished he would have slammed it.

"Fuck!" she yelled, kicking his chair into the table. Short, deliberate strides carried her from one end of the hotel room to the other.

Ringing sounded from the computer and she almost shot it. A new recording propagated. Julius answered on the second ring.

"Matthews," he said.

He's still in his office?

There was a pause before the person on the other line said, *"I've reconsidered your offer."*

Kiera's heart skipped a beat. She upped the volume as high as it would go.

"*Wise decision. Do you have credible intel?*" Julius asked.

"There's no way," Kiera said. "Brenna wouldn't!"

"*Yes,*" her friend said.

Seconds ticked by in silent agony, leaving Kiera holding her breath.

"*She's at the Sheraton on Eighth and Maple, or was twenty minutes ago.*"

Her heart stopped and the boulder in her throat threatened to choke her. Memories of Brenna flashed before her eyes – good times, bad times. They'd known each other since OPASA. They'd gotten out together. Brenna was practically a sister to her.

Betrayal's knife twisted deep. Kiera questioned what Julius could have said, what threat he held over Brenna to make her do this.

Energy coursed through her veins, potent and tangible. Overwhelming. She reached for the laptop. The instant her fingers made contact, a current of electricity arced through her. Static crackled a warning. Components began sparking erratically, heating her fingertips. She let go and the screen shattered. Smoke sizzled up from the fried remains.

She fanned blue-grey wisps away from the smoke detector. Wanting to blame Dajah for bugging the laptop, the electrified tingling running up her arms told a different story. Familiarity accompanied the sensation, something from her childhood. Kiera tried to pinpoint the memory but drew a blank.

She took the laptop to the bathroom and dropped it in the tub basin. Sparks and crackles flew when the shower water hit it, releasing scents of melted plastic. Leaving the tub stoppered and the water running, Kiera gathered her belongings. She eyed Dajah's messenger bag.

"The cat-eyed non-human's the only one I can trust right now. I'm fucked!"

CHAPTER 9

Dajah ordered a Baileys on the rocks and seated himself at the lobby bar. The location was suitably deserted, the only patrons a businessman three stools down and two women conversing at a corner table.

~Are you going to turn her in to Julius?~

Think I should?

~She's an unnecessary distraction for you.~

He wasn't going to argue with that one.

~I can take care of things.~

No! Dajah threw up his mental barriers and fortified them in case Queen fought for control. He doubted she was capable of the finesse required to subdue Kiera and get her back to OPASA, but he knew she'd be happy to go on a rampage. When Queen took over, people died.

~I'm just saying.~

I'd rather you wouldn't.

The bartender placed the tumbler in front of him, drawing him out of the conversation in his head. Taking a long sip, he savored the sweeter notes before swallowing. Muffled laughter from the women grew louder. A few others came and went from the reception desk visible in the mirrors behind the bar.

Wednesdays are slo— that was fast. Turning fully on the stool, he watched Kiera make her way from the stairwell with their stuff. As soon as her eyes met his, he understood enough to drop a handful of bills on the bar. One last sip and Dajah stood to meet her.

"Didn't expect to see you this soon," he said, defaulting to a casual tone while he scanned the lobby.

"We need to go."

She held out his messenger bag and he took it, noting the lightness. "Where's my computer?"

"Destroyed. Can we talk about it later?"

It wasn't the time for irrelevant questions; that didn't stop his eyebrow from lifting. "Garage?"

Kiera nodded, turning on her heels as a handful of men in suits entered the hotel.

Do they all wear those hideous cufflinks? Dajah ushered her directly into the restroom saying, "OPASA's here."

"We should have had more time," she said.

"What happened?" Though possible, it was highly unlikely Matthews's men followed him back with the route Dajah took. He hadn't smelled a whiff of a tail since getting dropped off at the restaurant.

"Right after you left another call came through," Kiera said. "Letting him know we were here."

"We or you?" he asked. "What did they say?"

Kiera pulled her holstered weapon, ensuring a round was chambered. "Me."

He could tell there was more to it the instant she broke eye contact. *Still, not the time.* "Alright, listen. Head back to the stairs all casual-like then pick up the pace. Go to the second floor. There's a vending machine alcove just beside the stairwell. Hide there until they pass and don't attack them."

"What are you gonna do?" she asked, studying him.

"Create a little chaos."

"What happened to not risking your life unnecessarily?" Her brow furrowed, nose scrunched up when she must have realized she wasn't dissuading him. "Do you need a weapon?"

"Kiera, I *am* a weapon. Give me five minutes after they pass you. If they go up another floor, take the hall straight to the secondary stairwell. If they stop on your floor, go down to the first. Make your way out from there and secure us a vehicle. Got it?"

"Yeah," she said, reholstering her firearm.

"Don't leave without me." He offered the messenger bag back. "Ready?"

Kiera took the bag with a nod, and he motioned for her to go first. Following a few seconds behind, Dajah hung back in the bar to observe. As anticipated, one of the men spotted her. He raised a hand to his earpiece, signaling his friends to follow. Eight more suits entered through the front doors.

Most activity the lobby's seen all evening. No way to know how many are waiting outside.

~Then you better cause enough of a scene to draw them all in.~

Dajah licked his lips, grinning. He snatched the serving tray leaning against the wall and eyed the bartender. "Hey! My buddies just got here. Extra fifty dollars if you can whip me up a dozen gin and tonics in the next two minutes."

Armed with a full tray of cocktails, Dajah waved to the main party congregating near the reception desk. "Joe! So glad you made it! I got drinks for everyone." He walked towards them, putting enough swagger in his step to suggest complete intoxication. The women at the table stopped talking and turned to watch. So did the receptionists. He let the drink tray teeter.

One of the suits stepped forward. "Private business, sir. Please stay back."

Dajah paused, visually choosing the person with salt-and-pepper hair. "Joe, what's up? This, like, your bodyguard or something? Quit messing around!"

"Sir," the bodyguard said, "no one in this group is named Joe. We're here on official business. Stay back."

"You're not Joe?" Dajah asked Salt-and-Pepper. "Huh." He spent a few seconds studying the group with mock bewilderment. "What am I supposed to do with all these?"

"She's on the second floor," one said.

The one talking to him turned away and Dajah frowned, taking one of the glasses from his tray. "Guess these shouldn't go to waste." He took in a mouthful and then launched the serving tray into the air. Everyone looked up, watching a dazzling array of tumblers, clear liquid, and limes go airborne. Dajah smashed his glass into the side of the nearest man's head, shattering it. Salt-and-Pepper gawked then choked as the serving tray slammed into his throat and he stumbled back. Tonic water and alcohol rained down. Snatching a glass from midair, Dajah chucked it at another one of OPASA's flunkies.

The man to the left closed in with a fist. Dajah danced around him, throwing jabs and punches that rendered body parts useless. Within seconds, half of them were down, groaning. Yells and shouts filled in the background as pandemonium ensued among the remaining staff and patrons. The next cufflinked drone pulled his firearm. If someone hadn't called the cops yet, that would certainly escalate it. A heel kick sent the weapon skittering across the floor and Dajah ended him with a palm strike under the chin, snapping his head back.

Everything was breath and body and motion. Dajah could have fought them blindfolded. Their moves were clunky, hurried, and unprepared. He could have finished them without the dramatics, but this was about causing a scene. In that regard, he succeeded.

When all were incapacitated and reinforcements failed to appear, Dajah grabbed the firearm inside Salt-and-Pepper's shoulder holster. *No point in stopping now.* The first headshot left a streak of crimson across the floor. Screams erupted from those who hadn't fled yet, but they were smart enough to stay down. Seven more rounds ensured permanent silence from OPASA's henchmen before the slide on the 9mm locked back.

Dajah snorted. *Not even packing a full mag? OPASA's definitely not Caerus.* He tossed the gun and headed for the stairwell. Footsteps rushed down from the second landing. "Turn around! Turn around! There's a lunatic in the lobby shooting people!" he yelled.

"Out of the way!" cufflink number nine demanded, shoving Dajah against the railing to rush past. Dajah dropped with the push, hooking the man's leg with his shin. Number nine went tumbling down the last five steps, and Dajah cleared the distance with a leap, landing with his knees in the man's back. Nine grunted, likely disoriented from the unpleasant meeting of his face with carpeted concrete. Blood oozed from his nose and mouth. Dajah grabbed his head and jaw, twisting vertebrae with a clean snap.

"Teaches you to be rude, huh?" He patted the dead man's head and plucked the communication device from his ear. "Let's find out where your other three friends are."

"—in. Come in! Anyone read?" a man's voice demanded through the equipment.

"I copy," Dajah said. "Where are you?"

"Third floor. We— Wait, who is this? Freddy?"

"Afraid Freddy's dead," Dajah mused. Discarding the earpiece, he paused at the doorway to listen. A TV played some kind of action movie nearby, complete with explosions and epic music.

We need soundtracks in real life.

~Pay attention to what you're doing. They're coming.~

Queen was right, of course. Three sets of footsteps closed in on his location.

Let's see. We've done the drunk and the panicked hotel guest acts. What should we do next?

~How about competent professional whose ride already left without him?~

Snorting, Dajah kicked the stairwell door open and ducked as bullets whizzed past. *Guess they don't care about collateral damage anymore.* He dove out into the hallway, summoning an excess of energy from his core. The blast left his palm tingling with heat, and the blue-green sphere decimated the closest shooter's chest cavity.

The last two shot recklessly before Dajah was on them. He

knocked one weapon wide, pivoting behind its wielder as the other fired directly into his friend. Dajah shoved his human shield away and dropped to sweep out two sets of legs. The men crumpled on top of one another. The other raised his firearm and Dajah took his hand off with another blast of energy. The resulting scream was deafening.

"Can't believe Matthews thought *this* was going to be sufficient to get her." Howling continued. His energy blast cauterized the man's stump instantly; he wouldn't bleed out from missing a hand, but his mind might have a hard time grasping what happened.

"Don't worry," Dajah said, picking up the pistol. He flicked the severed index finger from the trigger guard and put Howler out of his misery.

~You're gonna have the cops after you as soon as they pull the security tapes.~

They'll assume it's Organization business. Time to see if my ride left without me.

Dajah sprinted down the hall and turned, entering the secondary stairwell. He exited onto the side street and scanned both directions. Sirens wailed in the distance. An SUV backed up and skidded to a halt.

"Get in!" Kiera yelled from the driver's seat.

Mentally grinning at Queen, he hurried to the passenger side and opened the door. A corpse fell out with a single round through his head. Shiny gold cufflinks glittered in the setting sun. The instant Dajah's ass was in the seat, Kiera peeled off.

"You stole one of their cars?"

"It was just waiting there, engine running, driver oblivious," she said. "We'll have to ditch it soon. All OPASA's vehicles are rigged with tracking devices."

"Tracking devices, huh? I got an idea. How fast can you get to Outbrook Park and Ride?"

"Put your seatbelt on," she said, taking a hard right.

Dajah braced himself against the dashboard then followed her advice as she accelerated, weaving through traffic. Blood smeared his wrist after clipping in his belt, drawing attention to the subtle throb in his side.

"Did you get shot *again*?"

He lifted his shirt, noting the graze wound. It'd heal by morning. "And here I thought you were ready to shoot me upstairs. Didn't realize you cared so much."

Kiera opened her mouth but paused.

"I had the bullet I pulled out of you analyzed by someone I trusted. She confirmed OPASA's involvement. I called her in the hotel room when you took too long getting back but didn't tell her any details. After you left, she called Julius. Bitch traced the call. Gave me up. You can't trust *anyone* these days!"

"So, all your known contacts could be compromised?" he guessed.

"Can't believe I'm saying this," she started, "but you're the *only* one I can trust right now."

"Don't make it sound like a bad thing."

"Don't go out of your way to get yourself killed."

Kiera's eyes met his and he offered a smile. She returned the gesture half-heartedly.

~Don't like her too much, Dajah.~

CHAPTER 10

Julius knew it was a risk sending his closest team to the Sheraton. They weren't equipped with the sedative required to subdue Kiera easily, but the intel was too good to wait on. She was key to identifying their mystery guest. The sooner he got his hands on her, the better. Regardless of what it cost. In any case, he hoped the team could detain her long enough for proper backup to arrive.

Time ticked by without a word. Having little more to accomplish at OPASA, he packed his briefcase and notified his driver to be ready.

Twenty minutes away from Elizabeth, Julius's phone rang.

"We lost her, sir," Jaren informed. He must have drawn the short straw. "Tracked the stolen vehicle to Outbrook Park and Ride, but she ditched it. Eddie's trying to pull camera footage as we speak. I've already dispatched men to the next three rail stops in both directions. Santino's getting security feed from the hotel."

"Keep me informed." Julius dug his thumb in, ending the call. "How hard is it to capture one woman?"

Kiera's skills exceeded that of the teams he sent. She could have been one of his top assassins if she hadn't let morality get in the way. Short of that, she was an excellent test subject when it came to foreign substances, biological enhancements, and toxins. He never knew anyone, human or non-human, whose bloodstream purified chemicals the way hers did. Until Elizabeth.

He *had* to know more.

Julius was in the elevator when his phone rang again. "Matthews."

"I want to follow up on the individual who visited you," Sasha said, her voice bitter.

"Yes, ma'am," he answered flatly.

"I'm sending a picture to your phone. Is this him?"

A text message dinged; Julius spared a moment to open the file. "That's Dajah."

"Listen to me very carefully," she started.

Julius exited on the Sapola Wing, picking up the pace on his way to Elizabeth. If he timed things right, she'd be the perfect way to vent his frustration after having to listen to Bekarda speak.

"I need Dajah brought to me. Can you locate him?"

The words stopped him in his tracks. "Did you say brought *to* you?"

"Yes."

"In what condition?" He assumed Dajah had his motives, but hearing Sasha ask for him made Julius wonder what the president was up to. And what it had to do with his work at OPASA.

"Alive and unharmed," she said.

"Anything's doable. If he refuses your invitation?"

The pause raised a new level of suspicion.

"Julius, I'm making this a Code Red Priority. You're authorized to use whatever means necessary, but I insist on this being done as gently as possible. I need him *alive*." She emphasized that last word, knowing his methods could veer towards sadism for the sake of pleasure.

Code Red Priorities were rare. This afternoon, the president didn't seem to care less who Dajah was. It was presumptive, but he couldn't help but ask, "In exchange for this?"

She never hesitated. "Make this happen and I'll approve funding for OPASA's next project, no questions asked as long as it adheres to our code of ethics."

For once he was speechless.

"Julius?" she asked.

"Yes, Madam President. I'll get on it immediately."

Sasha hung up without another word, and Julius's night got a thousand times better. Elizabeth could wait; it was time he did a little research of his own.

Unlike the view from OPASA headquarters, this office only offered the illusion of being above ground. A simulation played on the screen that served as Julius's window here, accurately depicting the darkening city. He chose to keep his blinds closed and leave the illusions for the hundreds of other employees who didn't have the luxury of working in a real high-rise.

Only from here could Julius access Caerus's host files directly.

Every attempt to pull up information on Dajah returned roadblocks. Heavily redacted files. Lost data. He should have sought the information as soon as Dajah left OPASA, before Sasha decided to make him a Code Red Priority.

"First Elizabeth, now Dajah. What am I missing?"

His phone rang again. "Matthews."

"Sir," said Jaren, "we're forwarding you video from the Sheraton. Remember the man you met with earlier today?"

Julius stared at his phone, wondering if he was the butt end of some cosmic joke. "Yes, what of it?"

"Kiera didn't take out Ben's team at the hotel. He did. She picked him up a few minutes after we lost communication. Seems they're working together, sir."

"Thank you, Jaren. Call a meeting. I want everyone at headquarters eight a.m. tomorrow morning." Julius ended the call and sat in stillness. One deep breath. Two. Three. 'Access Denied' flashed across the computer screen. A ding signaled delivery of another file to his phone.

"Alive and unharmed? Not when he's interfering with *my* business. The hell with Bekarda!" Julius threw his phone and stormed off to Elizabeth's room.

Ethan was driving when the updated information came through. The Collective picked up two distinct essence flares in the same city, twelve hours apart. The latter was strongest, suggesting Elizabeth was in trouble – she'd never use her abilities for trivial things. Something prevented the Collective from giving exact coordinates, but knowing the city was enough for Ethan. His internal radar would be able to pinpoint Elizabeth's location once he got closer.

"I'll see you soon. Then our game of cat and mouse ends, and the world's better off for it."

He turned up the radio. Having been gone from Aetatisia for so long, Ethan didn't know any of the popular music, but the current song filled his ears with righteous pride. His fingers tapped the beat against the steering wheel as he counted down the miles.

CHAPTER 11

Kiera paid attention to the route Dajah took out of habit but was preoccupied with the past. Brenna gave her no reason to believe their friendship was easily thrown away. However, Julius was vindictive and cunning.

Loyalty gets you killed.

*

Suddenly she was eight years old, sitting in the front seat while her mother drove them to Granma's. Her brother circled another word in the word find book stashed in the back for long car rides.

"What's an Afgan?" Sammy asked, turning his book sideways.

"A type of crocheted blanket," Mom answered. "What other words are in your book, Sammy?"

Kiera fidgeted with her hands, only half-hearing the string of words relating to arts and crafts projects. "Mom, is Dad mad at you?"

The look on her mother's face was impossible for an eight-year-old to comprehend. *It was hurt and betrayal. I know it well, now. First time Dad lashed out at her. The first time we caught him drinking behind the house.*

"No, honey, your father just had a rough time at work. Remember what we talked about?"

Kiera remembered why they were driving, but she couldn't remember what they talked about. It nagged at her.

*

"Wait here. I'll get us a room," Dajah said, killing the engine.

They were parked in front of a Super 8. She didn't remember leaving the highway. "Sure."

Two hours had passed since they ditched OPASA's SUV for the Toyota Dajah stashed at the Park and Ride. She still wasn't sure what he was going to do with the data he copied from the SUV's GPS. Why he had an interface tablet in the trunk of the waiting car raised other questions.

Whatever he was involved in, it went beyond a simple hit. She suspected he had an entire network in place working behind the scenes. Part of her suspicion was confirmed when he let her into Room 17. He immediately started moving the cheap furniture, revealing a cache under the floorboards.

"Stayed here before, I see," she said, watching Dajah bring out one box after the next.

Removing the last case, he lined them up on the bed and began opening them. An assortment of supplies waited at their disposal – everything from weapons and cash to electronics and spare clothing.

"Before I go to a new city, I make arrangements," Dajah said, rummaging. "Always hope I never need places like this, and I almost always do." He brought a full-sized laptop and external hard drive over to the table where the interface tablet waited and started syncing up the electronics.

"What are you doing?"

"The guy that makes my ghost tech, Gary, he's a genius when it comes to anything electronic. Throw me one of those burners, would you?"

She did as instructed, snorting when Dajah caught the phone without looking. "Shouldn't we bandage your side?" Blood stained a significant part of his button-down shirt.

"It's not actively bleeding. I'll shower once I get this running." Dajah dialed a number and set the phone down on speaker, focused on the computer.

A male voice answered. "Kanto's delivery service."

"It's me," Dajah said. "Can you get in touch with Gary? Got a project for him."

"You know how he is."

"Yeah, well, I've got a lead. Solid one. Need everything he can pull up on a man called Julius Matthews. He runs Organized Protection and Asset Security Affiliates. They're partnered with Caerus."

"You sure?"

"Asshole was wearing Earth Beads. Offered to put me in contact with them. He knows too much to be bluffing."

"What are you going to do with him?"

"Kill him once I get what we need. I'm syncing data from one of their SUVs. Tell Gary to track the vehicles since six thirty tonight. He uses them as his personal escorts. Find a place Matthews goes where I can intercept him. I can't touch him in his office."

"You can't?"

Dajah's face scrunched. "Let's just say it'd be risky. Have Gary set an alarm. Let me know if any of their cars come within ten miles of my current location."

"File's coming through now. I'll get it transferred. Dajah, how is she?"

Kiera perked at the mention of 'she' and the sudden tension visible in Dajah's shoulders.

"Under control. I got this. Talk to you soon, Taron."

Under control? Her eyebrows peaked, narrowed, and her heart beat faster. *Who's under control?* When Dajah ended the call she asked, "Who was that?"

"My brother. I can't reach Gary directly, so he'll take care of things."

She couldn't detect a lie. "Who's the 'she' he asked about?"

Subtle tension rippled through his neck and shoulders again. "No one you need to worry about."

"It's not me?" she confirmed, unconvinced.

"No, it's not you."

Kiera decided to let it go for now. Whoever 'she' was, Dajah wasn't elaborating. "Now we wait around for your friends to do what, exactly?"

"You mentioned Matthews always uses company cars to travel."

Nodding, her eyes wandered back to the stain on his shirt. "When he does leave, it's with a convoy. Identical vehicles that split up and go off in different directions."

"We know he was at his office when we were at the hotel. Don't ask me how he does it, but Gary'll find a way to hack into the GPS and satellite systems. He'll track all the company cars going to and from OPASA since that time and look for discrepancies. We'll have a list within twenty-four hours."

"That's gonna be some list. What are we supposed to do in the meantime?"

"Lay low. Clean up. Maybe order some takeout. You want first dibs on the shower?"

So he can call Julius when I'm not in the room and screw me over? She recognized the callousness of the thought as soon as it surfaced and sighed. *He hasn't betrayed me yet. Then again, it took Brenna twelve years.* Kiera shook her head. "You can go first. I'm not the one bleeding and reeking of cheap liquor."

"I'm not bleeding." Dajah pulled his shirt open, popping several buttons instead of undoing them, and flashed his side to her. "See? Almost good as new."

She spent a moment studying the graze wound then took in the rest of his exposed skin. The wounds she helped patch up after the Raven were almost non-existent. "If you heal that fast, why do you have so many scars?"

Shrugging off his shirt, Dajah tossed it in the plastic-lined waste bin. "There's a limit on how much damage my body can heal at one time. Get too good at something, and Caerus finds interesting ways to make the same task more challenging next time around."

She frowned. "This is about revenge, isn't it?"

"Absolutely. But it's not only because of what they did to me. Some of it was... necessary, I guess. Caerus didn't raise children. They raised weapons, which, for the record, should come with a certain amount of respect. Treat your weapons carelessly and sooner or later they backfire."

"What happened to you?"

He sat on the opposite bed facing her, but his eyes were on his forearm, fingers tracing old scars. "We were raised in one of their training facilities out in Arizona. If you make it to eighteen and pass your final test, you get to leave. Go out in the world. Be one of their elite assets, or pay them back as a type of indentured servant. My brother was weeks away from graduation. We both knew I wasn't gonna survive a month without him, let alone two more years. So, he risked everything to get me out."

Dajah paused, looking thoughtful until he snorted with a tight-lipped smile. "Caerus didn't like that we destroyed their facility in the escape."

"Two of you did that?" She tried to hear all the things he wasn't saying.

"No, more like a dozen. Anyway, they hunted us. Still do, so we're making sure they leave us alone permanently."

Kiera could relate. She walked away from OPASA with stipulations, believing as long as she adhered to Julius's rules, she'd be free. But she was never truly free. *And look where it has brought me.* Another sigh escaped her lips. "I've never even heard of Caerus before. They sound capable."

Dajah's chuckle broke up the monotony. "They don't want people to know they exist. Companies like OPASA think they're big fish in the pond. They don't realize they're swimming in Caerus's aquarium. Your ex-boss must have close contacts with their elite."

"Because he recognized you as one of their projects," Kiera said.

"That, and the Earth Beads."

"You gonna tell me what Earth Beads are?"

"You gonna join me in the shower?"

Kiera stared at him, trying to decide if he was joking or serious. His smirk implied the former. "Is the shower somehow relevant to Earth Beads?"

"Not directly. Makes you curious though, doesn't it?"

"Go shower." Kiera shook her head but smiled. "I'll wait out here. Make sure OPASA doesn't storm the motel room in the meantime."

He grabbed a spare set of clothes from one of his boxes, looking far too pleased with himself.

"Hey, Dajah," she called right before he entered the bathroom. "Nice ass."

"Door's unlocked if you change your mind," he said.

"Maybe next time." As physically appealing as he was, and as much as Kiera could use a good distraction, she didn't need to complicate things further.

◆

Doubting either of them would sleep, Dajah ordered some late-night Chinese food once he was out of the shower. Kiera declined her turn. He attributed part of that to her lack of trust, but she still smelled faintly of lavender-scented soap every time he walked past.

"Now, in contrast to my substantial package," Dajah said, clearing his throat as he removed containers from the smiley face delivery bag, "Earth Beads are small. Ever notice the stone bracelet on Matthews's left wrist? Different shades of reds and yellows?"

"Sure, he always wears it along with his gold cross necklace."

~She's clearly not interested in your package, Dajah. Not even the hint of a smirk.~

She liked my ass, though. It's been a long day. Refocusing on the explanation at hand, he continued. "Each one of those quarter-inch stones is responsible for a magic spell."

Kiera opened the first container, releasing salty ginger and steam into the air. "You're telling me Julius can cast magic?"

"If he wants to. That bracelet's composed of elemental and self-enhancing magic. I can tell from the richness of the colors those spells are advanced, but how much experience he has using them is questionable. Caerus gifts Earth Beads to their favorite associates as a double-edged sword. They're easy to use but extract a toll on the caster's energy reserves. If someone's not prepared for it, casting an advanced spell could kill them."

"I've known Julius for a long time," Kiera started. "No one's even joked that he's capable of magic."

"He knows what Earth Beads are. I'd wager he knows how to use them, but since the magic's unique to Caerus, he probably keeps it a close-guarded secret. I haven't noticed Earth Beads on any of the assholes he's sent. Just those ugly gold cufflinks."

"What do you mean it's unique to Caerus?"

"Without going into really technical details, let's just say I've never heard of this form of magic being used outside their circles." He scooped up a heaping forkful of chicken and broccoli, savoring the aromatic flavors.

Kiera opted for chopsticks and a single shrimp. "I've never heard of Earth Beads, but jewelry possessing magic isn't uncommon."

"They don't possess magic. They *are* magic. Crystalized radiation that harnesses abilities science can't yet explain."

"Semantics," she said. "My granma used to tell us stories about *Yara'ista* when we were little."

A tremor passed through Dajah's hand. He dropped his next forkful as Queen's presence saturated every aspect of conscious awareness. *What the hell's up with you?*

~That word! She shouldn't know it.~

It'd been a long time since a word set Queen off. Dajah forced his hand down, spearing another vegetable like it wasn't a big deal. "What's *Yara'ista*?"

"Legend goes that a magical lake once existed high up in the mountains of Yunnan that held all the knowledge of our ancestors. Only the bravest and pure of heart could find the lake, seeking it out in times of need.

"In one of granma's stories, a little boy went to the lake to try and save his village after a devastating plague hit. He offered up his life in exchange for a miracle. The ancestors accepted this as a worthy sacrifice, instructing him to carry a handful of water back to the village. By the time he returned, only a single drop remained. The boy fell to his knees, called upon the ancestors, and every living thing in the village was healed in an instant. When the villagers found the boy's body, he held a tiny, solidified purple sphere in his hand. The villagers buried the boy with honor and placed the sphere on display so everyone would remember his sacrifice."

Kiera washed a mouthful down with her bottle of water. "In another story, an elderly woman brought a drop back from *Yara'ista* Lake to stop a fire threatening to consume all their crops. The wildfire went out instantly and, again, she was found dead with a tiny sphere in her hand."

"What color was the sphere?" Dajah asked. Queen had gone quiet, but she was listening.

"Red, I think."

"So *Yara'ista* is another name for Earth Beads," Dajah said.

~That isn't a normal word.~

It's the name of a lake from one of her grandmother's fairytales. Aren't you paying attention?

~That word doesn't belong.~

Dajah refrained from rolling his eyes, deciding Queen was having an off moment. It wasn't unusual, but these days, fortunately, it was rare. He continued, "Makes sense some older cultures would know them by another name. Caerus found a way to pick up their energy signatures and sent teams to secure all the naturally occurring Earth Beads a long time ago, but there's no way they got all of them."

"What can Julius do with those Beads?" she asked.

"You can't tell what a specific Earth Bead does without

touching it, but the magic's somewhat color-coded. If I had to take a guess, I'd say he's got the ability to cast shields for protection. Maybe enhance a few of his senses – speed, hearing... A handful of elemental spells, for sure."

Kiera held her chopsticks in midair.

"What?" he asked.

"Something I'm remembering. A sniper tried to take him out once. Accounts say the shot went wide, leaving most assuming it was meant as a warning, but it never added up for me. The sniper who took it was good enough to land the hit. I'm wondering now if it wasn't some kind of barrier that deflected the bullet. Can your Earth Bead magic do that?"

"Definitely," Dajah said, emphasizing it with a nod. "Did you ever talk to the sniper?"

"No, he turned up dead the next morning."

"We'll have to assume Matthews uses barrier spells, then. Good news? They're only so strong for so long. If we find one, we keep hitting him until it fails. Then go in for the kill."

"You really think this Gary can locate him?"

Dajah's grin was his answer. "We should try to sleep at some point."

CHAPTER 12

Dajah held the spoon steady and waited for Zayan to give a nod, indicating he was ready for more.

"Sorry, Zay, Taron's better at judging, but this spoon shouldn't be too hot."

Zayan's lips parted and Dajah eased in the broth. Then came the hard part. Staring. Waiting. Ensuring his oldest brother swallowed properly and didn't choke on their lunch. This was the worst Zayan had been in a while, but at least he could sit up straight. His left hand remained curled in a half-fist – Dajah had to help stretch out his fingers so they didn't get stuck like that. His right hand was limp. Useless.

Zayan swallowed and a tiny smile poked at the corner of his lips.

"Ok, good. Good temperature." Dajah lifted another spoon, snagging a few soft vegetables this time, and blew on it. "You gotta keep eating, Zay. Get your strength back."

"I should..." Zayan started, "...be taking care of you, little brother." The words came slow and with great effort, but it warmed Dajah's heart to hear Zayan speaking. His grin split his face so wide it hurt.

With his best monotone impression of Taron, Dajah said, "You have to take care of yourself first." He raised the next spoonful.

The cafeteria held half the normal occupants. Most of the older kids were undergoing some kind of team trial, Taron included. Zayan would have been with them if he could function. Dajah didn't know everything Caerus did to his brothers, but he knew Zayan was getting worse. *Every time the Other took over, Zayan recovered more slowly. This time it took him two days just to remember how to walk. He couldn't feed himself yet – he hadn't regained control of his hands.*

The scientists said that Zayan was sick, but Dajah knew the truth: Zayan was sick because of the Stream. If they just stopped injecting him so much, he'd be as good as any of them. Better.

"The cripple speaks," one of the guards joked. Dajah zeroed in on the speaker. Beady – the nickname they gave to the one always looking for someone to pick on. Zayan was an easy target when incapacitated.

"Don't listen to any of them, Zay. You're gonna get strong again."

Zayan took the next spoonful and swallowed quicker this time. "Little... too cold, D."

Nodding, Dajah prepared the next spoon.

"Three hundred bucks says he doesn't make it to the end of the month," Beady said.

Noah stood beside him. One of the better guards, he tried to mitigate hostility whenever possible. When Beady was on guard duty, hostility was guaranteed. "He'll make it."

Beady laughed. "Maybe till the end of the week if he doesn't become monster food. Then again, he's so scrawny they'd only use his bones for toothpicks."

Dajah couldn't suppress the tremble in his hand and lost half of the spoon's contents.

"Oh, are you getting angry?" Beady asked. Dajah knew the question was directed at him, but he tried to avoid eye contact. It'd only make things worse. "Keep feeding him. Fatten him up for those monsters. They appreciate a little meat on the bones."

"Leave it be," Noah said.

Dajah tried to calm the rage building inside with controlled breaths like Taron taught him. In for four. Hold for four. Out for four. Hold for four. Repeat.

Beady laughed again.

The spoon twisted in Dajah's hand.

"You're ten years old, kid. Don't know a fraction of the horrors out

there, and if you keep that attitude up, you never will," Beady said. "Monster food. Just like your brother." He made gestures with his hand, teeth chomping through the air.

The tremor rippled through Dajah's body to the point where he could feel it radiate into the table. Something whispered to him. Encouraged him.

"Come on," Noah said to Beady. "We should do our rounds."

Still laughing, Beady turned to follow.

"Dajah, don't listen... to her..." Zayan said.

Her. The Other. She flooded his body with need. Strengthened him. Made him fast. Immune to everything. Dajah leapt over the table, spoon clutched tightly in hand. He slammed into Beady before either guard turned. Clawed up his body. Dug the metal curve of the spoon into his eye socket. A satisfying wet pop-snap sent the juicy globe skittering across the floor and Beady screamed. Limbs batted at Dajah but the Other made him an invincible creature. He went for the second eye. Scraped at it. Stabbed. Sharp pins pierced through his clothes, adhering to skin, and Dajah's body started convulsing. All the strength and rage of the Other fled as electricity rendered him immobile.

◆

Thrashy, jerky sounds woke Kiera. She gripped the handle of the .45 beneath her pillow and let her ears pinpoint the source of the disturbance.

He's dreaming.

On a good night, she slept lightly. Between the cheap motel linens, the betrayals, and a strange non-human in the next bed over, she was surprised she fell asleep in the first place.

Daylight hadn't brightened the curtains yet. Dajah's computer ran in the background, its fan switching on and off while it processed untold data. She rolled over, eyeing the clock, and groaned. *They won't have fresh coffee out yet.*

Moving shadows caught the corner of her eye. Gun in hand, she squinted at the darkness. "What *is* that? Dajah, you awake?"

He mumbled something incoherent and trembled.

Kiera turned on the bedside light. Her eyes adjusted, going wide. A pen and several scraps of paper marked with the yellow Super 8 logo were drifting lazily above Dajah. She sat there for moments, watching the objects defy gravity while Dajah's face twisted in the tell-tale signs of nightmare.

Approaching carefully, she extended her empty hand above him. Palpable vibrations radiated off his body in short, rippling waves, making her hand feel weightless. She removed the pen from the energy field and released it over her bed. It fell with gravity as it should have.

Dajah's unconscious ability was fascinating, but non-humans were exceptionally more dangerous when not in control. She didn't know what he was fully capable of; letting the nightmare continue could end in disaster. "Dajah, you need to wake up."

Another mumble.

Kiera retrieved a glass of water from the bathroom and stood beside the head of his bed, figuring it was the safest place if he woke violently. She hadn't forgotten about the energy blast he was capable of.

Tilting the glass, she let a few drops of water rain down over his forehead. The droplets froze in midair like they were caught in an invisible web then started to swirl. Round and round. Sometimes gaining height. Sometimes falling. Always gentle and mesmerizing.

"That's not gonna work."

A random double BEEP caused Kiera to flinch; Dajah bolted upright. She crouched down, redirecting her weapon while praying he was lucid. Water droplets fell, leaving darkened marks on the bedsheet. Paper scraps fluttered away as he went to the computer.

Before sitting at the table, Dajah's eyes found her. "Uh, there something you wanna tell me?"

Kiera stood, lowering her weapon. "There something you wanna tell *me*? You were having a nightmare. Making shit float!"

Dajah tilted his head, eyeing the pieces of paper on his bed and the floor, then rubbed the back of his neck. "Did I hurt you?"

That's his first question? Kiera blinked in disbelief and came over to join him. "No, you didn't hurt me. Does that happen a lot?"

"Sometimes," he said, pulling out the chair. "Sorry. I didn't mean to wake you. I don't usually sleep with others around."

The frown came automatically, knowing what haunted *her* dreams. "Was it Caerus?"

He raised an eyebrow, his devil-may-care nature resurfacing in a half-smile. "You really wanna know?"

"Wouldn't ask if I didn't." Kiera took the other chair.

His smile faded. "Just some memories. When our older brother was still alive. One of the guards was... making fun of him. Zayan was getting worse from all the injections. Every time they experimented on him, he became... less." Dajah paused, staring down. "Anyway, I was young and reckless back then. Didn't understand the meaning of consequence. You asked about my scars. I attacked the guard and gouged out one of his eyes. They beat me good after that one, but the beating wasn't the real punishment. It was just to make sure I couldn't do anything to stop what came next."

Kiera feared asking, but when he didn't elaborate, she had to. "What came next?"

"They hurt Taron and made me watch. He wasn't even involved, but that's Caerus for you."

"How old were you?"

"Ten."

She gripped her weapon tighter; her heart went out to Dajah. "Caerus does this to children?!"

"They did," Dajah said, still not looking at her. "But we were never children to them. Just weapons. Tools. The monsters got treated better than we did."

"Monsters?"

"Genetically-engineered animals. They'd take the nastiest

beasts, splice them together, radiate them. Guards always argued with the scientists that we were too intelligent to train. That the animals were a safer bet." Dajah told it matter-of-factly, but she could tell it had a profound effect on him.

"How old are you now?" she asked.

"Thirty." He clicked on the laptop screen, waking it.

"And Taron helped you escape when you were sixteen," she said, remembering what he'd told her last night. "What happened to your older brother?"

"Zayan didn't see me turn eleven."

Her shoulders slumped. "I'm sorry, Dajah."

"It's the past. They'll get what's coming to them. Anyway, that beep should be good news."

"Gary found Julius?" She tried to layer some optimism into her tone but couldn't stop thinking about his upbringing. As unfortunate as the death of her parents was, her childhood was mostly normal.

"We'll see. Beep means an email from Gary. What do you know about a place called Heritage Heights?"

"One of the elite gated communities," she said, snorting. "It's the only place in Nu Philly city limits where you get your own country club and acres of manicured lawns for a hefty HOA fee. Not even delivery trucks get past the main gates. It's a no-fly zone. Even satellite imagery's restricted."

"Sounds bougie," Dajah said, clicking through something rapidly, "and also appropriate, I guess."

"What do you mean?"

He turned the laptop to face her and moved it closer. "Live satellite feed *is* restricted, but it's archived. Gary tracked one of OPASA's vehicles to a house in Heritage Heights and pulled images. See for yourself."

Nothing about the contemporary estate and its expansive patio and yard that backed up to the golf course stood out besides the fact that Dajah's associate came across these images too easily. She attempted recon on Heritage Heights once for a particular

Mark. In the end, it was easier to change locations and eliminate the target outside a movie theater. OPASA's connections and deep pockets couldn't override the security restrictions to get her the information she needed. She'd since rectified that.

Clicking the next image, Kiera drew in a sharp breath. Zoomed in, the screen showed Julius Matthews lounging on outdoor furniture while presumably entertaining a handful of guests. A series of images followed. Different days. Different weather patterns. All of them caught some glimpse or definitive image of the man that made it unlikely he was a guest.

"Julius lives here," Kiera said. "Dajah, how...?"

"Told you," he started, "Gary's a genius when it comes to this stuff. And he tends to know exactly what I need. Keep clicking."

Kiera did. There were design blueprints of the house, a detailed layout of the golf course, even notes about security rotations on the two main gates into Heritage Heights. Other data followed the tinted-window SUV that seemed to be Julius's escort. "Looks like he travels between this house and OPASA's headquarters. The other stops are somewhat random, but he's made several at... Saint Mary's grade school?"

"There's a kid in several of those images," Dajah said.

Kiera's brow furrowed and she scanned back through the images. "Maybe the daughter of someone he's dating? There's a blonde woman in almost every picture with the little girl. Not in a thousand universes does Julius have a *kid*. Look at the times the SUV is at the school, too. More likely it's a drop point. Can you tell where the car that dropped him off is at now?"

"Yeah, hold on." Dajah scooted his chair closer and angled the computer so they could both see it. He closed the email file and brought up the tracking program. The computer displayed a map view of the city overlaid with satellite feed. The vehicle in question flashed with an orange triangle icon smack in the middle of a greyed-out area.

"Heritage Heights," she said, checking the time stamp in the corner of the screen. "He's still home, but I've never heard of him getting to OPASA before eight."

"What time does he stay until?"

"On a Thursday? Probably till five or six if he's not meeting with anyone, but that's a guess. He never made a habit of having a predictable schedule. I just remember him wanting to finish up early as the weekend got closer. Mondays and Tuesdays he'd stick around till ten. Sometimes later."

Dajah leaned back in his chair; arms folded. "I'm confident enough to move on this intel. We need an easy way inside Heritage Heights."

"Actually," Kiera started, "I might have one. I tried to do a job in Heritage Heights years ago. OPASA couldn't get me inside to gather the intel I wanted... which makes sense now in hindsight, so I changed plans. Anyway, I swore I'd never have that problem again. Made friends with a couple that lives there. They've got... unique tastes."

CHAPTER 13

"Two minutes," Dajah said, closing out the program on his burner phone.

Kiera's contacts were happy to honor her request for a visit without asking too many questions provided she brought them a bucket of fresh eels from the river docks. They spent the afternoon hosted by the Treebums, an elderly, non-human couple who'd done well for themselves and mostly wanted to chat about the weather.

To be fair, it never used to snow in September. A light coating had blanketed the area and melted by mid-morning, but word of the phenomenon covered every radio station and news broadcast, and it was all the Treebums wanted to talk about. That, and how the Organization turned Old Philadelphia into something residents could be proud of again. Dajah wondered if they'd feel that way living outside of Heritage Heights. Nu cities and Old cities were the same – still run by a bunch of people who cared more about fattening their wallets than the livelihood of those beneath them.

Gary's tracking program indicated that two of OPASA's vehicles were en route in this general direction, and the predictability index that one of them carried their intended target was high. Dajah and Kiera made their move.

"When he rolls into that driveway, we need to be inside. You know what to do," he reminded her.

"Finish the job," Kiera said. She was friendly with the Treebums, spinning half-lies while keeping up a relaxed, easygoing demeanor. Now, as they crouched waiting under the cover of trees, she was all intense focus.

Dajah admired the way she studied some detail on the back of the house two hundred yards away.

~This is a bad idea. You should have come alone.~

Ten, maybe twelve personal guards, max.

~Don't forget about his Earth Beads.~

Dajah wasn't worried about Matthews's bracelet, but it was a good reminder for Kiera. They hadn't discussed Earth magic in depth. "Don't forget he might have a Shield in place. You come across one you either keep firing until it fails or go for a slow strike. Most barriers created by Earth magic react to force. You can't punch through someone's Shield, but you can slowly extend your hand and shake theirs."

Kiera gave a curt nod, never deviating her focus.

An impressive stretch of open ground complicated approaching the terraced landscaping of the estate, but the setting sun worked in their favor. A glass and iron dining table reflected the glare at the two guards conversing beside double French doors.

Dajah exchanged his phone for the handgun in his belt holster. Opting for a single .45 fitted with a silencer, he'd rely more on the stash of throwing knives sheathed around his waist. Kiera took two firearms and every spare magazine that fitted them in his collection.

She screwed the suppressor onto the muzzle of the Colt, saying, "Leave those guards to me."

Hitting targets over one hundred yards with a handgun and no sights required a healthy dose of luck or a lot of practice for the average human layman. Kiera might have been human, but she was far from average. Dajah never doubted her ability.

"Thirty seconds," he said.

Both guards paused in unison, with the man on the left

pressing two fingers against his ear. They stood a little straighter. Then the first one's head flew back with a splash of crimson. The second joined him, a fresh corpse crumpled on the patio before he could realize his partner was down.

Dajah smirked. *She's amazing with that thing!*

~You could be that good if you practiced.~

You know I prefer close contact. Sniping feels like cheating.

~Spoken like a true Caerus Weapon.~

"He's home," Kiera said, lowering her gun while Dajah snorted at the voice in his head.

"Let's go." With zero cover on approach, his plan hinged on security being distracted by Matthews's arrival.

No alarms sounded when they reached the bodies. Removing an earbud from each man granted them access to the team's audio channel. Dajah dumped the dead guards into one of the storage boxes used for cushions. Kiera got the door open.

With few places to hide among the contemporary accents and furnishings of the great room, he was glad to find it deserted. Movement and voices drifted from other parts of the house. He'd memorized the blueprints Gary provided, having a good idea where the main security room should be. Signaling Kiera with his fingers, he directed her down the hall and indicated his intended path.

"Boss has arrived," a male voice confirmed over the earbuds.

Kiera moved silently over rich hardwood floors and rugs. Crouching low, Dajah made his way across the great room to another hallway skirting the side of the house. They had seconds, maybe minutes before security protocols dictated some kind of check-in.

Measured footfalls neared him.

Pressing his back to the wall, he palmed two throwing knives and peered around the turn. A large, burly man faced the opposite direction. His associate, half his size, was moving towards him. Both wore tailored suits. Their hideous cufflinks glistened when they caught the light.

A well-timed throw embedded Dajah's knife into the thin one's skull, right between the eyes. He wrapped one hand around the burley man's mouth and nose, the other around his shoulder, and wrenched in opposite directions. A satisfying pop came from the man's neck and he sagged in Dajah's arms. The thud from the first body hitting the floor went unnoticed. Both corpses went into the nearest closet.

◆

Kiera's heart beat a steady rhythm. She felt it in her grip and the little vein beside her temple. Always on the right side. Years of training taught her to suppress that thrill and anxious uncertainty that accompanied any hit. She wasn't about to assassinate the man who named himself her enemy; she was shopping in the food store, strolling through a quiet forest. Keep the goal simple: *Kill Julius.*

A single, well-placed bullet would do the trick. As much as he deserved worse, she wouldn't allow revenge fantasies to creep in any more than she'd allow doubt to blindside her.

Slow, steady breaths.

The house was immaculate. Almost too... *normal* for someone like Julius. The sitting room she ducked into, complete with baby grand piano and bookcases, felt surreal. Cultured. Julius was always business and pleasure rolled into excess.

She dropped her index finger to the trigger as a dark-skinned male turned the corner. His eyes widened for an instant and death froze his features in surprise. The bullet passed clean through his skull, lodging into a hardback book. Red-splattered confetti fluttered around the impact. Kiera pulled the slumping corpse out of view of the hallway.

"Mister Kengee?" a squeaky, feminine voice called out.

Shit! The little girl!

Kiera made it a point to choose her targets carefully; she hated situations involving children. Soft footsteps picked up the pace, closing in, and Kiera's heart quickened.

Please don't come in here. There was no way to hide the blood and tissue oozing from the dead man's skull. It marred the plush, cream-colored throw rug and soaked her arms. Dropping the man on the loveseat, Kiera stepped forward and hid her gun behind her back, praying the child took a detour.

"Mister Kengeeeee," the girl called again, melodious as she entered the room and came up short.

A miniature blonde human in a garnet sundress and bare feet stood wide-eyed. She couldn't have been older than twelve. Loose hair fell around her shoulders. Deep brown eyes shifted between Kiera and the man on the couch.

"What happened to Mister Kengee?" the girl asked. "Did you kill him? Are you here to kill Daddy?"

Kiera stared. *No normal child responds like this.* A slew of scenarios raced through her thoughts, all leading to the same concerns: *What'd he do to you?*

Tucking her gun into its holster, she wiped her arms against the back of her shirt and brought them forward, crouching down. "What's your name?"

"Mikayla," the girl answered. "Are you... gonna kill my Daddy? Mommy said one day someone would come to kill him. He's not a good man."

The little human bore no resemblance to Julius whatsoever. "You're right. He's not a good man."

Mikayla's eyes dropped to the floor and she shook her head. Stray hairs concealed most of her face. "If you kill him," she whispered, "he won't be able to hurt us anymore."

Kiera's hands clenched into fists. "He hurts you?"

Mikayla sniffled and dipped her head lower.

"Listen," Kiera said, sympathetic. "Can you sneak out of the house? Maybe visit a friend that lives nearby?"

The girl looked up and nodded. "I can get out, but Daddy always knows where I am."

Because the possessive bastard is probably tracking her. And her mother. Now the mission was more than just Kiera's freedom.

Anxiety seeped its way inside with the added weight of purpose. "I want you to get out of this house. Now."

"Can Mommy come with me?"

"Can you get her to leave right now without your dad knowing?"

Mikayla's face brightened. "Yes." She paused for a moment then whispered, "I hope you kill him. But you won't be able to. He never dies." With that, she ran off.

Such a risk.

Kiera stayed low, listening, ready to act on a moment's notice.

"Mikayla, why are you running?" a woman asked down the hall.

"Mommy, come with me!"

"What's this all about?" a man asked. The voice blanched her vision, turning it red.

Julius!

"Hi, Daddy," Mikayla said. "I wanna show Mommy something I made!"

"Can it wait until after dinner?" the mother asked.

"No, now! It won't last that long."

"Might as well go see what it is," Julius said. "I need to clean up anyway. Where's Kengee?"

"He was just here," the mother said.

"Mommy, nooow!" Mikayla whined.

The chuckle escaping Julius sent a chill down Kiera's spine. She grabbed the suppressed Colt. Two sets of footsteps went off in another direction, leaving only one behind. No warning came through the earbud to suggest any of the bodies were discovered, but that was only a matter of time.

Each step brought her closer to her target until only a wall separated them. He was pouring some kind of carbonated beverage in the kitchen – she could make out the shadows reflected in the hallway and heard the fizz against glass. A chair pulled out, wood sliding on tiled floors. He sat.

"That you, Kengee?" Julius asked.

Kiera whipped into the opening, gun leveled at her target's head. His initial response was a tightening around the eyes, glass held halfway between his mouth and the table.

"Keep both hands where I can see them," she said, moving into the chef's kitchen and placing a solid wall of cabinets to her back.

Julius was sitting on one of the island's stools, phone on the counter, lips curled in sardonic malice. He lowered his glass while keeping his left palm up.

"I'd give you credit for this one, but you're not working alone. Well, Sweetheart, if you're going to shoot—"

Three rounds flew in rapid succession towards the sweet spots: Forehead, throat, center of the chest. The bullets rebounded off an invisible force that rippled in prismatic colors, outlining a sphere around his body.

Dajah was right about the barrier.

Julius laughed, standing. "Did you think it'd be that easy?"

Kiera rapid-fired, striking the same locations. Unfazed, Julius's gaze drifted to the hall before boring into her. "Guessing you dispatched most of my security team already. No matter."

A bolt of lightning struck her dead-on and the world froze. Her back slammed into the cabinets. Pots and pans jostled within while her muscles spasmed, leaving her wholly dysfunctional and convulsing in pain. The Colt fell from her grasp. Teeth clenched, threatening to break. Pressure raked up the back of her skull. Electrified tingling coursed through every vein and nerve.

A shadow hovered over her. New, sharper pain flared through her collarbone. A thin steak knife rendered her right arm useless. Sparks intensified around the embedded metal.

"Do me a favor," he said, landing a kick to her abdomen, "stay put while I deal with Dajah."

Kiera curled in reflexively. Residual tremors raced throughout her body and a faint sense of déjà vu surfaced. She grabbed her secondary weapon, aimed, and continued firing.

His magic barrier deflected the next four rounds. The fifth jacketed bullet penetrated, shredding muscle and shattering the bone in his leg. Julius dropped to one side with a curse then took off at a hobbled run.

"Shit!" Yanking the blade out of her shoulder, Kiera knew she was out of time. She snagged the fallen Colt, scrambling to her feet. Blood ran from the deep stab wound, saturating her shirt, but her fingers worked. She gave chase.

Julius raced around the corner and started up the curved stairwell. Another projectile grazed his side, causing him to stumble. If she'd had a clean shot, it'd be over. He retaliated with another spell. Kiera's feet slipped out from under her, and a bone-numbing chill made her gasp for breath. The sensation faded quickly, but the shivering was slow to dissipate.

By the time she reached mid-staircase, a series of clicks echoed from the second floor. Gritting her teeth as the last vestiges of frost left, she gained the landing. Down the hall, Julius stood in the threshold of an office watching her, arms folded in arrogance. His calf and side leaked dark red, leaving a trail anyone could follow.

Kiera fired at his head. A clear, bulletproof shield absorbed the impact, bouncing the projectile to the floor without the slightest scratch. Like a coward, he fled to the protection of a panic room. And like OPASA's arrogant CEO, he had *glass* acting as the preliminary barrier instead of the expected steel door. Odds were good she wasn't shooting through it. That didn't stop her from firing until the slide locked back and the next trigger-pull resulted in an empty click.

"Feel better?" he asked.

"Would if you stopped breathing."

"Unfortunately for you, I've a vested interest in surviving." Another bolt of electricity shot through her body, more like static this time around. Enough to feel, but not enough to become incapacitated by it.

He's running out of juice.

She slid the empty firearm into its holster and stepped closer. "Why? After all these years, why now, Julius? What do you want from me?"

Despite the barrier, Kiera caught whiffs of cologne mingled with copper.

He shifted his weight to his uninjured leg and studied her. "I always thought the redundant sequences in your DNA were junk. Random genetic defects that somehow led to a few enhancements. Less than a month ago I met someone who changed my mind. You might want to meet her. What do you say? Come along willingly for old time's sake?"

Willing consent never ranked high on Julius's priorities. "Who is she?"

"No one you know," he said, "but I think she'll inspire you."

"How?"

"She's gifted, Sweetheart. In ways you can't begin to imagine."

Footsteps raced up the stairs. Kiera drew her other gun and slipped into the nearest room. Someone paused at the top of the stairs before moving closer. She readied herself to drop down and fire, expecting Julius to give away her location.

"Where is she?" Dajah asked.

"You're becoming problematic," Julius said. "However, I'm never one to waste opportunity."

"Dajah!" Kiera called, leaning out to see him standing alone. Staring down Julius.

Cat-like eyes met hers. "We need to go," he said. "Now."

"What's the hurry?" Julius asked. "Stay and chat a while. Your friends are coming, Dajah. You wanted me to put you in touch with them, right? I'm doing you one better."

"What's he talking about?" Kiera asked, eyes darting between them.

"Caerus is coming," Dajah said.

Choppers droned in the distance as if on cue.

That fast?

"Better get running, Sweetheart."

Dajah took her hand before she wasted more bullets and led them down the hall to another bedroom. A balcony overlooked part of the golf course. "We've got twenty minutes to get out of Heritage Heights. Two air units coming from the north. Ground vehicles won't be far behind."

"What's the plan?" she asked, torn.

"Kill Matthews later. We follow the trees. Gary's deactivating security on the wall so we can get over it." Opening the balcony doors, Dajah stepped out and surveyed the drop.

Kiera checked the hall and turned back in time to see him jump over the railing.

He waited two stories down unscathed. "I'll catch you. Come on!"

"Damn it!" Kiera cursed to herself. She was so close to having Julius gone, but she knew she wasn't getting inside that panic room before backup arrived. Frustration fueled anger and she threw herself over the railing, landing in strong, deft arms. "Unnecessary," she said to him, "but thanks."

"Don't need that getting worse," he said, giving a nod to her shoulder before putting her on her feet. "Keep up, ok?"

Kiera was too annoyed to acknowledge the steady throbbing in her shoulder. They took off at a jog for the tree line.

Body aching, mind replaying every detail from the moment she entered Julius's house, Kiera hadn't said a word since they cleared Heritage Heights and stole a vehicle.

Electricity still resonated in her veins, sparking at random from the first time Julius zapped her. If it wasn't for that, she might have had a clean shot. One perfect shot would have done it. Two imperfect shots turned his smug expression sour until he felt safe behind glass walls.

Déjà vu lingered, but she wouldn't acknowledge it.

Dajah pulled over beneath an underpass. "We should tend to that wound."

Audible words shifted her focus back to the lightheadedness and blood loss consuming her physical body. "Are we far enough away? Don't think anyone's following, but they can track us just as easily with a satellite."

He thumbed out the window. "Auxiliary subway entrance."

"Convenient." A smile tried forming through dulled pain.

"No, planned. Take your shirt off." Before she could object, he continued, "It's ruined anyway. Gonna use it to make a temporary bandage. We'll stitch it later."

"Not sure how I feel about you stitching anything," she said. Groaning with the movement, she did as he asked.

"He nicked the subclavian artery. If we don't stitch it, it'll break open with the least amount of effort, and it's kind of important." Dajah pulled one of his knives and cut her bloody shirt into strips. "Hold this," he said, pulling a USB device out of his pocket.

A hissed curse escaped her lips as he pressed wadded fabric deep into the wound and began wrapping it. When she thought she could speak without threatening him, she loosened her grip on the device and asked, "What is it?"

"Gary pulled some valuable intel off the man's hard drive. We should be able to use it..."

She met his gaze, brow furrowed at the pause. "But...?"

"Matthews has enough clout to summon Caerus to his defense." He tied off the makeshift bandage. "I'm beginning to think he works *for* them, not with them. Which means it's time we had some backup."

PART II

CHAPTER 14

The sun was cresting the horizon when Dajah and Kiera entered the park. Up ahead, three men sat on a bench, newspapers obscuring their faces.

"Time to meet the transporters," Dajah said.

"Them?" Kiera asked.

"Pretty sure." He'd never seen these three before, but that was expected. At his words, they lowered their papers and their heads turned in unison. Their pupils and sclera were pitch black.

The man in the middle stood up. "You're early," he said.

"Early," the others repeated, monotone.

"Not operating on all cylinders, boys?" Dajah asked.

"Bodies acquired on short notice. Come." They started walking with the same awkward, stiff gait.

Dajah shrugged to Kiera and followed.

"Demons?" she asked, staying by his side. "What kind of friends do you have that summon demons to be our transporters?"

"Eccentric. You'll like Matt."

"He owns the place we're going to?" she said.

Dajah nodded. He'd given her a brief overview of the team during their drive, but he wasn't sure how much she paid attention. Kiera stayed quiet, keeping her thoughts to herself.

The trio led them out to the street where a short limousine waited.

"Rolling out the red carpet I see," Dajah said, opening the door for Kiera. He slid in beside her, followed by two of their escorts. The third made his way to the front.

"We need to scan you," the duo said, pulling identical devices from the cloth sacks they carried. Within, black stone tablets held an iridescent sheen. The demons angled the tablets in their direction. A light, invisible touch caressed the top of Dajah's head and spread down along the silhouette of his body.

Kiera must have felt it, too. "What the hell was that?" she asked.

"Sensor tablets," the demons answered. "You're both clean."

"They're making sure we don't have any tracking devices," Dajah clarified.

The limo rolled forward, turning onto a main road. Tinted windows obscured their surroundings, but Dajah counted eight right turns before they pulled over.

"Your stop," the duo said, gesturing to the door by Kiera. Someone opened it from the outside. A lightly tanned hand with black, glitter-coated nails reached down to help her out. She accepted, and Dajah exited after.

Dressed in upscale casual – jeans and a button-down shirt that likely cost a fortune – Matt gave Kiera a once over. An intricately woven plait barely contained a mess of auburn-colored hair, with a few pieces framing perfect, mascara-lined eyes and a bare face.

"Long night?" Dajah asked. He knew this look on Matt well.

"Got the last stragglers out an hour ago," Matt said, motioning to the club behind them.

Observing the front of the establishment, Dajah shook his head. "Seven Street Lounge? You never learned your lesson in Vegas."

Matt smirked, giving Kiera his full attention. "Who's this gorgeous lady hanging around with your sorry ass?"

"Kiera, meet Matthias," Dajah said.

"Matt," he corrected, taking her hand with a suave finesse and kissing the back of it. "Pleasure's mine. Allow me to welcome you both to my newest, humble abode!"

~He makes a better first impression than you do.~

Really? He wanted to argue but caught the edges of Kiera's mouth lifting in the first smile he'd seen in too long.

Matt gave an elaborate flourish to the club doors. "Sanctuary awaits!"

Seven Street Lounge was upscale, swanky, and offered various forms of entertainment from what Dajah could see. The daytime lights were on, but it was easy to imagine the bars and dance floor crowded. Workers moved about cleaning up last night's extravaganza. Matt paused to pick up a silver necklace peeking out from one of the couches by the poles.

"Definitely didn't learn your lesson," Dajah said, watching one of the DJs gather up personal belongings. His simian tail swished to some lively beat only he could hear. Cocktail waitresses helped a blue-skinned man behind the main bar wash up glasses, some of which were floating.

Matt waved his hand dismissively, pocketing the necklace. "Too much competition. You'd be surprised how many asinine CEOs show up throwing money around here. We've even got that whole organic, non-GMO thing going on. The locals love it, and it's *way* more lucrative."

"You're a better fighter than a businessman."

"I'd argue I'm an *equally* exceptional fighter, but the lounge keeps my nails cleaner and my head on my shoulders."

"Where's the fun in that?"

They passed a vacuum running itself on the way to a set of metal stairs.

Always over the top, but it's nice to see.

"Matt," Kiera asked, "is your club exclusive to non-humans?"

"No, but it's a judgement-free zone," he explained. "All are safe and welcome here. The locals know it. And we've got measures in place that ensure both privacy as well as discretion." He led them upstairs to a security room with an overview of the main dance floor and countless monitors. "Gary designed most of the equipment in here."

"Anyone else here?" Dajah asked.

"Steffi's downstairs. You didn't give much warning you'd be coming. Was hoping to surprise you with this place."

"You knew I'd be coming sooner or later."

"Last time it took you months just to narrow down the city. Anyway, the tour continues. To the basement!" Matt keyed in numbers on one of the computers. The adjacent wall slid open, revealing an elevator, and Dajah raised an eyebrow. Hesitated. It wasn't the most spacious of steel boxes.

"Still haven't gotten over that?" Matt looped his arms between Dajah's and Kiera's to usher them inside. "It's only three floors down. You could jump it... or take the stairs. This is the shortcut. Can't have some drunken patrons stumbling into my bedroom because they're looking for a toilet to upchuck in."

"You live beneath the club?" Kiera asked. Dajah didn't hear Matt's answer, too focused on movement until the car stopped.

The elevator opened to a wide hallway below and two risqué paintings impossible to miss. Stepping out, Dajah tilted his head and tried to decide whether the bright curves were the outline of a hip, a breast, or both.

"We posed for those just last week," Matt said.

"You and who else?" Dajah asked.

Their host grinned. "Left to the warehouse. Right to the new digs. We'll see the warehouse first. Then you two can get settled and clean up."

The hallway turned once, ending in double steel doors that required a handprint scan to open. On the other side, hundreds of boxes, crates, and pallets lined the floors and aisles in organized rows. Workers moved about with forklifts and dollies, checking off lists. Several saluted Matt or offered deep nods as they passed.

Not a single one looks disgruntled. He must pay well.

"What do you *do* with all this stuff?" Kiera asked.

Matt dipped his hand into a crate of precious stones, pulling up quartz and several eye-catching pieces of amethyst. The next open crate featured fine silks. Further down Dajah spotted ammunition shells. Silverware. Paper.

"Trade it, sell it," Matt said with a shrug, letting the gemstones tumble through his fingers. "Consider me a middleman. Thanks to all the farms and processing plants around here, goods are shipped all over daily. If there's something you want, odds are good I can get it."

"Don't let him fool you," said a sultry voice from behind them. "He can't get *everything*."

Dajah turned as Steffi approached. When it came to style, the vampire often followed the latest upper-class fashion trends. This was the least amount of clothing he'd ever seen her in. High heels tapped a confident click as she closed the distance. Curly black hair flowed loose around her. Makeup accented an otherwise flawless face, and the rhinestone top and skirt exposed far more than it covered. Any man or woman who laid eyes on her couldn't deny Steffi was a perfect sex symbol, especially in exotic dancewear, though Dajah considered her the sister they never had. A few inches taller than him thanks to the heels, he had to look up to meet her gaze.

Steffi embraced him in a strong hug and took a long whiff of his scent. "Nice to see you're still alive, Dajah."

He smirked, taking a step back. "You, too, though I'd question what Matt's intentions are."

"Hey," Matt said, folding his arms after motioning over Steffi's outfit, "this was *her* idea."

"Stefanie de'Llewellyn," Dajah started, making formal introductions, "meet Kiera Lin."

Steffi's bright hazel eyes found Kiera's and she offered a hand in greeting. "Please, call me Steffi."

"Kiera," Kiera said, shaking.

Before Steffi released her hand, she lifted it and sniffed. Her expression transformed into one of bliss. "How exquisite!"

"She's not for tasting," Dajah said.

Her laugh was alluring as much as amused. "Kiera, if you're ever curious come find me."

"Steffi comes from an ancient line of vampires with a highly developed sense of smell," Matt explained. "She can tell you what you ate three days ago."

"Don't make it sound so uncouth," Steffi said, letting go of Kiera with a wink.

If nothing else, Kiera looked pleased with the exchange. "I'll keep your offer in mind," she said. Then, turning back to Matt, she asked, "You're demonkind, right? Upper echelon?"

Matt bowed to her question. "Lucky guess, or did Dajah tell you?"

"He mentioned we'd be hanging out with a bunch of non-humans, but your eyes give it away. There are purple flecks in your irises. I've had enough lessons in demonology to know it marks you higher than a Knight, or a half-breed. Given the way I feel around you, I'd bet on the former."

"How do you feel around him?" Dajah asked, curious.

"Safe when I have no right to be," Kiera said. "He's manipulating the emotional fields within the club."

Dajah's brow furrowed. "Really? How do you know that?"

"Told you she's exquisite," Steffi said.

"Couple tricks I learned from my brother," Kiera said. "He's a relic hunter."

Dajah had no idea what a relic hunter was, but Matt gave a respectful nod. "There might be a spell or two on the lounge. Doesn't make it any less true. You *are* safe here, Kiera. Any friend of Dajah's is a friend of ours. Now, let's get the two of you cleaned up and settled in. This way."

"I'll have Paul prepare some refreshments if he hasn't left yet," Steffi said, heading off.

Matt led Dajah and Kiera back into the hallway.

"What's up with you and Steffi," Dajah asked Matt.

"Mutual business partners," he explained. "Steffi oversees the parts of our entertainment that cater to specific tastes. And she's done amazing things for the local misfits. We've been operational for three months and we have a *waitlist* of people wanting to work here."

"So business is good," Dajah said.

"Business is excellent!"

Matt placed his hand on another scanner at the opposite end of the hall. It unlocked a wooden door that opened into spacious living quarters. Each piece of furniture and artwork was distinctly unique yet cohesive. Designed to seat ten or more comfortably, the living room came complete with a fireplace and wide-screen TV along one wall. Flowing into the kitchen, an island separated the two spaces. Five bedrooms, a communication room with high-tech computers and monitoring equipment, and a full gym with a sparring ring completed their tour of the space.

This'll be perfect for everyone when we're not in the field.

Their last group headquarters met an unfortunate end at the hand of a misunderstanding and some powerful explosives. Dajah grinned at the memory, but it came with barbs.

Caerus was closing in on us. We would have had to move regardless.

"No one else's here yet, so make yourselves at home," Matt said. "Spare clothes in most closets and drawers, but if you can't find something that fits let me know."

"Can you get us some Earth Beads?" Dajah asked.

Matt's expression fell flat. "For you?"

"For Kiera. She needs a crash course in Earth magic, and theory only goes so far. The man we're after has a modest set. He'd be dead by now if we were outfitted properly."

"You weren't?" Matt's eyebrows lifted.

"Don't try to sound like Taron," Dajah said. "It was a rush job. So the asshole lives a little longer. Still worth it for the intel Gary pulled. He said you could transmit this to him when we arrived." He pulled out the USB stick and handed it off.

"I'll take care of it. As for Earth Beads, I'm sure there's a few around somewhere. Give me a couple hours. In the meantime, first aid kits are in every bathroom if you need them."

CHAPTER 15

The shower ran hot and steamy – Kiera's ultimate haven. Water beat down on her hair and skin, stinging when it touched the stab wound, but it was worth it. The amount of physical and emotional dirt that could be washed away always soothed her.

Why now? Who was the woman he mentioned? Why do I still *feel like my blood's electrified?*

She squeezed extra shampoo into her palm.

"You're special, Kiera, but you need to know when it's better to be normal," her mother's voice echoed from memory. Kiera tried recalling the exact moment it was said. She remembered her mother and father arguing about something she'd done. The 'what' still eluded her.

Clean and relaxed, she found a pair of pants and a shirt that fit well enough. She donned the new attire and laid down atop fresh sheets, grateful for the privacy of one of the guest rooms. Memories and questions kept circling. Plaguing her.

The vampire's off-handed comment about her being 'exquisite' might have been flattery, but Kiera couldn't ignore the pattern any longer. Breathing deep, she released any lingering stress on the exhale and closed her eyes. If she didn't rest now while things were relatively safe, the mental and emotional tax of the past week would cripple her.

The dream came too fast for her to have fully fallen asleep.

*

She was in her parents' living room. Sammy sat across from her with a puzzle between them. Bits of eyes and fur and bars stared up at them from the incomplete zoo scene. Her brother went about trying the same piece in every possible position, even when the ends wouldn't match up.

"Kiera, you're too bright!" Sammy complained.

She knew the markings on her skin were glowing. She was using them to shield her brother from the arguments coming from the kitchen. Forcing her eyes to stay dry, she picked up a random puzzle piece – black and white striped fur.

"You're supposed to match the colors and patterns, Sammy."

"Yeah, but this could go too many places. See?" He held his piece against the image on the puzzle's box and moved it around, oblivious to the raised voices and foul words. "You can't just expect to know things. Gotta try it in ways that make sense so you don't miss anything."

She nodded, slipping her piece into place.

"We can't do this anymore!" her mother yelled from the kitchen. "It has to stop now."

"It'll stop when I say it's time," her father threatened. He'd been drinking again.

"There's no time left! You know this. We know this. It's over!"

Something crashed to the floor and shattered.

Sammy heard it. He leaned back, craning his head.

"Sammy, I think your piece goes here," Kiera said, pointing.

"They're at it again, aren't they?" he asked.

She couldn't lie, dropping her head in acknowledgement.

"We should go in there," he said, moving to get up from the floor.

Kiera grabbed his arm. "Don't." Every time Sammy tried to stop them, he made things worse.

Another crash sounded and Kiera flinched.

Another.

Some kind of thud.

Spilled liquid.

A chair toppled.

She wanted it to be over. Willed the noises to go away. Willed her parents to stop fighting.

She wanted things back to the way they were.

The ear-shattering BOOM extinguished her glowing symbols instantly, and both she and Sammy were on their feet. He ran in first and froze in the threshold. Kiera's heart pounded so fast she felt it in her temples, pummeling her brain. Her mouth went dry. All she could see past her brother was red.

Red on the walls.

Red dripping off the cabinet.

Red pooling on the floor.

Sammy's wail broke her heart into pieces. He threw himself to the ground, cradling their mother's body. Her face was distorted in grim acceptance, almost serene. Gooey, corrugated material glistened within a crescent gap in her skull, the flesh surrounding it blistered.

Her favorite cast iron pan was still gripped in their father's hand. In his other, a 9mm. Kiera wouldn't have recognized it as more than a gun at that age, but the lucid part of her knew the exact model. She noticed other things, too. How the burner on the stove was still on. How her father must have mouthed the pistol before pulling the trigger to achieve that sort of exit wound. Their mother... he'd only hit her once. Hard. The blow must have killed her instantly. She'd hit her head on the counter on the way down, jarring her neck into that gruesome angle.

She was making breakfast. Dad had manned the stove while she chopped onions. The scent of fresh-cut onions and burnt flesh was something Kiera'd never forget. She couldn't eat raw onions to this day.

*

Rapid blinking brought her out of the memory. She laid there in the stillness, numb until a shudder passed through her. She'd recalled her parents' death plenty of times, but never in such vivid detail.

My skin was glowing. Using some kind of magic... She knew at that moment where the déjà vu came from. Her blood tingled then like it tingled now. *It wasn't the first time, either, but it was the last. I know that. Why can't I remember?*

Part of her died with her parents. The events of that night shaped her future, but dwelling in the past wasn't helping the present. Sitting up, Kiera surveyed the bedroom, backlit by the light she'd left on after her shower. She ran a hand down the smooth, unmarred skin of her forearm – no symbols or scars existed. A wrought iron wall clock contradicted the fact that it was barely noon. She wasn't sure what time her body thought it was *supposed* to be, but she missed her routine sleep schedule.

"Can't believe Julius was only yesterday," she groaned. "Or that the asshole's still alive. I was so close!" Before she started second-guessing every action from Julius's house, she left the bedroom to find Dajah.

The living room's giant flat screen played a news broadcast on mute – warning signs that a previously dormant volcano might become a major threat in Europe. Kiera watched it for a moment before realizing the remote was hovering above one of the couches. *Again?!* She moved to the center of the room, giving the furniture a wide berth.

Dajah laid on his side, brow creased in concern with his eyes closed, body jerking in subtle ways. He was otherwise silent. A drink coaster floated a foot above the table next to him, spinning slowly.

"I'm sorry they gave you nightmares," she said. "You're not alone in that regard."

Ensuring there were no weapons within reach, Kiera placed her hand on his shoulder and squeezed gently. "Dajah."

◇

Registering pressure dangerously close to vital arteries, Dajah reached up and grabbed the arm. He pulled back, simultaneously kicking out to disrupt the attacker's center of gravity, and launched himself over. They hit the ground hard, him on top, and the last vestiges of nightmare faded... just as Kiera head-butted him. His vision swam with black spots. She brought one knee up between them, twisted her arms to break his lock-hold, and threw him over her head.

Dajah landed on his back and Kiera came down on him, pinning his hips to the ground, arms to his sides. Leverage worked to her advantage. He stilled himself, eyes closed. "I'd apologize, but I'm equally impressed."

Her snort made him smile and he looked up as she leaned back, taking her weight off his arms.

"If this is the 'thanks' I get for waking you up from your nightmares, I'm gonna leave you to them next time."

"I am sorry," he admitted. "Didn't mean to fall asleep."

"What were you dreaming about this time?" she asked, arms folded.

"I was fighting."

"Maybe you shouldn't be in this line of work if it gives you nightmares." She was obviously trying to keep the tone light.

"I'll take it under advisement." He wasn't going to admit the reason people were dying was because sadist scientists forced Queen into a frenzy and unleashed her on those unequipped to defend themselves. Neither of his brothers was in that nightmare, but the lack of control, the feeling of being trapped... it was always the same.

A whistle came from the other side of the room. "You know there are *five* unoccupied bedrooms, right?" Matt asked, coming closer. He picked the remote up from the floor and turned off the TV.

Both Dajah and Kiera looked at him.

Matt waved between them. "Also, it's usually more satisfying when you're not fully dressed."

"Thought you'd be longer," Dajah said, grinning.

Kiera stood and offered a hand to help him up.

"More foreplay then!" Matt said, tossing something.

Dajah caught the bracelet – six marble-sized Beads knotted

along black cord. Three red, two yellow, and a purple-hued stone made up the collection.

"Earth Beads?" Kiera asked.

"Yep," Dajah confirmed. "You ready?"

"That depends heavily on his definition of foreplay," she said, "but I'm interested in how these work."

"Place is shielded," Matt said. "Use them anywhere here or in the club, though I would strongly encourage you to keep to the sparring ring."

Dajah's grin widened. "I'm not gonna destroy your new place, not with these anyway."

"You've ruined more with less," Matt said, eyes crinkling.

"Remember what I told you back at the motel?" Dajah asked Kiera, keeping the topic on track.

"Most of it," she said. "Having experienced Julius's attacks firsthand, I think I've got a pretty good idea how they work."

"You will," Dajah said. "As soon as you touch one of these and bring your awareness to it, you'll understand exactly what spells the stone is capable of."

Kiera moved to take the string of Beads but Dajah closed his fist around it. "Not so fast. Before you touch it, you need to understand what you're doing. Casting Earth magic is ridiculously easy. Out of respect for our host, we're going to the gym for this."

He explained the three steps to casting magic on their short walk. "First, you bring your awareness to the Bead and choose the spell. New Earth Beads will only possess one variation of a spell. Variants and intensities increase the more a Bead's used."

"And you'll get some idea of the cost of each spell," Matt added. "If it shreds your brain just concentrating on it, probably shouldn't cast it."

"I'll keep that in mind," Kiera said flatly.

"Second," Dajah continued, "choose your target. It can be an object or an individual, including yourself, and in some cases, you can target multiple. Lastly, you surrender your energy to the Bead to complete the sequence and initiate the spell."

"Balancing cost with desired effect is one of the hardest things to get used to," Matt said. "Gotta know your body's limitations. Never forget that you fuel those Beads with your body's energy. It'll feel like you sprinted a marathon at first, but it gets easier over time as you build up a tolerance for it." He grabbed a dummy and placed it in the center of the sparring ring. "Cast your first spell on this."

"Actually, I'm gonna cast the first spell," Dajah said. He pinched the purple stone between index finger and thumb, already knowing from the deep color the healing spell would be satisfactory. "As long as a Bead's in contact with your flesh you can use it," he continued, "but two people can't use the same Bead at the same time. The cord we string them with functions as a closed circuit. In other words, if you're wearing Earth Beads as a bracelet, I can't just come up, touch your bracelet, and use them."

He cast a mid-level Heal spell from the Bead's three variants, using Kiera as his target. It was overkill for the level of injuries she sustained but cost him nothing. He wanted her fully recovered from her confrontation with Julius Matthews.

Kiera's hand went to her shoulder wound and her face reflected the intensity of the healing. It wasn't a painless process, but it was fast. Twenty seconds later her body was hale. There wouldn't be as much as a scar from recent events.

"Now *that's* impressive," she admitted, rolling her shoulder and catching her breath.

Dajah tossed her the bracelet. "Touch them one at a time. Tell me what you sense."

She did as asked, describing the spell and associated variants within each Bead.

"Anyone ever tell you you waste too much time trying to explain shit?" Matt asked, then looked to Kiera. "Just cast one of the spells already. Earth magic's easier to learn through experience."

Kiera grinned, turning her attention to the target. A moment later the puffy white pad atop the dummy stick burst into flames.

She immediately extinguished it, encasing the structure in a layer of ice that burst into prismatic dust seconds after forming.

"I don't feel any different," she said. "Should I?"

"Cast the advanced Ice spell five times in a row," Dajah said.

After the third casting, he raised an eyebrow at Matt. "Enchanted targets?" The dummy hadn't suffered an ounce of visible damage.

The demon's face beamed. "Best kind!"

Kiera hesitated after the fourth spell but continued. When the last bit of ice shattered off the target, she took a deep breath. "Yeah, ok."

"We call it the Drain," Dajah explained.

"Feels like the early effects of some kind of sedative," Kiera said.

"Drain's cumulative and proportional to the types of spells cast and how you use the magic. Rapid-casting's rarely a good idea, but your body adjusts to the magic the longer you use it. Use it enough, and you'll reach a point where you'll have to cast a *lot* of magic before you feel the slightest Drain."

"How long does it take to wear off?"

"For what you just did? A few minutes tops. Just remember it's *your* energy powering these spells."

"So if I use too much, it'll kill me," she said.

Matt pointed at her. "You got it!"

"Julius didn't cast another barrier to protect himself when I finally broke through it. He ran to his panic room instead."

"He uses Earth Beads like most of Caerus's bureaucratic morons – showy, powerful threats that exceed their skill level," Dajah said. "Matthews ran because he couldn't cast another barrier capable of deflecting bullets without it significantly costing him more than he was willing to risk. We're gonna make sure you know how to use these properly."

"Don't forget about your barriers!" Dajah moved, casting

another Ice spell. Kiera's barrier manifested in time to absorb the magic, but the resulting Drain slowed her, and he landed a punch to her stomach. Tensing, she doubled forward and countered, stomping on the arch of his foot and sending a palm strike to the center of his chest. He took the hit and stepped back. She pressed her advantage, throwing a series of punches.

Kiera wasted a lot of energy with her physical attacks, but this exercise was about using Earth Beads for tactical defense. He'd teach her momentum flow some other time.

A Lightning spell hit the back of Dajah's leg, causing him to buckle at the knee and lose his current train of thought. Kiera threw him over her hip. He cast Fire, shattering her remaining barrier and singing the tips of her hair. Then he double-cast Ice, immediately halting whatever advance she had planned.

"I *hate* that damn Ice spell!" she yelled, vigorously rubbing the frost from exposed skin.

Dajah regained his feet. "You're a fast learner. Few would think to target—" Another Lightning spell struck him to the core, dropping him to his knees. Forked, tertiary branches of electricity sparked off his body as it spasmed, searing black rings into the mat. He fell forward, catching himself with his hands. Breaths came fast and labored as the residual effects of the spell subsided.

"Holy shit!" Matthias yelled. He'd been seated beside Steffi on the bench. Now he was on his feet, moving in.

"You ok?" Kiera asked, crouching beside Dajah.

Dajah sat back on his calves and looked at her. "How'd you do that?"

"What do you mean? I wanted to shut you up before you started lecturing again."

"Not what I mean."

Matt gave Kiera a pat on the back. "Might be the first time I've ever seen a novice take him down like that. Excellent job!"

"It was an impossible spell," Dajah said. "That Lightning Bead isn't capable of casting it."

"Kiera, were you using the Enhance spell?" Steffi asked.

"No." Kiera diverted her eyes to the colored stones on her wrist. "Did I do something wrong?"

"Let me see your bracelet," Dajah said, holding his hand out.

She slid the stones off, offering them. As soon as Dajah touched the Lightning Bead, he understood what happened. It was still impossible.

"Well?" Matt asked.

Dajah tossed the Beads to him, watching to see if Matt sensed the same thing.

"Double holy shit," said the demon. "She created an upgraded variant after three hours of practice?"

"Told you she was exquisite," Steffi said.

"Are you even Drained?" Matt asked Kiera.

"No. Maybe? What'd I do?"

Dajah stood as the pins and needles subsided. "You created a new variation of the base spell that exceeds the level of the previous variants without upgrading the Bead itself."

"In English?" she asked.

"You combined the two versions of lightning magic within that Bead and created something new."

"That's possible?"

"It's possible. It's also extremely difficult to accomplish. I've never heard of anyone intuiting it before."

"The woman's got natural talent! Where'd you say you found her again?" Matt asked.

"A dingy bar," Dajah said, "pretending to drink herself into a stupor before getting shot at just to avoid dancing with me."

"Is that how you recall things?" Kiera asked, eyebrow raised.

"My preferred version of it," Dajah admitted, smirking. He took the Earth Beads from Matt and combined them with his own, creating a six-Bead bracelet that he offered back to Kiera. "Here. You've earned them."

"Speaking of bars," Matt started, "are you two going to make an appearance at my club?"

"That even wise?" Dajah asked. "Kiera has a bounty on her

head till we off her ex-boss."

She lifted both brows. "Don't use my contract as an excuse. If you don't know how to dance, just say so."

"I can dance," he defended.

"Then you've got nothing to worry about. Steffi," Kiera asked, shifting her focus to the vampire. She'd since changed into casual attire. "Can I talk with you in private at some point?"

"I'm heading out on a few errands if you care to accompany me," she offered.

"Sure," Kiera said.

The two of them left the gym together.

"We should touch base with Gary," Matt said to Dajah, "see if he's made any progress with that USB."

"Sitting around a computer screen is sooo exciting," Dajah said flatly.

"What? You wanna get your ass kicked again?"

"She hardly kicked my ass, Matt. I wasn't prepared to defend against a spell like that."

"Unprepared for the spell. Unprepared for the raid on some guy's house. You're slipping."

"Been a bit distracted lately."

"Uh huh," Matt said, motioning to the sparring ring.

CHAPTER 16

Ethan considered himself many things. At the top of that list was 'patient.' He'd hunted Elizabeth for months. Sparing a day to plan out his next move cost nothing. The violent flares of essence last night confirmed her location. He sensed her even now. Weak. Barely stable. Stationary.

The problem was that she was somewhere *below* him.

Indulging in a greasy tuna melt, he sat at an outdoor table and observed the buildings across the street. A hodgepodge of jewelers and brand-name stores punctuated by the occasional coffee shop lined the sidewalk. Ethan was more interested in the double glass doors leading down to additional shops and the subway. People of all colors, dressed in outfits ranging from something someone found on the street to corporate lawyer, came and went from those doors.

Every Child of the Sect was born with the ability to sense nearby abominations, but they didn't gain their symbols until successfully eliminating one. Abominations wielded distorted forms of magic that scourged the very Realm they walked on. Only after that essence was taken in by a Child was it purified and worthy. Ethan had gained many useful abilities over the years. A gentle flare activated two symbols that gave him a form of radar capable of visualizing patterns of hollow and solid forms.

The feedback perplexed him.

Riddled with tunnels, pipes, basements, and miles of subway tracks, the city was comparable to any major metropolis with one exception. Two hundred feet below the buildings was a massive complex, impenetrable to his senses. One of the subway lines connected to it. Beyond that, he'd have to explore on his own.

Infiltrating locations was something Ethan had always been good at, even before gaining his Invisibility Bubble. Regardless, he'd be diligent in approaching this mysterious complex. The first step was ensuring his energy reserves were full.

"Some things are universal, regardless of the Realm." He popped a deep-fried onion ring into his mouth, savoring the crunch. Washing down the delicacy with carbonated water, he left a tip that was triple the price of his meal and made for the doors.

Nu Philly's subway lines operated in conjunction with their regional rail and bus services. Instead of dank, dingy tunnels littered with trash, homeless, and the unmistakable scent of urine, Ethan was greeted with a hub of activity. A handful of restaurants anchored the underground mall, with smaller newsstands and a plethora of average retail shops catering to locals. Automatic stares ushered him along to the transportation sector. Screens listed arriving trains and connecting points – organized chaos, not unlike the airport. He scanned listings and studied the elaborate map of colored lines while Elizabeth's essence pulsed on his radar. None of the marked tracks took him near her location, so he waited, observing those around him.

Patience always paid off.

The group of interest wore business casual attire, conversing amongst themselves while snacking on foil-wrapped sandwiches. Instead of moving to any of the listed platforms, their destination was a utility hallway labeled AUX27. Divine guidance encouraged him to follow, and he cast his Invisibility Bubble.

The ability could form a spherical shape large enough to accommodate two, or a tight silhouette around a single body. The Sect assured them that they were truly invisible – to eyes, to electronics, and to magic – when using this skill, as long as nothing disrupted the magic's field, but no method was flawless. Ethan kept his Bubble in close and his footsteps light as he continued past two doors labeled for employees. The third door was fitted with a scanner. One of the women pulled a keycard from her purse and ran it through the strip. A buzz and a green light granted her entrance. They headed through single file.

Ethan grabbed the lip of the door in time to make it appear as if it just closed slowly, and stepped out onto a private platform. A long bench provided seating. Numerous security cameras covered every aspect of the space. Ethan kept to the corners while everyone else scanned his or her keycard at a wall terminal. When the last one registered, a feminine computer voice announced, "Transport arrival in fifteen minutes."

Ethan slipped onto the near-empty train, choosing a space towards the back where no one should accidentally bump into him. If any of the occupants became alert to his presence, it would complicate matters.

Half a day wasn't nearly long enough to explore all of the facility he learned was called "Caerus." The complex was expansive. He lifted surface thoughts from regular office workers and high-level executives alike, each having a different perspective on how valuable their work was. None of it overlapped with the Sect of Preservation, which meant their acquiring Elizabeth was little more than an accident.

With minor exceptions, her essence signature hadn't moved. Still, it took Ethan careful scouting and some skillful pickpocketing to procure the right keycards to reach her. Securing access was the most challenging part. Now that he was here, the hallway was deserted. No guards patrolled, threatening to bump into his Invisibility Bubble, and he only passed two workers in lab coats leaving one of the other rooms. All the individuals housed in the Wing were either incapacitated, unconscious, or in no state to leave on their own.

He observed through the door's window for some time, watching an aid fuss over Elizabeth's current state. A thin gown kept her modest but did little to obscure countless wounds. Her symbols pulsed weakly. Ethan had eliminated enough of her kind to know that she was already on Death's doorstep. Those symbols were trying desperately to pull in enough energy from the surrounding environment just to keep her alive.

"Did they find you like this, or do this to you?"

A pang of regret flitted through him. Elizabeth had given him a good chase. Though not as skilled as her ancestors, she had the potential to be a worthy opponent. Now she was little more than a corpse. It didn't make his duty any less sacred, but it left a bitter taste in his mouth as he swiped the keycard.

The door slid open and the aid within looked up, perplexed. "Hello?"

Aware of all the surveillance cameras monitoring the room and all the equipment monitoring Elizabeth, Ethan had few options. He approached Elizabeth and placed his hand over her wrist, unable to help the snort that followed.

"Who's in here?!" the aid demanded. She backed up against the counter, searching.

"It seems you're in the right place at the right time," Ethan said. He flared the symbols under his ribcage and brilliant, blinding white light engulfed the room. Closing the distance, he had his hands on the woman's arms in an instant.

She gave a startled yell before her instincts kicked in. "Get your hands off me!"

"My using these powers on you would be frowned upon by the Sect, but it's the kindest thing I can offer," Ethan said by way of apology and explanation. He activated the symbols on his palms and started siphoning the woman's lifeforce. She went limp in his arms. A skinny thing, Ethan held her up without difficulty until his task was complete. Once the aid's condition mimicked Elizabeth's as closely as possible, he began the task of transferring the monitoring equipment. It took extra time, but this was a calculated risk. He wove an illusion spell over the woman, replicating Elizabeth.

"Who knows? They might even be able to save you if they find you in time." Ethan assumed he had until someone else came to check on Elizabeth or the aid was reported missing. Security cameras would show whiteout conditions temporarily. His task shouldn't trigger alarms unless someone happen to be watching this particular feed at this particular moment. In a facility this big, he doubted it – divine purpose guided him. Always.

"As for you," he said, shifting attention to the broken abomination lying on the floor. "Your time has ended. And the world becomes safer for it." He crouched down beside Elizabeth, pulling his ceremonial dagger – the one blessed by the oldest Teacher. "I take back that which never belonged to you," he said, placing his palm on her chest, symbols still active, "and transmute it into that which gives me strength to protect the Great Seal." Ethan absorbed what was left of her life essence, knowing the transfer would leave him with enhanced abilities once the assimilation completed.

The glow of Elizabeth's symbols faded. When the last trace of orange disappeared from sallow skin, he plunged the dagger into her heart. Her wound bled little. Her flesh faded to an ashen grey and took on a withered appearance. As the stain of Elizabeth was purged from the Realms, her essence mingled with that of many others inside Ethan. Given time, it would settle in, forming new patterns on his skin. He would have gotten far more had she been in an ideal condition. Nevertheless, Ethan was grateful.

As he pulled his dagger free, Elizabeth's corpse disintegrated, leaving piles of carbon dust and a handful of plastic medical instruments. He swept them away with a wave of his hand and a burst of air. The brightness of the room faded.

It was time to go.

CHAPTER 17

Dajah took the stairs, preferring them to the cramped steel box Matt used to get from his apartment to the club. All things considered; it was an ideal location for a base of operations. They'd move fast once Gary finished analyzing the intel, but tonight was for distractions, according to Matthias.

~Haven't you been distracted enough?~

Where've you been?

~Busy.~

He snorted outwardly. What kept a voice in his head busy when it wasn't in his head? Refusing to go down that path, Dajah opted for a different approach. *You gonna be a problem tonight?*

~While you procrastinate? ~

Procrastinate? This is the best lead we've had! Gary needs time.

~She's not who you think she is.~

And how the hell would you know who she is?

~She called Earth Beads Yara'ista.~

Were you paying any attention during that conversation? It was something her grandmother called them.

~And what nationality was her grandmother?~

How am I supposed to know? Asian?

~Yara'ista is from an ancient language. It means 'concentrated energy,' and it's not from any Asian culture.~

And what culture is it from? And how would you know if I don't?

~It doesn't matter. I pay attention. She created a third-level variant spell instantaneously. The energy reserves required to do something like that... Even you'd have a hard time with it.~

What are you implying, Queen?

~That she's keeping something from you.~

She's got a right to her secrets. Not like I've been forthcoming about you. Just let me enjoy this, ok? Once her boss's dead, it's over. She'll be gone.

~Lie to yourself all you want. You can't lie to me, Dajah.~

Are you finished?

~You're the one standing in a stairwell talking to yourself. I'll keep an eye on things.~

That was probably the best response he could hope for, and a sharp reminder that even when Queen's presence wasn't apparent, she was always around. How could she not be? She *was* him.

With his mood temporarily dampened, he continued up the stairwell. Heavy base reverberated through glass doors leading to one of the employee lounges. A swarthy, broad-chested bouncer held open the door as Dajah approached.

"Evening, sir," his gruff voice offered in greeting. "Boss secured the Opal platform for your group tonight. He asks that you meet him by the main bar. Straight through those doors. Hang left."

"Thanks," Dajah said, following the bouncer's instructions. The music was subdued within the lounge. He'd been preparing, dulling his hyper-senses to a point where the noises and flashing lights wouldn't overwhelm him. It was a delicate balance, being receptive enough to pick up the slightest hint of danger while not blowing out his eardrums or burning his retinas. Matt would have his demons spread out to make sure nothing got out of control, but Dajah still worried about Kiera's safety. Jackson wasn't under Organization jurisdiction. That worked both for and against her.

~Why are you worried about her safety?~

Because we need her, Queen.

~You don't.~
Go away.

Eight p.m. was early for a club that stayed open until five in the morning, yet dozens worked up a sweat on the dance floor. Others chatted in groups. Both the main and secondary bars had a healthy crowd, and close to half of the tables and booths were taken already.

Spotting Matt, Dajah joined him at the bar. The demon was impeccably dressed, with a silk shirt, leather pants, and silver jewelry accenting his neck and wrists. He'd left his hair half up, interwoven braids giving him fey-like attributes.

"Has Kiera seen you yet?" Matt asked, studying Dajah. "Forgot how well you cleaned up."

"Not yet. She was still getting ready. Insisted I meet her here. Steffi wasn't dressed yet, either."

"Ah, she's not working tonight. I've got a little surprise for us. Guests!"

"Guests?"

"Should be here in an hour or two. Meantime, we've got full bottle service on the platform." Matt raised his hand, summoning one of the women behind the bar.

"Lookin' hot tonight, Boss," she said with a wink. Tufted ears protruded from bouncy waves of snow-colored hair. Her gaze shifted to Dajah, and white snowfields reflected in her eyes instead of him or the club. "Friend's not bad, either. What can I get'chas?"

"Two Special Sevens, Valie," Matt ordered.

Nodding, she turned with a flourish to grab two bottles behind the bar. Her tail kept beat as the DJ switched to the next catchy tune. Dajah leaned his arm on the bar, scanning the club. Non-humans flaunted their features openly alongside the mundane.

"It's good to see this," Dajah admitted.

"Here ya's go," Valie said, placing two Collins glasses in front of them. "Enjoy!"

Dajah picked up his drink, appreciating the seven layers in

various shades of peach and lime. "Do I wanna know what's in this?"

"Deliciousness," Matt said, taking a sip. The layers remained suspiciously in place, just thinner. "All alcohol. Mostly rum. Little splash of something extra. You'll like it."

Dajah sipped smooth notes of fruity molasses and a touch of spice that kept it from being overly sweet.

"Well?" Matt asked.

"You're right." He took a deeper swig as his eyes caught sight of something truly magical. The rest of the club fell away into a background blur. He'd been instantly attracted to her when he'd first seen Kiera, but nothing prepared him for the bombshell swaying towards him.

Her hair was loose, blown out to give it volume and body with soft waves. Piercing hazel eyes sparkled between eyeliner and shimmery shadow, and her lips were accented in a matte ruddy pink. A teardrop necklace drew his eyes downward to the sequined silver cocktail dress fitting her like a glove. It showcased her perfect figure, flaring through the hips. Black stilettos completed the outfit, and Kiera most definitely owned the look.

"Shit, you both clean up well." Matt motioned for Valie with a lift of his drink.

"Matthias," Kiera said in greeting.

The demon bowed his head to her, "Kiera."

"You look amazing," Dajah said.

"Gotta say, this is a much better look for you than burnt coffee grinds and flour." She pulled aside the edge of his blazer, exposing the button-down shirt beneath, and pinched fabric off his chest. His focus followed her hand as she rubbed the material between her fingers then let her palm lay flat and slide lower. A simple belt, chinos, and leather shoes completed his outfit, all in black with a slate grey jacket.

Valie produced another Special Seven and Matt offered it to Kiera, disrupting her attention.

"House special," he explained. "See that tall, skinny gentleman over by the stairs?" Matt directed their gaze to a section of elevated seating blocked with a velvet rope. White couches lined the back wall with a few tables and a dozen backless chairs. The man standing beside it aptly fit the demon's description, wearing a crimson suit. He must have sensed the attention, raising his hand in acknowledgement.

"That's Papos," Matt explained. "I reserved the platform for us tonight. Best view in the club, and the entire section can be soundproofed. Wanna have a conversation without straining your voice, get away from the noise, change up the music, or have one-way screens lowered for additional privacy? All doable. Papos will see to anything you need, and my head chef's preparing a feast. Make your way up there in about an hour. Otherwise... keep yourselves entertained. Gotta see someone about a duck."

Dajah raised an eyebrow but didn't ask as Matt took off with his drink.

"He did say 'duck,' right?" Kiera asked.

"Yep."

Kiera didn't realize how badly she needed a distraction until the DJ switched to a slower song after the fourth set. She'd done nothing but smile and laugh for the past hour. True to his word, Dajah could dance, and he wasn't the least bit shy about whipping out some ridiculous move for the hell of it.

He led them into a slow, intimate groove without getting inappropriate or overstepping boundaries. His eyes glowed when certain lights hit just right, and when he looked at her, she felt like the only other person in the room. Adoration, mutual respect, and lust lingered in those green depths.

"Ready for another drink?" he asked, lips close to her ear.

A sly smile formed. "Let's check out our VIP seats." Taking his hand, Kiera maneuvered them through the bodies towards the Opal platform.

Papos unclipped the rope for them.

"Can we get a couple more of those Special Sevens?" Dajah asked.

"Right away, sir, ma'am." Papos lifted a hand to his ear, placing the order.

Hot, sizzling food reached Kiera's nostrils as soon as they crested the stairs. "Dajah, look!" A spread of appetizers and snacks lay before them. The instant watering of her mouth reminded her the last time she'd eaten anything substantial was too long ago. "This smells amazing!"

Wasting no time, she plucked one of the skewers off the plate, biting into a piece of roasted pepper and steak. "Perfectly seasoned." She went in for another bite.

Dajah selected one of the egg rolls, ripping it open to examine its contents before stuffing half into his mouth.

"You're particular about what you'll put in your mouth, huh?" she asked.

"I've got a *discerning* pallet. Shit like this can be deceiving." He grinned, inspecting the salsa before scooping a chip in.

"It's your friend's nightclub. You think he'd send us food he knows you hate?"

"Absolutely, look at that other dip. It just screams guac and cheese."

"Not everyone hates cheese," Steffi said, cresting the top of the stairs. Her dress was sapphire lace, modest compared to what she wore when Kiera first saw her but still chic. She carried a martini glass with dark red and black swirls, choosing one of the chairs adjacent to Kiera.

"You look amazing, Steffi," Kiera offered.

"And you're stunning." Setting her glass down, she scooped an excessive portion of the guac-and-cheese dip onto a strip of flatbread.

Dajah shook his head, selecting another skewer of chicken, beef, and vegetables.

"The twins are here," Steffi said. "Matt's giving them a brief tour. They should be joining us..." She leaned forward to scan the floor below. "Ah, over there."

Kiera spotted Matthias leading two men in their direction. Both were dressed similarly – dark denim with polos – but she'd be hard-pressed to call them twins.

"Mars is wearing red. Gunner's the one in blue. More of Caerus's reject experiments," Dajah said fondly. "They're spliced with over a dozen animal species between the two of them."

"Have all of you been wronged by Caerus in some way?" Kiera asked, genuinely curious.

"You could say that. Everyone you'll meet, save Martin, Gary's protégé, has a bone to pick. Gary and Martin are human, for the record," he said.

The trio joined them.

"Kiera, meet Mars and Gunner," Matt said, motioning to the twins. "Guys, this is Dajah's friend, Kiera."

"Nice to meet you," Mars said, a snake's tongue darting out briefly on the word 'nice' to give the man a subtle lisp. He was bald, with ears flat against his head and limbs that seemed a touch too long for his body. Mottled, dark skin was visible on his exposed arms and neck, evening out on his face.

"Heya," Gunner said with a wave of two fingers. He was all scruff. Scruffy beard, scruffy hair, pointed ears, and claw-like fingernails. A patchy wolf's tail swished leisurely behind him.

The twins were certainly odd. With tall, athletic builds, they could have passed for humans with a fetish for body modification provided Gunner hid his tail. *Skullz would be into either of them if he was still single.* The thought made her wonder if Rad Tattoos was still standing. *OPASA would've sent agents to ransack my loft by this point. Hope everyone else is ok.* Brenna was a topic best avoided, but Skullz and the others at the tattoo parlor had nothing to do with her past. Didn't mean Julius wouldn't try to use them if he thought it'd give him an advantage.

A sigh escaped her lips, but the creeping melancholy was soon replaced with curiosity. In addition to the Special Sevens on the waitress's drink tray, there was another martini, two amber-yellow draft beers, and a full bottle of unopened... something. The bottle lacked labels but came in the shape of a ram skull, and the clear liquid suggested vodka or tequila. A stack of shot glasses accompanied it.

This'll get out of hand quickly.

Matt, Mars, and Gunner took seats, helping themselves to the food.

"So, what brings you two out tonight?" Dajah asked.

"Word on the street," Mars started, "says we're due for another hit."

"Word on the street travels fast," Dajah said, glancing at Matt. "We only just got here this morning."

"Yeah, but you should have heard Gary over the phone," Matt said. "Kiera's former boss is our ticket in!"

"You worked for Caerus?" Gunner asked Kiera.

"No," she said. "I worked for a company called OPASA. Seems like my boss had his hand in a bit of everything."

"Matt said Dajah's helping you get rid of him," Gunner continued.

She nodded. "That's how this all started. Asshole put a contract out on me."

"Piss 'em off?" Mars asked.

"Who knows? Julius rarely justifies anything he does. He's got enough clout and financial backing to entice an endless number of mercenaries and goons. Best chance I've got short of uprooting everything is to get rid of him."

"He'll be dead soon enough," Gunner said. "If Dajah said he'd help, he'll help." Both twins looked at Dajah with adoration, leaving Kiera wondering what the story was.

"How many people are in your group?" she asked, keeping the conversation light.

"Count's up to fifty-seven now," Matt said, "but not everyone fights. You're looking at the bulk of the ground team, here. This'll be the third facility we've taken out."

"Small team's better. More efficient," Gunner added.

"How many facilities do they have?"

"Left? Maybe six more after this. We don't count their satellite stations," Dajah said.

"Chain of command trickles down," Matt elaborated. "Take out one primary and it effectively disables Caerus for a region, but if we could locate their island, we could end them completely."

"They have an island?"

"Rumors for the most part," Steffi said, finishing her martini. "We believe Caerus's headquarters is located on a heavily fortified island. Presumably, their president lives there. It's where all sensitive research is conducted, and where their servers are kept."

"Take those out and it's game over," Matt said, reaching for the skull bottle. He cracked open the seal and lined up the shot glasses. "Enough talk of business. It's a fine night for a party!"

Kiera lost track of how many shots they took. Halfway through the second ram's skull, the twins were wasted. Mars was on the stripper poles, and Gunner convinced one of the bartenders to join him elsewhere. Matthias was chatting it up with customers, making his rounds. Steffi eventually retired to a private room with a handful of men and women, leaving Kiera and Dajah alone.

He tried to match her shot-for-shot for a while until he realized this wasn't a contest he'd win.

"Are you even buzzed?" he asked, watching her finish her cocktail.

Kiera grinned. "Call it energized. Not sure I've ever been drunk. Not sure I can be."

"Well, I can't keep drinking like this without burning some of it off. Come on." He stood, offering both hands to her.

Dajah was tipsier than he pretended, and though he didn't stumble, he was less mindful about where his hands trailed on the dance floor. Kiera took full advantage, shimmying and shaking in seductive ways while guiding those hands. She deserved a good distraction at this point.

When the next song called for more intimate maneuvering, Dajah spun her in close and wrapped both arms around her. His gaze was hypnotic, wanting. He leaned in to kiss her and Kiera met his lips without objection, appreciating every nuance of his mouth. Their kiss deepened. His hands became more needy and possessive while their bodies continued swaying to the suggestive baseline. Then he stiffened the wrong way and took a step back. Confused, Kiera searched those green eyes for an explanation.

"Sorry, need some water," Dajah said, making a hasty exit off the dance floor.

She stood there watching him weave through the crowd as others continued their private and public performances around her. "What the hell?"

Kiera found him downing a second glass of water at the bar. She approached cautiously, placing a hand on his shoulder. "You ok?"

His eyes met hers and he shook his head. "Migraine. Not sure if it's Matt's cocktails, the lights, or the music."

Pressing her lips into a frown, she wasn't sure what to believe. *Something* sobered him. "Let's get out of here, then." Kiera considered taking his hand but thought better of it. Everything about Dajah's body language suggested he was a willing participant up until that moment. Either he really was getting sick, or he was using the oldest excuse in the book. She tried not to take it personally but couldn't help but wonder if she'd done something wrong.

"Yeah," he said, finishing off his water in a big gulp.

CHAPTER 18

The space below the club was quiet. Even with the party in full swing above, the demon ensured his domain was properly warded and insulated. Dajah was grateful for the privacy for all the wrong reasons.

~*You're exaggerating things.*~

I don't trust you not to hurt her. And we both know if it comes to that, you won't stop.

~*When was the last time I hurt someone who didn't deserve it?*~

Dajah winced as memories bombarded him. He knew Queen was trying to reference the incident two months ago when she 'helped' with the gang, leaving a slew of bodies to clean up afterwards. They deserved what they got. It didn't justify her taking over when Dajah could have handled it.

He'd never forgive her for the past.

He'd never fully trust her, even if she was trying to do better.

"Does it hurt that bad?" Kiera asked.

Dajah realized he was standing there, gripping the back of the couch like his life depended on it. Or hers. "I'm ok."

"Go lay down in one of the rooms. Keep the lights off. I'll get you some more water."

He watched her head into the kitchen and sighed. "I'm sorry. You don't have to keep an eye on me if you wanna head back upstairs."

Hazel eyes pierced him from across the room. "You trying to

say you're no longer enjoying my company?"

He'd offended her. Dajah made his way over while she filled up a glass. Gently reaching out, he turned her face to his and looked her in the eyes so there'd be no mistaking his next words. "I'm very much enjoying your company. Don't take this personally. You need to understand that sometimes I can't trust myself. These headaches come on and..."

Kiera waited.

~By all means, keep comparing me to a headache.~

Queen was too close. She permeated his consciousness, tingled from the tips of his fingers down to his toes ready to prove a point. Dajah dropped his hand and looked away. "People get hurt."

She offered the glass to him. "You don't need to explain anything, Dajah."

I should.

The half frown forming on his lips was an inadequate reply but the best he was capable of. He nodded, taking the water, and made for the first bedroom.

~Why are you ruining things? She would have slept with you.~

Better if things don't get personal. We've got a lot of work to do in the next few days.

Queen didn't trust Kiera, and he knew how close she was to pushing boundaries only loosely agreed to. He felt her potency on the dance floor. As much as he was enjoying himself, Queen tipped the scales into dangerous territories. Caring too much about anything was a liability when you had a manic voice in your head ready to annihilate people on a whim because she decided it was 'necessary.'

He pulled the door halfway shut and went through the dresser, selecting a pair of lounge pants from Matt's collection. Club clothes shed, Dajah slipped on the pants and then laid in bed. Alone.

Why do I care about protecting someone I don't even know?

Zayan wasn't the first person Queen killed, just the first that mattered. Dajah didn't want to wake up finding Kiera's mutilated corpse beside him, hands covered in her blood.

He closed his eyes, forcing himself to sleep. The nightmares were too close already.

*

"What is it?" he asked Taron, eyeing the cardboard box riddled with holes. His brother had just returned from a supply run. Dajah was getting better at staying by himself for longer periods, but paranoia always lingered, and being alone too long would send Queen into frenzies. It was part of the reason they built a house in the middle of nowhere.

"Something to help keep you calm when I can't be here," Taron said. He set the box down and opened the lid. A scruffy, grey-and-black mutt leapt out. She wasn't as tall as the wolves that populated the forest, but she was muscular and fit. The mutt made her way to Dajah, sniffing.

"You bought me a dog?" Dajah asked.

The mutt cocked her head, one ear flopped over while the other stood erect, then rubbed herself along Dajah's shins. He crouched down to pet her and the tail wag made him smile.

"She's a therapy dog," Taron explained. "She senses when you're starting to panic and helps calm you down. You can focus on her the same way we practiced when Queen gets worked up – breathe, feel her fur, sense her calm..."

"Are you sure this is a good idea?"

"You're getting better, Dajah."

"I want revenge. So does Queen."

"We'll get it," Taron said, "but first you need to learn to function properly."

Dajah hated being told he couldn't do something, especially when it was true. "What's her name?"

"They were calling her Takoda."

"Hey, Takoda." He scratched behind her ears, and she melted into his lap. "You gonna keep an eye on me when Taron goes into town?" Her tail beat happily against the dirt.

*

Takoda saved him dozens of times over the next few months. Until she didn't.

Just one more of Queen's victims when he couldn't stay in control.

The knocking made him question whether he was actually dreaming.

"Dajah?" Kiera asked.

"I'm awake," he said.

"Can I come in?"

"Yeah." He sat up, legs crossed. Light filtered in from the hallway as Kiera slipped through the door. The apartment was still quiet, but she'd changed from her dress into shorts and a loose tee shirt. She looked just as appealing without makeup and her hair tied back.

"You were having another nightmare," she said, resting on the edge of the bed.

Conceding the truth with a sigh, he said, "Just things from my past."

"Tell me about it?"

He considered how much was worth telling. Queen's presence was distant but never gone. "Like I said before, most of my nightmares are from the past. When I was younger. Caerus's methods were, well, effective, I guess. I could field strip a rifle by seven. Made my own sword at thirteen. Been fighting monsters since before I can remember."

"Monsters Caerus created," she said.

"Yeah. Some they'd sell to the highest bidder. Others were used to train us. When we got too good at fighting them sober, they'd pump us full of chemicals and construct elaborate mazes to push us harder. We had some normal schooling, but a lot of it was hand-to-hand combat, survival skills, extensive weapons training.... Some of their high-level challenges were straight-up torture. None of it was humane."

Kiera repositioned herself. Concern seemed to tarnish her

otherwise curious expression.

Why am I telling her any of this?

He knew the answer.

"But your brother got you out," she said.

Dajah nodded. "We found places to stay. Avoided their clean-up crews. It took me close to three years to recover from the withdrawal of not constantly having their poison running through my veins. There's still... side effects."

Her mouth stayed downturned for so long that he regretted saying anything. And that was the sugar-coated version. "Kiera—"

"It's ok," she said. "I get it. Do you care if I lay with you for a bit?"

Dajah turned to face her. Before he could say anything, she added, "I'm not asking you to have sex with me. I just... I want the company."

He felt that through every fiber of his being. "Ok," he said, moving over to make room for her.

Kiera positioned herself beside him and placed a hand on his shoulder. "Lay down."

"We can't fall asleep," he said, allowing her to coax him back to the pillows.

"Why not?"

"Because I'm not always in control when I'm asleep. It's not safe."

She stretched her hand across his chest and snuggled against him despite his warning. "Then you stay awake. As nice as your friends are, I'm not sure *I* can sleep soundly here by myself. The bed's plenty big."

"Not when you're sleeping practically on top of me."

"Just shut up and try to relax. I need this."

He took a deep breath and slid his arm under her.

Don't hurt her, Queen.

~Sometimes you're too paranoid.~

Weight roused Dajah, but he didn't overreact. Soft hair and a cheek rested against his chest, with an arm and a leg sprawled across him. The rise and fall of Kiera's breath suggested a shallow sleep if she wasn't awake already.

He offered a light hug, his arm still wrapped around her from when he'd positioned it.

A contented moan answered him.

Dajah sighed. "You're insane."

She shifted into a seated position beside him, pulling down the covers he never remembered climbing under. Queen was quiet.

"You're the one that wasn't supposed to fall asleep," she said, studying his face. "So, any nightmares?"

Sliding his forearms back, he propped himself up on elbows. "Didn't dream at all."

"But you slept."

"A little, I guess."

"Dajah, it's almost eleven. You've been passed out for a good nine hours."

Disbelief made him check the bedside clock. "Did you drug my water?"

She laughed. "I've got a theory. Your brain knew that your body wasn't alone. If you didn't trust me on some level, I doubt you would have fallen back asleep."

He just blinked at her, unsure what to say to something like that. "Did you sleep?"

"Enough. Now I'm gonna see what I can cook up for breakfast." The smile she flashed was infectious. Kiera climbed out of bed and left the room.

She's still insane. That could have ended terribly.

By the time he made his way to the living room, she had various ingredients out and was heating a skillet.

"Need help?" he asked.

"You're on coffee duty, barista boy."

As soon as she laid the third piece of bacon on the skillet, the next reveler stumbled out. "Smells delicious," Gunner said. White shorts hung low enough that very little wasn't exposed. His chest and abs were bare, tail swaying until he plopped himself into a chair and rested his chin in his hands.

"What happened to Valie?" Dajah asked.

The twin grinned. "You know Matt'd have a fit if I brought her back here. We still made the most of it."

"Your brother make it back?" Kiera asked.

Gunner shrugged. "He'll roll in sooner or later."

"That signs of the living I'm hearing?" Matt called. He emerged from the hall dressed in casual jeans and a shirt, still donning his jewelry and makeup.

"Are you all ok with pancakes and bacon?" Kiera asked.

"Under the circumstances, that sounds amazing," Matt said. "Carry on, but if you need any help..."

"Pretty sure I can handle it."

Matt joined Gunner at the table. "Gary wants to have a virtual conference this afternoon."

"It's happening?" Gunner asked, tail broadcasting his excitement.

"He found it?" Dajah asked.

Matt nodded. "Thanks to the intel stolen from Matthews, we've got ourselves a target."

<hr>

Kiera contemplated the mock blueprints on the screen in front of them and the two men on the secondary monitor.

Gary Lewis was a middle-aged gentleman with a receding hairline and a kind face. He seemed to pride himself not so much on his technology, but what he could do with it. After all Dajah's mentioning of Gary, Kiera pictured someone more like his protégé. Martin was easily ten years younger than the master hacker, with fiery red hair and a well-trimmed goatee.

The current blueprints came courtesy of something Gary called his 'Water Map.' In short, he dropped a device into a reservoir, and that device emitted a form of sonar. Combine that with other bits of information and he presented them with a fair representation of Caerus's Eastern Primary Branch.

It's a goddamn fortress beneath the city!

"How can something this big be down there and no one knows it?" she asked. The expressions of the others confirmed she was the only one surprised.

"Most of their primary branches are underground," Matt said. "This isn't even the biggest one we've come across. The people that need to know it's there do, trust me."

"Caerus's facilities are usually self-sufficient when it comes to power, but their water and waste lines feed into the city's," Martin said. "We've been seeking ways to exploit this for months."

"Martin came up with the algorithm to turn pipes and cooling tanks into useable data," Gary said, slipping a hand around the younger man's shoulders.

"Can we use this to find the other facilities?" Mars asked.

"Range is limited," Martin said. "You'll still have to narrow down the exact location."

"So, what's the plan?" Matt asked.

"Security's gotten tighter. The computer system in Matthews's estate was an open terminal link to their mainframe. Kiera, your former employer doesn't just run OPASA."

"I wanna say I'm surprised," she started, "but I'm not. Julius had plenty of secrets."

No one knew he had a wife and kid. If he can keep something like that to himself, working for another organization would be easy to conceal.

"Thanks to this data link," Martin said, "we've managed to create new ghost tech for the upcoming assault. It'll keep you invisible to their surveillance systems, but we'll still need a local access point to hijack them."

"How complicated is this in reality?" Matt asked.

"Simple for you guys," Martin said. "Someone needs to insert a piece of tech into one of their hardwired computers. Similar to an

Ethernet port. We've found a floor that looks like it's used for conferences."

"And you know that from studying sewer pipes?" Mars asked.

"It's an educated guess, but one with a statistically significant confidence level," Gary said.

"What, exactly, are you trying to do to this place?" Kiera asked.

"All the previous facilities we've found have a central core," Steffi explained. "Blow up the core and it cripples the facility, but not every floor has access. Gary and Martin point us in the right direction. We deliver the explosive and get out before the fireworks begin."

"And you've done this before? *Successfully*?" Kiera was beginning to suspect they were all insane.

"We've got it down to a system," Matt said. "Don't worry."

"You don't have to come with us," Dajah said, searching her face for something.

"Oh, I'm coming. That asshole's down there, isn't he?"

Gary spoke up, "As far as we can tell, yes. The security team delivered him. We've no indication he's returned to his residence, or OPASA, since you and Dajah visited."

"Good," she said. "Gonna make sure he never comes up again."

"I like this one." Mars made eye contact with her, grinning.

"Julius also gave us a way in." Gary focused on something off-screen. The blueprints on the main monitor disappeared, replaced with satellite imagery of two buildings. "Allow me to introduce Saint Mary's. Conveniently located on five acres of open ground, just south of Heritage Heights and three miles from Philadelphia's Old City. Two auxiliary shafts descend from the school, connecting to Caerus's main complex. You won't be able to reach the core from there, but the shafts go at least thirty floors down."

"When are we doing this?" Matt asked.

"We'll need eighteen hours to prepare. Meet at the strip mall off Exit Twelve before you enter the city. Eight p.m.." Gary said.

"You got it!"

CHAPTER 19

"We should get back to work," Dr. Ashley said. "It's been two days since I left your experiment in Flynn's care. Hopefully, she's managed to improve the subject."

Julius knew the haughty look was because of what he'd done. He wondered if she wore that same look when he had her bent over the desk.

"I'm serious," Ashley said. "You did a number on her, Julius. I don't know that we'll get her back to viable status."

"She had it coming."

"If I heard you correctly, it was your wife and that little brat you should be blaming."

"Oh, don't worry," Julius said. An amused smile found his lips. "They paid for it, too."

"The President will want an update."

"Fuck her."

Ashley grinned. "That's one you'll never get ass up over your desk."

"Nor would I ever want to." There were other things he'd rather do to President Bekarda. "Call me with an update on dear Elizabeth."

Ashley knew when she was dismissed and left like an obedient worker should. Caerus wouldn't let him leave the facility unsupervised until the security breach at his house was addressed. The President hadn't called him yet. She would have been informed of the incident immediately.

"What's she up to down there?"

Julius woke up his computer screen. There was more than one way to skin a cat.

He'd been at the computer barely an hour when the desk phone rang. Julius tapped his index finger on the space bar. "What's our mystery woman with glowing symbols have to do with volcanoes and hurricanes? Or Kiera, for that matter. There's no mistaking the identical sequences in their DNA." The ringing persisted until he finally answered: "What is it?!"

"Dr. Ashley needs you to come down to the Sapola Wing immediately, sir."

He slammed the phone back on the receiver.

"This better be worth my time."

Julius reached Elizabeth's room, finding two guards conversing with the doctor inside. When he entered, all three fell silent. His eyes went to the woman on the table. The woman who was not Elizabeth.

"Go," Ashley ordered. The guards left, giving respectful nods to Julius as they passed.

"What is this, doctor?" he demanded, fists forming.

Ashley looked lost for a split second. "I don't have an explanation yet, sir. She was unattended when I entered. As soon as I touched her to take readings, the illusion dissolved. Flynn was lying here instead. She hasn't made a report in over fifty hours."

"The *illusion*?" Julius asked, voice tightening.

"Some kind of magic," Ashley said.

"Our facilities are warded."

"I know, sir, but certain individuals still have access. Your cross enables you to override the wards. Perhaps her magic—"

He raised a finger, cutting her off before she uttered another word. "And the fact that Flynn hasn't reported in over two days?

No one thought that was relevant?! I want a full sweep of the entire Wing."

"Already ordered, sir."

"Find her, doctor. Or else."

Julius marched straight to Central Security, cursing under his breath the entire time. The incident at his residence would be seen as a slip-up. If word got out that Elizabeth was missing...

"Greetings, sir, what can we assist you with?" Adam, head of Central Security, asked as soon as Julius set foot inside.

"I need to view specific feed."

"Certainly, sir. You can use the spare office." Adam led him to the intended room and took a seat at the main monitor. "Which feed would you like to view?"

Julius stood behind him, arms folded. "Sapola Wing. Room thirty-eight B. Play it backwards, three times normal speed, beginning from live time."

The head of Central Security did as instructed, even though it was within his right to question Julius. They both watched the footage scroll. Prior to Dr. Ashley entering and unknowingly dissolving whatever illusion had been set up, Elizabeth lay still and motionless on the table. There was no sign of the doctor's assistant. Then everything turned white.

"Freeze it," Julius ordered. "Is this some kind of malfunction?"

Adam tweaked a few settings, but the recording remained unchanged. "Sorry, sir. It's not a malfunction. The cameras are whited out by an intense light source."

Julius gave him a flat look, refusing to justify a response. "Continue playback. Twice the speed. I want to know exactly when the *light source* appears." Mentally he scoffed at his own words. Celestials were known to be able to sustain such brilliance. Both Caerus *and* OPASA were working on ways to nullify their magic. Runes were overrated and easily circumvented. Regardless, Elizabeth was no celestial.

Adam stopped the feed a few seconds before the whiteout then played it back in slow motion.

"Hello?" the aid, Flynn, called.

Julius reached past Adam and upped the volume.

"Who's in here?!"

"It seems you're in the right place at the right time," a male voice said.

"Freeze it. Isolate that voice. Run it through our databases." Julius clutched his gold cross necklace, not because of any religious sentiment, but because the alloy was forged specifically to override certain wards. He cast a fortified Barrier Shield around himself and prayed he got the situation contained before Bekarda caught whiff of it.

CHAPTER 20

Electrifying adrenaline danced through Kiera's veins as she crouched on the roof of the descending elevator. It'd been a long time since she'd worked with a team. Normally she avoided team assignments – too many variables left too much room for error – but for reasons beyond sheer competence and skill, Dajah's team *felt* different. He and Steffi waited with her for Gary's word. Matt, Mars, and Gunner were securing access to Caerus's mainframe.

A brief crackle sounded in her ear before Gary's voice followed. "We're in. Team Mu, forty-sixth floor. Small group of employees down the hall to the left. Take either the first or second turn on your right. Team Delta, exit now. You'll need to switch elevators. Straight shot to a dead end, but move fast. Third elevator. First two are occupied."

Gaining access through the school was straightforward given the time of night. Now the real test would begin. Everyone was outfitted with tactical gear designed to help with Caerus defenses, encrypted communication earpieces, and a modified version of Gary's ghost tech. Kiera tuned out after Martin used phrases like 'shortwave EMP blasts' and 'simultaneous reversed Wi-Fi signals.' So far, no alarms sounded, but the instant human eyes sighted them all bets were off.

Dajah's friends were insane.

And I'm right here with them.

She knew she had to keep her mind focused on the task at hand. Somewhere down there, Julius waited.

"You heard the man," Dajah said, motioning for the women to enter the car first. He pulled the hatch closed while Steffi opened the doors and took point. They reached the next set of elevators without encountering a soul.

"Car's delayed," Martin informed. "Second door. Two employees."

Before the elevator fully opened, both men were dead. Steffi ended them with palmed throwing blades.

"We're invisible," Dajah said, "bodies aren't. Kiera, get that hatch opened."

They stuffed the corpses on top of the elevator car as it descended, and Kiera hoped no one watched the security monitors too closely. *Floating bodies* might *raise some suspicions down here.*

A tremor passed through, rattling the car, and the lights dimmed. Kiera braced herself against the wall. Dajah and Steffi opted for crouched positions.

"Earthquake," Steffi said.

"Since when do we get earthquakes?" Kiera asked.

"We're deep enough underground," the vampire explained. "Who knows how many tremors happen below the surface."

The disturbance passed and the lights regained their normal brightness.

"Team Mu's in place, but the gold mine is heavily guarded. Almost time to cut security feed," Gary said. "You'll have fifteen minutes before surveillance kicks in and whatever bodies you leave behind are spotted. They'll come at you fast and hard."

"No worries," Matt's cheery voice echoed in their earpieces. "You know we excel at this part. See you on the other side!"

Definitely insane.

"Get ready," Gary said. "Martin, isolate that thread. Give me full control over the encryption patterns."

"Team Delta," Martin added, "exit on the next floor. Most

rooms are storage. Minimal surveillance. You need to reach the other side of the facility. Elevator at the end of the wing will deliver you close to the weasel's lair. Floor twenty-one."

"You sure about this?" Kiera asked Dajah.

"I said I'd help you kill him. I meant it. He'll get trapped in the explosion and suffocate down here, but it's always better to be sure."

"Thank you," Kiera said. "All of you."

"We're a team. You're one of us, Kiera, at least until this is over," Steffi said. "What you decide to do afterwards, that's up to you."

Kiera nodded. She couldn't fantasize about life after Julius when she had to worry about what might be on the other side of those doors once the elevator opened.

"USB's in transit," Gary said. "Blow it on my mark. Teams ready?"

Matt and Dajah confirmed.

Kiera gripped the handle of her silenced HK45 and steadied her breathing. This was the ugly part. The part where people died because they worked at the wrong place. No one was innocent. That didn't mean everyone deserved to die, but people with morals made terrible assassins.

"Now!" Gary commanded.

◆

"Nothing matches our databases, sir," Adam informed. "Ren Kirby's card accessed the Sapola Wing two minutes before the incident, but he's clearly seen up on Floor Seven the entire time. I've ordered two of my men to question him. Still, we have no trace of anyone on surveillance at the time the Wing's accessed. Whoever this was found a way to circumvent our systems. We should notify Headquarters."

Julius paced the small office, waiting for luck to turn an eye in his favor. Instead, luck spit on him. "*We* shall do no such thing. I'll take the matter up with Bekarda personally. Someone, presumably a non-human using magic we're not shielded against, infiltrated our perimeter, made it to a high-security ward, and managed to replace my test subject with the woman tending her. This had better be a fluke."

"I take this very seriously, sir," Adam said. Julius could tell the head of security was sweating. The implications were disastrous, but it wasn't without salvaging.

"Run a scan for Elizabeth's energy signature," Julius ordered.

Someone knocked on the door. Then had the balls to open it. Julius glared at the individual – someone he didn't recognize personally but whom he wouldn't soon forget.

"S-sorry, sir," the peon stuttered.

"What is it, Mikees?" Adam demanded.

"S-sir, there's... There's been an explosion in one of the conference rooms."

Julius felt the muscles around his eyes twitch involuntarily as the peon continued.

"One of the orderlies found a network terminal running with a USB attached. He was bringing the USB here when the explosion happened. We believe the source was the device itself. Six men are dead, sir."

"Perform a system-wide protocol—"

"Adam! We just got a W-7 called in," someone yelled from the other room, "and lost feed to seventeen floors."

"Lock. It. Down." Julius ground out the words with his teeth.

◆

Red warning lights flashed around Dajah, forcing his eyes to scan everything. Tonal alarms bruised his eardrums. Eighteen guards and another four workers were down.

"This escalated faster than expected," he admitted, pulling his knife out of a skull. The body slid down the wall, leaving a trail of oozing blood. It was always a matter of time before someone called them in, but he didn't think anyone on his team was at fault. "Keep moving."

"We're out of time," Steffi said. She was right, but Dajah didn't get this far by always listening to reason.

Holding up his fist, he paused them at the next intersection. "Cameras are still down. Otherwise, they'd be all over us. We've got a job to do."

"But we have no idea if he's still in that office," Steffi said.

"Gary'll get the comms up and running again. It's the best place to start." They'd lost contact with the others as soon as the alarm triggered, but that part *was* expected – one of Caerus's security features Gary could only override after it'd been initiated. He just needed time.

Seeing no one in the immediate area, Dajah resumed a brisk jog. Windows offered a disturbing view of what waited behind the walls here. This floor wasn't storage in the conventional sense. It housed hundreds of bioweapons.

He recognized half of them. Mutated birds with rows of serrated teeth feasted on a nest of albino rodents. Tigers with shifting stripes and stag horns ending in pulsing, bulbous lesions lounged on elevated platforms. Another group must have been spliced with a great ape. They were human-sized, with ulcerated, peeling flesh that revealed bone-plated armor beneath. Four of them tore apart something with too many legs.

Two handlers pushed a cart down the aisle. One checked off a clipboard while the other threw numerous pieces of meat or the occasional live snack into a pen. Dajah suspected the pseudo-zoo was isolated from any alarms to keep the beasts calmer. One-way observation glass must have lined the halls. Neither monsters nor men seemed to notice them running past.

"When you said Caerus made monsters, I'm not sure what I was expecting. Not this," Kiera said, keeping pace.

"Must be one of their breeding floors," Steffi explained.

"Guards!" Dajah yelled, letting his knife fly. It embedded into the eye socket of a man with his head cocked, hand moving to his earpiece.

The second man grabbed his neck when Steffi's throwing star

penetrated it. He would have lived longer if he hadn't pulled the metal out. Three more rounded the corner, taken down with quick, precise headshots from Kiera.

Dozens of eyes watched. The grotesque, weaponized canines Dajah and his brothers referred to as Spots paced their cages in the next observation window. No one-way glass here. They saw. Waited.

Stay on that side.

The three of them entered a new section devoid of windows. Alarms were subdued here, and for that his ears were grateful. Every so many yards was a steel door with a sequence of numbers identifying it.

~STOP!~

A rigid bolt shot through Dajah's core, freezing him in place. Control slipped like sand through open fingers. The more he grasped, the faster he lost it. He barely registered the door Queen paused in front of. *What are you doing? We don't have time for this!*

~We're going inside, Dajah.~

He pulled out an electronic lock pick from his pack, slotting it into the keycard access port. Steffi said something. He couldn't make it out. Noises became muffled and dulled. His vision blurred, focusing on erratic, insignificant objects – the door frame, a tile on the floor, his fingers...

The pounding in his head intensified, obliterating him.

CHAPTER 21

"Dajah?" Kiera called, examining the door numbered 5378.

"We don't have time for this!" Steffi growled.

Kiera agreed with the vampire. Between the lack of alarms in this area and the horde of genetically engineered monsters they passed, all the tiny hairs on the back of her neck were raised.

Dajah didn't respond to either of them. The door panel flashed green and opened. He entered, never bothering to remove his equipment from the access port. Inside, empty cages and examination tables occupied the space. Glass cylinder tanks with unidentifiable dark liquid lined the near wall, with plenty of monitoring equipment and storage near the back. Claw marks and deep gouges were everywhere.

"Keep an eye on him. Someone's coming." Steffi drew her firearm and took off.

Kiera stepped inside after Dajah.

Two shots rang out, followed by a string of foreign curses before the automatic door closed behind Kiera. She hit the release button, drawing her secondary weapon. Something shattered within the room. Flinching, she aimed one gun at the newest disturbance, the other held level with the open door.

Dajah had used his fist to break into one of the storage cases. Fresh blood coated the edges of the glass.

"Dajah, what the hell are you doing?!"

Someone cried out down the hall.

Shards of glass stuck out of his glove, reflecting the lighting as he fixated on a compact refrigerator.

"We gotta go! Steffi needs our help."

As if he couldn't hear her, Dajah carried on.

Despite the warning that Earth Beads wouldn't work inside Caerus, she never removed her bracelet. Now she attempted a Lightning spell. Nothing magical happened besides an intensified tingling. Her mind insisted everything was falling apart. They were trapped underground, surrounded by the enemy...

On Dajah's next punch, something gave. He pulled out a handful of test tubes.

Kiera took a step closer and his eyes turned to her. Everything about that expression was feral. Slitted pupils narrowed, staring. He stepped forward, muscles tense, and drew one of his knives.

Training both guns on him, she dropped her index fingers to the triggers. "Talk to me, Dajah."

A toothy grin was her only warning before the knife came flying. She deflected it wide with her firearm, but a solid backhand clocked her square across the face. Kiera sprawled to the ground, getting a single shot off.

Dajah moved inhumanly fast.

"Jesus Christ, Dajah!"

He stalked closer and she crawled back, reluctant to shoot even though their clothing was reinforced with carbon nanotubes. Heart thundering in her chest, she applied pressure to both triggers. Quickened footsteps reached them. Someone else opened fire. Three rounds hit Dajah's chest, a fourth going wide. The rapid impacts caused him to drop the tubes bunched in his hand, and the rage-filled shriek released when they shattered made Kiera cringe.

Blue-green energy flashed overhead. A muted grunt followed. Dajah bolted towards the opening. Another man yelled out. Crimson sprayed the door as it slid closed.

Kiera's pulse beat a headache-inducing rhythm into her skull. More gunshots sounded outside. Staying low, she crawled closer to the doorway until her fingers brushed against one of the test tubes. *Intact?* She holstered her spare weapon and held the tube up to the light, squinting at the liquid within. *What the hell is this?* Securing it in one of her pouches, she continued to the hall.

Beyond the room, six men lay dead or dying – one groaned, blood sputtering from swollen lips. He was stabbed more times than she cared to count. Intestines leaked out from a gaping wound in the side of another man. A third's limbs rested in anatomically incorrect positions.

Things got worse the more bodies she came across, following the carnage.

"Anyone hear me?" she asked into her comm.

No response.

Setting the core explosive was contingent upon them being in communication with one another. Cell phones were an absolute last resort – theoretically, they'd work, but disrupt the tech that kept them invisible to the cameras. She prayed she had time.

A single set of footsteps approached. Kiera pressed her back against the wall and waited.

"Kiera?" the vampire called.

"Steffi?"

"I'm alone. Coming around."

She eyed the woman critically and found no visible injuries.

"Patrol was headed our way," Steffi said. "I took care of them. Where's Dajah?"

Another cold shiver raced down Kiera's body. "He took off that way. Something's wrong with him."

Steffi cursed. "He's losing control."

Both women turned their attention to a set of double doors smeared with fresh blood. They kept to the wall, minimizing their silhouettes. Repetitive thuds and cracks echoed up ahead. Kiera identified the source – oversized, malnourished canines covered in spikes. They broke out of their containment cages and were throwing themselves against the observation glass.

"Quickly," Steffi whispered, leading them onward.

Kiera prayed the glass held. "What are we gonna do when we find him?"

"Depends on what condition we find him in. Gary needs to get those comms back up."

A woman's body lay strewn across the floor. Head backwards, her radio and rifle were several yards away. Static crackled from the radio, resolving into a masculine voice: "Intruder secured."

"Shit," Kiera cursed, picking up the radio.

"Take him to the Sapola Wing and sweep the floor," a different male ordered.

Steffi moved to the opposite side of the hall and locked eyes with Kiera. They moved cautiously into the next corridor. Tonal alarms returned with flashing lights. Ahead, nine security personnel gathered around something.

"Down there!" one of the men yelled, spotting Steffi.

A barrage of ammunition flew their way. Kiera squeezed off five rounds to no avail. "They're armored like we are," she said.

Steffi smashed the door release, sealing them back in the previous hall. "More than that," she said, pulling a dart out of her arm for Kiera's inspection. "Must be what took out Dajah."

"We can't leave him," Kiera growled.

"We won't. Come on."

They backtracked, barely clearing the hall with the monsters when glass shattered and screams followed.

"Those things are loose!" Kiera said, glancing back. She caught the hint of a tail flicking into the opening.

"Not a concern right now." Steffi turned down the hall she'd come from. It was lined with non-sequential doors like the last one, but these had windows. Kiera counted ten bodies in passing. Unlike the butchered corpses Dajah left, these were clean kills. As they ran, Steffi searched the windows, eventually finding what she wanted.

"This one," she said, inserting her lock pick.

Static preceded another voice on the radio: "Containment alert in Sector V12. Two more intruders spotted. Additional backup requested."

Steffi grabbed Kiera's arm and pulled her inside as soon as the door unlocked. This room appeared to be a lab, with a row of ventilation hoods along the back wall and island workspaces complete with sinks. Dust coated everything.

"What are we doing in here?" Kiera asked.

"Going up," Steffi said. She leapt onto the central island, directing Kiera to the ceiling grate.

"This is gonna work?" she asked, doubtful.

"It better," Steffi said. She boosted Kiera up into the shaft then joined her and replaced the grate. "Turn the radio off for now."

Kiera secured the device, holstered her weapon, and began army crawling behind the vampire. Metal groaned against their weight and dented. Exit options were limited to sharp-angled turns, downshafts, and upshafts.

"How much time you think we have?" she whispered to Steffi.

"We're not leaving anyone behind. You wanna climb up or down?"

Kiera shook her head. "Does it matter?"

CHAPTER 22

"Trail leads back to room fifty-three-seventy-eight. One of the specimen cases was broken into." Adam explained.

"What case?" Julius asked.

"Labeled QZ-5. That's where things get interesting. All records of what QZ-5 '*is*' have been redacted."

The muscles around Julius's eyes tightened again. "You don't have access." It was more statement than question.

"No, sir. And if I don't have access, I doubt you will either. You're welcome to try."

Julius already knew what would happen if he tried. "Unnecessary. What do you think about that?" he asked, pointing to the device in Adam's hand.

"It concerns me," the head of Central Security admitted. He held the device up, scrutinizing the live feed on the room's monitor. Everything within the room showed true except the object – it was invisible. "Explains how they've been moving around."

"Can you neutralize it?"

"I'll get this to IT personally. If it truly masks them from our systems, it'll take time to locate any others."

"I want them alive."

"Understood, sir. Be careful with this one." Adam gathered up the equipment, clothing and weapons included, and took his leave.

Julius turned to the unconscious man on the table. The guards stayed back but kept their weapons ready.

Caerus's Weapons were durable. Fresh bruises spread across Dajah's flesh, with old scars serving as a reminder of the kind of punishments Caerus inflicted on its experiments. "Failed experiments," Julius reminded himself. Every one of those training facilities was either decommissioned or destroyed. Still, he respected what they were capable of.

Dajah's arms were secured out to the sides, resting on table extensions. Iron shackles fit snugly around his wrists and ankles, with thin spikes through each restraint. When placed correctly, major arteries were avoided but maneuvering free was nearly impossible. Julius had never seen it happen, but there was one report of a captive breaking her forearm trying to contort her wrist free.

Leather straps secured the Weapon's thighs, chest, arms, and forehead to the table. He wasn't going anywhere.

"Time for answers." Julius picked up a liquid amphetamine vial and syringe.

✦

A splitting headache was common after one of Queen's rampages. Either someone knocked him out, or she retreated of her own accord. Dajah's body remained mostly unresponsive. Wiggling his fingers was an effort, and forcing his eyelids open took more energy than he wanted to commit. He managed, greeted by a head backlit with harsh, bright light. The shadow moved, causing his pupils to narrow and his retinas to sting. Spots lingered long after he shut his eyes again.

"Time for answers," a man said, determination laced in his tone.

It took a moment, but Dajah recognized the voice. Attempts to turn his head in the same direction failed, and he knew only part of it was due to whatever sedative they'd given him.

Queen, you're an asshole.

Fighting against restraints in his condition would only prove futile; he needed to recover first. A pinpoint prick of heat flared in his arm. Sometime after, his senses grew more acute. The dull hum of electronics settled into background noise. Someone shuffled uneasily to his right. Bright light continued to sear through closed lids.

"Can you hear me?" Matthews asked.

Dajah snorted. "I hear a dead man."

"I won't insult you by making small talk, so I'll just ask it plainly: What are you doing here?"

"Actually, I'm here to get Kiera your head."

"A little late for that, Dajah. She's down in holding. Awaiting my... *ministrations.*"

"I'd pay to see it given she was three hundred miles away two hours ago." He guessed at the time. Based on the way his newest wounds felt, he doubted he'd been unconscious that long.

Silence encouraged Dajah to open his eyes. He hissed, squinting until they adjusted. A circular lamp was directly above his face, with tube lights and an off-white ceiling beyond that.

A door swished open. Unrushed, heeled footsteps followed.

"Ah, Dr. Ashley," Matthews said, "did you bring what I requested?"

"Yes, but you understand the risks," a woman answered.

Matthews's face came back into view. "You saved me a lot of trouble, Dajah, and for that I'll let you know what's about to happen. An experiment of sorts. See, I've read your file. As things currently stand, you're a hot commodity. I want to know why. Do you know what this is?" He reached across, accepting something from the doctor. She'd moved closer, but Dajah could only make out dirty blonde hair and a white lab coat.

A syringe dangled in front of him. Intense light made the swirling green liquid within translucent, and all Dajah could do was laugh at the irony. "Wouldn't recommend it."

"And why's that?" Matthews asked, passing the syringe back to the doctor.

"I'll need one of you to position his arm," the doctor said, instructing someone behind her. Another shadowed silhouette stepped forward.

"Queen hasn't exactly been cooperative today," Dajah said. Hands grabbed above and below his elbow, twisting his arm and applying pressure. It put additional strain on his wrist. A warm tickle ran down his forearm.

"Is that the *Other* you used to refer to?" Matthews asked.

"Don't say I didn't warn you." Dajah fought down the initial nausea Stream radiation caused when injected too fast.

Get us out of here.

Queen surfaced. Observing.

The doctor's assistant didn't release him. A second pinch followed, and he tensed. It burned up his chest, suffusing his torso. The room turned hazy, tilting until it began to spin. Dajah clenched his teeth and shut his eyes at the third injection. His head split.

"Anything to say now?" the arrogant male asked.

"*Your time is limited.*"

"Is that you or her, Dajah?"

Despite the restraints, Queen managed to twist Dajah's head, eyeing the male. "*Release me.*"

"Excellent!" the male said, pleased with this turn of events. He was truly foolish. "Ashley, give him more."

"Sir?" the female asked.

"Was that in some way unclear?"

Queen kept her eyes on the male, drinking in another dose of vibrant nourishment. She jerked Dajah's body, testing the limits of the restraints. Leather and metal strained against her efforts, almost breaking.

The male laughed in jubilation. "Who are you?" he asked, staring directly into Dajah's eyes.

"*Your destruction. You've no right to what you've taken. I have no more to say to a pawn.*"

Dajah went limp against the restraints. A blank, vacant stare took over before his eyelids closed. The male and the female continued conversing.

"Samples, Ashley! I want a sample after every subsequent injection."

"We've already exceeded the recommended dosage for a matured lifeform. Higher levels of Stream are neurotoxic. You could kill him or worse."

"I understand the risks. Continue!"

Another burst of vital energy coursed through Dajah's veins. Too much. His body began convulsing violently.

"Twenty milligrams of diazepam with X-sedative. Keep him still!" the female ordered.

The tremors slowed. Voices grew muffled until reality faded away.

———◇———

"I'm second-guessing this plan," Kiera admitted.

"No, it'll work," the vampire said. She sounded more confident than Kiera felt.

They'd found a women's locker room, donning scrubs and lab coats over their gear. The biggest risk was deactivating the ghost tech – their new clothes wouldn't be camouflaged. Security was more likely to notice disembodied articles of clothing than nothing.

Kiera led the way out of the locker room, reminding herself to act like she belonged. Few frequented the halls and corridors since the alarms were tripped, but those out and about seemed indifferent to the flashing lights and constant tones.

Must happen often.

Steffi approached two women conversing. One was dressed in a suit, the other wearing scrubs. "Excuse me. Could you direct us to the Sapola Wing from here?"

The women exchanged glances before the one in scrubs answered. "Sapola Wing? Floor eighteen. Take the primary elevators down there. Left once you exit. You'll see the signs."

"Thanks," Steffi said, offering a smile.

The women returned to their conversation – something about a production schedule – and Kiera and Steffi made for the elevators, passing others on the way.

No one looked twice.

Not everyone's some psychotic mastermind down here. These are just regular people doing their jobs. Still, she found it hard to view the employees as anything but complicit. Dajah's stories painted an idea of Caerus, and Kiera's experience with OPASA colored in the blanks. She wondered if the Organization knew this place existed beneath one of its cities.

They have to know. They probably help fund it.

Signs were marked clearly on the eighteenth floor. The Sapola Wing opened into a massive atrium. Glass windows and artificial light made for a sense of serenity. The plants caught her eye first: Varieties ranging from colorful shrubs full of flowers to tall trees swaying in a gentle breeze. Alarms were non-existent here, replaced by the sound of waterfalls and garden fountains that instantly transported Kiera back to her loft. Soft voices conversed in the background.

How does a company that makes monsters create a perfect space like this?

"Over here," Steffi said.

A floor plan was etched atop a decorative pedestal. Based on the layout, three hallways branched off from the atrium. One led to a series of laboratories double the size of anything they passed so far. The second accommodated smaller, staggered rooms, and the third hall was labeled 'restricted access.' It outlined rooms of various sizes, all along one side.

"Elevator at the end of hall three," Steffi said, tracing the lines with her finger. "Doubt they'd bring prisoners through the atrium. It'd ruin the aesthetic."

Kiera shifted her gaze from the map to the steel doors visible behind a grouping of fruit trees. Keeping their disguises made the most sense for passing through those doors. However, it significantly limited her ability to reach for any weapon quickly.

The hallway was devoid of personnel. Single doors ran along the right side, unevenly spaced but numbered sequentially with observation windows. The opposite wall was solid, unadorned down to the elevators at the far end.

I've executed riskier jobs than this. The reminder didn't calm the racing of her heart or ease the knot in her stomach. They walked the corridor at a casual pace. All her legs wanted to do was run for cover. They were too exposed. Any minute security would flood their location. She wasn't thrilled with their options once that happened.

A glance through the first window showed a padded room. Huddled in the far corner was a man clothed in a thin hospital gown. He twitched and shivered, lips moving as if reciting the same thing over and over.

The second room contained a similar scene, this one with a woman sleeping on the floor. Her ears came to points, fair complexion riddled with severe burn marks that exposed charred muscle and tendon.

Steffi paused at that window, expression grim, and Kiera could only imagine what memories it brought up. A simmering hatred leveled out the tension building within her. *They're no better than OPASA. Worse.*

Steffi grabbed her wrist, bringing her to a halt before they reached the next room. Shadows caught Kiera's attention. They approached cautiously, and what she saw inside turned her blood cold. Then made it boil. She clenched both fists.

Three guards stood close to the door, observing the happenings within, guns ready. Beyond them, a woman in a lab coat moved around a man strapped down to the table. In the corner, lifting a piece of paper stacked on a clipboard, stood Julius.

Kiera pulled one of the HK45s. Ejecting the magazine, she replaced it with a full one and dropped a spare into her lab coat pocket.

A hand grabbed her shoulder and wrist simultaneously. "Don't get reckless," Steffi said. "We still need to get Dajah out of there."

"Dajah?" Kiera was so consumed with the image of Julius, she ignored the others in the room. The woman's position obscured the face of the man on the table, but Kiera knew that pale skin and those black boxer briefs.

Tingling intensified in her bloodstream.

A voice screeched in her head. "...hear me?" Not a voice. Gary.

"Comms are back!"

"Switch to auxiliary channel immediately," Steffi said into her comm.

Switching her device over, Kiera listened as the others conversed in short, direct phrases. Team Mu had secured a location and was ready to set the explosives.

"Small problem." While Steffi explained their situation, Kiera moved back to the observation window.

The woman now stood by Julius's side. Their backs to Kiera, it appeared as if they were arguing. Dajah remained motionless on the table. Blood oozed around his restraints. Fresh wounds hinted that he was already unconscious when someone beat him.

Julius was less than ten yards away.

Kiera tightened her grip on the weapon. Remembering their last encounter too well, she palmed another fully loaded magazine and placed it in another accessible pocket.

"You don't get to walk away this time," she whispered.

CHAPTER 23

Steffi tapped on the window. Her expression, coupled with persistent waving and pointing, must have convinced the guards to come out and investigate.

More than likely, Julius told them to address it so he wouldn't be interrupted.

"The subject in room one is critical! We need a hand!" Steffi pleaded as the door slid open.

One of the guards stepped out, his neck instantly snapped by powerful hands. Steffi slipped into the room to engage the others and Kiera entered behind her. Her first shot was flawless. At that range, it should have borne a hole through Julius's skull, splattering brain out the back. She expected the magic barrier, unloading consecutive rounds.

Julius's expression seethed with annoyance as he moved forward, drawing a pistol from behind. The doctor dove to the floor too slowly and Kiera spared a bullet to confirm she wasn't protected by any spell. The ACP round punched clean through her chest, silencing her cry.

A bullet rammed into Kiera's firing shoulder with the force of a horse kick. She stumbled but kept her feet. Kept firing. Pain was a small price to pay for the death of Julius. When the slide on her gun locked back, she replaced the empty mag in a heartbeat. Another projectile scuffed her side with minimal effect.

"Enough!" Julius demanded. He pressed the barrel of his gun to

Dajah's head, eyes darting between the two of them. Steffi froze. Kiera's finger squeezed against the weighted trigger but held short of firing. "Ashley, get up! She grazed you at best."

Kiera kept her sight trained on Julius while the woman doctor, Ashley, gained her feet. Her hand pressed against her chest, blood oozing, dying her coat crimson. She looked pissed more than anything.

Non-human. Should have gone for the head!

Kiera's heart beat faster.

"Not gonna fire?" Julius asked, amusement turning thin lips to a grin as his eyes burned into hers. She hadn't lowered her weapon. "I'd be impressed if I wasn't so disappointed."

"Why are you working with Caerus?" she asked.

He laughed. "Working *with* them? I *run* this facility, Sweetheart. Soon you'll know it... *intimately*." Keeping the gun pressed against Dajah's head, Julius took out a phone and activated the screen with his thumb. "Security breach. Room Seven. Sapola Wing." He looked back to the woman. "Dr. Ashley, please sedate our guests."

Whatever type of non-human the doctor was, Kiera's bullet injured her. She moved stiffly, approaching the counter of drugs before selecting a bottle.

Kiera knew Julius's protective spell was weakened. Would one more bullet do the trick? Two? His index finger rested on the trigger guard, not the trigger. That bought her a second, but if her next two rounds didn't penetrate his shield...

His brow lifted as if reading her thoughts. Hand tilted. An unsilenced projectile snapped the air. Kiera flinched, eyes widening at the gory mess that became Dajah's shoulder. It could have been his head. Her heart threatened to explode, racing so fast she felt lightheaded.

Dajah's reaction was little more than a subdued groan. Whatever they sedated him with was potent. At point-blank range, bone shattered, and blood spurted, coating his skin and pooling beneath the table. Without intervention, he'd bleed out.

"You don't have enough bullets in that gun to stop me," Julius said. "Drop it."

The doctor had two syringes in hand, one of the needles uncapped and ready. She looked to Julius, awaiting further instruction.

"This only ends one way," he warned.

Kiera's pulse pounded. Her chest heaved with rapid, shallow breaths she forced out her nose. Memories came rushing back. Injections. Experiments. Pain. Loss. Her mother's head beaten in. Her father's lifeless eyes staring out. Blood. So much blood.

The tingling reached a crescendo; her entire body vibrated.

"No," she whispered.

Energy bombarded her from every angle. Bottles along the counter shattered one after the next. The whites of Julius's eyes were visible for an instant. Then the lights failed, raining glass and plunging the room into darkness.

Lightning split and forked in the air, freezing the scene in a flash of overexposure. Kiera darted at Julius, clearing Dajah's body in a leap, then tackling the man to the ground. His gun fired wide, ricocheting off something metallic.

She pistol-whipped him across the face, no magical shield protecting him from the onslaught this time. He got his legs between them, throwing her. Kiera hit the floor, her primary weapon skittering out of reach.

Inhuman hissing underscored Steffi's battle with the doctor nearby.

Emergency lights kicked on in the hallway, casting dim illumination through the observation window. It was enough to see Julius gaining his feet.

Kiera shed her coat and ripped the scrub top off for better access. She pulled another firearm, but a knee smacked into her forehead. Then he was on top of her, forearm pinning her neck to the ground while his other hand slammed her wrist into broken glass. A thick, sharp pain pierced the meat between her thumb and fingers. Grip failing, her gun came loose.

She pushed past searing pain and made a fist. It met Julius's skull and Kiera was able to throw him off with a roll of her hip. She palmed the first handle in reach.

Light caught the thin line of a syringe held in Julius's hand. The man was on his feet again.

She couldn't let that needle pierce her flesh.

"Come on, you bastard," she threatened, standing. "Let's end this!"

"With pleasure," Julius said, charging her.

Deflecting his strike wide, Kiera slashed up with her dagger, scoring a line along his forearm. She lashed out again, met with a blow to the gut that knocked the wind out of her.

His syringe missed her face by a hair. She stomped on his insole, following it up with a knee to the groin. He growled, trying to backhand her, but Kiera twisted outside his grasp and rammed her knife into his armpit. He dropped the syringe to grab the dagger and yank it free. Kiera pulled out another knife.

The blood pouring from the wound slowed him. His blade scraped along Kiera's armored ribcage, bringing her inside his guard. She caught his arm in a lock. Punched him square across the bridge of his nose, and tore her knife across the flesh of his throat in a split-second opening.

Julius stumbled back, mouth working as he grasped his neck with both hands. Dark liquid cascaded between his fingers. Closing the gap between them, Kiera plunged her knife into his chest. With a gasp, her enemy fell over backwards, knife hilt-deep at an angle that ensured she pierced his heart. Bending forward to catch her breath, movement had her reaching for the last dagger.

"It's me, Kiera," Steffi said, hands raised in front of her. She didn't appear injured.

"The doctor?" Kiera asked.

"In pieces."

Kiera approached Julius's body and crouched beside it. Staring. No air inflated his lungs. Blood pooled beneath his form. She reached out, pressing two fingers against his neck to confirm death. Checking his clothes, she removed his phone and a keycard, then snapped a picture of the corpse. With the rest of his pockets empty, Kiera retrieved her weapons.

The vampire peeled open Dajah's eye, and the glow of his iris was bright enough to reflect off the ceiling in swirling hues of green.

"What'd they do to him?" Kiera asked, helping undo the restraints.

"Find some bandages." Steffi lifted Dajah's good arm and sank her teeth into the puncture wound near his wrist. Moments later she pulled away, spitting blood to the floor. "Radiation poisoning. A bunch of chemicals... I can clean some of it."

While Steffi went through drawers and cabinets, Kiera retrieved her discarded scrub top and cut strips. She wrapped Dajah's wounds and created a sling for his arm.

"This should reverse the sedative enough for him to function," Steffi said, returning with a syringe. Kiera watched the contents disappear into Dajah's neck. Moments later he groaned.

"Dajah, can you hear me?" Steffi asked, close to his ear.

He didn't respond, but his breathing changed.

Steffi slapped him across the face with an open palm. "Dajah! We need you awake. Now!"

Though cringe-worthy, it did the trick. He reached up to touch his cheek and opened his eyes. Kiera'd never seen any creature with eyes that bright. If it wasn't so disturbing, it'd be beautiful. He looked between the two of them, pupils constricting.

"Can you walk?" Steffi asked. "We got to go. Matt's team's ready."

Slowly, Dajah pushed himself into a seated position, legs loose over the side of the table. He looked confused.

"Dajah?" Steffi demanded.

"Yeah," he mumbled.

"Gary, tell them to deliver the package," Steffi said into her comm. "Find us the fastest way out of here."

"Come on," Kiera said to him, offering a hand. He climbed off the table and his legs immediately collapsed beneath him. Fortunately, she caught him before he fell over. "Whoa! You really think you can walk?"

"Not easily," he admitted. Kiera helped him straighten, draping his good arm across her shoulders to provide extra support. Blood soaked through the bandages on his ankles.

Those restraints cut through his tendons.

"We're not leaving unseen," Steffi said.

"This might help." Kiera offered the keycard to her. "It was Julius's."

"He's here," Dajah said.

"He's dead." Saying the words lifted a weight off her chest, but Julius's death meant nothing if they couldn't get out of Caerus.

Martin's voice sounded in Kiera's earpiece. "Twenty minutes. Team Delta, take the elevators at the end of the hall. Floor twenty."

"Why are we going down?" Kiera asked.

"Only a few shafts reach the surface," Martin explained. "Straight shot till the path dead ends. Right. Then another right at the first intersection. Take it to the end and wait for Team Mu. Couple empty offices nearby."

"Got it," Steffi confirmed. "Just make sure those offices *are* empty and not full of mutations wanting a meal."

"Thirty minutes until critical mass," Gary said.

Steffi stripped out of her scrubs and reactivated her ghost tech. Unholstering one of her firearms, she ejected the magazine to check it before reloading. "Let's move."

Kiera held Dajah upright, providing support. Bare skin burned feverishly against her. She could imagine how he must have felt. His gaze remained unfocused, reactions delayed. He could pass out any moment. The fact that he functioned at all was a testament to non-human endurance.

We're getting out of here.

A crowd of fully armored guards stormed in from the atrium. Kiera shoved Dajah into the waiting elevator car, smashing the

CLOSE button while Steffi took aim. She took several potshots for all the good it did. A barrage of blue-tipped darts barely missed them as the doors sealed.

Kiera breathed, appreciating the temporary respite. "You'd think they'd run out of men sooner or later."

Dajah slouched on the floor, staring at nothing. Kiera shared a glance with Steffi who shook her head. "He'll get worse until his body processes the Stream."

"The Stream?" Kiera remembered him mentioning it in their previous conversations. "Why would Julius give Dajah radiation?"

"An experiment?" Steffi shrugged. Number twenty lit up and the elevator slowed. "Can you handle him?"

"Yeah. Come on, Dajah. We have to move again."

Steffi was ready to take out anything in their way as soon as the doors opened but the area was deserted. *Won't be for long.*

They followed Martin's instructions. Most rooms were empty or storage for equipment still in boxes; a few offices were sparsely decorated.

"Two patrols on the way. Coming from both sides," Martin warned.

"Alternate routes?" Steffi asked.

"Not without a lengthy detour," Martin confirmed. "Team Mu's on the way. Five guards coming from the left. Six behind you."

"In here," Steffi said, slipping into the next open office. "I'll take care of security. Be ready to move."

"Be careful." Kiera frowned, watching the vampire leave. She eased Dajah to the floor out of view, then took up position ready to fire.

Footsteps sounded in standard, start-stop procession further down as security swept the rooms. Someone grunted. Another shouted, "There!" Projectiles dinged against walls. A symphony of chaos unfolded – cracking wood, broken glass, thuds...

Kiera crouched low, peeking out into the hall. Steffi blocked an attempted shot, knocking the guard's arm away so forcefully it hung limp afterwards. She twisted behind the same man, using his body as a shield. Another tried getting around them. She tossed the groaning guard into his partner, charging at a third.

A red-feathered dart stuck into Kiera's arm, others missing as she leaned back in the room. "Shit!" She yanked it out, feeling over the divot in the fabric. It hadn't penetrated.

Footsteps rushed in and she fired blindly to slow them. Loading her last magazine, she pressed her back against the wall and waited.

A rifle tip entered the doorway. Kiera knocked it up, swinging into the opening, and pressed her HK45 against the guard's chest. Three shots nullified his armor. She shoved his collapsing body into the hall. A dart embedded into her chest, another in her left thigh. The shooter rushed her.

Bullets deflected off the guard's face shield, stunning him for an instant. Kiera dropped low to sweep his legs out from under him, but he overstepped her kick and shoved. She slid back on her ass.

Wind and heat rushed past her face as a concentrated flash of blue-green energy took the guard in the chest. He cried out, falling backwards, and Kiera spared a moment to study Dajah. Chest heaving, left hand extended straight out, he looked utterly exhausted. And was smirking.

A deep-throated growl resonated in the hall, stealing Kiera's attention back. An approaching guard was tackled by a blur with a tail before rolling out of view. Another body slammed into the wall, hitting the floor with a wet crack.

"Miss us?" she heard Matt ask.

"Bout time you caught up," Steffi said.

The group converged, and Kiera never felt so relieved to see a bunch of non-humans.

"Mars, carry Dajah. We need to go," Matt said.

Kiera turned at his prompt, finding Dajah passed out on the floor. The twin lifted him like he weighed nothing, balancing Dajah across his shoulders in a fireman's carry.

"That's it," Gary said as they approached the next elevator.

"Hurry."

Steffi and Gunner forced the doors open, denting them.

"Where's the car?" Matt asked.

"Ten floors below you," Gary answered. "Use the cables. I'll disengage the safety break and unlock the counterweights."

Hearing those words, Kiera imagined only one scenario where it'd be necessary. Her gut clenched in anticipation as Matt commanded, "Everyone on!"

Gunner leapt first, securing a rappelling device and climbing higher on the cable. Steffi went next, followed by Mars who maneuvered Dajah around to his chest for a more secure hold. Kiera cleared the distance to the primary cable, ignoring the void beneath her. Another glance up and she swallowed hard. The cable jiggled.

"Drop it," Matt ordered.

A too-loud click echoed up the shaft followed by the hissing of air and time froze.

One heartbeat. Two. Thr— they launched up at ridiculous speeds, wind deafening Kiera's ears. She clutched that cable for dear life. Hair and clothes whipped wildly. The glow between floors blurred past. Then came a stretch of darkness.

"Now, Gunner!" Matt yelled, his voice carried away instantly.

"On it!" The twin answered.

Kiera didn't dare look up. A loud growl competed with the wind as they catapulted skyward. Their ascent stopped in split seconds. Momentum thrashed and bounced the cable violently. Something smacked into Kiera's side, causing her to lose grip, but the harness kept her secured to the oscillating steel.

"Off!" Matt yelled, voice closer now.

Steffi disengaged, making short work of the doors. Gunner was braced against the overhead, countering hundreds of pounds of pressure with every bulge and strain of non-human muscles. The instant everyone else was clear, he released his grip and jumped to their side of the shaft. Cables tore out of the pulley system, catching Matt's chest and gouging a line through the overhead machinery. Sparks flew. The remaining pieces jangled and scraped down into darkness.

The school gym waited on the other side. Everyone bolted, negligent of any alarms they might trigger now. A low rumble shook the earth.

"It's going!' Matt yelled, blood trailing from his wound.

They made it to the van. Steffi took the driver's seat, the others loading into the back. Another tremor passed. Rattling. Shaking. She peeled off, throwing the passengers, A *crack*-boom deafened Kiera's eardrum. The van lurched up. Wheels burned rubber as Steffi floored it, but the earth split open and swallowed them.

CHAPTER 24

Ethan slammed on the brakes. He was a good fifty miles from the city, but there was no mistaking the massive energy flare exploding on his radar. Elizabeth's recent adaptations boosted his abilities. Still, the power behind this essence was exceptional. The Collective would certainly register it.

"Is Caerus housing other Anodorians?"

By now someone would have discovered the woman standing in for Elizabeth. Was the outburst because of that discovery? Were there other abominations concentrated in the city that managed to cloak themselves? And if so, what set off such a powerful flare?

He turned the car around and made posthaste towards his former destination.

Sirens greeted Ethan's arrival. Local radio stations buzzed about the unprecedented gas explosion, speculating that excavation for a controversial new subway line was at fault. At least twenty were reported dead, and authorities anticipated weeks before all victims were discovered. That the event happened late at night was a godsend, according to one reporter – Saint Mary's grade school was near the epicenter.

It didn't matter which Realm Ethan was in; those in power always fabricated half-truths to subjugate and appease the masses. He abandoned his vehicle in favor of his feet and made his way to the roof of one of the taller high-rise structures. Plenty of buildings here made the Lord Commander's Glass Tower in Novusia look minuscule, but what function did they serve other than to disrupt a beautiful skyline?

Ethan stood among other spectators observing the damage. At least a dozen buildings collapsed in on themselves, leaving piles of indistinguishable rubble. In the distance, helicopters shined light on the bulk of destruction – a blackened crater on the edge of a park.

He flared his radar symbols, knowing feedback would be subpar from this height. When those invisible waves hit the ground and penetrated, they bounced back solid interference.

"Some kind of generalized defense system?" Head cocked, Ethan found it hard to believe Caerus would go to this extreme because of one missing abomination. "Did they intentionally bury their facility? Or destroy it?"

He frowned at the unnecessary loss of life, but if the essence flare was any indication of the abomination's power, the loss was justified. He guestimated the timing of the flare occurred shortly before the explosion. Since that time, his Anodorian radar flatlined.

A buzz-ring brought his attention to the cellular device in his pocket. He wasn't surprised to hear Teacher Lydia's voice when he answered.

"Master Ethan, what's your status?"

"I'm still in the city. The abomination known as Elizabeth has been purged from this Realm."

"When?"

He sensed the urgency in the Teacher's voice. "Seventy hours ago. I felt the recent flare. I was on my way back to the airport when it hit. Upon my return to the city, I discovered that the structure previously housing Elizabeth had been demolished. The timing coincides with that flare."

Lydia was silent a full minute before saying, "I have concerns."

"I'll issue a full report on my return."

"Do you have any reason to believe other Anodorians were in this location?"

"No," Ethan admitted. He'd lifted thoughts from dozens of employees in the underground facility. None of them, including the woman watching Elizabeth, gave any indication they knew what she was.

"I've personally discussed this with the Collective," Lydia started. Ethan balked, unaware the Collective could directly converse with anyone. "We require your presence in the area until the matter can be sorted and confirmed."

"Sorted and confirmed?"

"We need total confirmation that this individual has been destroyed." She paused again before saying, "The essence flare came from an Unawakened."

"A child?" Ethan asked. Unawakened operated below their radar because their abilities were either dormant or intentionally suppressed. As such, they were of lesser concern to the Sect, but still required elimination when identified.

"I do not know. Regardless, it must be destroyed. You are our most gifted Master. The Collective will monitor for additional essence signatures. In the meantime, you must confirm that this abomination was destroyed."

"Of course, Teacher, but with all due respect, I sense a significance here you're reluctant to share."

Lydia remained silent for some time again, leaving Ethan wondering whether he should have asked. Or who she was consulting with.

"The Collective received but a glimpse into the pattern underlying this essence. The Unawakened carries the ability to break the Great Seal."

A chill washed over him. He had to use the wall to steady himself. Protecting the integrity of the Great Seal was the core of their mission. Only a highly skilled Anodorian or one of the *Eldarie* could break the Seal, releasing chaos and imminent destruction upon the Trinity of Realms. The *Eldarie* fled long ago, hunted to extinction by their enemies, and the number of Anodorians remaining on Earth had significantly dwindled thanks to the Sect of Preservation. Hearing Teacher Lydia mention the Great Seal aloud confirmed what he felt all along. Divine presence guided his mission. Fate brought Elizabeth to this realm, Ethan to this very moment.

"Yes," Lydia said, "now you understand the weight of this task. Though risk to the Great Seal is minimal, even minimal risk is too much."

Ethan placed his left hand over his heart and closed his eyes. "I swear to you, the Great Seal will be preserved at all costs. I will not fail."

"Keep this phone with you at all times. Should the Collective receive any more information, it will be directed your way. In the meantime, I expect a full report before morning."

The phone line went dead but Ethan kept his eyes closed, hand on his chest. He felt the potent energies mingling within him. "Great Teachers of the Past, guide my hand. Let me be your instrument of salvation."

He took a deep breath, opened his eyes, and departed the rooftop.

<u>PART III</u>

CHAPTER 25

Kiera remembered the van. The sense of weightlessness. The sounds of earth burying her alive. Though stiff, her body lacked pain. She was *comfortable*. Her Earth Beads and belt, complete with pouches and weapons, rested beside a stack of clothes on the dresser.

Where am I?

Movement caught her attention. She bolted upright and reached for the firearm beneath the pillow out of habit. No such firearm existed, and the rush of activity triggered a bout of dizziness, forcing her back down.

"Take it easy," Steffi said, entering the room. She held a large mug and was dressed casually, considering Kiera's last memories. "You're safe."

She sat up slower this time, folding her legs. Someone had put her in flannel pajamas.

"Drink this. It'll help." Steffi offered the mug and Kiera accepted.

"How long was I out for?"

"Six days. Matt had to get us out of the sinkhole."

She wasn't ready to ask questions, but that explained her sore muscles and dry mouth. Sighing, Kiera sipped warm, soothing spices that awoke her taste buds.

A solemn expression overtook the vampire. She sat on the edge of Kiera's bed, eyes downcast. "There's something we need to talk about."

Kiera's heart beat faster as her mind spiraled down the worst possible scenarios. "Is everyone ok? Did we all make it?"

"Yes." That simple word brought immediate relief while Steffi continued, "But Dajah's still unconscious. As soon as we cleared the debris, it was a blessing you had your Earth Beads. Matt used them to heal everyone. You should have woken then, but you didn't." Pausing, Steffi's eyes met hers. "Do you remember what happened in the room with Julius?"

Memories rushed back with a tightening of muscles. "He's dead," Kiera spat, the image of his corpse manifesting in her thoughts.

"Yes, he's dead, but what do you remember?"

"Lightning?" Kiera recalled hatred and desperation welling up within her. Everything was on the line. "I didn't *cast* anything," she admitted. "I tried using the Beads earlier when Dajah... It didn't work."

"You can't cast Earth magic inside Caerus, which raises the question of how he had a Shield in the first place, but that Lightning spell didn't come from your Beads. It came from you."

The words hit home. In that moment, Kiera knew beyond a doubt that she used to have abilities. She wasn't some non-human gifted with innate magic, but she *did* have abilities.

All of it ended the night Mom died.

"When you didn't recover after the healing, I sampled your blood. Please forgive me. It was the fastest way to assess what was wrong." The concern on Steffi's face hadn't dissipated and Kiera's anxiety crept back in.

"What'd you find in my blood?"

"Something ancient is entwined with your lifeforce. Older than any line of Kindred I'm aware of. I can tell it's passed maternally. What do you know about your family history?"

"My family?" Kiera's head threatened to split open with the information. She took another sip of tea and considered Steffi's question. "Not much. Dad was third generation American but his great grandparents were from Hong Kong. My mother's parents came from a village in Yunnan."

"Have you kept in touch with any of them?"

"Only Granma Meili. She moved back to Yunnan years ago." Remembering her last visit coaxed a partial smile. *All the stories Granma used to tell were real. Yara'ista are real. How much else?*

"She might be a worthy resource," Steffi suggested. "Next time you talk to her, ask about any stories involving lightning. Even legends she can remember from her childhood might provide insight. I don't have contacts older than the Grand Coven, but Matt might."

"I appreciate all the information," Kiera said, "but why are you bringing this up?"

"I sampled your blood without permission. It's customary to inform the offended party immediately and provide recompense."

Kiera had to think back to remember their initial conversation about her smell, and how Steffi had elaborated on it at Matt's club. Before the second Ram's skull was opened. That night had been punctuated by other highs. And lows.

"You think I'm offended that you bit me? Steffi, I'm grateful you wanted to help. Please, don't worry about it." There were more pressing matters than her ancestors. "Where are we?"

"Thank you," Steffi said, bowing her head. She stood, seeming more like herself. "This is Rita's house, an indirect cousin of mine. I'd like you to meet her once you've adjusted to being awake."

Between the tea and the conversation, Kiera was feeling plenty awake. "I've rested long enough. Can I see Dajah first?"

"Of course."

Kiera eased her legs over the edge of the bed, testing their strength before standing. She felt better than she had a right to. With a mental snort, she asked, "This is just tea, right?"

"Tea's one of Rita's specialties. She's an herbalist at heart. Wait until you taste her cooking." Steffi led her into the hall, stopping at the next door down. "Before you go in, you should know he's restrained."

"Why?"

A male voice answered, one Kiera didn't recognize. "So he doesn't wake up and try to kill us."

The man making his way up the stairs held a steaming mug that scented the hall with chocolate and coffee. Easily a foot taller than Kiera, and just as lean and well-built as Dajah, he also had the same intense, cat-like green eyes, and moved far too gracefully. Long, silver hair was loosely braided down his back.

"You're Dajah's brother," she said.

Steffi did the introductions as he crested the top of the stairs. "Kiera, this is Taron. Taron, Kiera."

Taron acknowledged them with his eyes and continued into his brother's room. Kiera and Steffi followed.

The furnishings were like Kiera's room with one notable exception: Chains ran from four eye bolts anchored in the floor to the four limbs of the man asleep on the bed. A loose tee shirt covered his upper half and a comforter obscured the rest.

"How long will he be like this?" Kiera asked.

Taron seated himself beside the bed. "Another week. Probably." His voice lacked all emotion.

Steffi brought over a wooden folding chair, placing it near Taron's. "Here, Kiera. I'm going downstairs to see if Rita needs any help. Join us when you're ready."

Kiera frowned as the vampire left and looked back to Dajah. Moments passed in awkward silence. Taron seemed content to sit and watch his brother, but Kiera felt compelled to say something.

Nothing came close to adequate.

"Steffi filled me in on most of it," he started, "who you are, the raid on Caerus... I'd hear your version of what happened to him." Like his monotone voice, Taron's expression was unreadable.

"We were clearing a hall when Dajah just stopped. Wouldn't answer us. He entered this room and went straight for a refrigerator. Smashed it open with his bare hands... It wasn't Dajah."

"And then?"

She summarized the rest, from the test tubes to finding him strapped to Julius's table and his last outburst of energy to stop a guard. Silence followed.

"It was Queen," Taron said eventually.

"Who's Queen?" Now she studied every nuance of his features.

"A presence. Capable of taking Dajah over when she wants to and he's distressed. He's gotten better over the years, but he can't keep her in check all the time."

Dajah's 'headache' took on a new meaning. "He has multiple personalities?"

"No," Taron said, pausing. His eyes never left his brother. "I've also heard Queen in the past. She's never had much influence over me."

"She's something Caerus put inside your heads?"

"Maybe." Taron lifted Dajah's eyelid and Kiera caught a hint of glow. "It's been years since he's been exposed to this much Stream. They used to inject him to trigger Queen, and this much at once is dangerous. We can't trust him until he's processed it. You should go introduce yourself to Rita. I'll keep an eye on him."

Kiera stared at Dajah a moment longer.

"You care for him," Taron said.

Hit by a torrent of emotion, she struggled to keep her response monotone, "He went above and beyond to help a stranger."

"Did you sleep with him?"

Kiera just blinked, unsure whether to be offended. She narrowed her eyes at the man studying her in turn.

"I'm curious," he said.

"I'm inclined to say it's none of your damn business."

He stared for a second longer then his lips curled into a smirk. Genuine delight surfaced. "You didn't. Tried to?"

"Is there a point?" she asked, folding her arms.

"Queen has her own ideas about what Dajah should and

shouldn't do. If he turned you down, it's because he worries about you."

"And if he didn't?"

"Then you're lucky to be alive, or Queen must like you. Wouldn't count on the latter."

Kiera snorted, leaving the room before Taron commented further. Dajah's change on the dance floor wasn't as drastic as the one he had inside Caerus, but it was similar. The nightmares, times when he seemed to lose focus in the middle of a conversation... all clues.

What did Caerus do to them?

The main living space was the cottage aesthetic at its finest. Knickknacks adorned shelving and oak display cases. Paintings of pastoral landscapes hung on the walls, not to be outdone by the river-stone fireplace and chimney that drew the eye up to an exposed beam ceiling.

Kiera followed the scent of savory herbs suffusing in the air to find a small Italian woman manning the kitchen. Freckles dotted her cheeks and nose. Her mousy brown hair was swept up in a bun, and fine lines crinkled around her eyes when she offered a welcoming smile.

"You must be Kiera."

"I am."

"Hope the tea and bed were to your liking. My name is Rita. No harm will come to you inside this house." Visually, Rita couldn't have been more than twenty years her senior. It was the fluidity of her movements that suggested something supernatural.

"Thanks for your hospitality. What can I do to repay you?"

"You are a guest in my home. My personal experiences with Caerus are limited, but enough that I support Steffi and her friends in any way possible. Right now, that comes in the form of stew and a warm fire. If there's anything you need, don't hesitate to ask."

CHAPTER 26

Among Kiera's recovered equipment was Julius's phone. She sent images of his dead body to the Organization, knowing it'd take time for them to confirm the kill and nullify the contract. For now, her life was in limbo. Regardless, she had no intention of going anywhere until Dajah woke up.

Do I care for him?

She remembered their meeting at the Raven. His cocky confidence. Technically, they used each other. *But he didn't know about Julius on that first night. And he didn't have to introduce me to his friends.*

Seeing Dajah strapped down to that table inside Caerus, Julius's gun pressed against his head...

"I *would* like to know him better," she admitted to the emptiness of her room. "If he wants me to." With Julius dead, she had time.

Kiera turned Julius's phone over to Gary by way of Matt and wondered if she'd ever meet the master hacker or his protégé in the flesh. Matt promised to inform her if Gary came across anything relevant. Left with too much free time, she tried to keep her thoughts productive. Whatever ancient force flowed through her bloodline, Julius developed a recent interest thanks to the woman he referenced at his house. Who was she? Would Kiera ever meet her? Was she even still alive? And how many of Julius's associates knew about his interest? How many would continue to hunt her?

It was easier to focus on other things. Like the test tube she found in her pack that survived. "Queen wanted this."

'Queen' was another topic that needed to be addressed. She filed a mental reminder to ask Taron about it later. Kiera might have had few allies left outside of Dajah's circle, but there was one man she could count on to tell her exactly what was in that tube. Hoping she could provide some answers for Dajah and his brother, she overnighted the sample to Chase Sanderson.

The next morning, she put in a call to her brother's oldest friend.

"Hello?"

"Hey, plant boy!"

"Kiera! Bout time you checked in. How are you?"

"Fine."

"Heard about the contract."

Eyes narrowed, she stared at the wood grain in the dresser without saying a word.

"Come on," Chase said after a moment, "you know I make it a point to keep tabs on you and Sammy as much as possible."

"Yeah," she sighed. "Contract shouldn't be a problem for much longer. Have you heard from him?"

"Sammy? No, but I'm not expecting to."

"Some job out in the middle of the jungle..." She remembered Sammy's last assignment and wondered how *he* recalled their past. *Does he remember those markings? The abilities?* Opportunities to speak with her brother would come few and far between.

"What's up now?" Chase asked, pulling her back into the conversation.

"I sent you a package."

"So *you* sent the mystery box."

"Did you open it?"

"Kier, the last time someone sent me an unlabeled package it was positive for traces of cocaine, cyanide, and human blood."

"This isn't that exciting. It's just a test tube. I need to know what's inside."

"Any background? Or is this one of those 'less I know the better' deals?"

"They were kept in a refrigeration unit. The other tubes were damaged, and this one hasn't been cold for... a while. Someone wanted whatever it was or is. The more information you can get me, the better, but I'd advise discretion. The people who had it aren't ones you wanna mess with."

"So more of the usual," he said. "If it was meant to be kept within a specific temperature range, whatever is inside has likely destabilized."

"Just see what you can do. Call me back at this number."

"Alright, give me a few hours," he said, ending the call.

She contemplated telling Taron, Steffi at the very least, but no one knew she had the test tube. If nothing came of it, they never needed to know.

The follow-up call came while she was helping Rita peel potatoes. Kiera excused herself to answer.

"Yeah?"

"How far away are you?" Chase's tone was off.

"Rural Ohio, near the Lakes. What's wrong?"

"Nothing's *wrong*," he said, emphasizing the word, "but I'm not comfortable talking over the phone. We need to meet."

"Is it bad?" Steffi entered the kitchen at that moment. Kiera had no doubt she heard Chase's side of the conversation, even when he spoke quietly.

"No, it's... it's a first for me." Excitement leeched into his voice. "We need to talk about it."

Kiera breathed – Chase wasn't in trouble; he was intrigued. "Hold on," she said, getting Steffi's attention. "Can I borrow one of the cars?"

"Of course," Steffi said. "Everything ok?"

"I think so." Then Kiera considered a thousand ways any side trip could go wrong. "Mind going on a short drive with me to meet a friend?"

"You're bringing someone?" Chase asked.

The vampire nodded.

"Yes," Kiera said to the phone. "I trust her, and whatever you need to tell me, she might benefit from hearing it."

"And you can't tell her when you get back?"

"*Chase...*"

"Fine, fine. How long will it take you to get to Buffalo?"

"New York?" Steffi asked. "Four hours, give or take."

"You hear that?" Kiera asked Chase.

"Yeah, meet me at Betty's for dinner. Six p.m."

"This better be worth it, Chase. I've still got a contract on my head."

"It will be! See you at six."

Kiera stared at the ended call before pocketing the phone. "Thanks," she said to Steffi.

"No problem."

"This is perfect!" Rita chimed. "I have a shipment of supplies waiting outside of Cleveland. Could you pick them up on the way?"

"Of course," Kiera said.

"We better get going then. Rita, do you need anything else?" Steffi asked.

"Find Taron," she said. "He can help finish with the vegetables."

"So how do you know him?" Steffi asked.

Kiera already explained why they were driving out to meet Chase, and Steffi supported her decision to keep the test tube a secret from the others. "Chase and my brother were the closest friends growing up. I usually tagged along. Anyway, when our parents passed, Chase's family took us in until we were old enough to legally make our own decisions. We stayed in contact over the years."

"And you became an assassin," Steffi stated. "What about him and your brother?"

"Chase has a background in microbiology and genetics. Does some fancy work with plants I don't understand. As far as I know, he's a freelance botanist."

"Which means?"

"No idea. His last project involved grafting a fruit tree with dozens of different kinds of fruit that will grow on it year after year."

"And you said your brother's a relic hunter, right?"

"Yeah. He works with a team that acquires preserved bones and ancient artifacts for individuals with unique tastes and excessive amounts of money."

"Interesting."

"You could say that. Ready to head inside?"

A bright red neon sign advertised Betty's Diner, emitting soft jazz from its speaker. There were a thousand restaurants Chase could have picked, from upscale to intimate. He always had a soft spot for diner food. Envisioning her friend, Kiera and Steffi entered the diner and Chase manifested almost perfectly from her thoughts. Messy, sand-colored hair, thick glasses, flannel, and loafers. He'd chosen a booth near the window side of the restaurant and waved eagerly the moment he spotted her.

Fried bacon and grilled onions saturated the air.

"Good to see you, Chase," she said, sliding into the booth. The man was outright beaming with excitement, but he took a moment to analyze Kiera's companion, squinting while he shifted his glasses up and down the bridge of his nose.

"Chase Sanderson, meet Stefanie de'Llewellyn."

He offered a casual wave. "Nice to meetcha."

"Kiera's had nothing but wonderful things to say about you," Steffi said.

Color flushed Chase's cheeks as he looked down. The server – a young man with an abundance of acne and a sky blue uniform with a brown bistro apron – came over. "Welcome to Betty's, home of the best loaded waffle fries four years in a row. Can I get you something to drink?"

"Pepsi, no ice," Chase said.

"Ice tea," was Steffi's request.

"I'm fine with water," Kiera said.

"Lemon?"

"Sure." Kiera waited for him to depart then focused on the man across from her. "So, you gonna tell us now, or keep us waiting?"

A huge smile split Chase's face. "The liquid within the tube was filled with a viscous, nutrient-rich media meant to support cells suspended inside of it. It *was* temperature-dependent. The cells were dead by the time I analyzed them."

"And?" Kiera prompted, knowing he'd drag this out as long as possible.

"I ran that sample through just about every piece of equipment I own." He reached inside his jacket, pulling out a piece of paper folded too many times over in typical Chase fashion. Opening it carefully, he smoothed out the creases over the edge of the table. "Just look at this!" He placed the sheet down facing them. A chemical composition and ratios ran down one side and a spiked line graph stretched along the bottom.

"What are we looking at?" Kiera asked.

"A list of the chemical breakdown of those cells. And *this*," he said, pointing to a section on the graph that flatlined, "is unreadable on any of my machines."

"It's part of the cell you can't identify," Steffi said. "Can you infer anything?"

Kiera studied Chase.

The server returned with their drinks, ready to take their orders.

"Give us a few more minutes," Chase said, dismissing him with a wave. "I can *confirm* plenty. The cells are tiny parasites, shed from the same lifeform. They adapt to an impressive range of conditions. The reason my equipment can't identify this section," he paused to tap the flat area with his finger, "is because it doesn't match anything in our periodic table of elements. Not even close. It's half carbon-based. The other part... isn't from here."

Kiera's brows pinched together. "When you say 'isn't from here,'" she started.

"Here. Earth. Our galaxy." Chase said.

"So it's an alien?" Steffi said. "What's Caerus doing with aliens?"

"Who's Caerus?" Chase asked.

Kiera said to the vampire, "The better question is: What did Queen want with it?"

"Who's Queen?" Chase asked.

The server came back.

"Can we get a large order of the loaded waffle fries," Kiera said.

"Anything else?" the server asked.

"Just the fries." When the server was out of earshot, Kiera explained, "Caerus is one of those groups you don't want to mess with. Queen... She's complicated. She wanted the test tubes." The words prickled, saying it so confidently.

Chase needed a moment.

The fries arrived, smothered in caloric decadence.

"Steffi, you said Dajah and Taron have unique cells inside of them. You think they're the same as these parasites?" Kiera asked.

The vampire plucked a waffle fry from the pile. Cheese stretched from the lone potato back to the basket. "It's possible, but I wouldn't know unless I could taste the parasites."

Chase's eyebrow shot up and he stared at her. "You wanna *taste* them?"

"She's a vampire," Kiera said. Chase wasn't naïve when it came to non-humans, but his exposure to them was minimal.

"Oh," he said, still looking confused. "But the cells are dead. I thought vampires needed blood."

"We do," Steffi said. "There's still a chance I could pick up something, even from dead cells."

"Why don't you just bring your friend to see me?" Chase

suggested. "If I had viable samples, I could tell you a lot more."

"Would a sample suffice?" Steffi asked.

"Possibly, but the less time between when the sample's taken and my machines analyze it, the better if we're looking for minute discrepancies."

CHAPTER 27

Dajah peeled open his eyes. When Taron's face was the first thing to come into focus, he groaned. Physically rested and renewed, his brain felt like swiss cheese. Vague flashes of gunfire and the tang of Stream filled his memory, but these new surroundings weren't Caerus.

"Where are we?" he asked, voice rough.

"Rita's," Taron said, holding out a glass of water.

"Was the mission a success?"

"Excluding the part where you let Queen take over and you got shot up with almost lethal levels of Stream? Yes."

Dajah winced, ready to smother his face with his hands. His hands didn't move. Craning his head forward, he saw the chains and sighed. "She's not here right now, Taron. You can let me up."

"Get yourself up."

A test. To be fair, it'd been a while since Taron or any of the others had to restrain him after an incident. When Queen took over, finesse was impossible – she had no need for it. *How* Dajah escaped from his restraints would tell Taron plenty.

Preparing, he propped himself up on his elbows and assessed the situation. It took a little maneuvering to free the covers from his body to better see the manacles. The key was conveniently placed on the bedside table. He might be able to reach it, but with Taron sitting that close, he knew his brother expected something more elaborate.

Padded metal bands. It ensured the shackles fit snug against his wrists, but gave him leverage. Dajah sat up and bent towards his left wrist, using his teeth to work out some of the padding.

"I told Kiera about her," Taron said, still holding out the water.

Dajah paused with a mouthful of padded fabric and eyed his brother. "*What?*"

"Someone had to tell her."

"She didn't need to know."

Dajah loosened the padding enough to give his hand some wiggle room, then used the bed as leverage to dislocate his thumb and slip free.

"And yet from her account," Taron continued, "sounds like Queen might have killed her had she not gotten distracted by the guards during your lapse of control."

"She doesn't trust her." Dajah popped his thumb back and swiped the key off the table.

Taron didn't stop him. "Do you?"

"Yes." Free of the remaining shackles, Dajah opted to stay seated on the bed. "I like her. She's got potential. Hell of a shot, too." A pang of sorrow tapped his chest. "Did she..." Experience aside, he knew from the stiffness of his body he'd been unconscious for a while.

The slightest hint of a frown graced Taron's features. "A trained assassin stands a better chance than the others, but you need to tread carefully."

Dajah snorted. He knew his brother meant well, but he made it sound like there were countless others, or that their brother was somehow... less.

He was... at the end. The memory of that day surfaced, threatening to break all composure. Dajah grabbed the glass from Taron and drank deeply.

"She has a friend she wants us to meet," Taron said. "Someone who might be able to help with Queen."

"How?"

"Wouldn't go into specifics with me. We had the option to

send some blood and skin samples instead, but I'm disinclined to give parts of ourselves out to strangers. I'll tell her you're awake. It's your call." Taron stood, pushing his chair back, and left the room.

My call. He sat there trying to sort through the feelings vying for attention. A small glimmer of hope sparked the grim reality of his life situation. He genuinely liked Kiera. Respected her skills. If she stuck around with him, there was a very good chance he was going to get her killed.

Dajah went to the bathroom and splashed water on his face. Green, bioluminescent rings surrounded his pupils. No wonder Taron insisted on a test – he still had enough Stream coursing through his veins that Queen could do significant damage.

A knock came from the bedroom. Stepping out from the ensuite, he found himself unsure what to say.

"Can I come in?" Kiera asked.

"Sure." Dajah motioned to the chair and perched himself on the edge of the bed.

"How do you feel?"

"A little guilty," he admitted.

Kiera's face scrunched with a note of levity as she took Taron's seat. "Could have told me you've got a split personality."

"Tends to send them running when I lead with that."

She smiled before her lips flattened. "Dajah, you kept your word. A bit unconventional, but Julius is dead. The Organization's reviewing all contracts he's issued since they can't get in touch with him. I sent visual confirmation; I doubt they'll ever find his body."

"Give any thought to what you'll do now?"

"I'd like to get to know you a little better," she said.

He searched her gaze, finding nothing but sincerity. "I'm not the best person to get involved with."

"Because you're not interested, or because you're worried about Queen?"

"What'd my brother tell you about her?"

"That she's dangerous. Usually listening." Kiera paused before saying, "He said she killed your oldest brother."

"Well, shit." Dajah massaged his temples, considering how much more Taron might have told her in the time he'd been unconscious. "And you still wanna get to know me?"

"You're not the only one with skeletons in your closet."

"No, and apparently my brother has zero qualms displaying them for you. I don't even think Matt knows about Zayan." He released his breath. "You should know I don't blame Queen fully. That was Caerus's fault. They put us together when he was in no condition to defend himself. They usually separated us before things went too far. Whether they weren't paying close enough attention or it was intentional, I'll never forgive them."

"They made you fight each other?" she asked.

"Not technically. They'd unleash Queen. Study different things. But they'd absolutely use each of us as incentive to complete tasks."

"What do you mean?"

"Get too close, care too much," Dajah started, realizing he was at the edge of an abyss. Another deep breath became necessary before he could finish his statement. "Let's just say I've got good reason to hate Caerus. Compared to Queen, they're far more monstrous."

Kiera leaned forward, placing a hand on his knee. It sent a pleasant spark up his leg. "I wanna help you, Dajah."

~Well isn't this cute.~

You're back already? Thanks for leaving me at the mercy of those disgruntled security guards.

~I knew you'd be fine.~

And after Matthews started feeding you?

~He was insignificant.~

"Is she talking to you?" Kiera asked.

~You told her about me?~

Taron told her about you.

~And yet she's still here.~

"Yes." Dajah said.

"I know someone who specializes in microbiology. Will you meet him? He might be able to help with Queen."

~And why does she think you need help with me?~

We had rules, Queen. You broke them.

~And yet, thanks to me her boss is dead and Caerus buries another facility.~

You're taking credit now?

Dajah shook his head, refocusing on Kiera. "Sure, I'll meet your friend. And, yes, to answer your other question. I *am* interested."

CHAPTER 28

Steffi came along for the ride to save Taron from being a third wheel, but Dajah knew his brother was here to make sure nothing got out of hand.

Chase Sanderson must have done well financially. His land was sizeable, with dozens of nurseries and greenhouses on the premises. The house, which was more like a small estate than farmhouse, could easily accommodate a large family. According to Kiera, Chase preferred plants to people.

Not a bad decision.

He wasn't winning any fashion awards with monotone argyle and slippers, all in shades of brown and offset by a shrub of unkempt, dirty blond hair atop his head. Clunky glasses made his eyes appear bigger, but Chase was most definitely human. Once introductions were complete, he invited everyone inside and put on a fresh pot of coffee. For someone whose 'casual' dining table was carved out of a single, massive tree trunk topped with glass and gold overlays, he could have afforded better quality beans.

Everything within the house looked hand-picked by a designer. On an aesthetic level, it worked. Most of the décor seemed to be an afterthought. However, Dajah lost count of the elaborate, exotic plants that were thriving.

"So you're the one with the voice in your head?" Chase asked, studying Dajah.

Very subtle. "Yeah."

"Can you hear her now?"

All of them were waiting for his answer. "She's around."

"Intriguing!" Chase said.

~*He doesn't interact with people often, does he?*~

I think he just has particular interests.

The ladies explained on the drive about the surviving test tube. Queen's response to why she took over his body to go after the tubes? *They didn't belong to Caerus.* She wouldn't elaborate, but Chase did.

"The sample Kiera brought me had some very unique properties to it. Your friends think there's a connection. I'd like to analyze some of your blood. Your brother's, too, if that's ok."

"That's what we drove out here for, isn't it?" Dajah said.

"Chase," Taron started, "how will you analyze our blood?"

"Kiera didn't tell you? I've got a whole lab in the basement. New combination spectrometer, diffractometer, plasmon resonance imaging system, and high-performance liquid chromatographer, custom designed, from Lumetics. A full electrophoresis suite – I can easily run ten different samples at once. Plenty of—"

"Any internet databases?" Taron asked, cutting Chase off before more words dribbled from his mouth.

"I have access to hundreds, why?"

"Don't use them," Taron warned. "Caerus flags certain entries. You don't want them knocking on your door with questions."

Chase seemed to consider it, nodded, then shrugged. "Shouldn't be necessary regardless. Now if you're both ready, let's head to the lab."

Dajah and Taron waited upstairs while Chase did his thing. The women joined them a little later, and they gathered in the great groom, occupying hardly used furniture. Kiera found some documentary to watch. Dajah contemplated his existence.

He wondered about Queen and her connection to those test

tubes. Thought back through the early years when his life was a mashup between her Stream-induced rampages and his failure to assert free will. Contemplation was a balancing act. Whatever she *was*, it was a part of him, privy to his musings. He expected an outburst any moment.

~Outburst? I'm interested in what the botanist discovers.~

Your interest is rarely good. Why'd you really want those tubes? You risked compromising the entire mission.

~It was a personal matter.~

He laughed out loud, drawing the eye of his brother.

~Taron's suspicious today.~

With good reason. How can you even have 'personal matters?'

~Let's just wait.~

Queen was amused, a welcome respite from her criticizing Kiera, but things could always turn. Dajah raised his palm to his brother and focused on the TV. The mild-accented narrator detailed the leopard's need to feed her cubs as she stalked a herd of antelope. A mother cat hunted more efficiently than a rogue, the narrator claimed. The antelope sensed danger, unable to pinpoint the source. Always a predator lurked, waiting for the perfect opportunity.

Dust and spotted flesh tumbled with horns and brown fur. Blood seeped from the big cat's mouth. Its prey twitched, fighting a losing battle against its own mortality. The rest of the herd ran for safety. In the end, the leopard dragged the dying creature to a suitable area and began indulging. A commercial started, and Chase made his way to them, dragging his feet. Something like awe graced his features. He wasn't stalling. His was the gait of someone who was allowed a glimpse into the workings of the universe.

"What'd you find?" Kiera asked, breaking the silence.

Chase took the open armchair. It was flanked by potted trees whose trunks wove back and forth in a curved, double-helix structure. Pink and green fronds formed a canopy above the chair.

"What'd they make us out of?" Dajah asked. He knew they resembled humans with few explainable exceptions. The eyes? Cosmetic lenses. Hair? Quality dye job. All the rest was every bit as human as the next person. Being raised alongside non-humans, he both appreciated and envied some of their physical characteristics. Queen made him unique, but even Steffi had no explanation for what he and his brothers were.

The question sobered Chase. "Someone made you alright. Did you tell them about the cells?" he asked Kiera.

"I didn't tell them anything," she said.

He looked to Steffi who shook her head in agreement.

"The unique properties I mentioned," Chase continued, "are alien. Part of their gene coding doesn't match anything on this planet. Or this solar system. The cells were parasites shed by a larger lifeform."

~I like this one.~

"Taron, roughly eighteen percent of your DNA matches the base code of those cells. Dajah, yours is closer to forty percent." Chase took a breath, releasing it in a forceful sigh. "I have two Masters and a Ph.D. This is what I *do*, and your genome contains amino acids never even dreamed up by humans. I believe the cells Kiera brought represent an original lifeform. The abnormal cells inside each of you were genetically spliced and forcibly mutated so they'd adapt to your human DNA and coexist. You match each other, but the original lifeform is... different. This is pure speculation, but it's possible the voice Dajah hears *is* the original lifeform."

Everyone was quiet. Even Queen. Aliens were no more far-fetched than werewolves, but the images Dajah conjured of a parasite weren't flattering.

~Do you think I look anything like that?~

So you're an alien?

~The correct term is Plyannian.*~*

Which means what, exactly?

Steffi spoke up. "Caerus found an alien, or parts of one, and experimented until they made you two. But if Dajah can hear her, then the original lifeform's still alive somewhere?"

So you want Caerus to pay because they took pieces of you?

~To simplify things, yes.~

Why'd you never tell me?

~You never asked. Not that it changes anything.~

It changes everything.

Dajah prepared for the backlash to his next question. "Chase, if the original lifeform's communicating with her cells, is there a way to block that connection?"

Queen laughed in his head.

~You don't think Caerus would have figured that out if it were possible?~

Her tone fostered suspicion, as if Caerus *had* figured it out. If Queen relied on others to survive, it further justified her desire to eliminate them.

Chase studied Dajah and Taron with narrowed eyes. "If I can discover how she communicates, maybe. But if you're asking me to stop her from communicating with *you*, I have no idea." He paused again, leaning forward and pushing his glasses up on his head. "It'd be purely experimental, with no way to predict how the block might affect you in advance. Dajah, you aren't a human infected with alien parasites. You're half alien. Trying to manipulate those cells specifically is like trying to alter half your genome."

"I've got good reason to believe it's doable," Dajah said.

~Then you're more of a fool than I thought.~

Chase shrugged. "To try, I'd need several vials of blood on hand and a couple weeks. But I've got other concerns. I know the types of people Kiera works with."

Kiera scrunched her face. "Meaning?"

Chase's sandy eyebrows peaked. "Really, Kier? I can count on one hand how many labs can do what's been done to them. None of them are government. What's Caerus?"

"An organization you don't want to get involved with."

Chase kept his eyes on Kiera, gesturing to Taron. "See? In over my head already."

She folded her arms across her chest, staring him down. "Don't pretend like it deters you in the least."

"Actually," Chase started, grinning, "I'd love to meet the lead scientist behind this."

"No, you wouldn't," Dajah said.

"If you're not interested, we'll take the sample and leave you to your plants," Kiera said.

"Oh, I'm interested, but I'm not attempting this solely to inflate my ego. I've got six projects awaiting completion."

"What kind of projects?" Dajah asked. "Is there any way we can help?"

"Not unless you can speed up the growth process of a genetically engineered tree."

A smile spread across Dajah's lips. "What if I could?"

Taron caught his eye, giving a subtle headshake.

"How?" Chase asked.

"Do you know what Earth Beads are?" Dajah asked.

"Beads made out of dirt?" Chase guessed.

"They're stones formed from specialized radiation with magical properties."

"Magic? Pah," Chase said, waving his hand. "I've tried spells in the past with the help of Kiera's brother. It never works the way I need it to."

"I can't compare it to what you've tried in the past," Dajah said, "but I can assure you Earth magic's unique. There's a spell for vitality that can enrich your plants. Speed up their growth in healthy ways."

"And what's required for this spell?"

"The Earth Bead for one. And a bit of your own energy that's replenishable."

"And the catch?"

"No catch. The Beads are easy to use," Dajah said. "If I get you one, would you consider trying to find a way to block or lessen that connection?"

"Provided it does what you imply? I'd consider it."

Kiera huffed and stood up from the couch. Approaching Chase, she pulled a folding knife from her waistband and flipped it open. Chase's eyes opened wide as her blade moved closer to the elaborate palm tree beside him.

"What are you doing?" Chase asked.

"Proving that Earth Beads work," she said, stabbing the point of her knife into the twisted trunk.

"That's twenty years in the making!" Chase yelled, up on his feet.

"Earth Beads," Kiera said, pointing to the bracelet on her wrist after carving a deep groove. "Watch the cut."

To be fair, Dajah never tried healing magic on plants. There was no reason it shouldn't work, but he was still impressed when the damaged trunk repaired itself before their eyes in a split second.

Chase lowered his glasses and observed the plant close up. The injury healed perfectly, leaving it impossible to tell where the cut had been.

"That's amazing!" he said, ecstatic.

"Agree to try," Kiera said. "I'll give you the basic rundown on how to use Earth Beads before we leave."

"And you'll give me them?" he asked.

"Kiera's Beads won't do what I mentioned," Dajah said. "But I can get the right Bead for you probably within a week. Ten days at the most."

Taron's expression remained neutral, but Dajah knew his brother's concerns. In contrast, Steffi looked intrigued. Dajah could only imagine what went on inside the vampire's head.

Chase walked over to Dajah and offered his hand. "Deal."

CHAPTER 29

Dajah left the car in a glade where the curve of the road obscured it from view. Colorful foliage flourished around them. A cool afternoon breeze carried birdsong and the scent of the morning's rain.

"Get your stuff," he said to Kiera. "Now we walk."

Unaccustomed to visitors, the wildlife was curious. Squirrels and chipmunks ceased activity to observe them with cocked heads and clicks.

"Spent a few years out here," he explained. "First time in my life I could just be me. There were rough spots in the beginning, but it was worth it. No experiments, no injections, not having to constantly watch our backs."

"That your cabin?" she asked, spotting the small house through the trees.

Natural features surrounding the area disrupted satellite and cell services, creating an electronic dead zone. Kiera wanted to get to know him; he couldn't think of a better place for it. With her contract still active, limiting their time in cities was smart. Of course, he had other reasons for needing to come out here.

~*If you give him an Earth Bead, he's more likely to destroy himself.* Then *how impressed will she be with you?*~

Since when do you care about strangers? Nervous about what he'll find out?

~*You're safe here. Don't do anything stupid while I'm gone.*~

Gone? Where are you going?

~I have things to look into.~

Her presence dissolved by the time they reached the cabin, but she was never truly *gone*.

Flat land surrounded the structure. Several boulders dotted the area, but most of the larger trees were cleared during construction. Plenty of saplings thrived in the space since.

Setting his bag down on one of the flatter boulders, he approached the single-story cabin and pushed the door open. How many times did they argue over the placement of the fireplace in the corner, or try to figure out the perfect height for windows?

Taron measured that chimney twenty-three times before cutting out the framework.

The bed frames, table, and chairs were also hand-crafted from materials around the cabin. Save for a few cobwebs and dried, decaying leaves, it was exactly as Dajah remembered.

"Well, it isn't the Ritz." Kiera observed the space with her hands on her hips, backpack hanging off one shoulder.

"Told you we'd be roughing it."

"No, you said you had a place in the mountains. If you would have been more specific, I could have at least gotten some sleeping bags or an inflatable mattress." The wry smile on her face suggested she was amused more than anything else.

"Give it a few hours," he said.

"To warm up to it?"

"No, to furnish it. Put your stuff down and follow me."

He led Kiera to the giant boulder around the side of the cabin.

"What?" she asked, eyes shifting between him and the rock as he folded his arms.

"Looks bigger than the last time we had to move it."

"You *move* this thing?"

"Yep. Now *we're* gonna move it." Her glare encouraged him to add, "Only a foot or so that way."

Getting the massive rock to budge a few inches proved

challenging, and they were sweating by the time Dajah judged it far enough over. He shook the numbness out of his arms while Kiera leaned against another rock and caught her breath.

"Explain why we did that again."

"Supplies." Crouching down, he brushed the dirt with his hand to find the latch. "Couldn't leave the place furnished in the middle of nowhere. We're off grid, but we don't need random hikers robbing us."

Dajah lifted the wooden hatch and climbed down the stairs. The supply cache would make veteran preppers jealous. Then again, Dajah and Taron's idea of survival was somewhat biased. He grabbed the bed rolls and some furs on his way back up.

Kiera waited, arms folded, eyebrow raised. "What else you got stashed down there?"

"See for yourself, though I'll warn you: All the high-end toiletries and fancy body soaps are in our desert cache."

"Dajah, if you have *any* soap, or a roll of toilet paper, I'll be overjoyed."

He waved her off with a chuckle and took the bedding inside.

◆

Kiera entered an impressive space carved from dirt and rock. As no-frills as the cabin was, the cache housed a surplus of surprising supplies. Modern weapons hung along one wall. Camping gear, animal pelts sewn into thick blankets, and folding chairs were all stacked in neat order. The giant stash of toilet paper made her smile. Canned goods, cases of bottled water, towels, spare clothes, and bars of soap occupied shelves. Below the shelves, tucked into a corner, she spied a weathered wooden lockbox that reminded her of pirate's treasure. Which subsequently made her think of Dajah on the bow of a ship with an elaborate, ridiculous hat and she laughed.

"Well?" he asked, joining her.

"I'm impressed. Certainly not what most people think of when they imagine going camping. What do you do with the swords?"

Five katanas rested in wall brackets beneath the firearms. One of the customized rifles with long-range scopes made her giddy. But, she refrained from touching it.

"Guns run out of bullets. And if you've ever tried shooting a vampire, or a bone ape for that matter, you'd wish you had a sword."

"Bone ape? We don't have to worry about those out here, do we?"

"No. But temperatures drop once the sun goes down. We should get the cabin ready. Gather wood for the fire."

Two hours later they had a cozy retreat. Furs made adequate throw rugs. Dajah lashed the bed frames together on her insistence, and she piled them high with pelts and blankets. A long folding table held what supplies they'd brought with them, and cookware now hung from nails in the wall.

"Where's the bathroom?" she asked.

"Outhouse is just beyond the trees over there. As for the shower, you need to be a little adventurous."

They passed increasingly rocky outcroppings before rushing water reached Kiera's ears. Above the next rise, a beautiful waterfall cascaded down from further up the mountain. Water collected in a pool at the start of a river. Stepping up to the edge, she crouched and dipped her fingers in.

"That's ice cold, Dajah. You shower in this?"

"*Brisk* is a nice word for it. *Refreshing* is another that comes to mind. But in the summer? Water's perfect."

"And in the fall?"

"This way," he said.

Guiding her along the river's edge, he approached the waterfall and began climbing up the boulders and cliffs. Some were broad enough to walk underneath the falls. Land leveled out at the top as the river continued uphill. Dajah stopped at one of the small collecting pools just before the water rushed over the edge.

"Feel it," he encouraged.

Pleasant warmth suffused her skin the instant she reached her hand in.

"Thermal vents. If you stand on that ledge below us and walk out to the water, it's warm enough to shower in winter. And these little pools are awesome when it's snowing."

Kiera found herself smiling again. "So, I've seen the outhouse and shower. No electricity, but you've got decent cookware. What do you eat besides canned beans and potatoes?"

"Everything from rabbits to deer. The river's got a healthy trout population, and there are plenty of edible plants and wild berries around. Also, you can't drink the water around the fall without boiling it because of the vents, but it's safe where it meets up with the river. We've also got a big rain basin."

She could imagine two teenage boys thriving here, but Dajah and Taron weren't average suburban kids that decided to rough it for a few years and learn as they went. They were trained survivalists. *Hiding from Caerus.* The thought sobered her, but she refused to let it ruin her mood. "You stayed here for three years. What brought you back to civilization?"

Dajah shrugged. "Never planned on living here permanently, but we needed the downtime to figure out what to do." He motioned for them to start back, picking up a branch. "Keep an eye out for sticks like this. They'll work perfect for the fire."

After a brief moment of silence, he continued. "Caerus made the decision for us to go back. Go after them. I guess Queen helped, too." His eyes took on that unfocused glaze, shoulders tensing. It passed with a subtle head shake and he leaned down, picking up another branch. "They found us during one of our supply runs in town. Long story short, I don't think they realized who we were at the time, or that we were armed with Earth Beads. Their off-site facility wasn't shielded from magic. We leveled it, killed all the monsters and staff, and put ourselves right back on Caerus's radar."

"So they hunted you."

"Caerus wasn't going to change. We had the skill to do something about it, so we started networking. Turns out we weren't alone in our opinion that the world would be a better place without them."

"You do this to make the world a better place?"

He laughed. "I do this for revenge."

"Revenge is tricky." She picked up a branch, snapping it in half before adding it to her collection. "Julius is dead, but I didn't go after him out of revenge. It was necessary. What happens next, though? How many others will come after me seeking revenge for his death? Where do you draw the line?"

"It doesn't matter; all lines are drawn in the sand. If you're lucky, no one'll blame you for his death. You're free."

"Am I though?"

Dajah got several steps ahead before realizing she wasn't following and stopped. "What is it?"

"Unhelpful thoughts." She started walking again. "If Caerus was destroyed tomorrow, what would you do?"

"You mean for the rest of my life?"

"Yeah. Ever think about it?"

"I'd open up another coffee shop with a bigger kitchen. Bakery on the side."

"Gotta say you're the first baking assassin I've ever met."

"We've all got our hobbies," he admitted. "Could I do it for the rest of my life, though? Nah. I was created to be a weapon. Part of me will always be that."

"I know what you mean. I was a smart kid. Not like Chase, but I could have gone any direction I wanted. I've always felt drawn to this life."

"You grew up wanting to kill people?"

Kiera met his non-judgmental gaze, finding only curiosity. She thought about it before answering. "I've got holes in my memories, but something's always been different. Saying I *wanted* to kill people isn't right. It's more the idea that death never bothered me."

"Dirty job but someone's gotta do it?"

She nodded. "Don't get me wrong, in the beginning it was a power trip. I had never liked the idea of following orders, but OPASA painted targets in ways that made you believe you were doing the right thing. Serving a greater good. And they paid well. When I became freelance, I had complete control over which contacts I took. The world *is* a better place without some people in it."

"Absolutely. Do you think you'll go back to working as an Organization assassin?"

"Don't know. Always imagined I'd own a home by an ocean. Raise horses. Ride from sunrise to sunset along the beach, waves crashing in the background..."

"Far cry from Death's Herald who lives above a tattoo parlor."

"Says the half-alien barista."

They gathered plenty of wood, returning just as the sun dipped below the horizon. Dajah set up the branches in a triangular-shaped arrangement in the main pit, then got the fire started with a striker from their supplies.

"Keep it going," he said. "I'll take care of dinner."

Kiera's smile came unbidden. "You're gonna cook for me?"

"Depends on what I catch. Might end up being canned string beans tonight." Looking far too pleased with himself, he headed back into the woods with a net and fishing pole.

"Hands down, best fish I've had in a long time," Kiera said. The flavors Dajah conjured with salt, pepper, lemon juice powder, and canned beans were shockingly delicious.

"Glad you enjoyed it. Now for the main reason we're out here." He left his seat and disappeared inside the cache while Kiera licked her fingers. Moments later, he brought up the lockbox she'd spotted earlier.

"Ah, the mystery box."

"Not exactly." He entered a code via rolled tumblers. The

locking mechanism clicked, and Dajah lifted the lid, revealing a metal interior and a kaleidoscope of richly colored Earth Beads.

"Shit, Dajah. How many do you have?" Meili's stories of *Yara'ista* and Dajah's explanation of how Caerus held the majority made Earth Beads sound as rare as some gemstones. He had a veritable fortune in a cache in the woods.

"Like I said, we used to use a lot of magic."

"You also said Earth Beads were rare. Where'd these come from?" She reached inside, pulling one out.

"With enough use an individual Bead maxes out and duplicates itself, restarting at the base spell. The variations any one Bead is capable of depend somewhat on the intention of the caster. In other words, you can start with one Ice Bead, max it with your own variant spells, and get a new Ice Bead to start over with. Create different variants with the new one."

"You make it sound simple."

"Maxing a Bead without creating variants isn't complicated. The more energy it receives, the more powerful the spell you can cast with it. When a Bead reaches the limit of how much energy it can take in, it uses the excess to replicate itself. You still have to supply energy to cast a spell with a mastered Bead, but you won't be able to enhance it further."

Kiera fingered each of the stones resting in her hand. "Richer colors indicate stronger spells," she said, remembering her earlier lessons. "I know reds are elemental magic." The Wind and Fire Beads she touched confirmed it. "Yellows are self-enhancing and protective, and purple heals. What are the other categories?"

"Dark purple heals," he corrected. "Lighter purples are considered miscellaneous magic."

"There's a category called 'miscellaneous magic?'"

"It's what we called it. The spells are extremely powerful, cast in multiples. Hard to explain. Orange is best thought of as non-elemental magic, similar to the blast of energy I'm capable of. Green's confusion and time magic. Blue transforms."

Of all the colors visible in Dajah's lockbox, she couldn't spot any blue-hued stones, and lighter purples were scarce compared to warmer colors. "Transforms what?"

"You'll see," he said. It was the same look he had when he told her to touch the hot springs. It made the butterflies in her stomach wary and excited in equal measure.

When he didn't elaborate, Kiera asked, "How do you know when a Bead's maxed?"

"It turns black." Dajah stuck his hand into the lockbox, rummaging deep. She heard another click, drawing her attention from the citrine stone capable of enhancing her strength ten-fold.

He removed three bracelets. Each contained twenty Beads or more, and every stone was onyx black. Slipping one of the bracelets over his wrist, a fondness graced his features. "This is my mastered set. This one's Taron's," he said, holding up the second bracelet, "and these are extras we've created over the years."

Kiera took the black bracelet when offered, visually appreciating the contrast from the rainbows. Pinching one of the Beads between thumb and index finger, she opened her awareness to it. Several dozen variations of a healing spell bombarded her mind. The next, a non-elemental spell, screamed raw, destructive power and almost shredded her thoughts. She understood how to trigger that spell to splice a wire with surgical precision or use it to decimate a building in seconds.

The idea of variant spells solidified the more Beads she touched. One Fire Bead cast progressively powerful explosions, while another would warm up an intended target by set intervals. Both of those Beads shared the same base spell – they could both create a spark leading to a flame.

"Don't do anything stupid," Dajah warned. "Just because you *can* cast something, doesn't mean you should."

"How long does it take to wield something like this without it killing you?" She recalled the Drain from casting consecutive minor Ice spells and imagined a mastered spell putting her on her ass. Or worse.

"Different spells have different costs. It's easier to cast a Water spell a hundred times than it is to heal the same cut on a hundred people. Your body adjusts to the Drain the more you use Earth magic. I was trained from a young age, so the Drain for me is minimal at best. For someone like you... I don't know." He paused, looking thoughtful. "No novice should be able to do what you did with that Lightning Bead at Matt's. You've got a natural affinity for Earth magic. We'll have to play around. See what happens after we make you a proper bracelet."

"Out of *these*?" The six Beads supplied by Matt were impressive in their own right, but nothing like the mastered stones. Her Ice Bead contained two variations. The equivalent black one contained seventeen, and the amount of energy required to cast every variation in that stone was astronomical.

She could only imagine how much time, energy, and practice it took for Dajah and Taron to master that many Beads, let alone use an entire bracelet of them in combat. It gave a new appreciation for his abilities.

"They won't all be black," he said. "I don't expect you to use mastered spells right away, but you should have access to them in case of emergency. Remember that a mastered Bead contains variations of its base spell. Just don't go for the most powerful spells first."

"Or it could kill me. Right. I remember."

His smirk returned. "I won't let you kill yourself. Go through all the Beads. Sense them. Set aside those you feel most connected to; we'll go from there."

CHAPTER 30

The forest exploded with magic. Lightning sizzled against Dajah's barrier then dissipated. He stepped back, slipping on a frozen puddle that hadn't existed seconds ago, and Kiera moved in. With her first high kick deflected, she followed up with a second to his ribs. He pinned her ankle between his side and arm with a twist.

Multicolored fractals shattered her magic barrier. An open palm forced her back as he released her leg and she hopped, regaining balance. Something snapped an instant before a massive branch crashed down. Dajah dove out of the way, twigs snagging in his shirt, and countered with a mild Poison spell. A shimmered distortion rippled around her, confirming she'd replaced her barrier in time.

"Nice! Way faster than yesterday."

"You're getting predictable." she taunted.

"What'd you cut the branch with?"

"Wind variant."

"Condensed to the point of creating an effective blade. I'm impressed." Dajah picked a tangle of leaves out of his hair, moving casually so as not to spur another round of attacks. "How do you feel?"

"I'm not tired if that's what you're asking. The elemental Beads leave more of a tingle afterwards compared to the others, but I still have no idea how to manifest lightning without them."

They'd discussed this in-depth – Kiera's contradictory memories, the odd, tingling sensation she described after using Earth magic, and Steffi telling her something very old mingled with her bloodstream. Based on what he'd witnessed over the last few days of training, he assumed her innate magical abilities were dormant, triggered only by high-stress scenarios.

"We need to up the intensity." He'd been going easy, providing ample opportunities to counter his magic and enough physical threat to keep her moving, and she excelled. The Drain limited her, but Kiera recovered faster each time.

To invoke latent abilities, at least according to Caerus, an individual had to be placed in authentic life-or-death situations. Dajah could cast spells to annihilate any barrier she could create at this stage, but he wouldn't take the risk of doing irreversible damage. He didn't want to hurt her. And she trusted him.

He spared a glance at the rich colors making up her bracelet. She'd chosen a majority of reds and yellows, with a few greens and the rare orange thrown in. The nine incorporated black Beads were ones he insisted on.

"Actually," she started, "I was thinking we take a break from magic. Spar with something a little more... interesting."

Dajah's brow lifted. "This isn't interesting? What'd you have in mind?"

"Knives."

"You wanna knife fight?"

"Yep," she said, walking towards the cache.

Dajah waited as Kiera brought up four daggers.

"You've got the advantage with magic," she said, pressing two blades flat against his chest. "I want something more on my playing field."

He took the weapons. "You can definitely outshoot me, but your hand-to-hand combat needs work."

"You haven't seen me fight enough to know what I'm capable of," she defended. "Shall we go until first blood?" Kiera took a standard offensive stance, right dagger pointed down, left up.

Dajah stayed relaxed. "With or without magic?"

"Without."

Nodding, he dispelled all magic lingering in the area including Kiera's newest barrier. "Need a minute for the Drain?"

"Nope." She launched a forward-sweeping attack. It would have done significant damage and ended their friendly wager instantly if he hadn't blocked.

So, she wants me to take this seriously. Grinning, Dajah tested her guard. Blades scraped and clipped off each other in a well-orchestrated song of steel. By the time they worked up a light sweat, the only casualty was her shirt.

"Watch your high guard," he warned, putting another diagonal slice through the loose cloth over her shoulder. She'd left herself open twice now. The three-quarters sleeve slipped lower on her arm. The other tear mid-torso offered rare glimpses of black lace.

"Point taken."

A barrage of stabs and swings followed. He fell for one of her feints, and Kiera managed a thin tear across his stomach. Knowing she only caught fabric, he lifted his shirt and fingered the opening. "Bout time you cut *something.*"

"You're one to talk." She switched both blades to her left hand. "All *you've* done so far is ruin my clothes."

He'd put a vertical slice into her cargos on their last exchange, exposing half her thigh.

"Are you complain—"

Kiera pulled her shirt over her head and tossed it aside.

"—ing...? Nope. Gonna take those pants off, too?"

Head cocked, she said, "You've seen me in less taking care of my wounds. Why should this distract you? Every time that sleeve fell it interfered with my range of motion."

"Ah, so it's a tactical decision." A light sheen of sweat coated tight abs, and the contrast between her tanned flesh, black lace, and the forest backdrop had him staring longer than necessary.

"My pants aren't giving me problems, so to answer your question, no. I'm not taking them off. Come get it if you want it."

Her lips curled in a tantalizing smirk. She waved two fingers, inviting the attack.

Dajah started forward and Kiera met his momentum head-on with renewed vigor. She feigned an upward stab, blocking his attempt to nick her exposed side. A punch at his jaw forced him back on the defensive, ruining his next string of attacks.

The woman could move. She wielded those blades with expert precision, and Dajah reminded himself to stay objective. Ignore how distracting those smudges of dirt on her forearms were from when he'd thrown her earlier. Ignore the utter enjoyment shining through her confidence. Ignore the rest of her clothing. Or lack thereof...

Flicking his weapon out, he aimed for a bra strap. She cross-blocked with force, deflecting his arm wide, and stepped inside his guard. Her dagger slipped down along his waistband, flat against skin as he moved back.

Kiera sliced through the fabric of his pants and barely scraped the surface of skin in one fluid movement. It was calculated, and either really skilled or lucky considering how much damage she could have done twisting the other way.

Waistband severed, Dajah's pants slid lower on his hips.

"Mm, looks like you lose," she said, eyeing the thin bead of crimson on the edge of her blade.

In hindsight, he should have stepped left, not back. Dajah lifted his shirt, exposing the one-inch scratch near his hip. "Not bad."

She tossed one of her daggers, embedding it in the dirt, and grabbed the bottom of his shirt. Pulling the fabric taut, Kiera ran her remaining blade up the center.

"That necessary?" he asked, eyebrow peaked as his shirt was split in half, exposing his chest.

"Fair's fair. You ruined my shirt. I get to ruin yours."

Dajah moved to take a step back and she dipped her fingers into the front of his pants. Her knuckles brushed against bare skin, pulling him closer.

"What do I get for winning?"

"What do you want?" Playfulness, but hints of anxiety kept arousal in check. All lines might be drawn in the sand, but they still existed. Queen hadn't returned yet. Didn't mean she was absent.

"You to stop thinking," Kiera said, never breaking eye contact.

"It's not that I don't want you," he started.

She pressed her fingers against his lips to silence him then slid both hands to his right wrist, taking the dagger. "I get it, Dajah."

He relinquished the weapon, but looked down the instant he felt the pull against the Beads magnetized to his skin. She slipped off his bracelet and placed it on her wrist, explaining, "Security incentive. If the crazy bitch in your head wants to interrupt, your brother gave me a few pointers on how to handle her."

"You had to bring up Taron right now?"

"I'll make you forget about him real fast," she promised. "Dajah?"

"Yeah?"

"Let go of the other dagger."

It made him smirk. The sarcastic comment on his lips disappeared the instant Kiera crouched in front of him, hands trailing along his sides and hips. Stubbornness and practicality warred against increasing desire. He dropped the dagger, focusing on the trees as she broke physical contact for a moment.

Weight slammed against his upper calves, buckling both knees and sweeping his feet out from under him. Dajah barely had time to break his fall. Laughing, Kiera crawled on top of him.

"That's so not where I thought things were going," he admitted.

"Because you're still thinking too much. Stop. Thinking."

"I don't want—"

Her lips pressed against his, stealing his next words with a skillful tongue before leaning back. "You were saying?"

"Nothing," Dajah said. "I was saying nothing." The knife fight was Kiera's way of proving she could handle herself. There was a fine line between caring and ruining the moment. He wasn't about to insult her. Reaching one hand behind her head and the other to her back, he pulled her close, meeting those lips for a thorough appreciation of what they offered.

<hr>

Kiera'd never seen a man struggle so hard against what he wanted. It was a risk she was willing to take. Dajah was the first one in too long to offer respect. Wanted to help her. Straight up *wanted* her. It felt good to be wanted.

She returned the kiss with all the aggressive, pent-up sexual tension she'd suppressed. Dajah responded in equal measure, and she could tell the instant he stopped thinking. Slipping her hands under the remains of his shirt, she dug her fingertips into his sides. Ground her hips against his. Ensured his thoughts stayed focused on the present.

Their tongues twisted and danced together. Claiming each other's mouths. She made space to dip her hand down, providing extra incentive for him not to think about anything else.

He groaned, and she pulled back to look at him. Wild eyes flaked in green sparkled with desire. She could lose herself in those eyes.

Dajah pushed himself up, forcing her to lean back lest they be nose to nose. Strong hands gave a decidedly appreciative grab of her ass then slipped around the backs of her thighs as he stood, picking her up with him.

A carefree laugh escaped as she wrapped her legs around his waist, arms around his shoulders. Dajah brought them inside the cabin while she lavished his neck and ear with affection. He unclasped her bra and let one hand travel the length of her back. Kiera moved her feet to the ground and stepped back, meeting his lips once more. She let the undergarment slip free and loosened her pants. Dajah was grinning.

Kiera stepped out of her clothing and Dajah pushed her hard enough to catch her off guard. Her legs met the edge of the bed and she fell back onto it.

"Fair's fair," he said with an expression so wickedly sinful she could have devoured him right there. Dajah spent more than a few moments exploring her with his eyes.

"This the part where you confess you don't know what you're doing? Because I'm more than happy to instruct you." Kiera wore amusement like an open invitation as she slinked back on the bed.

Dajah shed his shirt but didn't bother with his pants. Her eyes followed the lines and curves of his chest down, pausing on the tiny line of red by his hip. His pants were perfect for lounging, not for hiding *anything*. And the silhouette against the fabric had her body aching in all the right ways.

"Pretty sure I can figure it out," he said, stepping closer. "But by all means, feel free to voice your opinions." Dajah crawled onto the edge of the bed and gently lifted her foot, placing a kiss on her ankle. Then another, a few inches higher.

"Dajah," she started, voice failing into a satisfied moan followed by a tremble when his mouth reached the inside of her thigh. Too cool air caressed all the places he wasn't touching.

His hands kneaded her thighs, coaxing them wider apart. When his mouth found the sensitive spot between her legs she gasped, balling up the blankets in her fists. He didn't need any instructions. He knew exactly what he was doing with that mouth. That tongue. Those fingers.

Kiera's entire focus narrowed to the sensations he elicited. The building tension. The way he read her body and responded in perfect measure. "Mm, Dajah, don't stop."

He didn't, and she lost herself to a wave of pleasure and release that left her trembling. Wanting *more*. When she finally caught her breath and felt his absence, Kiera propped herself up on her elbows and studied the very amused individual crouched below her.

"Your reward for winning," he said.

"Oh, that's not nearly good enough." Kiera repositioned herself on her knees and curled her finger at him. "Come here. Lose those pants."

Dajah obeyed. The instant he was within reach, Kiera grabbed his face. Tangled her hands in his hair. His hands explored her body, grabbing and kneading. Before he could second-guess anything, she shoved him down and straddled his hips. A few strokes with her hand had him perfectly positioned and Kiera lowered herself down on top of him. Taking a long moment to savor how well he filled her. How perfectly they fit together.

Kiera rode him until nothing else in the world mattered. No Julius, no Queen, no ancient energies entwined with her lifeforce. Just the two of them. Dajah remained acutely aware of her needs. As she approached another climax, he rolled her onto her back and finished the job. Claiming *her*.

A slew of curses and demands left her mouth between hungry kisses. Then pleasure obliterated every thought in her head. She held on tight, body rippling with residual satisfaction until Dajah was spent and trembling on top of her.

She groaned when he pulled out and laid himself beside her, catching his breath.

"Better?" he asked.

Kiera rolled on her side to face him. A sly grin formed on her lips. "It's a start."

Dajah's returning grin, full of promises to come, was the best thing she'd seen in weeks. Maybe years.

"I'll have to kick your ass more often," she said.

One of his silver eyebrows arched and he leaned up on his forearms. "That's what you think happened?"

Placing a hand on his chest, she pushed him back down. "Semantics, Dajah. Now that I know what you can actually do with your mouth, I think less talking's in order."

He just laughed.

CHAPTER 31

After two weeks of squeezing himself in and out of a bomb site, Ethan concluded that Caerus was a dead end. Literally and figuratively. He surveyed enough of what remained to understand that the collapse was intentional. *Something* happened down there, and whatever that something was, it triggered a failsafe that effectively sealed off the facility then released a toxic gas that killed anything that might have survived the initial collapse. The first hints of gas almost crippled him. It took hours shielded in the darkness to heal when it should have been instant.

He couldn't find a way down to Elizabeth's room and doubted *anyone* survived this. The more interesting events happened afterwards, when a clean-up crew was sent in to investigate. Under the guise of federal employees, the official story was that subway excavations hit a gas pocket. Citizens at large needed to keep their illusions that a reliable form of government still existed, even though Ethan would have bet on them being from the Organization. It took little more than a brush of contact with those individuals, lifting recent memories to confirm they *were* federal employees. They were also part of Caerus.

"Another facility lies far to the north, across the border." The more Ethan looked into Caerus outside of those few individuals, however, the less he found.

"It's a ghost organization."

He wondered how many people outside the Sect knew of *their* existence, abominations aside. The Sect had a clear purpose. What was Caerus's? And what did it have to do with Anodorians? Fate brought him here for a reason, but he was beginning to suspect he sought answers in the wrong places.

That night Ethan returned to his hotel room and took out his cherished memoir. He closed his eyes and tossed the leather-bound book into the air, letting it land how it may upon the bed. Scooping up the object with reverence, he read over the page it opened to.

> I fear for our future. For all of us. The *Eldarie* put on a noble front, but their arrival woke the One Who Lies in Darkness. Realizing this grave mistake, they created the Great Seal and stalled Armageddon. But do not be fooled. The Great Seal was merely an attempt to contain the once-sleeping power until they could harvest it.
>
> The energy required to manifest such a protection rippled out into the Universe, alerting the *Eldarie's* enemies of their whereabouts. History will tell many stories – that the *Eldarie* left to confront these enemies, that they fled to avoid open war on a planet unprepared for such a threat... They left to draw their enemies away from the One Who Lies in Darkness, while many of their protectors, the Anodorians, stayed behind.
>
> We must rise up and protect this world. Protect the Trinity. For the sake of preserving the Great Seal for all time, Anodorians and *Eldarie* alike must be eliminated. The risk is too great. Should the One Who Lies in Darkness awaken, reality itself shall cease to be.
>
> I've written this memoir to guide those who come after me and have included as much detail as I dare risk should this fall into the wrong hands. The threats to this world must be contained and eliminated. The Great Seal must hold—

Ringing tore Ethan's focus from the book. He answered the call before the second chime sounded.

"Master Ethan," Lydia greeted. There was no warmth in her tone.

"Yes, Teacher."

"We have a lead. Sparks, blips. Hints that the Unawakened may be channeling magic."

"The signature is the same?" he asked. Ethan couldn't see how any Unawakened could have escaped Caerus's collapse. An abomination at full strength? Certainly. But an Unawakened? Doubtful.

"Similar, but significantly dwindled. The Collective suspects some kind of interference. We can provide a general location only."

"Send me the coordinates."

CHAPTER 32

Dajah surprised her with breakfast in bed: Wild berries and a stack of pancakes with tea. Kiera knew that the barista in him would never settle for instant coffee.

"What's on the agenda for today?" she asked.

Joining her with his plate, he said, "We should probably send a Vitality Bead to Chase as a sign of good faith."

"You had two in that lockbox if I sensed them correctly."

"You did. We'll be sending him the brighter Bead. The Drain from that spell is minimal enough that even if he casts the advanced variant it shouldn't set him back for too long."

"If there's a way to stop... her, Chase will find it." Kiera tread carefully around any mention of Queen or Caerus. He'd opened up to her. Been far more relaxed at the cabin than she'd seen him anywhere else, even at Matt's.

But where's this going? The thought hit hard, ruining *her* mood instantly. It triggered a cascade of unhelpful questions. What *was* she doing in the middle of nowhere with an unstable, genetically engineered weapon? So much had happened since declining Skullz's invite.

She was different now.

Dajah felt safe in a way she couldn't define, even if the rational part of her told her he was anything but. Still, she was a realist at heart. She wouldn't delude herself.

"You're not hungry?" he asked, halfway through his stack of

pancakes.

She barely touched hers. "Just thinking about what happens next."

"What do you mean?"

"Eventually your group will find another Caerus location. You'll go after them. Destroy them. You've got a plan. A purpose. When I think about the past few years, I'm not sure I had a plan. I was living to get by, doing something I was good at and not caring about much else."

"You know we can use your help, but it'll put you on their radar."

"Dajah, I'm already on their radar. My ex-boss ran their Eastern Branch, remember? Which reminds me... I should find out if the contract's been voided yet."

"We can drive into town. Ship out Chase's Bead, find out about your contract, maybe grab a bite to eat that isn't cooked over a campfire..."

She laughed. "These are good pancakes for what you've got to work with, but I'm dying for a cup of coffee."

"Let's get cleaned up and dressed, then. When we get back, there's something I wanna show you."

Her eyes widened then narrowed, studying him. "Something I'll like?"

Dajah seemed to consider his response. "It's... different. I think you'll like it. Have to wait and see."

They returned from their productive side trip into town and Dajah introduced her to transformation magic, starting with a lecture. As boring as his descriptions were, she could tell he enjoyed talking about it in an adorable, geeky sort of way. For that reason alone, she persevered.

"Transformation magic's duration-based," he said, finally getting to the topic at hand. "One hour is the minimum with a basic-level spell. A mastered spell will last for twenty-four hours."

"What are we transforming?"

"You."

Eyeing him critically, she figured this was another lesson he'd enjoy more than she would. He must have surmised her thoughts, continuing, "It's important you experience it. This one's fun, I promise. Just remember: When someone successfully casts a status spell on you, you'll need someone else to nullify it. Or you'll have to wait for the effects to wear off and improvise before you can use magic again."

"Let's get it over with, then."

Dajah nodded, casting his magic.

Pins and needles shot across her body, almost feeling every one of her nerves at once. The sensation lasted only seconds, but when it faded everything felt *wrong*. Her clothes became a trap. She shifted her weight and tangled further, hitting the ground with a grunt. Pawing at the fabric, Kiera finally got the shirt off over her head and observed the world differently.

Sounds reached her ears more acutely, and scent held visual substance. Furry black paws supported her weight. She had to crane her neck back to meet Dajah's eyes.

"What'd you do to me?" she asked, noting her how lips didn't quite feel the same. A long tongue assisted with the formation of words, her voice possessing an odd accent.

Chuckling, Dajah came over and helped her out of the rest of her clothing. "Would have told you to undress first if I didn't think you'd get the wrong idea."

She came to waist-height on him, turning in a tight circle to better view her body.

There's a tail.

He cast an Ice spell variant for her benefit, creating a solid, opaque block that reflected. Familiar hazel eyes stared back through fur an identical match to what used to be her hair color. Cocking her head, she observed how dog-like the motion was.

"You turned me into a dog." The mirror image of a speaking animal was surreal.

"A wolf, actually. Or at least the Earth Bead equivalent of one."

Watching Dajah strip in the reflection she asked, "Is the form an illusion?"

"No. You've got all the traits of that animal. Just start accepting the wolf as your own." He cast a spell on himself and began to sparkle. Then his lines blurred, his form faded, and he morphed into a silver wolf with intense green eyes. Shaking out his fur, Dajah moved naturally in his canine body.

Ignore the Earth Beads around his wrist and no one would mistake him for a man disguised as a wolf. I wonder if Shifters could even tell the difference.

"Some say a transformation Bead exists for every animal out there. We only ever found two."

"What was the second one?" she asked.

"A fish. It's in that box somewhere close to the bottom. The transition from breathing air to water and swimming isn't easy. Tried it a couple times then decided the effort wasn't worth it. This one's mastered, however. Taron and I spent a ton of time in the woods like this. Gives you a new perspective."

Kiera stood and stretched, mindful of the nuances of her new body. "I'm guessing you maxed the spell."

He dipped his head in a wolfish nod. "Takes a few hours to adjust your first time, but I think you'll find it fun once you're used to it. Should warn you about the smell, though."

His words brought her attention back to her new senses. Smell was often taken for granted. In this form, she breathed in. Faint traces appeared on the air, deciphered as easily as one could name colors.

Dirt, trees, squirrel? Campfire ash, wood. ...a hawk? Oh, a hint of the river. Visually sweeping her surroundings, she paused on one scent in particular – a complex blend of rich and subtle flavors she could only define as *Dajah*. Instinct linked the scent to some unnamed memory, at once evoking a fierce desire to protect him... and jump on him. Underlying the stronger drives was something akin to contentment.

There wasn't anywhere else she wanted to be right now, and she'd be lying if she said mounting him didn't cross her mind. Or him mounting her.

Thank god he doesn't smell like this normally. We'd never get anything done.

"You're drooling," he said.

Kiera blinked, realizing her tongue lolled out of her mouth and shut it.

"Come on." He trotted off towards the trees.

Before long they were sprinting through the forest, jumping off lower branches and rocks. They chased rabbits and deer. Hunted. Dajah let her lead, and her nose had no problem keeping on the trail of a large hare. How to ferret it out from its warren, how to pounce, and where to bite so death was quick all came naturally.

No way does just-dead rabbit taste this good as a human. It put their earlier lunch of salad and burgers to shame.

After sharing the carcass, they traveled upstream and drank fresh mountain water. A new scent found its way to her nose.

"What's *that* one?" She grinned in her wolf way and took off after it, flicking her tail to encourage him to follow.

<hr>

Dajah spared a moment to appreciate how grateful he was for everything these woods provided. Sitting to scratch behind his ear, he recalled the time spent here with Taron. Those were some of his most revered memories. Now he had new ones.

Taking a deep breath in...

What is *that?* The scent didn't belong. And the fact that he couldn't identify it raised every hair on the back of his neck. Growling a curse, he leapt into a full sprint, chewing up ground. Kiera's potent fragrance overlapped the foreign one.

He intercepted her before she ran out into the opening, giving a warning that was part verbal, part body language, and all wolf.

It stopped her instantly, mouth open and panting as she studied him. "What is it? What's wrong?"

"Whatever that is, it doesn't belong here."

They stalked it carefully, crouching behind the rise that marked the boundary to the field and the road beyond. A red sedan was parked a quarter-mile down with three creatures surrounding it. They appeared human, but the smell was off.

"That's what I smelled?" Kiera asked. "That's a nice car, Dajah. I've never seen a four-door Maserati."

He snorted, paying the vehicle little mind. "Guarantee they aren't local."

"Pleasure cruise?" she suggested.

The creatures seemed to be consulting some kind of tablet. Dressed identically in dark brown pants and black zip-up sweatshirts, only their hair color, height, and varied skin tones distinguished them from one another at this distance.

"They're looking for something. No one stops here without reason. We need to get back to the cabin. Hide." Dajah turned and took off, all tranquility vanished.

Shouldn't have maxed the spell!

He cursed himself for getting sloppy, for thinking they were safe, for letting his guard down... Little could be done about it now. Only one thing mattered: Protect the stash of Earth Beads.

Kiera caught up shortly after he reached the cabin, and luck was on their side. The block of ice he'd cast earlier melted, putting out their campfire.

Still no way of knowing if they spotted it earlier.

"Now what?" she asked, sniffing the air.

"Put as much as you can into the cache."

They made countless trips, carrying whatever possible in their mouths. There were limitations to how effectively two wolves could make a place appear deserted, but Dajah hoped they did ok. In the end, the cabin looked like hikers used it, not that anyone had been living in it.

He flipped the trap door over and covered it with dirt, scratching up the ground in various locations to make the cache less obvious.

Both of them froze when the scent returned.

"They're close," she whispered.

"They're not looking for wolves." All he had was a gut feeling. If it was a false alarm, it cost them nothing besides burning calories. "This way," he said, leading to an area they could watch from.

The creatures approached with nightfall, no flashlights, but the near-full moon provided exceptional visibility. Their clothing was accented with guns and blades.

Dropping his head, Dajah pulled his lips back to expose powerful, sharp teeth. His hackles raised. Adrenaline pulsed a steady beat through his ears as a brunette and a redheaded woman examined the landscape. The third, a dark-skinned male with his face and exposed hands covered in tattoos, approached the cabin.

"What are you doing?" Kiera asked.

"You know what I'm doing. We can't let them leave here."

"Please don't. We don't know what they are, let alone what they want. How are you gonna fight them?"

He wasn't dignifying that with a response. Eyes narrowed on the redhead as she moved to one of the game trails leading to the river. Dajah followed, crouched low, each step placed with the care of an apex predator. The woman remained unaware of him, reacting minimally when a twig snapped somewhere up ahead.

She turned to face the disturbance, pulling a knife from a thigh sheath. A whiff of bobcat floated in the air. The moment her back was to him, Dajah pounced, sinking teeth deep into the soft flesh of her neck.

They both went down. Dajah locked his jaw and shook viciously, vertebrae cracking and shifting under the force of his bite. Tangy crimson flooded his mouth.

He left the body limp and bloody, circling back to the cabin.

One down.

The second knew he was coming.

"Find anything?" she asked, turning to face the Dajah.

The blood staining his chin and neck contrasted his silver fur. He kept his ears pinned back, teeth bared, and approached with deliberate steps.

The brunette made no sudden moves, standing with indifference. "This is not your claim. Go away and we won't eat you for supper."

Dajah gave a deep warning growl. Kiera howled in the distance, and a third wolf, one of the local packs, echoed her call.

They're miles off.

The noises brought the male out of the cabin. "Wolves are getting closer," he said, laying eyes on Dajah before going still. "Lil?"

The woman, Lil, gestured for him to stay back. "If you help us hunt the people staying here, there may be a reward for you."

If she hadn't smelled so unusual to begin with, the fact that she tried bargaining with a wolf would have seemed odd.

They have power over the animals here.

He was neither an animal nor under the influence of these creatures. He snapped his teeth and stalked closer.

"Careful, Lil, the bastard caught me from above." The voice came from the trail behind him. Twisting an ear first, Dajah glanced back to see the redhead standing there, a hand against her bloodied neck.

Should have taken the extra time to dismember her body.

"You let it catch you off guard, Beth?" Lil asked. "You're getting slow."

Dajah lunged at the brunette. Taking his full weight, she went over backwards. He snapped just shy of her face. The male moved in to help.

"Don't," Lil warned. She managed to keep Dajah off her throat at arm's length, but his back claws dug into her thigh and abdomen as he pushed for leverage.

Kiera rushed out from the trees in a black blur, tackling the redhead. Claws tore chunks out of the woman's back. Dajah saw her teeth sinking into Beth's shoulder and Lil faltered, allowing him to chomp down on her arm. She clocked him with her fist, stunning him enough that he had to let go.

The male picked Kiera up off the other woman and threw her like she weighed nothing. At the same time, the brunette maneuvered her knee between them, launching Dajah over her head.

He landed on all fours, ready to lunge again, but caught Beth raising a gun in Kiera's direction.

"Stupid bitch," she said, her finger squeezing the trigger.

Dajah rammed into her legs, toppling her as the shot went wide. Nesting birds startled into flight. Something else rushed through branches, away from the percussion.

"Enough!" Lil yelled.

Before Dajah reached Kiera, every joint in his body stiffened. He face-planted, skidding along the dirt mid-run until coming to a stop. Immobilized.

They have innate magic. Guns would have been bad enough in this form. Now we're screwed!

This was the perfect time for Queen to make an appearance if only to mock his current predicament, but Dajah couldn't sense any trace of her. Beth approached and kicked him in the side, aiming the barrel of her gun at his head.

"Don't shoot them," Lil said.

"Why not? We should skin both of them. Eat their meat and save their bones. They deserve no less."

"If we did that the boss would be displeased. Look at their feet."

Unable to lift his head to see Beth's expression, Dajah knew what the brunette referenced – his black bracelet stood out as much against silver fur as blood did, but he'd never risk any environment Transformed without them.

"Earth Beads," Beth said.

Lil stepped closer. "You should have realized when he took a chunk out of your neck, sister. Take them back to the car. Tie their mouths shut."

The tattooed male hefted Dajah up under one arm, Kiera under the other. Dajah couldn't move if he wanted to, but his senses still functioned. This close to one of the creatures, he appreciated what was so wrong with their scent. *They don't have one. They're picking up the odors of everything around and distorting it into something else.*

They shouldn't exist.

They were thrown into the trunk of the red Maserati sedan. Beth tied rope around their muzzles, and Lil did... something. Dajah assumed she extended the duration of the immobilization spell. All he felt was a mildly perceptible shift in numbness.

The male slammed the trunk closed and someone started the car.

CHAPTER 33

A single gunshot echoed through the forest. Ethan flared multiple symbols, his Invisibility Bubble going up first. Enhanced speed boosted his run while his radar confirmed a structure in the distance.

"Enough!" a woman yelled.

The Bubble kept him shielded from unwanted eyes; Ethan still needed to be mindful of his surroundings. The Sect's coordinates covered hundreds of acres, including deep forest, mountains, and a small town. He hadn't picked up a single spark of essence, but the right combination of rock, water, and flora created an energetic buffer. It'd be as good a place as any to hide an Unawakened.

Slowing, he approached the clearing and observed the strange scene unfolding. Three humans. Two wolves. All lies. The humans were no hunters in any traditional sense. And the animals wore a bracelet each on one of their front legs. Their limbs were stiff and immobile, easily mistaken for stuffed trophies when the man picked up one under each arm.

Except for a dugout and a roughly constructed single-story building, Ethan's radar found no trace of any elaborate underground structures like Caerus. It was pure wilderness beyond the log cabin. Which begged the question of what, exactly, brought these individuals together. He fine-tuned his radar, sending it out like a soft wind on invisible currents. What it brought back to him was... frustrating. The animals were alive, cocooned in layers of magic that obscured any truth of what they might have been. The humans were walking voids. Their fields both consumed and repelled in a way Ethan had only seen once before. Only a true immortal manipulated the fabric of reality like that. Finding three of them in the same general area as Anodorian essence spikes made Ethan's skin tingle with sacred purpose.

He followed the group until a vehicle became visible in the distance. Having ditched his own miles from here, Ethan had to make a reckless but necessary decision. If those beings were true immortals, they would see right through his Invisibility Bubble. But *only* if they decided to look. Even immortals could be duped if they weren't actively seeking out illusions. Ethan offered up a silent prayer while the wolves were loaded into the trunk. The immortals took their seats inside, preparing to leave.

Energy lines shot out from Ethan's palms, tying him to the vehicle. Flexing and relaxing those lines would keep him elevated off the ground. The effort to keep from getting dragged while ensuring his Bubble stayed active would deplete his reserves in no time. He offered up another silent prayer as the car lurched into motion and hoped for a short drive.

CHAPTER 34

Kiera knew the spell was close to fading when it was easier to narrow her eyes at Dajah. Every tense, over-extended muscle relaxed at once and crampy spasms followed, forcing her to twist around inside the trunk to alleviate discomfort.

Dajah laid there longer than she did taking heavy breaths until he pawed the ropes off his muzzle, reminding her to do the same.

Anger simmered within. They could have run off into the woods and avoided all of this. Keeping her tone neutral, she asked, "What do we do now?"

He started sniffing. Then made an attempt to explore the minimal space allotted, including squeezing over her. The longer he went without answering, the more frustration mounted. Kiera clenched her teeth and suppressed a growl.

He must have sensed her mood because he said, "Depends on whether the transformation spell wears off before we get wherever they're going." Dajah flopped down on his side. Strong, silver paws began scratching at the grain leather upholstery lining. His teeth joined in, his back pressed against her body for leverage, and she let him destroy the trunk for a few minutes.

She highly doubted teeth and claws were dexterous enough to trip the locking mechanism and release the trunk latch. However, Dajah's actions bordered more on frenzied than calculated. "If it does?"

Yanking another strip of leather free, his claws scraped metal. "We get out. Take cover."

She shifted position, resting her chin on her forelegs to better observe her stubborn partner. Additional minutes passed. He managed to expose the tail light. "What happens if the spell doesn't wear off in time?"

"Attack as soon as they open the trunk. Go for the throat."

"Because that worked so well last time."

Penetrating green eyes flashed at her.

"We shouldn't have attacked them," she said, daring him to challenge her.

"You don't understand."

"Understand what? That they weren't some random hikers? That you needed to make sure they didn't leave your cabin alive? That they called our bracelets Earth Beads, and, according to you, only one group knows them by that name?"

He resumed clawing rapidly at the taillight, and the pheromones coming off him reeked of panic. "Won't be the first time Caerus found me."

"And how'd they find us?"

"One of the traffic cams in town, probably. Tracked the car. Spotted the campfire." Another robust kick loosened the taillight. Light from passing vehicles leaked in around the frame.

She considered his logic and current state of being. "Not saying it's impossible, but we were barely in town three hours. Caerus has a long reach if they identified us *and* sent a task force that quickly."

"Great, so we've just been kidnapped by random non-humans wielding innate magic!"

He got his foot stuck trying to wedge his front claws into the gap. The growl released when he wrenched free concerned Kiera more than their current predicament.

"Dajah, talk to me."

He snapped at her. "What do you want?!"

Kiera lunged, pinning him against the side of the trunk. The back end of the car swerved. He bared his teeth viciously and let out a warning growl. Unfazed, she flexed her claws against his fur. "Get your shit together," she warned. "I know how you feel about Caerus, but this isn't like you."

She backed off, ready should he try something stupid.

Dajah's eyes darted around the perimeter of the trunk and he started panting again. "I don't like small spaces. And if this turns out to be Caerus, we're not friends. You barely know me. We hired you as a means to an end, using your bounty as leverage. You're expendable to us. Always were. Understand me? If you get the opportunity to run, take it."

Kiera needed a minute to process his words. He wasn't angry at her. He was claustrophobic. And trying to protect her from Caerus. Or protect himself. *Just like with Queen.* Sighing, she said, "I can do that. But let's focus on getting out of the trunk right now."

It was pointless. Even working together, they couldn't get the trunk open. The Maserati slowed, turning off the highway. A short time later it came to a stop and a whooshing roar consumed every other sound in the background. With no good options, she prepared to attack.

The trunk swung open. They leapt out, teeth bared, and landed in a net. A jumbled mess of limbs, fur, and deafening engine sounds distorted Kiera's focus, but she spotted the waiting cargo plane. And couldn't do a damn thing to stop her and Dajah from being tossed into a sizeable cage together.

Kiera untangled them while Dajah snapped wildly at the men and women moving about – two more in addition to the three from the woods. All had the same odd fragrance.

Beth approached their cage. No hint of the neck wound Dajah gave her marred her fawn-colored skin. Red dreadlocks framed green eyes that observed quietly. Dajah was ready to lunge into the bars.

"You gave it a fine effort," Beth said, pushing a metal bowl through the slot in the bottom of the cage. She filled it with a water bottle, never flinching when Dajah snapped at her.

The others took turns monitoring them. Kiera memorized their features, connecting faces with the names she overheard.

Lil was undoubtedly their leader, with a fit frame, straight black hair, and sepia skin. Rin, the male from the cabin, had tar-like tribal tattoos that blended with his dark skin and Kiera swore they moved on his flesh. His eyes were equally black, matching ebony hair tied up in a half-knot.

Alex was the tallest of the five and the biggest. She guessed some two-hundred-fifty pounds of pure muscle accented his frame. His bald head vaguely reminded her of Skullz.

Markus, the last male, was so white he was almost translucent. Green-blue veins shone through his flesh, emphasized by blue eyes and platinum blond hair.

They're a perfect melting pot of ethnicities.

Their body language underscored confident, capable professionals, but nothing else hinted at who might have sent them. Or why.

Attempts to pull Dajah into conversation failed. The most she got out of him was in response to their location – he thought they were headed south. At one point he remarked that the transformation spell should have worn off hours ago. He said little more than that, but his scent wasn't saturated with the same level of panic from the trunk. Now it held something worse: Fear.

It was a *long* flight.

<u>PART IV</u>

CHAPTER 35

When the plane touched down, Dajah didn't bother getting to his feet. He laid there, Kiera by his side, as the cargo doors vented. Heat, humidity, and tropics filtered in, leaving him unable to match the scents and flight time to any known Caerus location.

Maybe he'd been wrong.

Unlikely. When this damn spell wears off, we'll have our Earth Beads... which won't work here... and our skin. Don't have high hopes of that lasting. He snorted, stood, and stretched.

Pacing the space afforded by the cage, Dajah evaluated the man in uniform driving a miniature transport truck into the cargo hold. He smelled human, at least. The entire cage was loaded onto the flatbed. Then Lil and Rin relieved the driver.

"Try to calm down," Kiera said once they were on the road.

He glared at her then settled on the ground. Theirs was the second truck in a series of five. The others followed in the SUV behind them, always watching.

"We don't know where we are. What they want," Kiera continued. "Getting information's crucial."

He chose to focus on their surroundings rather than comment.

Sun's too close. Must be near the equator.

The road curved around the perimeter of an extensive military airbase, snaking through patches of rainforest before skirting the edge of a cliff. Green, volcanic mountains rose in the distance. To the left spanned waters so clear Dajah could make out fish and stingrays swimming through a complex reef system. The water touched every shade of turquoise, blue-green, and white.

Visually, it was beautiful.

He felt like he swallowed ten kinds of poison.

"Dajah?"

"It's their island." His mouth went desert dry. Confidence fled in the wake of memories of what Caerus was capable of.

"Why would they fly us out to their headquarters?"

Kiera didn't understand and he couldn't bring himself to speak the truth aloud. His throat constricted. *Can't climb off an island. The odds of swimming suck. Stealing a plane or a boat? Worse.*

Gary never accessed more than hints related to Caerus Headquarters from any of the buildings they crippled. That told Dajah all he needed to know about security here. Swallowing hard, he reined in his imagination.

I'll be damned if I'm going down without a fight. Focus allowed him to slow his heart rate, but the only thing to fight right now was the cage. This was the perfect time for one of Queen's snarky comments. The voice in his head was quiet. Had *been* quiet.

Where are *you?*

The road turned back into a rainforest. When it cleared, Dajah stopped breathing. Three massive buildings of glass, steel, and concrete rose in the distance with paradise as the backdrop.

That one's easily forty stories tall... Probably twice that underground.

Their caravan split as it approached the tallest building, with one main entrance and a dozen smaller ones visible. Lil drove them through one of the secondary entrances after flashing a badge. Glass doors slid open to admit the vehicle, and they descended a ramp into a loading bay, stopping near a group of elevators.

A handful of guards, fully armed, waited with a dolly.

Dajah waited to get shot.

Two elevator rides and a series of hallways later, they reached their destination. Honestly, they could be in any upscale hotel, as long as you ignored the high-tech security panels and locks on every door. The seventh one on the left was opened with Lil's badge and a nine-digit push-code. Dajah forgot to breathe again, expecting a steel table. Radiation injections. Queen screaming manically before they unleashed her on Kiera.

It was an apartment.

The guards slid the cage to the floor in the middle of the living room. Dajah scrutinized every inch of space. Minimalist furnishings included a tan leather sofa and low-rise coffee table on a black-and-white patterned area rug. The floors were concrete, continuing into the kitchenette where a center island functioned as both counter space and table.

Clean white cabinets without fixtures, quartz countertops, and three stainless steel bar chairs lined the visible side of the island. A hallway branched off from the living room, presumably the entrance to the maze.

Fittingly twisted for them.

He refocused on Lil when she crouched in front of their cage, hackles rising.

"That spell will wear off in less than an hour," she said. "You'll be meeting with the boss in two. I suggest you spend the remainder of the time cleaning up and getting dressed."

He growled, adrenaline motivating him to attack, but held his ground. The brunette removed the padlock from the cage, and everyone, including her, left the room. The apartment door clicked shut.

Kiera ventured out first. "Not what I expected. What do you *think* they want from us?"

To torture us, experiment, use us as bait to catch the others... Pick one.

Sighing, he stepped from the cage and sniffed. In the back of his mind, Dajah knew those thoughts were not productive. Based on the reality of his past, yes, but he wasn't a child at the mercy of men in coats. Every interaction he'd had with Caerus since had been on his terms.

Kiera wandered down the hall and he followed close by, expecting the first trap to spring any second. They didn't enter a maze, just a bedroom with an ensuite bathroom and floor-to-ceiling windows.

"Dajah..." she said, voice trailing as she sat by the glass. The view overlooked coral reef waters and a pristine white beach at the bottom of a cliff. They were over twenty stories up.

Bet the window is unbreakable.

He continued his sniff of the perimeter.

"Too clean," he eventually concluded. "Others have been in here, but any scent remaining tells me nothing." At a loss, he laid himself in the middle of the living room floor opposite their cage. A flat-screen TV and floating shelves lined the wall beside the door.

Kiera flopped next to him. "Talk to me."

"I'm sorry I got you into this."

"We don't know what this *boss* wants," she said, level-toned. "They put us in an apartment, not a cell, and they haven't hurt us. We need to be smart about this."

"Yeah, they haven't hurt us. *Yet*."

She turned enough to narrow her eyes.

Caerus loves their games.

The magic wore off, turning them back into humans. Dajah wondered why no one confiscated their Earth Beads, but his attempt at a basic Wind spell confirmed what he already knew.

"Will you shower with me?" Kiera asked. Naked, dirty, with a few knots and twigs tangled in loose hair... she was beautiful. And he was going to get her killed.

"Yeah," he said, taking the offered hand.

Dajah went through the motions, washing off the remains of forest in their oversized shower. Afterwards he towel-dried and dressed in the grey scrubs and flip-flops provided. Kiera pushed him against the wall. He saw it in her eyes, in the tightness of her shoulders. The idea that she'd ever fear *him* caused shame to well up within.

She pinned his arms to his sides, pressing her entire body against his.

It's not fear.

Soft lips kissed him deeply, but he didn't return it. After a moment, she stepped back.

"I won't pretend to understand what being here is doing to you, but I need you with me." Taking his face in her hands, Kiera fixed her eyes on his. "The only way we're getting through this is together. Do what you have to, but I'm not leaving you. Understand me?"

All he could see was her strapped down to some chair, drowning and bleeding while he completed an impossible task under the surveillance of sadistic researchers.

"Dajah?"

"I understand."

She led him back to the sofa.

A triple knock sounded. Neither of them moved to answer it.

Lil entered with a handful of guards. "Boss'll see you now," she said. "Come along. We won't restrain you, but try anything and you'll both be unconscious faster than you can blink."

"We'll cooperate," Kiera said, hands on her lap.

For now.

CHAPTER 36

Dajah walked with the usual confidence Kiera came to expect from him, but he was colder.

He's afraid of this place.

She didn't survive Julius to succumb to some megalomaniac organization. Someone brought them here for a reason. She'd bide her time, learn the reason, and plan accordingly.

Following Lil and the guards, they never saw another soul in a building that had to be full of employees. Plenty of voices echoed down corridors. Caerus wasn't taking chances with them.

The brunette stopped at a set of double doors. A buzz preceded their opening into a waiting room. Floor-to-ceiling windows overlooked a different part of the reef. The reception desk was deserted.

"Sit and wait," Lil said, motioning to the chairs and couches lining the far wall. The guards moved to the opposite side of the room.

Dajah sat. Kiera joined him on the same couch, keeping enough distance to suggest professional acquaintances. Lil nodded to the guards and headed through a second door after it buzzed open. She was barely inside for a minute before coming back.

"Boss wants to see you first," she said, finger pointed at Kiera. "Let's go."

She followed without sparing a glance for Dajah, praying he

didn't do anything stupid.

Two low-back chairs faced an ornate mahogany desk, reminiscent of Julius's office. Windows took up the left wall, but Kiera was more interested in the woman seated behind the desk than the view.

With a perfectly tailored suit, hair swept back in a tight bun, and an attractive face and body, she was the type that liked to get other people's hands dirty. Kiera knew plenty just like her. She adjusted thin-rimmed glasses then folded her hands on the desk.

"My name is Sasha Bekarda," she said. "I'm the president and CEO of Caerus Enterprises. I hope your trip here was acceptable."

Hate her already. Kiera kept her tone level with a sprinkling of sarcasm. "I was kidnapped. Is that your idea of acceptable?"

"It's my idea of necessity," Sasha said. "I'm going to ask you a question, and I'm encouraging you to be honest."

Kiera waited.

"Does Dajah trust you enough to let you give him an injection without causing a scene?" She slid a tray across the desk, some sort of injection gun atop it.

Kiera saw the president's black stone bracelet. She'd never mistake Earth Beads for cheap jewelry now. Sasha was more than a company figurehead.

"I could better answer that question if I knew what it was and had an opportunity to explain it to him first."

"What I need to tell you only a few dozen people in the world are aware of. My words are for yours and Dajah's ears alone, and I need to ensure he's the only one listening."

"You're talking about Queen."

Sasha regarded her, eyebrow piqued, and Kiera immediately regretted using the name.

"The formula within that gun will temporarily block her connection with him after five minutes. He shouldn't experience any side effects."

Kiera's heart dropped. Ice ran through her veins. *Chase! Are you the reason they found us? What'd you do? Who'd you contact?*

Other explanations were possible, but the compound Sasha described was exactly what Chase was working on. "Is this experimental?"

"No," Sasha said. "We created Dajah. We have always been able to suppress his less desirable attributes."

She wasn't sure if she felt better or worse hearing where it came from. Dajah shared enough stories about the substances they injected him with. It was entirely plausible that some of those shots suppressed Queen. If they never told him, he'd never know the difference, thinking Queen was merely... preoccupied with something else.

He's been living with her in his head unnecessarily.

Eyeing the gun, Kiera promised herself she'd smuggle a sample back to Chase. He could replicate it.

"The longer he sits out there, the greater the chance the anomaly taps in if she's not observing already. What's your decision, Kiera?"

She took the gun.

◇

Dajah wasn't sure Kiera took his warning seriously, but she entered that room with confidence. She was only betrayed by the tightness around her eyes. The device in her hand was one he knew too well.

She never took her eyes off him, approaching. "I have to give you this, and if you trust me, you'll want me to. Don't make a scene, Dajah."

What choice did he have? Caerus wouldn't go to these lengths just to kill him accidentally. He'd purposely chosen a seat on the edge of the couch. The guards were less of a threat than the brunette woman, whatever she was. If her magic worked here, he'd be unconscious before reaching the door.

With a steady breath and slow, non-threatening movements, Dajah held his forearm out. One wrong move or a startled surprise and someone'd start shooting.

The injection caused a minor sting and left five reddened punctures behind. He rubbed the marks absently and waited to feel sick.

"Back inside. Both of you." Lil said, motioning to the door.

Kiera waited until he stood and followed.

"Sasha?" Lil asked the woman behind the desk.

"We'll be fine, Lilly. Wait outside."

Dajah and Kiera sat before the desk. As soon as Lil left, Sasha checked her watch. Earth Beads rested just below it, and it made him wonder. He contemplated trying another spell in the office, ultimately deciding against it. Until Caerus forced his hand, cooperation *was* their best defense.

"My name is Sasha Bekarda," she said, "I run Caerus now. You're here because we have a problem, and I hope that at the end of our discussion you realize I'm not your enemy."

All thoughts vanished as Dajah stared her down. "That's rich. What'd you make her inject me with?" He caught Kiera glancing his way out of the corner of his eye but refused to drop his gaze from the president.

"We'll get to that," Sasha said. "Things will go smoother if we agree to be honest with one another."

"You want honesty?" He leaned forward. "Caerus is a sick, diseased animal that needs to be put out of its misery. All I ever get from you people are scars. *What* do you want?"

"Your views are limited and biased, but that isn't entirely your fault. If you spent more time learning what Caerus is now and less time trying to destroy my facilities, perhaps you'd think differently.

"Our health department is in the final human trials for a novel anti-cancer drug. If successful, the drug will go to market. The latest studies show ninety-five percent efficacies in curing four different types of cancer.

"Our agricultural department has representatives in thirteen countries. They've managed to increase grain production with a new, genetically modified species, cutting overall famine down by seventy-five percent in those locations.

"Some of the weapons we supply prevented a third World War. We do plenty of Good, Dajah."

Adrenaline leaked into his muscles despite his best efforts. "I'm not interested in your statistics. What. do. you. want." In two seconds, he'd take his chances, send a blast of energy through Sasha Bekarda's chest.

Her eyes flashed to her watch again. "To kill time while the injection works its way through your system. It blocks your connection with the anomaly."

"What are you talking about?"

"The creature you call 'Queen.' This is about her." Sasha tapped a few keys on her computer. Blackout shades lowered over the windows and a screen projected onto them. Clips from various newscasts showed extreme natural disasters.

She let things play silently for a couple minutes before bothering with an explanation. "There are over a thousand counts of disasters all over the world that scientists agree are unprecedented. Consensus is on Climate Change being the driving force behind this, but it's not."

She hit additional keys, changing the projection to show a 3D model of Earth. "Our planet's made up of three layers. The crust we live on is roughly eighteen miles thick. Below that is the mantel, and much closer to the center is the core. The boundary between the crust and mantel is known as the Mohorovicic discontinuity. It has some notoriety, but most important to us is the radiation stream that runs through it. We use that radiation in many of our experiments."

Dajah tensed and relaxed his fists below the level of the desk, letting Sasha ramble on for Kiera's sake.

"My uncle did extensive research on this," she continued. "He found that changes in the radiation reflected changes on the planet. S-radiation, or the Stream as we sometimes call it, is unlike other forms of radiation. Depending on how it's collected, its usefulness varies. Suffice to say it's a direct indicator of the health of the planet.

"Fifty years ago Uncle Jameson identified an anomaly in the Stream and investigated, tracing the source to the Falkland Islands. He dug up what he thought was part of the root structure of some exotic plant species mutating from exposure to S-radiation. After taking several samples, the root retracted underground. Jameson brought the samples back to Caerus for analysis, finding it wasn't a plant after all."

The images changed, showing an enlarged diagram of five cells.

"This is anomaly QZ-5 – an alien lifeform, older than the planet itself. What Uncle Jameson thought was a root, we now suspect was a tentacle from a much larger creature. He ran experiments, determined to incorporate some of QZ-5's traits into subjects for his Weapon program." Her eyes returned to Dajah. "For the record, Caerus no longer experiments on children. Jameson's research was deemed unethical, most subjects too unstable for practical use."

He snorted.

"Several attempts failed before you and your brothers. Only human embryos with Y chromosomes would accept the genetic coding. Female specimens were non-viable. Your first brother was predominantly alien and completely unstable, thus he was destroyed. Taron was considered too human. He exhibited some characteristics of QZ-5 cells, but not enough for Jameson's satisfaction. So, he made you. You maintain the highest percent of QZ-5 cells Caerus could manage that resulted in a stable, rational being."

Dajah was ready to prove the rational comment wrong. "What's your point?"

"My point is that you have a unique relationship with the anomaly. You can communicate with her. The mutated cells inside you react to her presence."

"What does his genetic makeup have to do with any of this?" Kiera asked.

Calculating blue eyes settled on her and Dajah spared a glance for the room.

"We need his help," Sasha said. "Ever since Jameson began experimenting with QZ-5 cells, the anomaly in the Stream has intensified. Now we're at a tipping point. QZ-5 is poisoning our planet."

Some graphs appeared on the projection screen; Dajah couldn't care less.

"You said we're blaming this on Climate Change," Kiera said. "No one else has this data?"

"If other companies are measuring the Stream, I'm not aware of it. I assure you they're accurate."

Relaxing the strain in his forearms, Dajah opened his fists and rested palms on the arms of the chair. "So, your uncle pissed off an alien hiding inside the planet. Congratulations. What, exactly, do you think I can do about it?"

"We need you to find her."

The laugh bursting out of his mouth was pure.

"How's Dajah supposed to find her?" Kiera asked, practical.

"We know her general location," the president said. "The problem is that she's buried beneath a labyrinth of underground tunnels and caves. We've sent two teams already. Neither could successfully locate her. Once Dajah's cells are in close enough proximity to the anomaly, they'll react to her presence. He'll be able to lead us straight to her."

"Why not just use the cells you have left over from your uncle's experiments?" he asked.

"When talks of shutting down the Weapon program came up twenty years ago, Jameson began splitting up his research, spreading it among several of our primary and secondary facilities." She paused, studying Dajah before saying, "The remainder of viable QZ-5 cells were sent to our Eastern Primary Branch."

"That's a shame," he said. "Heard there was a gas explosion. Some kind of massive sinkhole."

"Yes... But even if we had them, the cells are dormant outside a host. And without full genetic incorporation, the host is useless. You're the best chance we have at finding her."

"Then what?" Kiera asked. "What are you gonna do when you find her?"

"QZ-5's threatening the existence of everything on this planet. At the rate we're going, global catastrophes are expected within six months. No one hides from this. Assuming we can find her, we're going to eliminate her."

"How?" Kiera asked.

"With compounds that are toxic to the QZ-5 cells. All the team needs to do is locate her and inject them."

Never that simple.

Dajah caught himself, annoyed he was even considering Sasha's plan. "I'm guessing these compounds are toxic to me, too?"

"Technically," Sasha said like it was a moot point. Technically, it was. Caerus had plenty of ways to kill him.

Where's the leverage?

"You wouldn't go through all the trouble to bring me here for a request. So, what do I get for helping you?" Dajah asked.

"Immunity," Sasha said. "For both of you."

Brow furrowed, Dajah glimpsed Kiera before looking back to the president. "We commissioned Kiera for a job in exchange for Beads. Your lackeys just so happen to catch us testing out one of the spells. What's *she* supposed to contribute to this?"

"It'll do you good to have a familiar face around. And if you think Kiera would be safe if I released her from this island, then you're either a fool or a liar. You should know that the former head of our Eastern Branch had a very unhealthy obsession with this woman. Death won't stop his plans, but I can.

"Assuming no more of my facilities are destroyed, you'll both be left alone. We'll set you up financially wherever you'd like. No one will touch you, not even the Organizations. You can start over, make a new life, or not. The choice would be yours."

He had to ask, "And if either of us refuses?"

Sasha folded her hands and leaned forward. "Choose to cooperate and you'll be given leave to explore the island, a stipend to buy new clothes, food, entertainment. You'll train with Special Tactics. And you, Dajah, will take injections twice a day to make sure QZ-5 remains in the dark."

A humorless gaze passed between them.

"Choose *not* to cooperate and you'll spend the next few weeks in a cell chained to a wall. We'll make sure you receive your injections and keep you in a chemically-induced coma. When time comes to leave, you'll be transported under heavy guard. And when you arrive on-site, you'll be given an injection that renders you capable of following the call of QZ-5 and little else.

"We don't need your consent. I'm offering this as a sign of good faith, a reminder that I'm not the enemy, but we've passed the point of no return. I'll use whatever means necessary to see this through."

Sasha maintained that matter-of-fact look, and Dajah offered it right back. "What's supposed to stop me from jumping over this desk right now and choking the life out of you?"

"Besides the fact it'd be a waste of both our time? This," she said, hitting another key. The projection changed to a live feed of two cells – no-nonsense rooms with a single cot, toilet, and sink in each. Taron sat in one. Chase paced the other.

He sensed Kiera tensing beside him and forced himself to lean back. The leverage. "What was all that shit about you not being the enemy?"

"Frankly, I don't care what you view me as. The threat is real. I will not let this planet fall to this creature when I have the means to stop it. Your willing cooperation benefits many, but the choice is yours. Make your decision before you leave this room." Sasha cut the feed to the cells and the shades rose, letting in daylight.

"What kind of choice is this?" Kiera asked.

"It's not one," Dajah said. "Welcome to Caerus."

"Follow the rules, show up on time for training. You'll each be allowed an hour of visitation daily. They'll be taken care of.

However, the first time I catch wind of anything suspicious or have any reason to doubt your full cooperation in any way, they'll be put to death immediately. You," her glacial stare fell on him, "will be made an empty shell."

Taron and Chase are on the island.

"And as for you," she said, eyes now on Kiera, "Julius Matthews had some interesting theories that many would love to follow up on."

Already Dajah's thoughts veered towards escape. Cooperation bought them time. Sasha Bekarda wasn't a fool – she'd use Kiera against him if she thought it'd help – and she already had plenty of leverage. *No such thing as no-win scenarios*, he reminded himself.

"You have my word on these things," the president continued. "*Now*, are we clear?"

Dajah wanted her head on a stake. "We're clear," he said.

"Miss Lin?" she asked.

"Crystal."

CHAPTER 37

"How'd you end up in a cell on *this* island?" Dajah asked, stretching his legs out.

"I received a call from Chase, only it wasn't him. Remember the rumors about the White Team? They're shapeshifters capable of lifting memories. I fought one pretending to be him when I arrived at his house. They're good, Dajah. Really good."

"He beat you?"

"I was sedated in the middle of our fight. Had the upper hand... it would have been a near thing."

"How'd they get to Chase?"

Taron sat upright on his cot, arms resting on his knees as he explained, "Flagged something he was researching. They showed up, lifted his memories, and reached out to me claiming they had something testable and needed more samples. Since you were off-grid, I went over. When the sedation wore off, I woke in Chase's lab with our last conversation being replayed in my head. It was easy for them to pull memories. Analyze them. They knew exactly where you were."

"How much of your memory do you think they pulled?"

"No idea. Potentially all of it, or just what they thought was relative."

"Which means the White Team might know everything. We're *all* compromised."

Taron dipped his head in acknowledgement. "We're not dead yet and you're still wearing your Beads. What do they want?"

"They didn't tell you anything?" he asked.

"You're the first person I've seen since they put me in here."

Dajah summarized Sasha's ultimatum.

"Queen," Taron said. "Are they aware of what she's capable of?"

"Is anyone? The President's convinced she's destroying the planet." Dajah studied the three concrete walls of Taron's cell and the fourth long wall of solid glass. Vertical metal bars created another barrier to the hallway beyond. Additional staggered cells were only visible from the very corner of the room.

An energy dome protected the camera mounted in the hall opposite Taron's observation window. The view was boring. Not a single guard passed, leaving Dajah wondering what the hall led to. He'd entered the cell through a sliding electronic door opposite the glass where an abundance of security waited.

Every structure within the cell was concrete, with a four-inch mattress placed atop a solid raised base as the only exception. The sink and toilet were molded out of the wall. Zero access to plumbing.

Getting Taron out was going to be a nightmare.

Leaning his head back, Dajah caught sight of tiny, open vents lining the perimeter of the twelve-foot ceiling. "We don't have a lot of options right now. Where's the hallway lead?"

"Glass slides into the wall and the bars rise to provide access. Right leads to the showers. Left to an exercise room and outdoor courtyard. Meals get delivered through that slot by the door."

"And?" Dajah asked.

Taron made eye contact. "The room's secure, Dajah. Twelve other cells line either side of the hall, but the glass becomes opaque when someone's walking through and the timing's varied. Given the number of times my glass turns dark, I'd say there are five other guests in this wing."

"Well, as long as I behave you get to see this handsome face daily."

Dajah considered the slight raise of his brother's eyebrow a win.

"Generous of them."

The start of Dajah's grin turned downward. "They do anything...?"

"No one's touched me," Taron assured him. "Can't say I've been mistreated as much as I've been ignored. Food's decent. I even get a menu."

"Huh." Relief eased the tension lingering in Dajah's muscles, but the reality was that his brother's condition could deteriorate at any time now that he was here. "We're supposed to be meeting with this team tomorrow."

"Be careful."

"Aren't I always?" Dajah tried keeping the mood light. Taron knew as well as he did how far they were in over their heads. *Let's hope we both remember how to swim.*

A buzz signaled the end of their allotted meeting time. Taron remained on the cot while two armed guards escorted Dajah out. One punched a code on the control panel to the right of the door once they exited. The other encouraged Dajah to keep moving back to the entrance hall.

A brown-skinned man with a five o'clock shadow and freshly pressed suit and tie waited for him. "Greetings! My name is Liam. President Bekarda asked me to show you around." He offered his hand.

Suppressing a scowl, Dajah took the hand and shook it. "Dajah."

Liam returned a professional grip, then pulled a tri-fold pamphlet out from his inner jacket pocket. "We'll wait for your associate here. She should be along shortly. In the meantime, feel free to look this over."

CAERUS ENTERPRISES ran across the top in bold print. A generic greeting thanked and welcomed new business to the island. Dajah plucked the brochure from Liam's hand. The interior flap provided a list of rules and regulations to be adhered to, while the inside spread contained a map with information on key areas.

Caerus's island was over six hundred square miles, shaped like three round-ish circles merged poorly together and squashed in on the bottom. The main buildings were located on the northern aspect – three massive properties containing the bulk of activity – with other structures throughout. The lower west quadrant hosted the airbase, and a cove on the southern shores protected a marina. A small chain of mountains ran through the center. Rainforest blanketed the interior of the island.

Dajah memorized it, aware this was more theme park map than blueprint.

The fresh click of combat boots accompanied muted slaps from flip-flops. Keira's expression remained neutral and gave no impression that she had been harmed in any way. Sasha didn't need Kiera for additional leverage. Nevertheless he couldn't afford to show an ounce of concern whenever she left his sight.

Hazel eyes met his and she nodded, turning to their escort. Liam introduced himself and offered her an identical pamphlet.

"Mr. Dajah, Ms. Kiera, this way, please. Your identification badges should be ready by now. You're required to carry them with you at all times as they serve as both access passes and our form of currency. Everything is debited to and from the accounts linked with your cards. You'll also need them to operate any of the transport carts. Walking trails and roads are marked on the pamphlet, and there are signs at every major crossroad."

They followed Liam outside and climbed into a glorified golf cart. He used his ID card to start the vehicle. "As I understand it," he continued, "you're part of Special Tactics. The remainder of the day is at your leisure. Someone will collect you from your apartment at six a.m. tomorrow morning."

The detention hall was housed in a security ward, nestled within rainforest roughly a mile from any other structure and far from the main buildings. Plenty of time for Liam to give an abbreviated tour on their way back. He explained how the majority of people who worked on the island also lived there. Because of that, Caerus catered to numerous tastes.

Building One hosted most of the living quarters and offices, with a mall and entertainment sector occupying the entire fifth and sixth floors. Almost everything needed or wanted would be found there. Building Two was reserved for Caerus's Research and Development departments. Building Three contained the island's hospital, as well as Medical and Communication centers.

The exposition sounded rehearsed like Liam had said those same words hundreds of times while wearing the face of Caerus's public relations representative.

"Remember, six a.m. sharp," he said after they picked up their ID cards inside Registration on the ground floor of Building One. "Any questions before I go?"

Dajah ran his fingers over the pearlescent credit card-shaped plastic showing his face with a barcode beneath it. A series of dots, dashes, and a black stripe embellished the reverse. "Nope."

"Thank you, Liam," Kiera said.

The man nodded and took his leave, climbing back inside his golf cart.

For the first time since they arrived, Dajah and Kiera stood alone. Unsupervised. "Now what?" she asked.

Men and women came from the building behind them. Numerous accents reached Dajah's ears, though everyone passing by spoke English. No one seemed interested in the two of them.

"Guess we buy clothes and... maybe stay outside for a while?"

Kiera's lips pressed into a thin line and she nodded.

After the chaos of activity that was the shopping district, Dajah appreciated fresh air. They found some boulders on the eastern side of the island to sit on, far enough from the buildings that it gave the illusion of freedom. It'd also provide a superb view when the sun rose the next morning. Currently, it continued its descent behind them, bathing the sky in rich pinks and oranges.

"Where do you think we are?" she asked.

Breathing in sulfur and sea, Dajah stared out at the horizon. *Nothing but water for miles. Not even a trace of another island or mainland in the distance.* "South Pacific, maybe."

"Do you believe what the president said?"

"About letting us go afterwards if we cooperate? Not a chance."

"Not that," Kiera said, staring out at the water. "What she said about the anomaly."

"Queen." Dajah closed his eyes. Time would tell whether Caerus's injections completely blocked her. "We should assume the worst-case scenario."

"That Berkada's right?" she said, voicing what he was reluctant to admit.

Leaning on the ridge behind him, Dajah added, "We still need a contingency plan. We'll meet the team we're working with. Go from there."

"Think *he's* part of the team?"

A uniformed young man approached from the road. "Excuse me, sir, ma'am," he said with a polite bow of his head. Offering a flat, zippered case to Dajah, he continued, "President Bekarda insisted this be delivered. Instructions should be inside."

Dajah accepted the case, turning back to Kiera. The man left without another word.

"Are you even the least bit surprised Sasha knew exactly where to find us?" he asked.

"No."

The immediate area was deserted, with an occasional rumble of tires passing in the distance. *We're no better off than Taron or Chase. Our cells are just bigger.* He unzipped the case. Fourteen injection pens and an instruction card rested within.

Kiera removed the card, reading, "To be given intramuscularly. Two injections every twenty-four hours. Do not administer injections within four hours of one another or exceed eighteen hours between injections. If any injections are missed or lost, contact the number below."

"You know I hate this, right?" he asked, sliding one of the pens free. "These could contain anything. No guarantee they *only* block Queen."

"Like you said. What choice do we have?"

"Right now? None." He injected the contents into his bicep.

CHAPTER 38

Dressed in practical pants, tee shirts, and hiking sneakers appropriate for most situations, Dajah and Kiera awaited the representative from Special Tactics. Kiera sat comfortably beside him on the sofa he slept on last night. He wouldn't dare share the bed with her, convinced the only reason they shared a one-room apartment was so the president could further assess their relationship. And find the best ways to exploit it.

Cooperation gained them a panel on the inside of their door, allowing them to come and go as they wished after programming a personal code.

Illusions of freedom.

The knock came at 5:58 a.m.

"I'll get it," Dajah said.

The man standing outside had two inches on Taron and skin that seemed to eat light. Not even a highlight shone on his blackened flesh from the hallway lighting. Ice blue eyes, tight braids, and a muscular build screamed special forces. He gave a respectful bow of his head in greeting, attired in a sleeveless cable knit sweater vest over trousers. Before the man uttered a word, another masculine voice called out down the hall. "Come on, Ron! Move your ass so we can get a look at the newbies."

Dajah opened the door wider, observing the eclectic group gathered. The one who spoke was dressed in silk black shorts with gold dragons and a fitted tank top accenting a flat, sculpted chest and abs. Bright blue-and-green hair looked like it was either very expensive or very cheap, with long and choppy unkempt strands serving as a rugged frame for a mildly feminine face. His skin was fair, ears coming to twin points at the top that stuck out noticeably from the hair. The subtle glow of grey-purple irises piqued Dajah's interest most. He knew Stream exposure when he saw it.

Compared to the first two, the third man was normal: Tapered pants, polo shirt, and brown hair with a punkish undercut. His skin was lightly tanned, eyes a darker hazel than Kiera's.

A woman also accompanied them, about Kiera's height, with light skin, freckles, and a mass of curly red hair barely contained within a ponytail. Toned, muscular legs matched her arms in emerald shorts and a loose white blouse. Green eyes stared Dajah down, unintimidated and only slightly offended. "Invitin' us in, or leaving us standin' out here holdin' yer hat, lad?" The thick accent confirmed her Irish heritage.

Kiera joined Dajah by the door and the Irish woman's gaze shifted to her. "Ah, thank the God! 'Bout time we had another lass." She glared at the men beside her. "The amount of testosterone 'round here is enough to make a girl sick."

"We were told to expect *one* person," Dajah said.

"It was supposed to be me, but word travels fast. Name's Ron Laurence," said the black man, hand offered in greeting. "That's Ginny," he gestured with his left to the woman, "Hobbs," the normal one, "and Elwood."

Before Dajah could release Ron's hand, Elwood closed the distance and grabbed his forearm, whistling. "Look at those!" The colorful-haired non-human turned Dajah's arm back and forth with a light touch. "He's got you and Xant matched, maybe even beat," he said to Ron, who'd stepped aside.

Ron Laurence wore a completely black set of Earth Beads. The other two men had bracelets consisting of seventy-five percent black stones, and Ginny's bracelet held a handful of mastered

Beads. Between the three of them, every other stone was deeply colored, spanning all seven hues.

"Who are you people?" Dajah asked, pulling his arm back.

"Special Tactics Problem Solvers," Hobbs said.

"Please, come in," Kiera said. "Unless... do we need to be somewhere?"

"Nah," Ginny said, accepting her invite, "not until eight."

"What are you all doing here? *Now*?" Dajah layered in a hint of skepticism with good reason.

"Well, Ron here's Xant's second," Ginny said. "Meets all the new recruits personally. But Elwood overheard last night, and Hobbs did some diggin' and, well, we wanted to meetcha."

"Why?" Kiera asked.

"Cause we're the ones that matter!" Ginny's mouth, cheeks, and eyes lit up in cheerful affirmation. "Two of ya joinin' makes twenty-seven o' us nuts goin' on some damn suicide mission."

"You were recruited?" Dajah asked. He closed the door once everyone was inside. Kiera resumed her seat on the sofa and Ginny joined her. Ron leaned against an empty wall. The other two helped themselves to chairs from the kitchen island.

"Xant hand-picked this team," Ron answered. "But, a handful of Bekarda's sycophants will be joining us. You're the last two recruits."

Dajah folded his arms across his chest, eyes focused on the dark man. "And as far as you know?"

The room fell silent.

"Official word is that you're spliced with QZ-5 cells and will be able to lead us to the anomaly."

Elwood added, "You were part of Caerus's Weapon program. I recognize that glow in your eyes."

"And you're here by choice?" Dajah asked, shifting focus to Elwood.

"I'm half Fey, half human. Let's just say I was volunteered to one of those programs when I was five. Once we completed the training, they released us out into the world. Not exactly the kindness they intended when you look like this." Elwood gestured from his neck up, head tilted with a wry grin.

"Non-humans are coming out of the shadows more and more," he continued, "but it doesn't mean we're liked or accepted. My options were limited, and I refused to get surgery on my ears. After the odd job here and there, I got word of Caerus's Special Tactics division. Heard plenty about you, though."

Dajah raised an eyebrow.

"You and your brother wiped out that breeding facility in Illinois nine years ago."

The approval on Elwood's face had Dajah grinning. "You heard about that?"

Ginny turned to Kiera, waving her hand. "See? Testosterone. Who casts the strongest spell, who's got the biggest stones, who blew up the most buildings... it goes on for hours."

Now Kiera grinned.

"Also heard your brother ended up here," Elwood said, taking on a more serious tone.

"And this is common knowledge?" Dajah asked.

"Nope," Hobbs answered. "Elwood sleeps with half the security personnel."

"They have my brother and Kiera's friend. So, I wouldn't exactly call us willing."

"Ah, but we could *so* use your help!" the half-Fey stressed.

Hobbs shook his head back and forth, eyes rolling. "He hasn't shut up about you since getting word you were coming."

Elwood snorted. "As if he's not the best bit of eye candy since we lost Aaron."

Again, Dajah's eyebrows lifted.

Ron pushed away from the wall. "We should be going. Elwood, you need to dress properly. The rest of you can meet at the training grounds. Dajah, Kiera, I'd speak with you alone on the way."

A twenty-minute walk brought them to the training grounds. Fully gated and accessed via ID badge, the grounds hosted two sizeable buildings and ample outdoor space ranging from thinned-out rainforest with obstacle courses built in, to cliffs that overlooked the eastern coast. A stairwell led down to a pristine beach.

During the walk, Ron admitted to knowing the ultimatum the president gave them. He emphasized the fact that Special Tactics had one of the highest clearance levels on the island. As long as no one gave him a reason to doubt their cooperation, Ron believed they had little to worry about concerning the president.

The man spoke candidly, but Dajah didn't know these people. He needed to better understand their motives before coming to any conclusions.

By 8:00 a.m. everyone gathered in one of the lecture halls, waiting for the commander to make his appearance. As Ginny mentioned, Dajah counted twenty-four individuals seated throughout the room, excluding himself and Kiera. Half weren't human. A third wore some combination of Earth Beads. Thirty Beads was the max any individual could carry on their person at one time. Any more and the Beads reacted with each other, leeching the wearer's energy constantly. Few of those present wore complete sets, and rarely did anyone have more than a handful of mastered stones.

Conversations quieted when the commander entered. Hardened eyes scrutinized the room's occupants as the uniformed man stood before them. With a full set of mastered Beads on his wrist and the build of a military veteran, he exuded raw, naked power, like the feeling before a thunderstorm cuts loose.

"Most of you know me by reputation," he started. "For those who don't, I'm Commander James B. Xant, and I'll oversee this mission. You've all heard rumors. Let me start by assuring you our reality is far bleaker. We have lost two teams already. I'll be damned if we lose a third."

Xant went on, summarizing what Caerus knew, which, in Dajah's opinion, was minimal. Queen was located somewhere beneath the Vinson Massif, a mountain near the base of the Antarctic Peninsula. The first team discovered the cave, reporting high levels of S-radiation in the area before communication went dark. The second team fared only slightly better. Out of fifty people, only two made it back alive: Commander Xant and a Stream Analyst named Carley Hanes who sat opposite Ginny.

And she supposedly signed back up voluntarily.

The woman looked visibly haunted, with distant, staring eyes and trembling hands she kept folded in her lap. Ginny occasionally reached out, placing a hand on top of Carley's when the tremors returned. It calmed her temporarily.

Xant's description of the horrors they faced justified the woman's composure. His last team was decimated. The fact that he dragged himself and Carley out of a frozen wasteland and was now going back for more meant he believed in the cause. Or he was a lunatic.

"This ain't no pleasure cruise or a free ride," Xant continued. "We went through hell down there. Twisted, mutated beasts tore us apart like we were nothing. This time everyone here was selected for a reason."

As far as the commander was concerned, this was their last chance to stop Queen.

He painted a convincing, albeit desperate picture.

Three distinct groups made up their team; the majority were warriors. Caerus was also sending scientists to compile data and serve as their medics when magic failed. The gearheads took care of the equipment and would be responsible for getting everyone from Point A to Point B in one piece.

Sasha wanted Dajah and Kiera to act solely as advisors, but Xant had other ideas and grouped them in with the fighters. It got weapons in their hands and improved their odds of making it out alive.

"We've got three weeks to whip all of you into shape," the

commander said, "This is how we'll do it." He outlined a rigorous training schedule that elicited more than a few groans.

Special Tactics's building hosted a hall of simulators at their complete disposal. Everyone had a list of simulations to finish by the end of week two, and plenty of conventional training to accompany it.

Xant picked up a flat box sitting on the side table that'd been there since Dajah and Kiera arrived. Approaching the closest individual – one of the scientists who probably spent most of his existence staring at a computer screen – he instructed: "Everyone takes one. These are Caerus's Flat Space watches, and they come fully loaded."

The scientist removed a watch, passing the box to the next person.

Dajah's eyes widened, following the movement of the box. He'd heard rumors Caerus perfected the tech but never expected to be gifted with one. FS shrunk down objects and stored them in a subspace dimension contained within the device. When the box came to him and Kiera, they each took one for themselves.

Similar in appearance to popular smartwatches, this one was likely worth more than some countries' entire GDP. Dajah secured his on his right wrist, below his Beads, and clicked through the inventory. Weapons, survival gear, and other supplies that'd come in handy for the mission had been included. Operating the device was point-and-click simple, with room to add more inventory and ways to customize lists for quick access.

Sasha'd never agree to us having these.

Weapons and supplies stacked the odds in their favor, but would never be the ultimate deciding factor in escape.

They needed a solid plan.

And allies.

CHAPTER 39

Ethan was utterly fascinated by the island. Concealing himself on the plane was riskier than his stunt with the car, but nothing ventured nothing gained.

Five true immortals bringing two wolves to an island wholly owned and operated by the company that held Elizabeth confirmed this was exactly where Ethan needed to be. He was forced to abandon the caravan of vehicles when he felt the attention of the brunette on him. For reasons unknown, she didn't act. Enduring her indirect, silent scrutiny proved uncomfortable in ways he couldn't explain, so he opted for a stroll through the rainforest.

By the time Ethan found the main buildings, his energy reserves were depleted. Until his abilities functioned fully, he was forced to do things the hard way. Fortunately, many of the workers on Caerus's island spoke freely. All he had to do was keep his ears open.

It took two days to discover that the group he arrived with was known as the White Team. Beyond that, all anyone had were rumors. People dreaded crossing paths with them. Some called them devils.

Ethan knew the difference between a true immortal and a non-human that lived a long time or could only be killed under specific circumstances. The Sect would want to know that Caerus employed five of them. But, why? Immortals concerned themselves only with things that interested them.

Cold foreboding washed over him. He removed the memoir from his satchel and tossed it high, letting the pages land open where they may.

"The Five that Remain," Ethan read, "search eternally for a way to release the Great Seal. Fear not their presence, for their means are limited to a singular realm. It will take One capable of traversing the Trinity freely to threaten the work of the *Eldarie*, but this day will come. All I can do is pass down my knowledge in hopes that future generations will prepare. Surviving Anodorians must be eliminated, lest Chaos be unleashed. Heed the words that follow. I will leave detailed instructions on assembling a Collective."

Ethan looked up at a cloudy sky. "The Five that Remain. The Unawakened carries the ability to break the Great Seal, and the animals they brought here were cocooned in magical distortions."

He was running out of time.

CHAPTER 40

Dajah seemed better, even optimistic regarding some of their teammates, but he wasn't the relaxed, free Dajah from the cabin. He studied every room like it held hidden traps, and engaged in conversations with particular, open-ended questions bordering on bizarre. Kiera had the advantage of approaching her teammates with an open mind, unbiased by any history with Caerus, and Special Tactics was focused more on saving the world than politics.

When it came to her, Dajah was polite and friendly, but all tenderness and intimacy vanished. They shared an apartment and a brief backstory, little else. Only on rare occasions did the man she'd come to care for shine through.

Kiera respected his need to act like this but wondered if he wasn't doing it just to protect himself. For the time being, she'd play by his rules. Didn't mean she had to like it.

"Will you do the first simulation with me?" she asked before Dajah opted to go it alone or choose another partner.

"Sure," was his response. He would have given the same answer to any of the others.

They stood in front of one of the Sim rooms. Dajah swiped his ID and the doors opened to a loading room with a computer touchscreen and a massive steel gate beyond. Both of them swiped beneath the screen to register, and the list of required scenarios appeared.

"We have to go through these three first before we can access others." He read the description of the first scenario out loud. "Terrain Tester. To complete the simulation, party members must travel from beginning location to beacon. Simulation is geared to replicate real-life terrain and environmental dangers of Antarctic Peninsula. All registered participants must reach the beacon within four hours to successfully pass. Magic is restricted."

"Straightforward enough," Kiera said.

Tapping to the next screen, Dajah perused the list of equipment they could choose from.

"Average temperature's listed as minus twenty," she said, pointing out the extreme-weather clothing. "Start with those."

They had to pick everything from boots, with or without crampons, to food rations. Kiera assumed Caerus would have their gear ready in advance, so the selection process was unnecessarily tedious. Eventually, Dajah hit the *Start Simulation* button. A tray slid out beneath the screen, providing two quarter-sized discs. Each came with an indicator light in the center and attached to their right temple.

A computer-generated voice came from unseen speakers as Dajah attached his disc. "Party member one registered." Kiera followed suit. "Party member two registered. Enter simulation chamber."

The steel gate hissed and parted, revealing a white arena with black sensors on every square foot of floor, walls, and ceiling. Once they stepped inside, the gate sealed behind them. Lights flashed in time with the computer voice counting down. The space went pitch black for the last two seconds before everything changed.

White light appeared, shaped like a curved opening. It took Kiera a moment to realize it was the mouth of the shallow ice cave they now stood in. She and Dajah were dressed in their selected clothing, the rest of their gear spread out around them.

"We have to pack it ourselves? Cheap," she said. "And time-consuming."

After marveling at the technology required to craft an FS watch yesterday, Kiera still found herself in awe of the simulation. Her clothes felt as real as any fabric, the weight and movement realistic. The ground was solid, the walls frigid to the touch. While Dajah started packing, she ventured to the opening.

Winds hit first, whipping through the channel created between the cave and a mammoth wall of ice several yards ahead. It stretched for miles in either direction.

"Guess we're supposed to climb?" she asked aloud, unable to see the top.

Dajah stepped up beside her, offering the second pack. "Assume the dangers here are as real as they come. Do you have any free climb experience?" He clipped into his harness, uncoiling rope from their supplies.

"Not like *that*."

"I'll lead," he said.

She doubted he ever climbed anything similar, but that was Dajah. He approached the cliff face while Kiera prepared her climbing gear.

Their anchors came loose twice due to shifting ice, but Dajah had enough cams jammed into cracks that slippage remained minimal. Still, Kiera underestimated how difficult it was to lift her body weight under those conditions.

Brutal gusts stole any comments she wanted to make after pulling herself up over the lip of the wall. The glacier stretched out indefinitely. If not for the digital countdown timer floating in the upper left corner of her periphery, she would have forgotten this was a simulation. Muscles ached. Her core remained warm, but her cheeks were frozen. Ice crystals formed on the tips of her hair and on the inside of her nose, stinging sharply when winds threw everything into a frenzy.

The barren expanse left them exposed. An occasional lump of rock dotted the surface, but nothing substantial enough to provide shelter. No wildlife. Just stretches of ice, frozen dirt, and countless fissures ready to collapse beneath their weight.

This is ridiculous.

Exhaustion reared its ugly head before long. If they had any hope of reaching the beacon in time, they had no choice but to push through. Kiera couldn't speak for Dajah – he moved with steady purpose – but she sincerely doubted her ability to make the final climb.

She should have said something, knowing any team was only as strong as its weakest link, but the timer ticked down. Tethered a few yards below him, she missed her grip. Her foot slipped, her support hand refused to hold on, and she fell. The sudden tension on the line jerked Dajah down with her. Fortunately, belay devices and figure-eight knots saved them from a catastrophic fall.

Dajah regained leverage on the side of the mountain. Kiera's body protested, muscles burning with fatigue. Any exposed skin suffered the consequences of second-degree frostbite, and she was bone-cold despite the clothing.

Time ran out. The computer voice echoing "Simulation Failed" over the landscape provided a tangible sense of relief. Everything went dark. Recognizing the painful tingling of healing magic, Kiera remained still until her perception of gravity shifted. Sturdy ground supported her back and she laid there, enjoying the post-healing bliss as the lights came on.

"I never wanna do anything like that again," she groaned.

Dajah was on his feet, studying the nearest sensor. "Explains how they can program these scenarios and not risk lives in the process. The room heals everyone when it's over." He walked to her, offering a hand. "I've got a few ideas for the next run-through."

"I'm sorry," Keira said, taking his hand to gain her feet.

"It's not your fault. Check the time. That scenario's impossible to accomplish the way we tried. It felt like four hours because of how we exerted ourselves, but we were only in there for half that.

Wanna try again?"

The thought of freezing was the furthest thing from appealing right now. "Lunch first?"

Dajah obliged.

Their second attempt passed with flying colors after taking full advantage of all available equipment. Dajah spent a half hour going through every option before initiating the Sim. Grappling guns made short work of the initial wall, buying them time to camp out mid-glacier, and sheltering within a terrain-appropriate tent provided almost as much of a recovery as magic.

After a brief respite, Kiera was ready to tackle the final ascent. Reaching the beacon and completing the scenario boosted her confidence so much that she suggested they try another.

Dajah agreed before she could reconsider.

———◇———

The next simulation replicated a survival challenge, putting them in the middle of a snow field with clothing not warm enough by half. The backstory was that their transport vehicle caught fire and needed to be evacuated in a hurry. Remains of it smoked in the distance, with gear scattered everywhere. The goal was to survive for three hours.

Kiera's teeth chattered so loudly Dajah worried they'd crack. She moved her arms over her body, trying to stay warm.

"D-d-d-d-daj-ah, we're not gonna l-l-last long out here l-l-like thi-thi-this."

Every second of exposure dropped their core body temperature. The shallowest breath felt like inhaling daggers. If he forgot to move his fingers or toes for a minute, they went painfully numb.

"We've got maybe twelve minutes like this. If we're lucky," he admitted.

After the last simulation, he realized the scenarios were a test of physical endurance, creativity, and critical thinking. Magic was unrestricted this time around, and after surveying the strewn equipment nearby, finding most of it useless, he couldn't imagine surviving without it.

Kiera collected a thermal blanket big enough for one while he approached a buried pickax, frozen solid beneath the snow. A targeted Fire spell sparked around it, melting ice enough to free the object.

"Your Ea-Earth Beads w-work here?" she asked, lips blue.

Despite the cold, he grinned. "Yep. Now let me show you how Earth magic saves your ass."

Dajah crafted an igloo in the middle of the snow field by manipulating Fire, Ice, and Wind spells. Once the basic shelter was built, any scavenged supplies became useful. They had a signal fire going within minutes. All that was left was to wait out the remainder of time, the translucent clock counting down at the edge of his vision.

Time presented an opportunity for Kiera to practice tweaking her elemental magic. When the simulation ended, she could form perfect, sustained Ice sphere variants. Her Bead turned a richer garnet, and the Sim's end healing would relieve any Drain.

"That was pretty awesome, Dajah, but I've had enough freezing for one day."

They returned their discs to the tray in the loading room and exited into the hall.

Xant waited.

"Commander," Dajah said.

"I saw your run," Xant said, shrewd eyes passing between them. "The scenarios aren't meant to be impossible. Some require magic. Some require a specific thought process or skillset." His words mirrored Dajah's earlier thoughts. "They reinforce teamwork as much as anything else. If even one person learns something that could help save a life, I'll consider them a success."

"What really happened to your last team?" Kiera asked.

"They weren't prepared," Xant said.

"And this time's different?" Dajah asked.

"This time the team was hand-selected. By me. Everyone offered a position was fully briefed on the failure of the previous missions. They've all volunteered willingly. Except you two."

"What's your point?" Dajah asked, careful to keep his voice neutral. "Sasha's holding my brother and her friend as collateral. I understand why Caerus wants Queen out of the picture, but I won't pretend like I'm doing this for any reason other than the fact that we have no choice."

"Bekarda and I rarely agree on the means, but the ends are justified in this. The threat is real and this may be our final chance to stop it. The last thing I need or want on this mission is prisoners to babysit. I need strong, dependable team members, and I won't have you two sit the sidelines when you have the needed talents and ability. However, don't mistake that for trust. Trust is earned."

Dajah couldn't agree more. "She knows you gave us these?" he asked, raising his wrist to emphasize the FS watch. "Our ID cards ban us from the purchase of any weapons or communication equipment, and you handed us an arsenal. That requires some degree of trust."

"I'm in charge of Special Tactics. It's my call, and you'd be foolish to try anything that'd put you on Bekarda's shit list."

The irony made him want to laugh. All the weapons and equipment he should need and free run of the island, and there wasn't a damn thing he could do with it until he figured out how to get Taron out of that cell.

"Let me ask you something," he started. "Did Sasha give you orders to kill us or leave us behind if this mission's successful? Did she tell you her plans for us if we refuse to cooperate?"

Xant's stoic expression as he looked between them told Dajah plenty.

"Kind of hard to be respectful when you know people you're supposed to respect are ok with killing you on someone else's orders."

"You misunderstand my hesitation," the commander countered. "The president's only orders are to make sure the two of you stay in line. If at any point I deem you a risk to the mission, I'm authorized to take certain steps. Those steps wouldn't involve killing you, but they're not in your best interest. Or mine."

He continued, "However you feel about the company or the president, the only thing that'll matter once we're down in that frozen shithole are the decisions made by the people on this team. I'd rather you fight with me than against me."

"You want my loyalty? When the time comes to leave for the mission, make sure Taron and Chase are on the plane with us."

"I'll see what I can do," Xant said, no trace of sarcasm. "You're both dismissed."

Scrutinizing the commander's body language gave away nothing as he left. Xant was firm and determined in his actions. His entire conversation was pragmatic.

"That was... unexpected," Kiera said. "You think he'll help us?"

"I think he doesn't want to worry about us. Beyond that, I've got my doubts."

CHAPTER 41

When it came to first impressions, Kiera trusted her gut. She took time to introduce herself to each of her teammates and kept note of the way they reacted to her, to Dajah, and how they treated one another. Definite cliques existed, and two other things were clear: Most of them were passionate about the mission, and this was Xant's team with few exceptions.

Ginny introduced her to the other women immediately. Between the five of them, no one felt the need to prove she was better than anyone else – a stark contrast to the games the men played.

"Nice o' ya to be helpin' Carley with that shootin' earlier," the Irishwoman said.

Swirling her bourbon, Kiera considered the redhead seated across from her. She felt a connection with Ginny. Ginny told her about her ability to read and manipulate auric fields. Though human, the gift let her see past the masks people wore. It also meant her intuition was impeccable.

The woman called everyone out on their bullshit. She was an almost perfect ally, with the potential to be an amazing friend if Kiera allowed herself to make the connection. Brenna's betrayal still hurt. It didn't negate the years of friendship they shared, but it served as a reminder that loyalty was a fickle thing.

"Carley needs all the help she can get," Kiera admitted. "I still don't understand why she's going back. That woman looks like death walking, and I swear, every time I see her it's worse."

"Nightmares," Ginny explained. "Lass canna sleep without dreamin' o' what happened."

"Did she have any clue as to what she was getting into the first time?"

Ringlets bounced as Ginny shook her head. "From what we figured, Caerus told everyone it was a research expedition. Goal was to investigate rumors of the anomaly's presence and find out what happened to the first team. Don't think any of 'em knew what they were gettin' into."

"And they were all Special Tactics?"

The bar was crowded enough for Kiera not to worry about anyone overhearing.

"No. Commander Xant went as a military advisor. The security team sent with them was standard issue. The first group was nearly all researchers. Makes little sense if ya were ta' think about it. Caerus had to have *some* idea of what could happen. They're messin' with an Earth-killin' alien."

"Do we know what *we're* getting into?" she countered.

"A damn fine fight?" Ginny raised her glass. "We get ta' try and save tha' world!"

The woman's enthusiasm had Kiera smiling. "To saving the world." She clacked glasses, swallowing deep.

Special Tactics was an elite strike force. Potentially Caerus's best. Ginny had an impressive right hook and specialized in chakram. Kiera'd seen her split a lemon at three hundred yards then wield her circular blades as well as any knife expert in close quarters. She bested the men nine times out of ten.

If Special Tactics failed, it wouldn't be from lack of ability.

"What do you think about the anomaly, Ginny? Can one creature threaten the existence of an entire planet?"

"It *is*. Don't know about where yer from, but back home tha weather ain't been right for years. We've 'ad earthquakes, crops lost ta' unprecedented heat waves and cold fronts. Even tha' animals sense it. But either way, should be a helluva adventure!"

"Is that why you signed up?"

"Way I see it, if the world's endin' and I've got a chance to protect what's precious, gotta give it a go, yea?"

Protect what's precious. The words touched her. Whether getting rid of Queen would fix the planet or not, it'd help Dajah. She allowed herself a moment to fantasize about what their relationship could be if he wasn't constantly worried about losing control. Of course, Caerus was a bigger threat currently. Getting rid of Queen seemed easy compared to ridding the world of Caerus. *We've got a better chance of an armistice.*

"Time for another round," Ginny said, drawing Kiera's attention to her dwindling glass. Before she could object, the redhead moved to the bar and was returning faster than she should have been able to with the number of patrons waiting to be served.

"How'd you get it so fast?" she asked.

"Bar tender's a good friend with a better memory. Tell me. What's tha' situation with tha' lad ya came here with?"

As far as Kiera knew, none of the others viewed her and Dajah as a couple. Three of them already made suggestive passes that she politely declined, and there was no question Elwood would happily sleep with Dajah if the opportunity presented itself. Ginny, on the other hand, saw too much.

"Complicated," she admitted. "Half the time, I don't understand it myself."

"But ya care about 'im?" Ginny affirmed.

"I care. We had something for a while. And if there's anything left..." She watched the swirling liquid in her glass. Mincing words was pointless. Admitting she cared cost nothing, and Kiera longed to confide in someone. "Dajah hates Caerus, and I know he's worried about his brother. Unlike Elwood, they didn't finish the program. Caerus never gave them leave to go."

Ginny's nose scrunched up, lips frowning. "Just cause we work *for* 'em, doesn't mean we *are* them. Those lads with me when we first met? I trust 'em with me life! Gone on a dozen other missions with 'em over the years. Xant's a right bastard at times, but he won't risk yer life unnecessarily. We're all comin' out a this alive. Don't give up on 'em, Kiera."

Kiera offered a smile of gratitude, unsure what to believe. "Thanks."

Training progressed uneventfully. The biggest problem was Dajah. A few of the guys convinced him to drink with them last night. He stumbled back to the apartment reeking of beer and liquor but made an impressive recovery after a shower. Kiera didn't believe for a second he'd compromise his faculties on Caerus's grounds by choice, which meant he was faking it. They barely said a word to one another. Pretending was one thing, but now Dajah was shutting her out completely.

Chase was an equally frustrating problem. All he talked about was how impressed Caerus had been with his research, never mind that they were holding him prisoner in a windowless cell. He seemed convinced they'd offer him a job once she and Dajah departed the island. He even boasted about receiving private tours of some of their laboratories and consulting with their lead scientists on a new project.

The man was delusional. Attempts to reason with him failed spectacularly. It wouldn't be the first time ambition put Chase in a dangerous situation.

Kiera channeled all her frustration at both Dajah and Chase into her sparring match with Hobbs. Another basic human like her, but with a background in medicine, engineering, and mixed-martial arts, Hobbs put up a hell of a fight. He was skilled enough to seamlessly switch styles. The fight left her a mix of grateful, pissed off, and temporarily sated even though neither of them won.

Commander Xant pulled her and Dajah aside. Worried her issues with the men in her life were becoming too obvious, she prepared an explanation and apology.

"I've watched enough of your training to get an idea of your preferred weapon," Xant said to her. "Your skill with Earth magic is also improving. Where we're going, firearms will have limited effect, so, I had this commissioned for you." He removed a wooden box just over two feet long from his FS watch.

Curiosity overrode all other emotions. Inside rested a hybrid machete with distinctive Damascus steel wave patterns showing on the blade. It was perfectly balanced for one-hand use. Equally tactical and decorative, the blade was one of the most aesthetically pleasing weapons she ever laid eyes on.

The handle's perfect. The black handle had red veins running through it – Kiera's two favorite colors. She spared a glance in Ginny's direction. The redhead winked back before throwing Alyssia over her hip, never missing a beat.

"This is a beautiful weapon, Commander," Kiera said, removing it from the box. She made a few slow practice cuts in the air, finding no flaws.

"That's Heaven's Dust forged into the steel, isn't it?" Dajah asked.

She had no clue what Heaven's Dust was, but it was the first time she witnessed unadulterated emotion from Dajah besides anger and contempt since they arrived. He was in awe.

Xant cracked a smile. "You know your weapons."

"Should I know what this is?" she asked.

Dajah answered. "When the Stream moves on from an area, it leaves behind a thin layer of sediment. Over time the sediment is compressed, forming the foundation Earth Beads grow out of, similar to how pearls are formed. The material is rare enough by itself. They call it Heaven's Dust because it twinkles like the stars. It's the only material we are aware of that will consistently deflect and contain Earth magic."

It sounded like Dajah wanted to impress Xant. Still, his words encouraged her to examine the weapon more closely. "This holds magic?"

"I expect you can show her," Xant said to Dajah.

"Yeah, I can."

"Then I guess you'll want something of your own."

"It'd certainly make things easier." The smirk was classic Dajah. As much as it warmed her heart to see a tiny bit of the man she knew existed, she wanted to smack him.

Wish I knew all it'd take was a fancy knife.

Xant removed a longer box from his watch, offering it to Dajah. "You're an excellent swordsman, deserving of a weapon worthy of that skill."

Calling the chunk of metal in that box *just* a sword didn't do it justice. The same wave patterns were folded into forty-one inches of exquisite, deadly steel, the handle wrapped in silver over black.

Picking it up with his left hand, Dajah studied the blade before his eyes locked on Xant. He nodded, right hand out to the commander.

Xant took his hand and shook.

I'm missing something.

"Better get started if you're going to get her efficient with that blade before we leave," Xant said. His smile remained as he walked past her and clapped his hands.

"Come on," Dajah said. "We'll have to use one of the simulations that allow magic. I'll show you what makes these unique." Excitement brimmed, and Kiera allowed herself to share in a bit of his joy.

They loaded one of the monster combat scenarios and she stood back, inspecting Dajah's form as he sliced through the man-sized centipede like a hot knife through butter. As soon as the edge of his sword made contact, the entire creature went up in flames. The katana glided through its body without a hint of resistance, completely bisecting the beast. Both pieces burnt to a charred mess in seconds.

"Any weapon tempered with Heaven's Dust can hold a magical charge," he lectured. "When you cast your spell, you channel into your weapon instead of your opponent. The magic won't fire without intent. You have to command activation."

He cast another spell on the sword, holding it out horizontally. From the right angle, the katana sparkled like someone dipped it in glitter.

Dajah stuck the tip down into the snow. "You also can't charge Heaven's Dust with all types of magic. Offensive spells work the best, for obvious reasons, and charging a sword with healing magic is just... counterproductive?" Gripping the handle, he caused flames to consume the surrounding area. Snow melted into an instant puddle.

"Are these blades stronger than regular Damascus steel?"

Both weapons came with scabbards.

"They're indestructible to anything other than another Heaven's Dust blade." Pulling his sword from the ground, Dajah flicked it dry with practiced ease. "In a swordfight between two Heaven's Dust blades, the better-forged blade is more likely to damage the other."

"How long can they hold a spell for?"

"Depending on the spell and how much energy you put into the casting, sometimes hours."

The implications hit her. "Xant gave us weapons we could charge here with magic and use hours later?"

"He did."

No wonder his mood changed! If they charged their weapons with advanced spells and left the Sim room... *Doubt it's enough to get us off the island, but damned if this wasn't the best chance we've had so far.*

"What's he thinking?" she asked aloud.

"He wants us to have the right tools for the job," Dajah said, always choosing his words carefully. "Ron's sidesword is tempered with Heaven's Dust. So are Ginny's chakrams."

She came to her own conclusion: *Xant wants Queen dead. He's a hard-ass who wants to save the world... and he needs help.*

She spent hours practicing various techniques with her machete under Dajah's guidance. For a time, she imagined they were back at the cabin. Having him close, listening to his explanations, even the unrestrained smile when she pulled off a series of attacks reminded her that what they shared wasn't gone.

Then Dajah remembered it, too, and the illusion shattered. His demeanor shifted on the spot. "Enough for now," he said, voice hard. "You should recover from the Drain. Good work, Kiera."

"Good work, Kiera," she mockingly repeated, staring him down. "*That's* what you have to say?"

His initial reaction was confusion. Frustration made her want to stab him, and only conscious willpower made her sheath her sword. The thrumming energy in her blood intensified three-fold with the addition of the weapon.

"What do you want me to say?" he asked.

"You have to realize it. You're not that stupid." She folded her arms, nails digging into her elbows. When he continued staring silently, she shook her head. "Forget it, Dajah."

That elicited a rise out of him, muscles tensing as he leaned forward. "You think I'm playing a game?"

She knew she should let it go. Instead, Kiera took a step closer. Dropping her arms, she motioned to the space between them. "What are we? You and I?"

His hesitation was brief. "Two people in an extremely dangerous situation who need to be careful."

As if she wasn't already aware.

"That's it?"

"That's it."

So much finality lingered in his statement that Kiera had to clench her teeth. She stabbed her index finger at him. "You're an asshole."

Leaving the room without another word, she let anger mask her breaking heart. Charade or not, she couldn't keep doing this.

CHAPTER 42

Dajah avoided everyone. Damp dirt and fresh, sweet flora cloyed his nostrils. Buzzing. Croaking. Chirping wildlife. A random helicopter passed somewhere above the canopy, and he focused on every physical sense possible.

It wasn't enough.

The guards in the detention hall gave him a wider berth than usual.

"What happened?" Taron asked moments after he entered.

Dajah leaned against the empty wall, keeping the door and glass in his periphery. "I'm running out of patience." Not even the boon of Heaven's Dust weapons could overshadow the fact that he was intentionally hurting someone he cared for. And he wasn't even sure it was necessary.

Taron's lips pressed together. "Regarding...?"

"All of it. The island's secure." Admitting that was another failure. The more Dajah learned, the more impossible it became to circumvent Caerus's security from within. He banged his head back against the wall.

"Shall we talk about it?" Taron asked.

He released a sigh, meeting his brother's eyes. "You're the only one that understands how precarious things are."

"I've seen you worse than this. Whatever *this* is," Taron gestured over him, "it's not just Caerus."

"It's Kiera," Dajah admitted.

"What about her?"

"I can't be what she wants."

"Doubt she wants you to be something you're not."

"You know what this is about," Dajah stressed.

"Better than she does, I'd imagine. How's the rest of your team?"

"Unsure... Ginny's more perceptive than others."

"Do you trust her, or any of them?"

Dajah laughed. "I'll go as far as to say most *probably* won't stab me in the back."

"Not sure I've ever seen you this conflicted."

"She's here because of me."

"She understood the risks."

Dajah cracked an eye. "Think any of us are walking out alive?"

"We don't believe in no-win scenarios. What's this going to cost for us to walk out of it alive? That's what you need to be asking."

Queen would have mocked them. He had a plan, but that plan involved more risk than he was comfortable with.

"A lot," Dajah said, closing his eye again. "Maybe everything."

"Then mitigate the damage. Can you get this Xant to visit me?"

Both eyes opened. After a moment, he shrugged. "Can't hurt to ask."

"Ask. And in the meantime...?"

Neither doubted Caerus recorded, analyzed, and deciphered their every word and action. It necessitated prudence. Kiera didn't seem to understand that, and he had no way of explaining it.

"I'll do what I can."

When all the mandatory simulations were completed, Xant ran squad-based drills. Those scenarios more accurately depicted what they'd encounter, providing a better indication of how well

Special Tactics functioned as a unit.

Overall, Dajah was impressed. When push came to shove everyone took roles as felt natural. They followed a loose chain of command, rarely having to repeat a simulation twice.

Outside of required training, he offered to help Kiera with her Heaven's Dust skills. She refused him every time, opting to train with Ginny or any of the others. Everyone had a unique style. She benefitted from a variety of advice, but he wasn't sure if he was more relieved or disappointed his plan was working.

Unless Xant paired them up on certain activities, they did their own thing as much as possible. Cordial in public, behind closed doors Kiera avoided him. She was pissed. All it'd take was an explanation and apology to mend things.

The benefit of destroying their budding relationship came in the form of Kiera's camaraderie with several team members. She inadvertently made herself a greater asset to the mission, and Dajah believed Xant and others would argue if the president attempted to pull her last minute.

That left Taron and Chase. From what little Kiera shared, Dajah learned Chase was fascinated by Caerus. It was highly unlikely he'd leave willingly given the opportunity.

If their offer's genuine.... The idea that Chase could be their inside man was a stretch. It hinged on a lot of things going right, and the *only* thing currently going right was that Dajah wasn't locked up in a small cell fighting off sedation.

◆

Ginny's face lit up, chattering on about the newest gossip among Special Tactics. Carley, Jen, and Alyssia declined to join them for the usual after-dinner drinks, but Kiera didn't mind.

"...then Alyssia and Charles Green, I dunna particularly fancy tha' lad, tried arguin' with Ron over some daft computer system. Ya kiddin' me? Like Caerus has na' tested this equipment countless times." The redhead leaned across the table, whispering, "We all know Green fancies Alyssia. What he doesn't know is she couldna' give two shits 'bout 'em."

Ginny could turn anything into an engaging story. Unfortunately, Kiera's thoughts drifted.

"Ya listenin' to anything I'm sayin'?"

"I heard you, Ginny." She lifted her glass, finishing off the drink in one swallow.

The redhead stared her down. "Havena' been yerself since Xant gave ya that nifty cutter. Problems with tha' horse you ain't ridin'?"

"You mean jackass?" She clenched her empty glass.

"Know why he's ignoring ya?"

"Honestly? No. I'm sure he's got some twisted logic to justify it." Kiera was over trying to keep that secret, at least to Ginny. "Lately I've been wondering if I imagined it all along."

Kiera sensed the lightest touch of *something;* she'd come to associate it with Ginny's talents. She didn't know if others felt it, too, but she knew when the woman utilized her abilities. Her pupils constricted and dilated in succession three times. Then Ginny leaned back in her chair.

"Try talkin' to him?"

"Briefly. Days ago."

"And?"

Kiera sighed. "And I walked away and have been ignoring him since." It was childish, but she couldn't deal with another failed attempt at communicating with Dajah.

"What'd he say?"

Brief as it was, Kiera recalled the scene with vivid clarity. How he stood there, how cold he was. The stubbornness... "I asked him what we were. He said we're two people in a dangerous situation that need to be careful."

"Well," Ginny said after a moment, "he's not wrong."

"I'm not an idiot. The President has some moron watching us every second we're not in our apartment or on the training grounds." She motioned to the loner at the bar. "Sasha's looking for any excuse to make good on her threats, but Dajah's taking things too far."

Ginny's eyes slipped past Kiera to the man she referenced. Black jacket, clean-shaven face, short brown hair, maybe early forties... His eyes were unnaturally dark in the lighting, and he didn't attempt to hide the fact he was watching them. A creepy smile and nod met their stares. Everything about that man felt greasy.

Turning back, Kiera caught Ginny's pupils returning to their normal size.

"Gettin' late," Ginny said, standing. "We best be off if we're doin' our last sim 'fore tha' evenin' over." Her scotch was a quarter-full.

Flagging down the bartender, Ginny had him close out their tab.

"Gonna tell me what that was about?" Kiera asked once they were outside.

"Jesus, Mary, and Joseph!" Ginny stopped walking. "How long you been seein' that lad around?"

"Four days. Who is he?"

"No idea, but I can tell ya he doesn't belong. *Not* one of the President's. All her tools give off a vibe. This one's trouble, Kiera. Promise me you'll be careful round 'em."

"Think I picked up a stalker?"

"Dunna like 'em in the least."

Looking back at Building One, Kiera waited for the man to make an appearance outside. This was one thing she could deal with at least. "If he follows, I'll see if I can lure him away from the crowds. Find out what he wants. Doubt he'll approach if you're with me, though."

The wink confirmed Ginny's unspoken excitement. "Go on then! Meet ya in there." She headed down the walking trail that looped back around, and Kiera followed one of the smaller paths into the rainforest.

She made it halfway to the training grounds when distinctive rustling came from the foliage up ahead. The Irishwoman could move in perfect stealth when needed. Kiera only spotted her once on the walk, and that was intentional.

Stopping on the widest part of the trail, she waited. Leaves gave way to a man walking out of the rainforest like he was on a casual stroll.

"Figured if I came out here alone, you'd find me," she said.

He faced her with a smile that didn't reach his eyes. "I deemed the risks worth the reward at this point. You and your girlfriend left so suddenly from the restaurant."

"We have things to do." Kiera glanced at her FS watch, noting the time. "I'm meeting her soon. What do you want?"

"I've been searching for you," he said. "Wasn't sure it was you at first. I'm sure now, though the spell you carry is potent indeed. Whoever cast it paid dearly."

Kiera searched her memories, trying to match the stranger with anyone from her past. His voice caused her skin to prickle. "Do I know you?"

"Not in the way you're thinking." He spoke leisurely, posture relaxed and unthreatening. It made him dangerous. "It's such a pleasant night. Will you walk with me for a bit? I'd like to talk."

"Do you have a name?"

"Ethan," he replied.

"Alright, Ethan, if you promise to get to the point sooner than later, I'll walk with you."

He chuckled, turning back to the rainforest. "This way."

"To where?" Going off-path would eventually cut through to the marina if they continued straight. However, the marina was miles off with no known buildings in the heart of the forest.

"To a place we won't be disturbed," Ethan answered. "This island comes with ears, and our business isn't for them."

Kiera questioned whether this could still be a gambit on Sasha's part, or if one of her teammates put Ethan up to it. Caution stroked the back of her neck with claws, but only a vague sense of familiarity surfaced. Something encouraged her to follow, like he had all the answers she forgot she was searching for.

On Caerus's island? Thoughts immediately shifted to Julius, remembering his connections. *Only one way to find out.* She gestured into the rainforest and prepared for the worst. "Lead the way."

CHAPTER 43

Despite having little to update Taron on, Dajah never missed an opportunity to visit. They could sit in amiable silence the entire hour and it'd still be worthwhile. No telling when it might be the last time they saw each other. One wrong move, one careless word... He tried not to let it get to him.

"Training's going well. They're one of the most organized groups I've ever worked with. You'd like them."

"Think they stand a chance?" Taron asked.

"Of destroying Queen?" He still checked himself every time her name came up, finding nothing. "We've got a fair chance of reaching the caves. Beyond that, no idea. No one knows what to expect. I know how they *think* this will go, and you know how well that works."

Taron nodded. "When do you leave?"

It was a touchy subject. Dajah loathed the idea of leaving Taron behind, and he'd yet to come up with feasible alternatives. "Five days, give or take. Caerus is monitoring weather patterns."

Silence resumed. They sat on the cot until the door unlocked sixty minutes to the second from when Dajah arrived.

"See you tomorrow, Taron."

"Night, Dajah."

Security always waited until he turned away to seal Taron's cell. Sometimes it was six digits, sometimes eight. The combination changed daily.

Twenty-some days of the same thing and he gave the guards credit: They never missed a beat. Staging a successful prison break with what he had to work with held obscenely high risks. And getting Taron out of the detention hall was only the first in a slew of impossible tasks.

Only way is after I'm off the island.

Mentally reviewing his FS inventory, he started on the footpath to the coast. Clear skies made every star in the sky visible. It was the first evening in weeks he considered pleasant.

Footsteps reached his ears before Ginny appeared, sprinting in his direction. Nothing about her expression boded well. Adrenaline kicked into overdrive, tensing his muscles. She stopped before him and caught her breath.

"What happened?"

"Needin' ta come with me right now. Somethin' happen' ta' Kiera."

Dajah clenched his fists. The invisible walls of his prison were shrinking fast.

"Start talking, Ginny." His Heaven's Dust katana materialized after two quick button strikes.

"Come on," she said, turning back. The explanation began.

"What do you mean they disappeared?"

Ginny slowed, reaching the place she lost sight of them. "Swear it, Dajah. I was close enough to hear 'em give 'is name. They turned into the trees here, then whoosh! Gone!"

Crouching down, he examined the forest floor beyond the lip of the paved walking trail. "And you looked for them?"

"Aye, of course! Looked fir 'em over fifteen minutes. Possible there's some tunnels or somethin' beneath the ground I'm not savvy to, but ya know what I'm capable of. Tellin' ya. They up and disappeared!"

Resting his palm on the dirt allowed for another perspective. "There's a trail."

"That's the trail *I* made tryin' to find 'em."

"No. He's using some kind of cloaking magic. Smell the burnt ozone?"

Ginny stared into the darkening forest, sniffing the air. "Dunna smell anythin.' Can't see another trail, either. Ya sure about this, Dajah? Magic outside the Trainin' Hall?"

"Go get Xant. I'll leave a path to follow." He swung his sword, shearing a bundle of vines.

"Whacha gonna do?"

"I'm going to find them. And if this man has done anything to hurt Kiera, I'm going to cut his head off." Stepping off the walkway, Dajah ventured into the heart of the rainforest.

❖

Kiera stood, arms folded, as Ethan removed his jacket and laid it across the nearest boulder. He brought them to a clearing with several giant rocks dotting the landscape. Moonlight shone brightly.

"What is this place?" she asked. Their walk consisted mostly of silence.

"One of the few locations where natural features disrupt Caerus's security systems. They can't track us here. Or hear us."

"How would they hear us?"

"Think that ID card you carry is strictly for opening doors and buying shoes?"

The plastic card rested in her back pocket.

You can't go more than ten feet without having to swipe this on something.

Dajah's short, abrupt conversations finally made sense. *They're always monitoring us!* Kiera suppressed her anger while Ethan rolled up the cuffs of his dress shirt. She couldn't afford to think about Dajah right now. "What do you *want*?"

"Ah, the million-dollar question," he mused. "I have a unique set of skills, and it's my divine mission to hunt down and eliminate threats to the Trinity of Realms."

"What's the Trinity of Realms?"

"You wouldn't know. You don't even know what you are, do you?"

"I know I'm losing interest in this conversation."

"You're a threat that needs to be eliminated."

She snorted, dropping her hands to her sides. "Did the President send you?"

"I don't answer to Caerus. Now, I prefer a sampling of what I'm getting before I take it. The last three were hardly worthy of my talents. You're Unawakened, but from what I've learned about Special Tactics, you're not without skill. Make this challenging, ok?"

Kiera stared at him. Dozens of weapons waited a button-click away. *Would Sasha believe me?* A frustrated growl escaped her lips. "Think I've heard enough."

"Agreed," Ethan said. Symbols lit up along his forearms and neck in a variety of colors. Childhood memories bombarded her. It was the symbols. Always the symbols. And those symbols were what allowed her to do things the rest of her family couldn't. They were part of what her mother and father argued over. They were—

"You recognize these."

"I've seen them in my past," she admitted.

The twisted grin forming on his face opened a pit inside her stomach. Ethan extended his left hand, eyes trailing down his arm before that black gaze bore into her. "I'm not what you are, but every time one of your kind is destroyed, the victor gains new abilities. Every color you see once belonged to an abomination. Now they all belong to me."

Tingling triggered in her bloodstream with a surge of adrenaline. Kiera took a step back, removing the Glock from her watch. She attempted a Shield Barrier, but her Earth Beads didn't function.

"You're not gonna walk away, are you?" she asked, knowing the answer.

A line of yellow energy shot out of his hand and snared her

neck with a snap. Kiera grabbed the line with her left hand, raised her Glock, and fired. Bullets found Ethan's hand, chest, and head in rapid succession. The hand shot disrupted the energy line, causing it to disappear. Other shots were minimally effective – his wounds healed instantly. His body *ate* the bullets. The projectile in his forehead broke apart as if devoured by tiny insects. It spread out in thin black lines before fading.

"Try harder," he said, sending another line at her.

Kiera dodged, squeezing off two consecutive shots while putting distance between them. She had Xant's gift out in a second, removing the Heaven's Dust machete from its sheath in time to block Ethan's next energy whip. The blade sliced through the line, and it disappeared, wiping the sadistic look off his face.

"That's no ordinary weapon," he said.

Kiera attacked, moving through a fury of slashes and stabs Dajah would be proud of.

She never came close to cutting him.

Self-enhancing magic? Something connected to those symbols?

Firing at his head while simultaneously thrusting her sword, she gouged both shirt and skin. The wound to his ribs bled freely, the first credible injury that healed slower than the bullet holes.

Coming at her again, Ethan moved inside her guard, rendering her sword useless. She deflected a palm strike outward. Punched with her Glock. The gun grazed his cheek and he locked her arm at the elbow under one arm.

A sharp crack brought pain and she lost the grip on her firearm. His next open palm connected with her solar plexus. Breath fled her lungs in a forced exhale as multiple somethings broke. Doubled forward and gasping for air against stabbing pains, she felt the *snap* around her ankle.

Ethan released her arm the same time her leg was ripped out from under her. The energy whip hurled her into the closest boulder. A series of short, flat glowing discs followed her graceless crash into a rock. The first missed her face, scoring deep into stone. The next grazed her shoulder and pain intensified.

Kiera rolled over the top of the boulder, ducking down to catch her breath.

Stone shattered, raining volcanic dust. Her cuts were minor, but the broken ribs made breathing and movement nearly unbearable. She rallied.

"Losing patience," Ethan said in a sing-song voice, moving closer. "Thought you were some kind of elite warrior."

His form blurred in front of her. Kiera dove to the side before his fist collided with her skull. Gaining her feet, she raked the edge of her sword across his back. Ethan retaliated with a handful of energy discs, forcing her to block. Again, he was inside her guard. She went to smash her pommel against his head. He caught her wrist with one hand, stalling the blow, and grabbed her throat with the other.

"You're disappointing—" A knee to the groin silenced him. She broke his hold and shoved him back. Flipping hand over feet with inhuman speed, Ethan avoided her horizontal slash. He raised both palms and dozens of energy lines shot out. Some snapped at her face and limbs, leaving small lacerations in their wake. She blocked what she could, finding her arms pinned in moments. One of the lines wrapped around her chest and constricted, suspending her in the air. If she didn't find a way to significantly injure him soon, it would cost her everything.

Wind whipped past Kiera's ears, freeing multiple strands of hair from her ponytail as she flew through the air. Momentum came to an abrupt stop against a tree limb. Then another. Wood cracked and shattered. Disorientation followed until her body met ground and she rolled with the impact, having lost her sword. Gasped breaths came in painful waves. Adrenaline did little to subside it.

"*This* is slightly impressive," Ethan said. Her sword was in his hand now.

Kiera removed two daggers from her watch and stood, willing her body to function. Eyes locked on his.

"Afraid we've wasted enough time." He adjusted his grip on

the sword and advanced.

It took every ounce of training Kiera had to stay one step ahead and avoid being beheaded. Energy buzzed in her veins. She racked up several wounds against him with her daggers, but they healed faster than those delivered with the Heaven's Dust blade.

An energy disc almost took her hand off, and she lost the first dagger. Attempting to block a downward strike cleaved her second dagger in half and split her thigh open. She screamed through clenched teeth as white-hot pain rendered her leg useless.

Countless lines ensnared her. Ethan's fuzzy silhouette approached. His hand weighed heavily on her shoulder while his other, the primary source of the binding lines, kept the sword out of reach.

"You might have been quite the challenge once Awakened. Alas, we'll never know."

He leached energy from her shoulder and the concept of pain vanished, replaced by waves of intense weakness. Wounds throbbed but didn't sting. Blood oozed in rivulets from her leg, soaking her pants. She clung to her broken dagger like a lifeline as her vision blurred. The world faded. With no recollection of falling, her consciousness registered the ground again. Mind-numbing cold emanated from Ethan's touch, sapping everything.

"It'll be over soon," he said.

Blue-green light flashed. Dirt and leaves exploded. Ethan's touch and silhouette disappeared, but the energy bindings remained. A second blast of energy flew overhead. Something splintered behind her, too fast for her addled mind to follow.

All she wanted to do was close her eyes and surrender, but something within resisted. She saw another figure move into the clearing. It took her brain a moment to connect the silver hair and the man she came here with.

Ethan stood tall, sword in hand. "You're interrupting us."

"Gonna do more than that," Dajah said, his voice dead calm.

The two collided, swords clashing in violent precision. Ethan had skill; his swordsmanship was excellent. Dajah's was better.

They were almost too fast for her to follow. The assassin parried one attack after the next with a cool smugness until Dajah changed tactics on the fly. Ethan paid in flesh before laying into Dajah with the energy lines. Kiera's eyes widened, too weak to call out a warning.

Dajah sliced through the lines repeatedly until one caught his ankle. Another snared his arm midair and Ethan sent him flying into a boulder. He recovered, charging Ethan the moment he gained his feet. Several quick, deep strikes added to Ethan's injuries. If it wasn't for his enhanced healing, the fight should have been over.

Need to do something.

Her broken dagger had zero effect against the energy bindings, and her heart skipped beats when Ethan's blade came too close for comfort. The swordfight turned bloodier. Oblivion beckoned, offering peace and rest until a lack of movement demanded her full attention. Both men stood. Dajah's katana protruded out of Ethan's back, through his stomach. Her machete sword was embedded in Dajah's shoulder. They pulled away, spraying the forest with blood.

"No!" she cried out, feeling that electric tingle intensify.

Dajah stumbled. Ethan moved in.

A voice echoed in Kiera's head, vaguely familiar: *"You strong girl. Wake up!"*

Knowledge blossomed within. Time slowed. Shifting focus to her restraints, Kiera *breathed*, sucking their essence into her body through every point of contact. It provided substantially more energy than Ethan took. More than she'd felt in a long time. The lines disintegrated and the world came into crisp focus. Kiera stood and ran to the fight. Her feet hit the ground with each step but she felt weightless. She *flowed*.

Ethan turned, his expression a mix of hatred and desire, but he had to block another strike from Dajah. Kiera drove the remaining half of her dagger between his shoulder blades, hoping to sever his spine. He howled in pain as she twisted, silencing his noises.

Dajah's sword passed clean through Ethan's neck in a perfect, level slash. His head separated from his body as a forking bolt of lightning hit all three of them.

Kiera lost consciousness.

CHAPTER 44

Based on how fantastically terrible his body felt, Dajah couldn't have been out for more than an hour. Kiera's lightning knocked him out cold.

Aches and pains aside, the rest of his senses told him he wasn't still in the clearing. It didn't occur to him to wonder where he was until he opened his eyes.

This is a joke, right?

Someone handcuffed him to a hospital bed, wearing the same clothes caked in blood. A few bandages dressed major wounds. For better or worse, he didn't have any painkillers.

A quick scan revealed he was alone. Rage came unbidden, nullifying any sense of bodily damage. He snapped the handcuff at the chain joint, bending the rail of the bed in the process. Guards stationed outside his room had their guns trained on him as soon as he touched the door.

"Where is she?!" he demanded.

"Sir, you're not supposed to leave your room," one guard said.

"I *asked* you a question."

His tone garnered uncertainty and an answer: "Down the hall. Now please go back to your bed and wait."

"Do you have orders to shoot me?"

Their hesitation said plenty. Dajah shoved past the closest guard and started down the hallway. No one fired. Ahead, six armed guards waited outside Kiera's room. Inside stood another three, Sasha Bekarda, and a man and woman wearing lab coats.

He saw red.

"Sir, you're not authorized to ent—" The man never finished his statement. Dajah knocked him out with a swift strike to the temple, immediately dispatching the others. In fifteen seconds all six were down. More were coming. He kicked open the door, slamming it so hard its glass window shattered. Everyone inside turned to face him. Everyone except one.

"Dajah, go back to your room. Now!" Sasha ordered.

He barely saw her, eyes settling on Kiera – unconscious, with symbols glowing on her skin. Neither of the scientists standing nearby had syringes in their hands, only a stethoscope and a tablet.

"What'd you do to her?" Every nightmarish scenario associated with Caerus came to a head.

"They're examining her," Sasha said. "Return to your room."

"Not. What. I. Asked." Dajah glared at the president. She maintained a level gaze in turn while the guards shifted nervously, guns pointed in Dajah's direction. He knew they considered how close he stood to their boss.

"Madam President?" one finally asked.

Before she responded, Dajah said, "Better be prepared to kill me, Sasha, because that's what it's gonna take to stop me if they don't get away from her *right now*."

He had no idea what these guards were prepared for, but Sasha was aware of the kind of damage he could do. She didn't have enough men and she knew it.

The president took a slow, deep breath. "Stand down," she said to her guards. Control shifted in Dajah's favor. "All of you outside. But if either of them tries to leave, shoot them."

Security hesitated while the scientists fled fast. Dajah's eyes lingered on the president, keeping the others in his periphery. Sasha scowled at her guards when they didn't move. "That's an order!"

"Yes, ma'am," they said in unison, moving to the door.

Dajah went to Kiera, checking her vitals. He examined every inch of her body, assessing wounds and markings, ensuring no needle marks punctured her flesh.

She fought him longer than I realized. Two minutes more and he might have been too late. Guilt plucked at his insides, kept in check by the growing hostility ready to consume him.

"What'd you do to her?"

The president looked wholly unimpressed, folding her arms. "We didn't do anything to her. What happened?"

Promises and threats meant little at this point. They'd already broken her rules. If taking a man's head wasn't enough to condemn Taron and seal Dajah's fate, Caerus wanted him cooperative for other reasons.

"By the time I found them, he was ready to kill her. I killed him first." Simple. To the point.

"Dajah, an investigation's underway. Whoever that man was, he didn't work for Caerus. I gave explicit orders for the two of you to be left alone if you obeyed the rules. I didn't send him."

"Then you've got a bigger security problem on this island than you realize." Catching his reflection in the window, he saw his eyes glowing brighter than Kiera's markings. Had they injected him with Stream while he was out?

If she doesn't recover, I'm sinking this whole fucking island.

"Out of my way," Xant ordered, pushing past the guards.

Dajah put his back to the wall behind Kiera's bed, observing the commander as he entered. Xant's attention went immediately to Sasha.

"What are they doing here?"

"They're under investigation, Commander," she answered.

"They're my responsibility. I discipline members of Special Tactics."

The tension between them was thick enough to cut through.

"Are you sure you want to take this path, Xant?"

The commander didn't waiver under haughty stares. "I take full responsibility for whatever consequences result."

"They murdered someone on the island. Dajah's already admitted to it."

"Does it look like either of them fought someone without cause?" Xant asked, throwing his hand in Dajah's direction. "They defended themselves. It was *our* responsibility to make sure they were safe. We failed. The man that attacked them didn't belong here. You should see what Simons found on that body."

The president's projected authority eased, and mild satisfaction soothed Dajah's rage.

"So be it," she said after another moment. "They're under your watch. I expect you'll treat them the same as any other member of Special Tactics under investigation." She left the room, reminding the guards of Xant's jurisdiction.

A thin frown formed on the commander as he looked over Dajah. "Let's get the two of you out of here and patched up right."

Dajah carried Kiera, climbing into one of the transports Xant activated with his badge. He drove them back to the training grounds where a third of their team waited outside.

Special Tactics could stare all they wanted as long as they kept their hands to themselves. No one spoke aloud. Dajah refused to meet their eyes.

The commander led them to the Sim Hall. "You didn't want to heal the old-fashioned way, did you?" Moments later they stood in an open field with a mild climate. "Magic's activated. Do the honors, unless you're not feeling up to it."

"I'll do it." Besides the fact Dajah didn't want anyone else messing with Kiera, he figured this was Xant's way of allowing him to burn off excess energy. He laid her down in the grass and cast a Full Heal over both of them.

Cuts, bruises, and broken bones repaired at a painful, near-instant rate without leaving a scar. The spell was over fast enough. Kiera never flinched from the healing, and that was cause for alarm. He cast a Refresher spell next, similar in action to smelling salts.

She woke up screaming.

He crouched down, almost touching her shoulder when another lightning bolt struck him. Cursing, Dajah pulled his hand back and shook out the painful numb running halfway up his arm. The commander took a step back.

Kiera sat up, catching her breath and scanning the area like some wild-eyed animal.

"Calm down. We're in a Sim," Dajah explained. "I healed you with magic. You're safe."

Hazel eyes met his before finding Xant. "Ethan?" she asked.

"Dead," Dajah said. "Are you ok?"

Hugging her knees to her chest, she stared at the glowing symbols along one arm and traced her finger over them. Each shimmered in response to the contact. Dajah had never seen anything like it before. The markings covering Ethan's flesh resembled unknown runes, glowing a dozen different colors. Kiera's were more elaborate in design, but all had the same soft purple hue.

When she didn't answer his first question, he gently asked, "What's happening to you?"

"Not sure," she said.

Xant cleared his throat. "You've both got explaining to do. You'll give a debriefing as soon as we leave this room. Then you're confined to quarters until the investigation is over. *End Sim.*"

Kiera stood from the bare arena floor, leaving Dajah unable to decipher her expression.

"You came for me," she said, meeting his eyes.

It broke something in him he didn't realize was there to begin with. Actions always spoke louder than words. His actions, or lack thereof, almost got her killed.

"Let's go," Xant ordered.

Dajah offered her a half-smile and nodded. There was so much he wanted to say, but not here. Not now. He followed the commander out of the room, Kiera trailing behind them.

The fallout from pushing his luck with Sasha was minimal. Being confined to the training grounds meant Dajah couldn't visit his brother.

The apartments within the training grounds were a far cry from prison cells. No frills compared to their other accommodations, but no coded locks either. Dajah and Kiera could come and go as they wished from the room. The building came fully equipped with a cafeteria and general store.

No one confiscated their FS watches or Earth Beads, and Dajah discovered someone returned their Heaven's Dust weapons to their watches. They were banned from the Sim Hall. However, training was still mandatory.

It was a small price to pay.

The day after the attack Kiera kept to herself, providing only short responses to any questions. She confirmed the symbols related to something from her childhood. Getting her to talk about much else was difficult.

Thirty hours later, her symbols stopped glowing. The markings didn't fade entirely, but the residual lines became faint enough to go unnoticed without close inspection.

"What happened to them?" he asked.

She pulled on a fresh shirt, keeping her back to him. "I burned through the extra energy. Did you hear anything more about the investigation?"

Sighing, Dajah said, "No."

"Tell me if you do. I'm meeting Carley and Ginny after training tonight. Don't bother waiting up." She grabbed her ID card, slipped it into the side pocket of stretch jeans, and left.

Now she was intentionally avoiding him. He leaned back against the couch he'd slept on and contemplated the best way to dig oneself out of a crater.

CHAPTER 45

When mandatory training concluded for the day, Xant pulled Dajah and Kiera aside.

"Any word on the investigation?" Dajah asked.

"Nothing," Xant said, "but I wanted you aware, I spoke with Taron and Chase. They'd have no way of knowing why you missed your daily visits. I kept details brief."

"Thank you, sir," Kiera said.

Xant's gaze passed between them, eyes narrowed. "Do I need to worry about the two of you?"

"We're good." Kiera said. Dajah wasn't sure he believed it, but the commander didn't press them. He walked away, and Kiera turned towards him.

"Later, Dajah." She exited the briefing room.

Elwood stepped up beside him, draping an arm over his neck. "You owe me. And whatever *that* was, you definitely need to punch at something."

That obvious, huh? Dajah gave him a sideways glance and pushed the half-Fey's arm away. "Think you'll fare better than last time?"

"Hobbs is betting two-to-one against you."

"Is he aware of something I'm not?"

On cue, Hobbs joined them. "Yep. You're fighting blindfolded."

"I am?"

"I mean, Elwood would prefer you fight naked."

Elwood vigorously nodded his agreement.

"I'm still not having sex with you."

"Does that mean you'll fight naked?" the half-Fey asked.

Dajah had to laugh. Elwood reminded him of Matt, who'd definitely sleep with him.

"You're thinking about it aren't you?" Elwood asked.

"I'm not fighting naked," Dajah said," but if we make it out of this alive, I know someone who'd love to meet you."

"Let's go, boys," Hobbs said. "Vance and Olivera want in."

Two of Sasha's, Vance and Olivera had enough skill to back up the harsh criticism they offered everyone. They loved to study Dajah in action. In turn, he refrained from outward animosity.

A fight was a perfect distraction. The added challenge of being blindfolded kept Dajah's mind on the present. Fighting stripped the world of complexity.

Hobbs gave the signal to start.

Breathing deep, Dajah centered his weight between both legs and waited. Currents moved on the air. Limbs came within proximity. One, two, three feints... the strikes were never in danger of touching him.

Elwood scoffed, giving away his location. Surrender allowed Dajah's body to respond automatically, blocking here, stepping there. The half-Fey never held back in training. His weakness was in the noisiness with which he moved. His feet scuffed the mat. His clothes carried a distinct scent and audible ruffle. Still, Dajah's reactions lacked perfection, gaining him bruises in no time. The trick was not overreacting and losing focus.

The goal wasn't to knock out your opponent. Each round was capped at three take-downs or one foot off the mat. As long as Dajah maintained his balance and didn't stray too far from the center of the ring, he could counter most of Elwood's moves.

After two rounds they were tied.

The final bout ended when the half-Fey outmaneuvered him, forcing him back until his left foot slipped out of bounds. Cheers and claps went up in response, with more spectators gathered by the end. Dajah removed his blindfold and nodded to his opponent. A giant grin spread across Elwood's face.

"Which one of us you think would win in a real fight?" Elwood asked.

"Hope we never have to find out." And he meant it. If they were both human, their skills would be equal. Whether half-Fey trumped half-alien in an all-out fight to the death... Dajah shook his head, patting Elwood on the shoulder.

Hobbs made his way over after settling with the others. "Hell of a show, gentlemen. Joining us for a drink, Dajah?"

"Stuck here, remember?"

"We can always bring back a few cases. Commandeer the commissary since the girls took over the roof," Elwood suggested.

"Thanks, but I'm gonna retire early."

"Want company?" Elwood asked, eyebrows waggling.

A forced smirk appeared. "Alone. Until Kiera gets back." *Whenever that is.* He needed to talk to her sooner than later.

The apartment was empty upon his return. Rumor had it the ladies were trying to help Carley remember what it was like to have fun. He hoped it helped for Carley's sake. She was more than a little unhinged.

Making himself comfortable on his couch-bed, he settled in to wait. Hours later the door opened, bringing in aromas of fire pit, liquor, and underlying notes of sugar. Kiera didn't so much as look at him before heading into the bedroom and closing the door. Knowing how quickly she metabolized alcohol, he doubted she was still buzzed. He also doubted she thought he was asleep.

He'd give her till morning.

Kiera was already in the shower by the time Dajah woke. Blaming frustration for the restless night, he stretched out and made his way to the bathroom. Knocked. When she didn't respond, he let himself in. She hadn't locked it.

"Can I join you?" he asked.

Kiera turned enough to acknowledge him then continued rinsing her hair under the water. It wasn't a denial. He started lifting his shirt when she said, "Be done in five minutes. Please wait outside." Her tone stoked his anger more than her words.

"Are you serious?"

"Yes, Dajah."

Lavender-scented shampoo filled his nostrils and he closed his eyes. It took an impressive amount of self-control to walk out of that bathroom and not slam the door, but he managed. Then paced the room until the water stopped.

Kiera came out with her hair wrapped in one towel, her body covered with another.

"We need to talk," he said, arms folded.

Hardened hazel eyes contemplated him for a moment. "Can it wait until after I'm dressed?"

"*No*. You're avoiding me, and we're running out of time."

Kiera resumed walking towards the bedroom. He grabbed her forearm more forcefully than intended.

"Get your goddamn hands off me!" she threatened. At least it was a genuine emotion. Dajah could work with anger. Still, he released her immediately.

"What the hell's wrong with you?" he asked.

"With *me*?" White-knuckled fists and fierce eyes declared her outrage. "What makes you think you can help yourself to anything now that you want something?"

Dajah blinked, convinced he misheard.

"Why do we need to talk, Dajah?" she countered. "You ignored me this long. What's a few more days?"

He slammed his fist into the wall. "I'm trying to keep us alive!"

Kiera didn't back away. "God, you don't even realize what's wrong, do you? Get out, Dajah. Go away. Anywhere but here. I don't want to deal with your shit right now."

"You're unbelievable." Nails dug hard into his palms to provide some other sensation to focus on. He slammed the apartment door shut behind him, ignoring the frustrated scream that followed. If he stayed within the training grounds another second, someone was getting hurt.

Turning down the hall, he stopped short of running into their commander.

Xant took a step back, giving him a once-over. "I was on my way to notify you charges were dropped. Caerus is looking into the background of the assassin. You're no longer restricted."

"Great." Dajah continued walking before Xant said another word.

❖

"Thought I told you—" Kiera bit off her words as she yanked the door open, ready to clock the idiot stupid enough to come back. Commander Xant stood before her.

"Sorry," she stammered, trying to compose herself in short order.

Xant's expression remained impartial. "I'm here to inform you the charges have been dropped. You're free to come and go." He didn't linger after delivering the news.

Kiera shut the door and counted to ten in silence. Then she screamed, grabbed a drinking glass, and launched it at the wall. Several controlled breaths later, the rest of her anger sizzled out.

"Aye! Comin,'" Ginny called. The Irishwoman opened the door and blinked, taking in Kiera's appearance. "Jesus, Mary, and Joseph, what the 'ell happened?"

Ginny wore pajamas – shorts and a tank top covered in horses with her hair unbound and disheveled. Kiera imagined she looked equally unkempt, having thrown on the first pair of pants and clean shirt she found. Her hair was still soaked.

"Sorry. Didn't know where else to go."

"First, how ya nae still hammered after everything *ya* drank las' night?" Ginny pulled her inside and shut the door. "Second, never apologize. Coffee's brewin.'"

Five minutes later they sat on the couch. Ginny's apartment had a more personalized layout, with expansive living room windows facing the east. The sun crested over low-rise clouds, bathing the space in orange-red highlights. Eclectic knickknacks, the occasional weapon, and bottles of whiskey decorated the main room.

Kiera summarized the latest Dajah drama through sips of a strong French roast, loathing the fact she knew he'd approve of Ginny's beans.

"So ya mad cause he tried joinin' ya in tha shower, or cause he wanted to talk?"

"I'm mad because he's the king of double standards. He ignores me the whole time we're here until *he's* ready to talk."

"Sure, 'e's got reasons," Ginny said, ever the devil's advocate.

"Yes, Ginny. Dajah's got nothing but reasons. He thinks he's been protecting me this way, but it's bullshit."

"Well," Ginny started, head cocked as she observed something behind Kiera before meeting her eyes. "Most important thing is what 'er ya gonna do about it."

Sipping coffee, she considered Ginny's words. The answer was as simple as it was obvious. That didn't make it easier to swallow. "I have to talk to him."

"Dajah cares about you. Clear as day to anyone payin' attention. Should have seen the lad when I found 'em after losing you in those trees. He would have taken on the entirety of Caerus if he had to. Heard he threatened the president. Beat up some of her guards, too."

Kiera raised an eyebrow. She hadn't heard about Dajah threatening Sasha, but rumors always spread fast among Special Tactics. She sighed. "I know he cares. I'm just not sure *why*. Sometimes I think he feels like he owes me. Like it's his fault I'm here. Ginny, you should have seen him at the cabin. He wasn't anything like this."

"Are ya listenin' to yerself?" Ginny asked. "We all know tha stories of what Caerus used to do to people like Dajah and

Elwood. Wouldna call it kind. New president's better than her uncle, but it's not like the two of ya volunteered to be here."

"What are you saying?"

"I'm sayin' Dajah's probably doin' the best he can, given the circumstances."

"By mostly ignoring me until he wants something?"

The redhead shrugged. "You're mad cause ya care about tha lad. Just talk to him, Kiera. And for God's sake, do it before we get on the bloody plane. Meantime, ya might wanna speak with Ron."

"Why?"

"I was there with Xant when we found you and Dajah half dead, but Ron saw ya afterwards. He says he knows what happened to you."

"What's that mean?" she asked, brows pinched.

"Hell if I know. Something about tha marks on yer skin. Ron's a true immortal. At least, we're pretty sure he is. He's never admitted to it, but he knows all sorts of shit he keeps to himself. And the bastard's notoriously difficult to kill."

"Alright..." Unsure what else to say, Kiera had thought long and hard about her symbols. Some of her memories were crystal clear now. Each symbol was linked to an inherent ability. She had full control over lightning and electricity when she was little. Remembering it didn't help her now.

The voice she heard when Ethan almost... It was her granma's.

"Kiera?" Ginny asked.

She shook her head. "Just thinking. I'm gonna talk with Ron."

The redhead eyed her questioningly.

Kiera found Ron doing paperwork. She knocked against the side of the open door and waited.

"I was hoping you'd pay me a visit," Ron said. "Come in."

"Ginny told me you know something about my symbols."

"I know a lot of things."

"She said that, too." Kiera took one of the chairs along the wall and moved it up to Ron's desk. "Are you busy?"

The black-skinned man gathered his pages and tapped them into a neat stack with a deep laugh. "Going over the latest weather reports. If this holds, we'll be airborne in seventy-two hours."

Regardless of the lighting, no visible shadows appeared on Ron Laurence's skin. If it weren't for the sheen on his Earth Beads, it'd be impossible to notice them without looking closely. Much like her symbols when they weren't glowing. Ron's Heaven's Dust sidesword rested in its scabbard leaned against his chair.

"I believe that knowledge needs to be gained in the proper order for it to have impactful meaning," he said. "Do you think that's true?"

Kiera hadn't come for a philosophical discussion, but she gave Xant's Second due consideration before answering. "It's true within a certain context. You can explain to a child how to drive a car, but the knowledge's meaningless if the child's not old enough to even understand what a car is."

"What do you know about the markings on your body?"

"Are you asking me as a representative of Caerus?" she countered.

Another deep chuckle left him. White teeth smiled. "Caerus doesn't know what you are. I dare say few do."

"That's not entirely true. Before I got involved with Dajah's group, my ex-boss ran a company called OPASA. He also ran Caerus's Eastern Primary Branch. Long story short, he developed a renewed interest in me recently, claiming it had something to do with my DNA. The president implied she knew something as well."

"Sasha Bekarda was raised by true immortals after her parents' death, but I'd guess even the White Team wouldn't have recognized you before now. I didn't."

"The man who attacked me said I was a threat to the Trinity of Realms."

"All knowledge in its proper time. You haven't answered my question."

Kiera thought about her childhood and sighed. "I know I had them when I was little. I was able to do things. Innate magic, I guess. My memories only started coming back in the past year. It was like I forgot about my parents and childhood entirely."

"And now?"

"I understand each symbol correlates with an ability, and using different combinations of symbols will produce different results. The energy's similar to what I feel when I use Earth Beads, but it's not the same. What am I?"

"You're Anodorian, an ancient race of powerful beings. A long time ago the *Eldarie* came to this planet to help humankind's evolution. The Anodorians were their protectors."

"What happened to them?" She decided to let the part about *coming to this planet* slide.

"Their enemies found them. The *Eldarie* were forced to flee lest they bring great destruction upon the Earth. Most of their protectors went with them, but some were entrusted with the safe-keeping of what the *Eldarie* left behind."

Another memory surfaced. Kiera raised both hands to her mouth.

"You've heard this before?" Ron asked.

"Granma Meili. Her village had a temple in the mountains. The few times I've visited she told me the temple was cursed, that to set foot within it would threaten their entire village. Given how superstitious they are, and what I know of actual curses, I never wanted to go near it. They called it 'Anodoria Temple.'"

"It's very likely the Anodorian line comes from your grandmother's ancestors, then."

Steffi was right. She needed to speak with her granma. Then something else occurred to her. "Ethan said I had a spell over me. That it cost someone dearly to cast it."

Resting his hands atop the desk, expression sympathetic, Ron said, "That's something I don't know. Perhaps you'll find the answers in time."

"How much *time* do I have? We're leaving on a suicide mission to fight an alien parasite hiding in a frozen wasteland. And I'm pretty sure it hates me."

Amusement brought out another toothy smile from the man. "Look at it this way. You're going with the people who stand the best chance of surviving it."

"Easy for an immortal to say."

"Who said I was immortal?"

"Are you?" she asked.

"Let's just say I'm old."

Kiera knew when to leave well enough alone. "What about my abilities?"

Ron shrugged, still smiling. "I don't know any Anodorians personally. From what I understand, a skilled wielder uses the energy around her to power her abilities. Sort of like a reverse Earth Bead. You're probably picking up some of that energy without realizing it every time you cast Earth magic. Does that help?"

Again, she considered his question and the way their conversation started. Did it help? It connected some of the dots while drawing a thick red line around others. Truth existed, one she wasn't ready to face and might never be. There was no point in jumping to conclusions. Dwelling on the past, wishing it was different... none of it changed the present.

"Yes," she concluded, "but not in the way I thought it would. Thank you."

Ron dipped his head. "If you have any loose ends to tie up, I'd encourage you to do it sooner rather than later."

Knowing exactly which *loose end* he referenced, Kiera took her leave.

CHAPTER 46

Opportunities to speak with Dajah were non-existent. Kiera showed up for afternoon training to find him missing. With sessions mandatory, his absence meant any number of things, none of them good.

"Where's Dajah?" she asked Elwood.

"Commander dismissed him from training today. Carley Hanes, too."

"Why?"

Elwood shrugged. "Neither were in the right mindset? Most of today's work is technical recon. Guess Xant didn't think they'd suffer from missing the lecture, lucky dogs."

Though practical, Xant wasn't a sympathetic ear. Kiera imagined Carley was still hungover after last night, but for Dajah to be in enough of a mood to warrant dismissal...

Don't do anything stupid, Dajah. Please.

Dedicating her focus to the lesson, Kiera joined several others for dinner afterwards. She saw no point in rushing to confront Dajah when he sought solitude, but it left her meal a blur. The only clear moment came when Hobbs commented on Dajah fighting monsters in the Sim Hall when he left.

Ultimately, Kiera decided to wait for him in their original apartment.

Time crawled.

When 1:30 a.m. came and went, she worried he might not

return at all.

"This is stupid. I need to just go find him."

Returning to his last known location, she found the Sim Hall deserted. Every room was dark, the computers on standby. Primary hallway lights always stayed on, but the secondary corridors operated on a motion-sensing relay system. She wandered until she spotted a light down a darkened corridor leading to the sparring rooms. Silence blanketed the area save for the hum of refrigerators from the kitchenette up ahead. LEDs activated in response to her movement.

She hovered in the threshold.

Dajah wore a pair of loose-fitting pants, no shirt, and moved barefoot through an advanced sword kata. Sweat coated his skin. His eyes remained unfocused and intense. Trance-like. Every action was precise, every movement intentional. Ron watched from the benches. He offered a nod when her eyes met his, then returned his attention to Dajah.

Never seen a man move so perfectly before.

Dajah swept his sword out fast and countered with a slow, circular block from his right arm while stepping. Each form flowed into the next like a dance. Beautiful. Deadly.

The kata went on for some time. Then Dajah bowed, facing away from the entrance.

He repeated that so many times it created a pattern on the mat.

Ron's voice cut through her thoughts. "What do you call it?"

"Doesn't have a name," Dajah said. "Just a way to direct energy through the body and enhance focus."

"I recognize most of the forms, but I've never seen those techniques combined in such a way before. How long did it take you?"

Dajah returned his sword to his FS watch and grabbed a towel, wiping his face off. "Four months to learn it. Ten years to perfect it."

"I'm honored to witness it from a master, then. Thanks, Dajah. Since you have company, I'll leave you to it."

Kiera cringed as Ron called her out and then left the two of them alone. Things worsened when Dajah merely stared, neutral.

"We can talk now?" she asked, mentally questioning how smart this was.

"What do you want me to say?"

She sensed the forced control in his tone and remembered one of her earliest martial arts lessons: *Don't counter force with force.*

"I'm sorry about earlier. I wasn't ready to talk." She dared to take a few steps closer. "You've pretty much ignored me the whole time we've been here without an explanation. It's like you decided I became unimportant." That hurt more than anything.

"You had a choice," he said. "You chose to stay with me, and now you're stuck in this. I'm not trying to make things more difficult than they already are. Xant's allowing me to stay here until we leave. You can have the original apartment. I won't bother you."

She grit her teeth. "So, you're gonna keep this shit up?"

"I'm trying to keep us alive."

Fingers curled into fists and she had to release them, letting her hands hang loose. "You think you're protecting me? Or do you not give a shit anymore? We came here *together*. Sasha knows it. Xant knows it. Our whole team knows it! Pretending to not give a fuck about me now isn't going to keep either of us alive."

He stood there. "You don't understand."

Her eyes went wide. "I understand plenty!" She didn't want to yell at him, but he was asking for it. "You have a history with Caerus. Whatever they've done to you and your brother in the past, you're afraid it's going to happen again."

"It *is* happening again." Finally, the slightest break in his level tone.

"No, it's not. We're trapped here, yes, but you're not locked up in a tiny room having to fight Queen for control, and Taron's not being tortured." A frustrated, sympathetic sigh escaped her lips. "Xant's on our side, Dajah. Even Sasha's given us more freedom than she needs to. She could have used Ethan as an excuse to imprison us, kill Taron and Chase, anything. But she didn't. You're not protecting anyone like *this*." She motioned with her hand then folded her arms, waiting for reason to sink into his thick skull.

Stubbornness rested just below the surface of Dajah's expression, but it was beginning to crack. On the verge of either freaking out or shutting down, he tried to walk away.

"Damn it, Dajah! Why won't you talk to me?"

Each step was another stab at her heart, and he showed no signs of stopping.

He wants to play this game? Suppressing every emotion except anger, Kiera removed one of the throwing knives from her watch.

She sent the knife flying, close enough to cut him. That stopped him in his tracks.

"Don't walk away from me," she warned. "If you don't wanna talk, I can think of other ways to solve this."

Dajah yanked the knife out of the wooden frame it stuck in and sent it back. Fast. She expected as much. After catching it by the handle, it occurred to her that his trajectory wasn't fatal, only threatening. There were hundreds of targets on an individual's body.

"What do you *want* from me?" he asked, voice raw. Thin beads of crimson ran from the slice in his cheekbone.

"Do you care about me?"

"I can't answer that."

"Bullshit. You *won't* answer. Because you're afraid you'll hurt my feelings, or because you're afraid of your own, or maybe Queen's? But you really can't use her as an excuse anymore." Walking over to the weapons wall, Kiera grabbed two combat knives. She kept one for herself and tossed the other to him. Dajah caught it but looked ready to leave.

If he tries, next one's going into his ankle.

"Fight me," she said.

"Why?"

"Because you need to be reminded that I don't *need* protection.

It was my choice to stay with you. I don't regret it, but I'm not continuing like this."

He started to respond, but Kiera attacked before a word left his mouth. If he didn't take her seriously, he was getting hurt. Never mind that he deserved it.

Dajah blocked her first strike easily, so she kneed him in the groin. Backhanded him. Sliced open the inside of his arm. Short of killing him, she was prepared to do what she had to. Kiera put *everything* on the line, hoping deep down she hadn't misjudged him.

Retaliation was imminent. When it came to a fight, Dajah never disappointed. He might have held back in their training sessions, but not here. Punches weren't pulled. She blocked and countered near-fatal moves while time ceased. Anger and determination kept her attacks sharp. He was faster and stronger than her; she had to fight smarter. Creating an opening was key.

A violent storm of slashes and blade scrapes followed. Kiera attacked high then low, leaving an opening Dajah went for. Moving to block, she still screamed when his dagger pierced through her forearm.

He hesitated.

Game over, Dajah.

Dropping down, Kiera took out his legs and dove on top of him, pinning his ass to the ground. She slammed her dagger into the mat by the side of his neck, cutting a few millimeters of skin, then ripped his dagger from her arm and jammed it into his opposite shoulder.

Grunting, he was smart enough to stay still. A twist from either of those blades would cause significant damage. Without magic or immediate medical attention...

"You sacrificed your arm to catch me off guard," he said. "If it didn't work, you'd be dead." They both breathed heavily.

"But it did." She kept her hand on the center of his chest, legs on either side of his hips should he try anything. "I can't fight as long or as hard as you, and I'm not immune to pain, but I've got my strengths and weaknesses, just like you. Our best chance to survive any of this is *together*."

"But you're—"

She backhanded him with a closed fist. "You're not hearing me and I'm not sure how much clearer I can make this. Pull the stick out of your ass, get over yourself, and work *with* me. We leave in two days! I can't do this without you, Dajah. But I won't do it with you if you're not with me, too."

⸻ ◇ ⸻

He stared up at her. Kiera wasn't going to let him up without another fight, and he hated to think what she'd do to herself to get the upper hand again. Blood dripped down her forearm, pooling on his chest.

"I'm sorry," he said.

"Sorry for what?" She refused to drop her guard for an instant.

"You know they're listening to all of this."

"I don't *care*! I care about *you*."

"They'll only use you. Hurt you to hurt me. It's better this way."

She dug her nails into his chest. "No. We're not children! And half our team would go fight with you if you let them. Don't you see?"

He couldn't verbally justify the thousands of reasons he had for doing what he did when Caerus got involved.

"I know you care," she said more softly. "If we're dead by the end of the week, I don't want to spend my last days fighting with you."

It was the one variable he hadn't considered.

Dajah thought beyond the island, how he'd enact his plan to rescue Taron and Chase once they left, but he never considered the possibility of no tomorrow. Tomorrow was mandatory. An absolute. It was how he'd fix everything.

Kiera knew he was trying to protect her.

But what if they ran out of tomorrows?

Moisture welled in her eyes as she pulled the daggers and tossed them. Her fingers pressed against his neck wound, staunching the bleeding.

No more tomorrow.

"I'm sorry for everything," he admitted. "I didn't want to see you hurt because of me."

She laughed through tears, slipping her hand behind his neck to help him sit up. "I know. But it's too late for that."

The reality of her words hit hard. In trying to protect her, he'd hurt her worse than Caerus could have. Wrapping his good arm around her, he hugged her tightly. Pretending like his eyes stayed dry. Pretending like holding her would make everything better. Pretending that, somehow, he could save them both.

She leaned back, taking his face in her hands and stared into his eyes. Dajah lost himself there. He wouldn't spend his last days shutting out one of the best things that ever happened. Kiera wasn't Taron, and as his brother said, she didn't walk into this blind.

He didn't deserve her.

Dajah kissed her with equal parts passion and desperation, and she returned every ounce of it. He couldn't deny her now. Not after the lengths she went to prove her point. Giving in might damn them both, but he was done playing the game by someone else's rules.

<u>PART V</u>

CHAPTER 47

"This is it. If we're successful, Caerus gives us a full pardon. You might be walking out of here as early as next week."

Taron pressed his lips together. "Believe it?"

"I believe she'll keep you alive until she's got confirmation we've succeeded or I'm dead. If I fail, you're the only one left with Queen's cells. That's worth something. She can't use you as leverage once I'm on that plane."

Taron leaned forward, maintaining eye contact. "I don't want you worrying about me when you're down there. Caerus aside, you need to take this seriously. Whether they can kill Queen or not, she'll try to control you the first chance she gets. You know she'll be pissed after not being able to communicate for almost a month."

"I know." For a moment, Dajah allowed himself the fantasy of everything going right. Then he laughed. They might not believe in no-win scenarios, but they were realists.

"Dajah, I'm serious. Don't worry about me. Worry about yourself. Worry about Kiera. But promise me you'll stay focused on what you're doing. I don't like any of this."

"Neither do I." He embraced his brother as the guards buzzed the door open.

"See you later," Taron said.

Dajah nodded, memorizing the way his brother stood there confidently regarding him. Taron always made him feel like he could accomplish the impossible. "Later, Taron."

Security escorted Dajah out, and he refused to look back as the door sealed shut. *Ten digits this time. What are the odds this all works out?*

He didn't delve further into the question because the odds were dismal. Getting in touch with Matt, giving the others adequate information to successfully infiltrate Caerus's island, orchestrate Taron's escape, and doing it without raising suspicions from his team would be challenging. Combine that with all the potential problems of Antarctica, or what Sasha'd do once they departed, and Dajah faced his most impossible task yet.

He met up with Kiera, and the guards ensured they left on the waiting transport.

"How's Chase?" he asked.

"Better than he should be. He thinks he starts his new job tomorrow. For his sake, I hope he's right. What about Taron?" Kiera was reserved when asking. She sat beside him straight-backed, palms on her thighs.

"As good as can be expected."

"And you?" Hazel eyes met his, showing more than concern. He couldn't make his smile feel genuine, but he wrapped his arm around her. She leaned against him.

Most of the team was assembled at the airbase and the mood was optimistic. Only Caerus would find people excited about a suicide mission. Time would tell how helpful all their training would be.

Commander Xant arrived last. Alone. Up until that moment, Dajah held out hope that Taron and Chase would accompany him.

Hope never stood much chance in Caerus's world.

Even if he wanted to, Sasha would never allow it.

Dajah's price for cooperation and loyalty was Taron and Chase leaving with them. Xant failed him. Now Dajah would do everything possible not to fail his brother.

Five thousand miles to figure out how to execute Plan B. Better get started.

Plan B fell apart as soon as they were airborne. The plane was shielded from all interference. Dajah couldn't get radio or satellite signals in or out except inside the cockpit, and he wasn't getting in there without major suspicion.

During the first quarter of the flight, he recalled maps of Antarctica. Countries all over the world had research bases on the frozen continent, which meant satellites and possibly Wi-Fi if they were close enough. It was a long shot, but so was everything at this point. Any message sent needed to be condensed into short, coded words the others would understand. Trying to organize all that in his head killed plenty of time.

Halfway through the flight, the alarm buzzed on his watch. Removing one of the injection pens, he clicked it into his arm and stared at the empty cartridge afterwards.

No idea if this will stop you.

Queen didn't respond.

Kiera placed her hand over his, giving a squeeze. "Hang in there."

Her words caused Ginny, seated to Kiera's right, to lean forward and peer at him. "Thinkin' ya can find this thing, Dajah?"

Before he could answer, Elwood turned around, leaning over the back of the seat in front of them. "Seriously. Can you track it?"

Dajah looked from the redhead to the colorful half-Fey. "No idea," he admitted. "Caerus thinks so. Guess we'll find out." No one advised him to terminate the injections. At this point, he wouldn't dare.

"What do you think it'll look like?" Elwood asked.

"No one knows," Hobbs said, chiming in.

"Maybe it's a blob of tentacles and fangs," Elwood said. "Met something like that once."

"Sleep with it?" Ginny asked.

The half-Fey smirked. Then Xant's voice resonated over the intercom: "Five hours till landing. Prep gear and get changed."

Five hours was plenty of time to run through systems checks on the all-terrain-transport-vehicle they'd travel in. An impressive piece of machinery mounted with enough weaponry to storm a small country, and it fit everyone comfortably. Ammunition had been preloaded on the island, but the computer systems took three people to operate and required programming once it was within a certain distance of the target destination.

Unlike the simulations, Caerus provided custom, extreme-weather clothing consisting of an underlayer and an outer. The material was breathable, easy to move in, and offered plenty of options for storing weapons and personal supplies. Everyone outfitted themselves with their favorite gear and weapons, Dajah and Kiera included.

"All right, we're on the express elevator to Hell!" Xant announced. "Back to your seats!"

The landing was smooth. Minutes after touchdown, everyone jumped into action. Fortunately, Dajah didn't have a specific job until they reached the massif. He stepped off the plane to assess their location and potential opportunities to transmit his message to their allies. The instant he had both feet on the glacier, a skull-splitting migraine blinded him.

Fuck! The intensity dropped him to his hands and knees.

"Dajah?" someone asked. He barely heard. Every sensation came muffled like his head was trapped underwater. Concentrating was impossible... until he focused on the pulsing.

What...?

He felt it through his palms, through the very core of his body. Something pressed against his mental walls. The tiniest fissure would let it come crashing through.

Queen?

Far from a presence in his mind this time around, Queen

saturated him. Weighed him down. The sensation passed, leaving Dajah with a dull headache.

The pulse continued.

That's not Queen. What the hell is it?

Something existed within the pulses. Vibrant flashes of color glimmered in his mind's eye. A *feeling* accompanied it.

It wants help.

Is it the planet?

Sitting back on his calves, he stared at frozen dirt until Kiera crouched beside him.

"You ok?" she asked, placing a hand on his shoulder.

Others stood nearby. A bullet slid into a chamber. Dajah grit his teeth, steeling his nerves. "She knows we're here," he said.

Xant moved closer. "Can you find her?"

"Yeah." With the initial bombardment over, he *could* sense Queen's general direction. "We're still far away, but..."

"But what?" Kiera asked. She rose with him.

Scanning the horizon first, Dajah settled his gaze on Xant. Three individuals stood behind him, guns drawn. *Never liked them to begin with.* They were Sasha's. Behind them, Ron kept tabs on everyone. His hand rested close to his sidearm, and if he pulled his gun, Dajah doubted *he'd* be the one getting shot.

"Xant," Dajah said, "this isn't just some parasite hiding in a cave. Queen's presence is all over this continent."

"Like she's many pieces?" the commander asked.

"No, like she's the size of Antarctica. Don't know how else to explain it."

Vance scrunched his face, relaxing the pistol grip of his battle rifle. "We're after something as big as a continent?"

Not what Sasha signed you up for?

"Size doesn't matter," Xant said, "we find her, shoot her, and verify the job's done. Everyone clear?"

A unanimous "Yes, sir!" came from everyone nearby except Dajah and Kiera.

"Get moving!" Ron ordered. "We're burning daylight."

Dajah looked at the sky; it was summer here. The sun never truly set.

"Come on," Kiera said, taking his hand.

Offering one last look at their cargo plane, Dajah didn't expect to see it again. The transport truck worked as a kind of Faraday cage in regards to Queen's influence, but they were over a hundred miles from the caves. It could only get worse.

Vance and Olivera watched him like hawks.

Opportunities to save Taron dwindled every mile.

After hours of travel, Elwood called their commander over.

"Sir, you need to see this," the half-Fey insisted.

Xant went over, face hardening. "Interference?"

She's closing in on us. Dajah didn't need radar to confirm anything – he felt it.

"No, sir, look. They're individual readings. Twenty miles out."

"What is it?" Vance asked. Xant and Elwood had most people's attention.

"An army," Xant said. "Hobbs, engage shields. Alyssia, weapons hot."

"An army of what?" Ron asked, moving closer to see for himself.

"Monsters," Xant confirmed. "What took out the first two teams. We'll churn right through them."

The situation was almost identical to one of the scenarios they trained for with one exception. As the transport closed in, Dajah saw them on the horizon. The monsters held a perfect line.

"Queen's controlling them."

A few of the others turned his way, but it was Carley who commented in a detached way. "She didn't want to be bothered."

That's one way of putting it. Dajah watched her stare at the floor, tapping her fingers on her knees.

"This thing understands tactics?" Olivera asked.

Dajah met his gaze. "She's been in my head for thirty years. I'd wager she knows more than that."

"Everyone get ready!" Ron commanded.

CHAPTER 48

The monsters held their line. Dajah identified half of the animals those creatures mutated from. Some resembled arctic foxes with glistening ice shards replacing fur. Others passed for small marsupials with exaggerated limbs and tails. Many kept marine origins, deformed by their land counterparts. Larger beasts sported four or six fins jutting out at odd angles, and various permutations of overgrown bears that shouldn't exist this far south. However, few were tough enough to withstand Caerus's rolling fortress.

A hundred yards out the beasts charged, attacking without regard for self-preservation. Massive treads crushed dozens. Screeches and screams filled the air. Gunfire followed.

The bigger creatures failed to penetrate the transport by force, but they continued throwing themselves at it. Others wielded innate magic. They bombarded the transport with everything from lightning strikes to fireballs. Enormous icicles jutted up at random. Fissures cracked open. Air exploded in shimmering fractals.

The pilots did their best to avoid obstacles. Caerus's vehicle moved fast, but it couldn't change directions instantaneously.

Smaller monsters eventually found ways inside, and Caerus's team was on point. No one flailed or panicked. They handled the disturbances with efficiency, and creatures died by the hundreds.

"We're two miles from the entrance," Elwood advised.

The pounding in Dajah's head intensified. Boom. Boom. Boom. Turning to one of the side windows, he tried pinpointing the source.

Ginny spotted it first. "Check out tha' one!"

The beast galloping at them was twice the size of their transport. A cross between mangy bear and dragon, it displayed tuffs of white fur over a scaly grey body and fangs three feet long. Its claws tore deep grooves with every step, and each footfall coincided with Dajah's headache.

Getting closer.

"Take him out!" Xant ordered. Gunners directed all available firepower at the bear-dragon, including several impressive spells cast by Xant and Ron.

Nothing slowed it.

The creature rammed the side of the transport, sending them flipping into the air. Anyone not secured to his or her seat, which was over half of them, went flying. Dajah grabbed a support rail, bracing himself between his seat and the window, and managed to grab Carley's forearm when she tumbled past.

"Hang on," he said, helping her reach the rail to stabilize herself. She looked offended, but he chalked it up to confusion. Kiera stayed beside them.

Seconds later the vehicle crashed and continued to roll, cutting a wide swath of monsters in its wake. Loose equipment and supplies banged around, occasionally meeting a body that gave a grunt or curse in response. Momentum ceased, leaving them upside down but intact.

A loud, splintering crack sounded nearby.

BoomBoomBoomBoom. Crash! The bear-dragon slammed into them again, sliding the transport downfield until everything teetered, shifted, and dropped. A jarring stop followed.

"We're lodged in a damn fissure!" Elwood yelled.

Dajah closed his eyes, pressing palms against temples. Something smacked the upward side of the vehicle, scraping metal. Explosions vibrated along the walls. A colony of tiny long-legged marsupials with rows of shark teeth invaded, going after electronics.

Another smack-scrape dented metal while a third of their team busied themselves with critter management. Dajah kicked and swatted a few, more concerned with what was happening above them. No one was in their seats anymore.

Theoretically, the tank treads could be rotated around all sides, enabling the transport to climb sheer surfaces. Frustrated gestures between Ron and the primary panel implied malfunctions or worse.

"Commander, we can't stay here," Ron advised.

A bird-like creature hopped past Dajah with broken wires hanging from its beak.

Elwood added, "Hundreds more are closing in, and *that* thing will be through the exterior in no time."

Bangs reverberated.

"Where are we?" Xant asked, calm and level-toned despite the chaos.

"Less than a mile to the entrance," Ron confirmed, blasting a group of colorful, winged mice with a flashy spell. The critters dropped dead.

"So be it," Xant said. "Everyone grab what you need."

Four razor-sharp claw tips penetrated the wall and raked massive tears through the steel. When the claws retracted, nostrils took their place, covering the gaps. Sniffing. Rancid smells wafted in, worsening when Vance and Olivera unloaded a full magazine each into the bear-dragon's head. It pulled back and roared, black-red blood spraying everywhere.

Ron led the vanguard team out through one of the side hatches to secure their escape then signaled for the others to join. Dajah climbed up onto the ice field to find an impressive Barrier holding around them. Mutated avians dove on the concave shape from above and skittered off. Emaciated wolves pawed and rammed the sides. Every impact caused a white shimmer to ripple over the near-clear surface. It was impenetrable, but wouldn't hold forever.

Dajah mentally prepared himself for what came next. Thousands of creatures spread between here and their final destination. Fortunately, the bear-dragon ignored them, determined to destroy their transport instead. Unpleasant noises echoed up from the fissure.

"Ready?" Xant asked.

Dajah counted to seven on each inhale, held it, and repeated on the exhale. Three cycles helped drown out the headache, enhancing his focus. His senses were already hyper-tuned. Pulling his katana free of its scabbard, he scanned the horizon.

"Move out!" Xant ordered.

The barrier faded.

Special Tactics trained for weeks, anticipating this very thing. They knew how to rotate formations, keeping the non-fighters in the center of their group. Still, Kiera never saw so much carnage in her life.

Earth Bead experts wielded magic to deadly effect. Others attacked with blades and guns, and monsters fell in clusters. Not every creature bled red.

Commander Xant and Ron led the team on a straight shot to the bend in the massif where the entrance allegedly waited. Everyone else kept the beasts at bay. Ginny held her own, charging her chakrams with magic and mowing down groups of monstrosities at a time. On the rare occasion her throwing blades stuck in a hide and she had to retrieve them, she showed how deadly her close-quarter skills could be.

The others were just as impressive.

When Dajah told her Caerus raised him to fight monsters, she assumed he referenced the various non-human species. This was something else entirely.

Dajah defeated dozens of beasts in the Sim Hall, but his actions on the glacier showcased his true abilities, wielding magic as fluidly as his sword. Exploiting weaknesses in his opponents with ample time to improvise, he never wasted an ounce of energy.

One minute he took off the head of some oversized bear. The next he disintegrated a scale-covered wolf with flames while blasting back an entire wave of creatures trying to flank them.

Kiera slowed, crippled, and defeated countless foes, taking out their eyes, pulverizing thin skulls, and distracting others. Rarely did she have to use her blade – the monsters never got that close – but she opted for the occasional spell, putting her Earth Bead training to practical use. The risks of Drain in battle were intensified by the hundred other things demanding attention.

They reached the cave without casualties. Xant, Ron, and Hobbs sealed off the entrance with an Ice Spell, crafting a wall over a foot thick. Creatures bombarded it, their attempts muffled.

"Won't last," Ron said.

"Give it another..." Vance started, staring at his watch. A grin spread across his face. "Four, three, two..."

The explosion rocked the foundation, showering the party in icy debris and loose pebbles. The Ice wall held.

"Nice!" Elwood cheered. Nothing attacked after that.

"Anyone need healing?" Xant asked.

Four of them sustained significant injuries during travel, mostly lacerations. Xant inspected the wounds personally, using magic on Cemond and instructing their medics to bandage the others.

Kiera used the downtime to study their surroundings. She'd seen images in Xant's lectures, but images never did reality justice. Thick layers of ice coated the cave interior, with countless crystalline arrangements. Soft light filtered in from areas still open to the outside.

Further in, snow and ice gave way to slick stone and immense caverns. Stalactites and stalagmites grew over generations, with flowstone frozen into curtains, and crystals jutting out with geometrical precision.

The cave was damp but substantially warmer than the glacier.

Several people retrieved supplies from their FS watches, illuminating the space in short order, and Kiera's breath caught. The intricacy of paths and tunnels laid before them was as gorgeous as much as daunting – a true labyrinth, with plenty of shadows where anything could lurk in the darkness.

Uninjured physically, Dajah appeared to be putting effort into concentrating. He touched the floor, nearby walls, and other structures. Kiera stepped up beside him, catching his gaze.

"I know which way to go," he said.

"What's it feel like?" she asked.

"Pressure. A heartbeat. I can feel it through the cave. It's everywhere, but stronger in one direction." Dajah turned to their commander, inclining his head. "This way."

"Don't like any of this," Vance said. "Look at this place! Beasts could be anywhere. One wrong step and those crystals will gut you."

Elwood placed a hand on Vance's shoulder. "Don't slip then, right?"

Natural phenomena carved out the labyrinth thousands of years ago. Some spaces were so large even their best LEDs couldn't penetrate every corner of darkness. Other paths narrowed considerably, forcing them to walk single file. Water dripped. Ice crackled. Tiny bits of stone randomly tinkled down ledges. The musical backdrop of near-silence was unnerving compared to the number of monsters waiting outside. It left Kiera ill at ease, and she wasn't the only one. No one jumped at shadows, but tension was evident in hunched shoulders, tight grips on firearms, and the slow, sure-footed placement of boots.

They continued downward, leaving the wider caverns, and entering a series of tunnels that branched off every so often. Dajah frequently paused to touch things.

Kiera touched some of the same things out of curiosity. Feeling nothing but the coolness of ancient rock, she wondered why

Queen would leave the caves unguarded.

It feels like a trap.

Identical passages led in opposite directions with stepping hazards and dead ends. Carley charted their progress on her tablet – the task keeping her tremors to a minimum – while Alyssia and Edward scored the walls to mark the path along the way.

The next passage funneled them into a box canyon that opened up into another cavern. Mineral crystals dotted cathedral-height ceilings, and a dozen tunnels branched off.

Xant called a halt. "Good place to set up base camp."

"*This* is a good place for base camp?" Olivera said to his buddy, Vance. "More like a good place for an ambush."

Kiera overheard a tech adding his two cents. "No other movement since we left the surface. Thermal imaging doesn't pick up anything alive down here besides us."

"You do realize that if the monsters are ectotherms, you're not going to register a heat signature," Vance said.

"It scans for movement fluctuations as well," the tech countered. "If they're ectotherms and they're frozen to the walls, then no, it won't pick them up. But if, say, they all start running for us ...."

"I get it," Vance said, waving him off.

The tech smirked and rejoined his buddies.

Dajah called Xant over to one of the tunnels.

CHAPTER 49

~ *Did you think it'd be that easy?~*

Dajah refused to acknowledge her as Xant approached, but it was absurd to think that somehow lessened her awareness. Queen knew exactly where he was. If she had the ability to control him, she would have seized it instantly.

"We've got a problem," he said to the commander. "I'm getting inconsistent readings from four of these tunnels."

"What do you mean 'inconsistent?'"

"Sensations are identical. Could be more than one correct route."

"Show me which tunnels," Xant said.

~How long do you think you can keep this up? I know you hear me.~

The passages lacked any distinctive features that suggested one was better or safer than another. Xant flashed his light down each in turn, coming to a similar conclusion. He returned to the bulk of their group and said, "We're splitting up."

Expressions amongst Special Tactics mixed from skeptical to indifferent, with several eyes finding Dajah.

"Laurence, you, Olivera, Paul, and Carley stay here," Xant said. "Secure the camp. Establish a better perimeter and find out what you can do with some of that equipment. The rest of us will split into four teams. Scout for an hour. Thirty minutes in, thirty minutes out. I want someone on radio at all times. Someone else mapping. Eyes and ears open. You find anything suspicious, anything that looks like a promising opening, you call it in. Clear?"

"Clear!" most responded.

Then Xant handpicked the teams and several men groaned. The commander's choices ensured each group had an acceptable ratio of fighters to scientists and gearheads. The cliques weren't thrilled, but social politics had little sway when lives were on the line in enemy territory. Dajah doubted a single scientist wanted to go down any of those tunnels without one of Special Tactics's fighters with them.

When Xant indicated that Kiera would accompany his group, not Dajah's, relief washed over him. He couldn't trust Queen this close. The safest place for anyone he cared about now was far away. Ginny and three others he spent minimal time with would be his companions. They shouldn't mean anything to Queen, but if she took hold of him? *Less than half of Special Tactics survive the first wave.*

He alone had a fair sense of what she was capable of, and Dajah didn't presume to understand a fraction of it.

Xant required everyone to switch their primary firearms over to anti-anomaly ammunition. The bullets acted as carrier shells, loaded with a concoction supposedly fatal to QZ-5 cells. It was a reasonable call considering how close Queen felt. Still, Dajah knew Sasha intended at least one of those projectiles for his skull. He'd take one semi-competent gearhead and two moderately skilled combat medics over her minions any day.

Kiera pulled him aside while the groups organized. He expected her to argue in favor of them being together, but maybe she understood after all.

"Promise me you'll be careful."

"As much as I can be."

The frown said plenty. She didn't like the idea of splitting up, but it was more than that. Kiera searched his eyes. He'd never acknowledge the obvious out loud, but Kiera knew Queen was up to something.

"Dunna worry, lad," Ginny said to Edward, close enough to be overheard. She wrapped her arm around the quiet man and whispered something in his ear. He smiled afterwards.

"Keep an eye on Ginny, too," Kiera said.

"I will. See you back here in an hour." The words felt like a lie. He turned, ready to join his group, and Kiera gripped his arm. Before he could ask, her hands were on his face, lips against his. Despite plenty of eyes on them, he didn't hesitate to return the gesture.

"Make sure you get your ass back to me," she said after pulling away.

"Is that a promise for later?"

"Might be. Now go." She shoved him lightly.

As commanded, Dajah led his group down the second tunnel. Xant and Kiera's team took the first one.

The path sloped upward, snaking around sharp bends before narrowing and making them travel single file. Dajah took point, with Ginny bringing up the rear. The walls were close enough he could touch them with both hands, but the ceiling rose into endless darkness.

If she sends anything, it's coming from above.

Casting a Shield Barrier above them, Dajah extended it to either side of the passage. The barrier wouldn't stop anything substantial, but it'd buy them a few seconds.

Fifteen minutes in, Alyssia informed everyone their tunnel suffered a collapse. They weren't going to make it back to base without digging or blasting.

"Continue and assess whether the route doubles back," Xant replied over their radio. "If not, warn us before you resort to explosives. The tunnels need to be assessed for integrity. Laurence, you copy?"

"Copy, sir," Ron responded.

"Have Carley scan the walls. If we need to blow something up, make sure it won't bring the whole damn mountain down on our heads."

"Seems like ya picked the borin' tunnel, Dajah," Ginny said.

"I'll take boring over the alternative."

"What's the alternative?" Edward asked. Ryan and Frank remained quietly alert, scanning the darkened abyss above.

"Let's just say we don't want to fight something in this passageway," Dajah said. "Keep moving."

Eight minutes later Ron was back on the airways: "Commander Xant, copy?"

"I copy," Xant said. "What is it?"

"Base camp's lost contact with Tunnel Three."

"Charles Green was leadin' tha' tunnel," Ginny said.

"Everyone check in," Xant ordered.

"Tunnel Four's clear," Alyssia responded. "Branches into another opening we might be able to backtrack through."

"Copy," Xant said. "Dajah?"

Unhooking the handheld radio from his hip, Dajah pressed the transmit button. "Tunnel Two's clear so far."

No response came from Tunnel Three.

After a minute, Xant's voice returned. "Five more minutes. Laurence, keep the camp secure. Under no circumstances are you to investigate. Wait for our return."

"Copy, sir," Ron replied.

Transmissions fell silent.

"Do you think another five minutes will make any difference down here?" Ryan asked.

Dajah observed the calm combat medic. Ryan was always reserved during training. He'd state opinions but never objected to going along with what was asked of him. He was the complete opposite of Vance and Olivera, and nowhere near as reserved as Paul, or as distant as Carley.

"Probably not," Dajah admitted, "but it opens up ahead. Might as well check it out before we turn around."

Queen probed again, pressed up against his walls so close that her essence smothered everything outside his mental fortifications. She wanted control. Short of that, she attempted persuasion.

~I'm not the enemy, Dajah. They are. You know this.~

You can't hear me, can you? Can't see what I see. Hear what I hear. His theory proved plausible as she continued her commentary.

~They made you incomplete, you know. I can complete you. Make you whole.~

~If you think to stop me, you'll need to be stronger. And you should know there are worse threats to your planet than me.~

The walls fell away, their path opening into a wider corridor. Ginny, Edward, Ryan, and Frank scanned for openings. Lights failed to illuminate any ceiling above them. Sighing, Dajah crouched and brushed the ground with his hand.

~Too bad your brother's not here with you. He isn't safe. Neither's Kiera. You think Vance will follow the commander's orders? Leave her alone? You'll need my help to save them.~

That stopped him, far too specific for comfort. If Caerus's injections worked the way they were supposed to... *How do you know who Vance is? Or that he's with her?*

~Why are you ignoring me?~

Either Queen couldn't hear him, or she was playing all of them for fools.

Ripples pulsed through the ground, intensifying further ahead. Queen *was* this way. He shook his head, peeling his palm off the ground, and stood. "Time to head back."

"Boring isn't so bad," Frank said, his first words since teaming up with them.

The faint reverberation of gunfire echoed up the passage.

"Dajah?" Ginny asked, hand close to the circular blades hooked to her belt.

"Came from base camp," he said. "We need to hurry."

Whatever was happening back there, Dajah felt the walls closing in. He picked up the pace until a flash of movement halted him. "Quiet. Listen."

Another gunshot broke the silence following. He unholstered his rifle, using the LED targeting sight like a flashlight. Something slithered nearby. "Whatever's attacking them, it's here, too. Be on your guard. We move slowly. Stay in line."

The passage was too narrow to spread out, but the men between Dajah and Ginny did an excellent job covering the walls as they proceeded forward.

Thin, vine-like tentacles lashed out from cracks. Dozens fell from above and ricocheted off Dajah's barrier. Gunfire exploded from his teammates. Stone pelted them every time someone's bullet missed, which was too often. Dajah dropped his rifle, drawing his katana in a diagonal strike to sever numerous offensive strands in the same motion. One of Ginny's chakrams skidded up the wall, downing others.

Hundreds more scratched and grabbed viciously at whatever they could. Edward, Ryan, and Frank switched to bladed weaponry, keeping an opening around them while percussions rained from above.

Sparing a glance for his barrier, Dajah cringed. "We need to get out of here!" Vines blocked visibility in both directions.

He cast a Blast spell, sending a three-foot fireball of white light spiraling down the passage. It disintegrated countless enemy appendages, clearing a path.

"Move!" he yelled, ready to take off.

The others stood motionless with vacant, glassy eyes. Stringy tentacles continued wriggling, but all pounding on Dajah's barrier ceased. Discarded LEDs threw unnatural shadows around the box canyon. The friction from a thousand non-snakes retreating sent a chill down his spine. Oppressive silence followed.

Four sets of eyes turned to him at once.

"You've gotta be kidding." Gritting his teeth, Dajah angled his sword across his body and considered his options.

"Don't you see how futile this is?" Ginny said. "You can't stop me. And if you won't listen, and you won't join me..." She sent her chakram whizzing at his torso.

Dajah blocked, causing the circular blade to career off several walls and clatter to the ground. He cast an instant Drowse spell, dropping Ginny mid-step. One of the others – Ryan, he thought – cast something against him. As richly hued as the combat medic's Beads were, most of the colors spanned purples and yellows. Dajah knew the spell the moment he attempted another casting – Queen temporarily disabled his magic.

Armed with machetes and knives, the men attacked.

CHAPTER 50

Kiera flanked Xant as they approached base camp. The gunfire rattled her nerves, but the eerie silence following it was worse. She doubted an alien hiding underground would attack with firearms, making one of her teammates the likely culprit.

Xant tried the radio three times. All he got was static.

Don't be Dajah. It was all she kept thinking. As soon as someone found Queen, Dajah became unnecessary. Sasha's loyalists could end him with a shot to the back of the head while he was crouched down, feeling some rock. She shut her eyes, banishing the vision, and opened them to find Elwood beside her. The half-Fey placed a hand on her arm and searched her face, concern emanating from those purple-grey eyes.

"I'll be ok once we know everyone else's ok," she assured him.

Everyone was *not* ok. The scene unfolding at base camp was the aftermath of mayhem. Ron cast a healing spell on Olivera – his wounds knitting together in seconds. They sat beside Paul, who looked visibly traumatized, and Carley, who kept wringing her hands one over the other in constant, rhythmic fashion as she stared at nothing.

Bullet holes peppered everything, with equipment strewn recklessly. Halfway between camp and Tunnel Three, the members of Charles Green's team lay motionless.

"What in the great fucking hells happened here?" Xant

demanded.

His Second answered, standing. "Best we can tell? The anomaly found a way to infect them." Ron waved at the deceased. "They weren't themselves, sir. It controlled their bodies."

A tremor passed through Carley and clarity returned to her sight. "It's true, Commander. They came out and attacked us. No explanation. No warning. They were just like the monsters."

Kiera went to her, taking Carley's hands. The woman's eyes met hers and she mouthed a silent "Thank you."

Hobbs examined the bodies. "They're dead now," he said. "What are the scratches from?"

"Might be how she infected them," Ron said with a shrug. "Your guess is as good as ours."

"We had to use the anti-anomaly ammunition," Olivera added. "Only thing that stopped them. Regular bullets didn't cut it."

"You shot them with regular bullets first?" Elwood asked, a blue-green eyebrow raised in challenge.

"*Obviously*," Olivera said. He folded his arms across his chest.

The half-Fey snorted, moving to the nearest body. "Dajah said she knows we're here. They're dead because you effectively killed them *before* you tried the anti-anomaly compound."

Olivera's hands dropped to his sides, close to several weapons. "It wasn't like we had time to reason with them. What's your point, Elwood?"

"My point, Olivera, is that if she can infect them, she can infect us." He nudged the limp body with his foot, oblivious to Olivera's scowls. "Do we have any of Dajah's drug to spare?"

"No guarantee it'll work," Vance said, adding something besides the hostile, defensive stance he took near Olivera.

"It works for Dajah," Elwood said.

"Or so he wants us to believe," Vance countered. "This was his idea to split up, insisting all these tunnels held potential. Look what happened. Where's *his* team?"

Kiera wanted that question answered, too.

"Enough," Xant ordered, trying the radio again.

Vance and Olivera stood tense, hands in easy reach of weapons while Elwood studied them with a curious tilt to his head. The half-Fey wasn't easily threatened. If it came to physical blows, Kiera'd put her money on Elwood.

Carley placed her hand on Kiera's, giving a squeeze. Kiera returned the gesture before making her way to the commander. Xant tried several locations within the cavern to get a signal, finding only static.

"Listen up, all of you," he said, checking his watch. "We wait another fifteen minutes for Dajah's teams to make it back. If they don't, we go looking together." His attention shifted to Hobbs. "Does Elwood's suggestion have merit?"

Hobbs cocked his head and paused like he was doing some advanced calculus mentally. "Not as it is. Caerus manufactured that formula exclusively for Dajah's genetic makeup. For it to work on the rest of us, it needs to be altered. I can do it, but I need time."

"How much time?" Xant asked.

"To do it properly? A few hours."

"To do it quickly?"

"Without testing it first? Maybe forty minutes."

"Now just wait a minute," Olivera demanded, throwing his hand in Hobbs's direction. "How's he gonna whip up some kind of inoculation down here? What's he even know about it?"

Hobbs looked amused. "*He* knows a great deal about it. While some of us were busy bitching and complaining, others studied that compound inside out. And I've got all the equipment I'd need right here," he said, tapping his FS watch.

"What's the downside of not testing it first?" Ron asked.

The man shrugged. "No guarantees. I'm ninety percent confident I can make it work. Once the formula's changed, it won't last as long. We'll have six hours, give or take."

No one else had the expertise to match Hobbs's and provide a valid argument against his suggestion. Except for Paul, Carley, and Cemond, the remaining scientists and gearheads were either dead or missing with Dajah and Alyssia's teams.

Kiera settled down beside Carley and sighed.

Where are you, Dajah?

Hobbs talked while he worked, reminding Kiera of her mother. The woman always spoke aloud when thinking through a riddle or assembling some complicated piece of furniture that shouldn't be complicated in the first place. It brought back a fond memory: The two of them putting together a bookshelf in the spare bedroom. No magic, glowing symbols, or blood-soaked floors, just a genuine mother-daughter moment.

I'm not dying in this shithole cave at the bottom of the world.

Kiera caught the tail end of Hobbs's explanation of how he needed to make the compound stay in their bodies in the absence of QZ-5 cells and still be able to mobilize quickly if anyone got infected. He wasn't changing the base formula – he was fusing it with a carrier.

Xant's arbitrary fifteen minutes came and went. Elwood investigated the collapse in Alyssia's tunnel, mostly scanning equipment, and concluded that explosives were too risky.

Radios continued broadcasting static.

No one returned.

Time twisted Kiera's resolve into knots. She paced the perimeter, studying rock formations and shadows. *She's watching us.* All the little hairs on her arms prickled at the thought.

"Done!" Hobbs called.

"Christ, Hobbs!" she cursed. A glare was sent to the man and the various glass bottles, syringes, and hot plates scattered around him. Others snapped to attention, a few grabbing their firearms. "Was that outburst necessary?"

He was grinning. "Absolutely. You're all acting like we're dead already. Liven up! Compound's finished, and I'm impressed with myself. Now, who's getting the first shot in the arm?"

Hobbs drew up liquid from the largest vial into a fresh syringe.

"You are," Vance said before anyone volunteered.

Hobbs rolled his eyes and stabbed himself through his clothing, injecting it. "Perfectly safe if anything. Who's next?"

Only Vance and Olivera refused the injection, and Xant didn't force them. Kiera imagined he shared her sentiment: *Let Queen have them. I'll happily bury a bullet in either of their skulls.* They pretended interest when it suited their needs, but they were against her and Dajah from the beginning. And it was no secret they reported to Sasha Bekarda behind Xant's back.

Kiera allowed Hobbs to inject his concoction into her bicep then waited near Tunnel Two. The obtrusive darkness kept its secrets, consumed hope.

Something's down there.

The rest of her team readied themselves to move while Carley received the last injection. She collapsed in spasms before the needle was out of her arm. Hobbs dropped to her side, supporting her head through a violent seizure.

"That supposed to happen?" Vance asked.

"She's infected!" Hobbs said, holding Carley down.

Shock hit Kiera like a cold shower.

Queen's inside Carley.

She's been inside Carley.

All the tremors, the unusual stares and vacant expressions... Ginny and the others attributed Carley's duality to post-traumatic stress disorder. When the woman had clarity, she was an entirely different person.

Kiera met Xant's eyes, reading the same conclusions. *She knows everything!*

Carley's episode diminished until the woman lay still, head in Hobbs's hands. After a few moments, she rolled onto her side into the fetal position and began crying.

"Hey, can you hear me?" Hobbs asked, resting his hand on her arm.

A double nod was his response. "*I don't want to be here,*" she whispered.

"What can you remember?" he asked.

Kiera moved closer to listen.

"*All of it.*"

"Paul, stay with her," Xant said. "The rest of us need to keep going."

"No!" Carley said. She wiped her cheeks with the back of her hand, determination in the look she gave Xant. "I'm ok. I want to continue. I want to end this. I need to." She rose to her feet. Though visibly shaken, she persevered. Her resolve bolstered Kiera's spirit, though Kiera wasn't sure anyone would trust Carley now.

All ten of them entered the tunnel in standard formation. Twenty-five minutes later they came upon the first body, its head and part of a leg removed. Further ahead lay two others, also missing limbs.

Ample light revealed tacky, dark puddles and crimson spray narrating the tale of a swift battle. None of the corpses displayed obvious bullet holes, but Kiera didn't look too closely. She spotted a forth body and ran to it. "Ginny!"

"Explains plenty, doesn't it?" she heard Vance remark. "Dajah slaughtered all of them. He's the only one *not* here."

Dropping by Ginny's side, Kiera felt for a pulse in her neck. The Irishwoman survived, clothes perforated with tiny cuts extending into her flesh. Her pulse beat strong.

"She's alive!" Kiera yelled, spurring Hobbs over.

He checked Ginny more thoroughly. "She's enchanted. Dajah knocked her out with magic."

"Why?"

"Because of this," Ron said, pointing out the nicks. "Same markings on the others."

"So why'd he knock out Ginny but butcher Frank, Ryan, and Eddie?" Olivera asked.

Kiera had a theory that made her blood run cold.

"Why didn't Dajah return to camp if he's got nothing to hide?" Vance fired back.

Kiera's right hand dropped close to her .45. One more word out of Vance and she'd put him out of everyone's misery. As luck would have it, he got the hint. He gestured to Olivera and the two of them lured others into a conspiratorial debate while Ron and Elwood secured the perimeter.

Paul and Carley hovered nearby, constantly looking between the groups as if none of them were safe to stand with.

When Xant finished his inspection of the other bodies, he approached Ginny.

"Commander," Hobbs said, "if she's infected we need to cure it before attempting to heal her."

Xant nodded. "Give her one of the injections. Kiera, hold her down."

Unlike Carley, there was no revolt from Ginny's body. She lay completely motionless, breaths coming in slow, regular intervals. Five minutes later, Hobbs gave the commander the go-ahead to reverse the spell.

Ginny woke with a start, flailing but grasping reality fast. She sat up, narrowed her eyes at something past Kiera, and raised both hands, flipping her middle fingers. Kiera craned her neck in time to see Vance and Olivera lowering their guns.

Christ, if they're that ambitious to shoot her, *Dajah doesn't stand a chance.* She looked back to the redhead. "Ginny?"

"Aye, t's me. What happened?"

"Hoping you can tell us," Xant said, offering a hand.

Once she was back on her feet, Ginny took a moment to compose herself. "Heard gunfire," she started. "From camp. We were headin' back then somethin' attacked us. Out of the ground, the walls... Ceiling, too." Pausing, she tipped her head back to study the darkness.

"What happened after you were attacked?" Xant asked.

Green eyes looked down at an open palm, flexing and extending her fingers before she contemplated the others. Her pupils dilated, brow creased. "Tha' part's a bit blurry, sir. Where's..." Ginny's words trailed off. Mouth gaping, she darted past them and stopped at Edward's body. "Oh, no. No, no. What happened to 'em?"

Kiera's heart went out to her, but it was Olivera who answered. "Looks like they got sliced and diced with someone's sword. Any idea where Dajah is?"

"*Olivera*," Xant warned.

Ginny's wide eyes met Kiera's, her face an open plea for forgiveness. "Don't understand it. They were all with me, not two minutes ago!"

"Ginny," Ron said, gentle but firm, "You've been unconscious longer than two minutes. You were knocked out with magic."

Ginny's shoulders slumped. "The others?" she asked Ron.

"Still no word from anyone that left with Alyssia. The tunnel's sealed. If they're still alive, they're on their own for now. As for the others..." The black man pressed his lips in a tight frown, shaking his head.

CHAPTER 51

Queen could infect others, but she controlled them only as well as the monsters – lacking the fluidity an individual typically possessed. They didn't move the way he did under her influence. That was the difference between parasitic QZ-5 cells... and him. Dajah understood that now.

However, it left him no choice but to finish off Edward, Ryan, and Frank. She wasn't releasing them, and if he failed to engage, Queen had them hurting themselves. A quick death was the only kindness available on short notice. His magic didn't return in time to save them, so he continued alone, mind racing.

What if Kiera'd been with him?

What if everyone's compromised?

What if Taron's already dead?

What if Queen gets control?

Going back held too much risk. His only hope now was to end it. The others wouldn't be able to find Queen unless she wanted them to. His tunnel branched three times, and Dajah ensured no trace of his passing lingered. When he was confident the only noises around were natural ones, he removed several communication devices from his watch.

Opportunity came too late. None of the equipment received a signal, and any attempt to transmit to satellites this deep underground failed.

Returning everything to his FS watch, he prepared to face the inevitable. *No such thing as a no-win scenario, right?* Pressing his empty palm against the wall, he let the pulses guide him.

Queen's presence grew potent the closer he got. He no longer needed to *touch* to sense her, but anyone relying solely on vision would miss the entrance to her domain. Obscured behind a curtain of flowstone, a manmade doorway was carved into the rock. Even he had to double back when the sensation lessened, exploring the area carefully to locate it.

"Looks ancient," he whispered. Beyond the open frame, a stairwell led down. Countless symbols adorned the walls, etched with precision. They reminded him of Kiera.

Emotional ache was an unaffordable weakness, so he banished it. Only one thing mattered, and it was waiting for him somewhere nearby.

Descending into a vast, complex structure, his lights were a dead giveaway to anything living. Even the quietest steps echoed loudly. He kept the LED pointed down and relied on other senses to traverse what was starting to feel like a temple.

Antarctica wasn't covered in ice when she came here.

He imagined what the land might have looked like and the people that constructed this place. The life-sized statue in the next chamber hinted at an answer. The woman depicted appeared human, styled like a typical mother-goddess. Writing inscribed around the base matched the style of symbols lining the stairwell. Behind the statue, another set of stairs led up. The faintest glow of blue light touched the uppermost steps. Water flowed somewhere beyond.

Dajah turned off his LED, letting his eyes adjust to the blue-white of the stairs. Temperatures were adequate for him to remove his outerwear – the less constricted his movement, the better – and the air was surprisingly fresh. Compared to the stale, limited oxygen of the tunnels, he could close his eyes and imagine this place high up on a mountain or out in some expansive field.

Taking a deep breath, he loaded everything except his katana and a single firearm equipped with anti-anomaly bullets back into his FS watch. Then he cast a combination Earth and Ice spell. The magic followed his intent, sealing off the room.

Should slow them down long enough if anyone makes it this far.

Time to put a face to the voice I've heard all my life.

The images he conjured since learning Queen was an extraterrestrial hadn't been kind. He placed his foot on the first step and ascended.

A grand receiving room spread out at the top of the passage. White marble floors, matching free-standing columns, and organically shaped groupings of crystals gave off plenty of light to see by. Pools of colored water flanked the marble on either side, flowing towards the back of the enormous cavern housing the space.

Earth and moisture filled Dajah's nostrils. It was the scent of the world after a rainstorm, beach-like, with faint hints of electrified gasses and a sharp, mineral tang.

He stepped closer to the edge of the marble between two columns. The water's surface sheened iridescent with smoky wisps of greens, blues, and purples rising off like colored steam. Hypnotizing. Reminiscent of oil on water, but a far cry from both. Caerus believed a Stream deposit existed somewhere beneath the massif. Queen's throne room was built on top of it.

"I'm not surprised the *Sa'Nar* calls to you," Queen said. Out loud. Hearing her voice outside his head was surreal enough. Her gaze pierced his back and he turned to meet it.

Near the end of the marble floors, a woman sat atop an elaborate crystal throne on a raised dais. His imagination was definitely unkind. Queen rose to greet him and moved closer, a perfect, flawless woman. Waves of silver hair cascaded down her back. The same green-glowing eyes Dajah and Taron shared studied him. A gown of crystal beads accented her body, tinking and shimmering with each barefoot step.

"So you've come all this way, under the orders of your enemy... for what?" She stopped just out of reach, confident and unconcerned.

Dajah stood his ground, more relaxed in her presence than he had a right to be. They might have been old friends, visually sizing up what became of the other.

"Is it true?" he asked. "Are you destroying the world?"

She circled him once, always staying far enough away that she'd have time to react if he dared attack her. Queen knew *exactly* what he was capable of.

"What did they do to you?" she asked, ignoring his question as she stepped back in front. "I can sense my cells... Communicate *to* them... This isn't the same compound from the past."

"You can't control me anymore, Queen. It's over."

Her laugh was musical. "Queen. That was a nickname long before I came to your planet. I've learned much about your Earth since then. Once there existed a people here that treated me like a god. Be that as it may, I haven't had subjects to rule over for some time. My true name is Quen'ethellia. You should hear it at least once."

Dajah raised an eyebrow and she matched his gesture.

"Ironic, isn't it?" she continued. "You blame me for controlling you when you're part of what I am. I didn't make you, Dajah. Yet you're siding with those who've forced you here and hold your brother hostage. We have different ideas of what control means."

He had to snort at that. "You're the same as them. Using me when it suits your needs."

"And how many times have I saved your life?"

"That's not a denial, Quen'ethellia. Answer my question."

Another laugh. "I'm not destroying anything yet. Your world will end with or without my influence."

"Why?"

"Humans love that word. As if everything requires a reason. Walk with me." Queen strolled past casually. He'd seen that look before on plenty of faces. Nine out of ten times it was an act. With Queen, he wasn't so sure.

What do we really know about her?

He followed to the edge of the marble. Queen crouched by the

Stream pool and dipped her fingers in. Like her, he kept a reasonable distance while she stirred the surface. Colored wisps congregated, drawn to her presence. They circled up her wrist and arm, absorbing into her skin. A faint, temporary glow was left behind.

"You view this as radiation from the heart of the planet," she said. Cupping a small amount of liquid in her palm, Queen lifted it. "Where I come from, and on many other worlds, it is known as the *Sa'Nar*."

The Say Narr? Sparing a glance at the pool, Dajah kept the alien woman in his periphery.

"The collective consciousness of all things born of and given to a planet. The *Sa'Nar* contains your planet's past, nourishes your planet, and subsequently feeds all lifeforms. Without *Sa'Nar*, this world would be dead. It's a source of much power, but it's damaging to your physical shells and thus stays buried." She sipped the liquid in her hand.

"*Sa'Nar* sustains my people," she continued. "It nourishes *us*, and we, in turn, can access its knowledge. From any source, I can gather information about your planet. I could tell you what's happening in any part of your world right now. It's how I've learned all your languages and histories, and how I can tell you that your planet's damaged."

"Why are you even here?" he asked.

"As a race sustained by *Sa'Nar*, we must constantly replenish that of our planet. We're sent out into the Great Universe from a young age to gather *Sa'Nar* from other worlds. We move from one to the next, consuming lifeforce until we can make our way back home and return that energy to *Plyanna*."

"So you're a damn parasite that feeds off planets."

"If you prefer stripped-down, simplistic explanations, then yes. But don't look so concerned. We're not monsters."

Willpower kept him from snorting that time.

Queen smiled. "We can't suck up a planet's lifeforce in a matter of weeks. Compared to yours, my people are eternal.

Generations of your kind would live and die countless times before one of us absorbed enough *Sa'Nar* for your planet to start feeling its absence."

"But I've felt the planet hurting," he said. "If you're not the reason behind it, what is?"

Standing, Queen turned to face him.

Dajah took a step back.

"You've known me your entire life and yet you don't trust me."

"Taking over my body and turning me into something I hate has *nothing* to do with that, I'm sure."

"Would you blame a fire for burning? I didn't create you, but I can help you now."

The sincerity in her voice made him trust her even less. He kept his arms loose by his sides, posture relaxed, feet grounded. From here, he could draw his sword in milliseconds. If he did, it wouldn't come with a warning. "How do you think you're gonna *help* me?"

"If I told you why your planet's dying, you wouldn't believe me. It requires an understanding of knowledge long lost. These days, only the rocks remember. Fortunately for you, the answers are all right there." Queen gestured to the pool with graceful elegance.

"You're insane," he said, though she seemed anything but. "That's radioactive."

"To your human half, perhaps. But you're a child of my cells and they require your human half to sustain them. They won't let the radiation kill you."

"You're out of your damn mind if you think I'm touching that."

"It's not a trick. Hold your hand out over the surface. This isn't the sacrilege Caerus uses on its experiments. This is pure *Sa'Nar*, and it calls to you, Dajah. You can hear it if you listen." Queen stepped back far enough that she couldn't easily shove him in.

She knows me too well. And on some level... I know her.

Logic and reason screamed in the back of his mind. Regardless, something about her words *felt* right. He didn't crouch or turn his back, but he extended his arm out past the edge of the marble. Dozens of colored, sentient wisps rose higher off the surface and licked his fingers.

A smile curled the corner of his mouth. *They're warm.* Something comforting and intelligent flowed within the Stream. *It's not a trick.* He crouched down, moving his hand closer.

"The *Sa'Nar* reacts to the cells inside you."

More colored tendrils coalesced and wrapped around his hand. Traveled up his arm. Absorbed into his skin right through his clothing. "It feels..." Unsure how to describe it, Dajah understood what he perceived and it fascinated him.

Queen put those sensations into words. "It's power, Dajah."

It's more than just power. It's necessary, intoxicating, undeniable... Inevitable.

"Touch it," she said. "Learn what's wrong with your planet. Learn who the true enemies are."

Her voice faded into the background of a waterfall. Dajah couldn't peel his eyes from the colors interacting with his hand. Each vapor tendril assimilated through his flesh, strengthening him. Fueling him. Parts of him craved more, nourished in a way he'd never experienced.

He wasn't so far gone that he thought he'd survive falling into the liquid. *Sa'Nar* or not, it was still radiation. *But what if I can access the information? What if she's right?*

"Go ahead, Dajah," she said softly, her voice resuming that melodic tone.

This is a terrible idea. He lowered his hand anyway.

CHAPTER 52

Special Tactics came across the first tunnel branch and no one could say with certainty which path Dajah took. Rather than order them to split up again, Xant removed a tablet from his watch.

"What's that for?" Kiera asked, immediately disliking the look and timing of it.

"It's a receiver coded to the tracking device in Dajah."

She dug her fingertips into her hips. "Does Dajah know there's a tracker inside him?"

"No," Xant said, impartial.

Asking if she had one was pointless – Caerus cared less about consent than OPASA ever did. As much as it was a violation, the fact that Xant received a signal encouraged her. And brought on other suspicions. "How come that works when the rest of our equipment's useless?" It wasn't just the radio static. Most electronics besides their FS watches failed. They'd turn on, go haywire, and bounce back undecipherable data.

"It runs off a different kind of system," Xant said. He took the path to the left and Kiera fell back to Ginny.

"Wha's wrong?" Ginny asked.

Kiera relaxed her face and dropped her shoulders. "Nothing that should have surprised me at this point. Just hope we find Dajah soon."

If she was being honest, it wasn't the tracking device that

grated on her, though it didn't help. Dajah made decisions based on what he thought was right at the time, and he stuck with those decisions regardless of how they affected others. He went after Queen alone, intentionally.

As a distraction from progressively depressing thoughts, Kiera focused on the intricate charges of energy traveling occult pathways through her body. All the magic cast out on the glacier vitalized her, and with excess energy came an innate understanding. She was confident she could use a handful of abilities as well as her Earth Beads, lightning especially, but this wasn't the time to test it.

The team kept their surroundings lit, checking for cracks and other openings Queen's tendrils might come through. The deeper they went without an attack, the more tension mounted.

Xant found the stairwell.

"Well *this* is a bit ominous, no?" Elwood said. "What do you think all this writing says?"

"Something along the lines of, 'Abandon hope all who enter?'" Hobbs said. "Who puts stairs underneath a mountain range?"

"Those who delve too greedily," Elwood said, grinning.

The half-Fey was probably right. All the same, Kiera couldn't imagine Queen as some hairy little dwarf. Someone's light flashed on a particular symbol and she was immediately drawn to it. "Wait! I know this one."

The others paused with her.

"What?" Xant asked.

Kiera couldn't explain where the knowledge came from. Reaching out to brush her fingers over the symbol's indentation, it lit up in a white-blue glow as soon as her skin made contact. The effect rippled outward. Within seconds, the entire passage was illuminated, with brighter lights coming from below. Kiera's symbols glowed faintly in response.

"The hell'd you do?!" Olivera demanded.

"I didn't *do* anything! I just touched it," Kiera snapped back. Electricity buzzed at her fingertips, ready to be unleashed.

"No one touch anything else," Xant ordered.

"She turned on tha' lights," Ginny said. "Kinda helpful, I think. Makes this place a wee less gloomy, no?"

"And announces our presence to anything down there," Vance said.

Xant got them moving before it came to physical blows.

"This place was built by the *Eldarie*," Ron said, stepping up beside Kiera.

"Distant cousins of yours?" Elwood asked him.

"Hardly. Their spirits are restless here. I can sense them."

"Do you think Queen's one of them?" Kiera asked.

"No," Ron said confidently, "but as one of their guardians, this temple will respond to your presence. Be careful what you touch."

"Little late for that," Kiera said under her breath. Ron smiled. His brief explanation made it sound like the *Eldarie* were a peaceful type with Earth's best interest at heart, but Kiera got the feeling that whatever this temple was built for was forbidden. Like Granma Meili's warnings about Anodoria Temple, she didn't want to be here.

The stairs ended at a palatial entrance. Crystal chandeliers gave off the same white-blue glow as the symbols, illuminating the space in detail and rendering LEDs unnecessary. Clean lines, high ceilings, and geometric patterns made the place look ancient as much as futuristic. From crisp corners to patterned arches, every surface was smooth to the point of being glass-like – a striking disparity compared to the caves they'd come from.

"Cities used to exist all over the world where ancient people would go to learn from the *Eldarie*," Ron explained.

"You think a whole city's under here?" Carley asked.

"No," Ron said. "This is... something different."

"Something's creating interference," Xant said. "I can't track Dajah. Last reading suggests he's a floor above us. Keep your guard up. Eyes open. Anyone sees another set of stairs you do *not* go further. We're going to..."

Kiera followed the commander's line of sight as he trailed off. A man stood in the threshold of another doorway. Wearing a monk's garb with a crystal pendant necklace, his ethnicity was difficult to place. Light filtered through him without casting a shadow. His eyes found hers and the monk nodded before turning back down the hall.

"Restless spirits," Ron confirmed.

"Are we supposed to follow him?" Kiera asked. "He stared right at us."

"Kiera and Laurence with me," Xant said. "The rest of you set up a perimeter. Four-by-four. See what you can find but do *not* engage."

The three of them followed the monk, crossing into the temple's monastery where a bizarre scene unfolded. Living quarters, a central dining area, and a kitchen were all populated with apparitions seemingly reenacting their daily lives.

Every room thrived with ghosts, and it was eerily silent. Women brought meals with visible steam out to the dining room. Groups of children waited at tables while others played. Monks performed menial tasks, one of them sitting in a corner reading to three wide-eyed kids, another carving soapstone in the form of some beast.

The absent aromas and noises had Kiera looking to Xant and Ron to gauge whether they witnessed the same thing. Their observant, scrutinizing gazes said yes.

One of the girls ran through Xant, oblivious to his presence. The crystal-wearing monk saw them, though. He stood beside an empty table, watching.

"Kiera, try and talk to him," Xant said.

"Why me?" she asked.

"Besides the fact that he's staring at you? The symbols on the walls reacted to your touch."

"They could have reacted to anyone who touched them."

"They didn't react to my touch," Xant said.

Kiera looked to Ron for backup. He shrugged.

"Fine! Just... fuck, watch my back." With a slew of warnings running through her head, she avoided the path of other specters on her way to the monk.

"I know you see us," she said to him. "Sorry if we've intruded, but we're looking for a friend who passed this way."

The monk held his hand out to her. Kiera glanced back, and Xant went so far as to nod like she had his permission to interact.

She recalled some of her brother's lessons on dealing with spirits. Protocols existed, steps one took to ensure nothing went wrong.

What are the odds Sammy's advice applies to the ghosts of aliens?

The monk waited patiently, hand extended.

Kiera couldn't remember a single helpful thing from her brother. She reached for the monk's hand. Nothing physical remained to grasp, but coming in contact with his silhouette caused every symbol on her body to flare brightly. She snatched her hand back and the monk motioned to the table.

She shook her head. "You think I'm one of your protectors, but I can't join you right now. I have to find my friend. Have you seen someone else come this way? About my height, silver hair?"

"Sir!" Hobbs called from down the hall. He approached the scene.

Xant's voice snapped him out of his open-mouthed stare. "What is it, Hobbs?"

"Sir," he repeated, "we found something you need to see." His eyes met Kiera's and his head tilted.

"Alright," Xant said. "Kiera, get back over here."

Following orders allowed her to excuse herself from the monk's presence and filled her with relief. "If I can come back later, I will. I have a lot of questions, things I don't understand, but right now I have to find my friend. He's in danger."

The monk bowed his head and went to join the spirits at a different table. Kiera scanned the location once more, ensuring Dajah – or Dajah's ghost – wasn't among the dead.

They found the room sealed off by a wall that didn't belong.

Besides the way it stood out compared to the walls of the temple, Earth magic left certain patterns when used to create structures.

Vance and Olivera had plenty to say about Dajah's wall.

"Carley, Paul, and Cemond stay here," Xant said. "You'll secure our escape. Whatever's on the other side of that wall isn't going down without a fight, and you'll serve us better here."

Paul *could* fight – Kiera'd seen him in action – but he wasn't on the same level as the others. Carley and Cemond were decent shots with a gun, but were liabilities in a true fight.

Paul can safeguard them well enough, and if he can't...

Electrified magic sizzled the air. Ron plunged his sword halfway into the wall and began carving out an opening.

Kiera pulled the commander aside. "Sir, just so we're clear, we're not gonna do anything to Dajah, right?" People she absolutely mistrusted armed themselves with ammunition fatal to half of Dajah's DNA.

"We're here for Queen, not Dajah," Xant confirmed. "As long as he doesn't interfere, he's got nothing to worry about."

And if he interferes? She didn't dare ask. Xant harbored no ill will towards them, but he'd see this through at any cost. If it meant sacrificing his entire team to get the job done, he'd do it without hesitation. *I've got too much to lose now. I'm walking out of here with Dajah, even if I have to drag his unconscious ass halfway across Antarctica.*

Ron finished his magically-charged slicing and a heavy rectangle of ice and dirt crashed inward. The opening was big enough for two at once, but they'd go single file. Xant stepped onto the fallen piece of wall and entered the chamber first.

Everyone spared a glimpse at the statue as they passed it, continuing up the stairs. The room at the top was grandiose, and certainly appropriate for a creature that called itself Queen, but it wasn't Queen sitting on the throne at the back.

Kiera's heart pounded in her chest. Radiation surrounded the marble floors. Rushing water echoed from the back of the cavern. All of it was secondary to the man on the throne. His eyes glowed brighter than she'd ever seen them. Form-fitting, silver-white armor adorned with glowing green veins replaced Dajah's uniform.

The eyes and the armor weren't even the worst part.

Where the hell did he get wings from?

Two sets of black, raven-feathered wings jutted out of his back, accented with the same silver armor. He sat comfortably with one leg over the side and the other bent at the knee. The pose and the smirk were quintessentially his. So was the Heaven's Dust katana naked in his left hand.

"Dajah?" she asked, taking a step forward. Everyone else held their ground.

Casually, Dajah dropped his legs and stood. "I think I'd make a good king, don't you?" His smirk was wrong. The group fanned out in defensive formation.

"Dajah, where's Queen?" Her level voice surprised her. Inside, Kiera was anything but controlled. *Someone tell me I haven't lost him completely.*

"Doesn't matter," he said, approaching. "She's not the problem."

"What did she do to you?"

What kind of aliens have wings like that?

"She gave me power. Now I suggest you all turn around and leave if you want to keep your heads."

"Dajah, whatever she told you it's a lie! Come over here. Help us destroy her."

"Last chance," he said.

Please don't do this! Tears welled in her eyes.

"Dajah," Xant said, "if you don't stand down you're leaving us no choice but to stop you."

"You'll try." Pushing off his back foot, Dajah sprinted the remaining distance, sword angled for attack.

Olivera and Vance opened fire. The invisible shield more than a yard out from Dajah's body deflected every projectile. He closed in on Vance first. Before the man had a chance to defend,

Dajah's katana fell in a swift strike, slicing off three-quarters of Vance's head. The body toppled limp and lifeless, blood and brain matter oozing onto the marble.

Madness unfolded and Kiera watched with horrid fascination. Olivera shot from multiple angles, but bullets failed to penetrate Dajah's shields. Elwood and Olivera pulled bladed weapons, engaging Dajah in direct combat.

"You need ta be snappin' outta it!" Ginny said, taking her arm and shaking it.

"I have to find a way to help him, Ginny. They're gonna kill him."

"No, they're not," Xant said. "We prepared for this contingency. Help us find Queen. Killing her is the only way to sever her connection to Dajah. If you get involved with them, he'll only attack you, too."

Kiera's eyes darted back and forth between the fighters. Having been the farthest from Dajah to start, Hobbs cast several spells. The magic was neutralized instantly and countered with powerful attacks. Columns crashed around them. Dust and rock sprayed into the air. Dajah held his own against all four of them and these men were *not* amateurs. One wrong move, one failed block...

Waving, Hobbs yelled to her. "Go! Buy us time!" He dove behind a fallen column.

"Fuck!" she cursed, peeling her eyes away. "Let's find this bitch and kill it."

"There's a path behind the throne. This way," Xant said.

CHAPTER 53

They moved strategically to keep from becoming targets in the battle against Dajah. A series of crystal platforms floated behind the throne. It was the only other direction to go in.

Xant jumped on the first platform, testing its balance. "Watch your step, ladies."

The overlarge step-stone path connected with a passage in the back of the cavern, and the surrounding currents churned, racing through an opening near the tunnel. It was the source of the waterfall noises – cacophonous, with high-pitched tings of metal carrying over everything.

Someone screamed and Kiera missed her next step.

"Whoa!" Ginny yelled, catching her arm.

Wispy tendrils rose off the surface, circling Kiera's dangling arm and unbalanced leg before falling back. She checked herself, regaining balance. "Thanks."

Another cavern three times as big as the chamber above opened on an expanse of black sand and a lake fed by the waterfall. The colors given off here were rich and stunning. Crystal geodes in the ceiling far above reflected those hues like psychedelic, twinkling stars. Whatever otherworldly beauty the space might have held was negated by the woman standing waist-deep in the lake.

"If it isn't the fledgling Anodorian whipping the ancestors into a frenzy," she said, glowing green eyes taking in Kiera. No one could mistake the resemblance.

"What'd you do to Dajah?" Kiera asked, staring her down.

The alien laughed. "I didn't *do* anything to him. I'm not controlling him. He's doing what he's doing all on his own."

Ginny and Xant exchanged glances. They were up to something, so Kiera kept the alien verbally engaged. "That's not Dajah. He'd never attack us."

"That's *all* Dajah. The cells he shares with me have finally been nourished properly. He attacks his true enemies."

Pulling her machete from its scabbard, Kiera simultaneously drew the SIG from her hip holster. "Hope you know you're going to die down here." She fired off a test round of anti-anomaly compound at Queen's chest, expecting the same barriers Dajah had.

The bullet punched a hole through the alien's gown, right where her heart would be if she was as human as she appeared. Queen cried out, covering the wound with her hand. She stumbled back once, twice, and fell into the lake.

Xant and Ginny took positions around the shore, both wide-eyed.

"Kiera, ya just—" Tumultuous laughter echoed off the radiation, silencing Ginny.

"Guards up!" Xant yelled.

An enormous root-tentacle surfaced and smacked down on the shore, causing everything to tremble. As thick as Kiera was tall, the appendage tapered down into an oscillating, dexterous weapon. A second and third crashed down. More followed until a dozen-plus tentacles of varying sizes occupied the beach, walls, and blocked the only visible way out of the cavern.

No one hesitated to open fire.

The center of the lake seethed. From its depths rose a vertical, disc-like creature over twenty feet in diameter. Twelve radiation-soaked wings jutted out at angles that would make flying anatomically impossible. Smaller, vine-like tentacles framed the edges of the disc, rattling and hissing like snake tails.

Queen's human half grew out of the center from the torso up. Crystal scales radiated out from her body, coating the front of the disc in geometric swirls. There was no way to know how deep the bulk of her form went below the surface, and Kiera couldn't see around it. That didn't stop her from identifying numerous targets. She hit all of them, hoping to find a weakness. Lingering fear dissolved into purpose. All that mattered now was destroying the monster in front of them.

Combined, they emptied six magazines of anti-anomaly bullets into Queen's core before a shockwave of energy knocked everyone off their feet.

"Watch it!" Ginny yelled, rolling in time to avoid being crushed by one of the larger tentacles.

Kiera ran, dodging as the alien made various attempts to ensnare her. After slicing through several thinner appendages, she reloaded her .45 ACP. Nothing seemed to significantly damage Queen, but the hope was that Caerus's chemicals would do the job once they got enough inside her.

She used up every anti-anomaly bullet in her primary and reserve stashes, sending the majority of spread into Queen's humanoid parts. Xant and Ginny did the same, but it still came down to physical blows. Swords, knives, chakrams... even conventional ammunition. With everything they threw at her, the alien was unconcerned. Amused, even.

She's toying with us!

Queen caught Ginny in one of her skinnier tentacles, wrapping the Irishwoman so tightly Kiera heard bones snapping. Hurled into a wall, Ginny hit hard and landed just shy of the lake.

Xant risked Drain to cast a healing spell on her. Before he recovered, another tentacle sent him skidding sideways until he struck rock.

The Irishwoman stirred.

Kiera sliced the next tentacle in half with a frustrated scream. Static sparked around the handle of her sword.

Dajah froze. Abhorrent, blind rage abandoned him for confusion and pain. He dropped to his knees, grabbing his head with both hands as mind-numbing throbbing raced from the needle embedded in his neck.

As his head cleared, he saw Ron, Elwood, and Hobbs. All were critically injured but standing. Lying several feet away was Olivera, his head bent to the side and Dajah's katana protruding out from his chest. The throne room was destroyed. Chunks of floor were missing. Columns toppled. Blood splattered everywhere.

"Dajah?" Ron asked, sidesword in hand.

Dajah pulled the syringe out of his neck and tossed it. Parts of the battle stayed fuzzy, but he knew it wasn't the first time they injected him. He also knew how close he'd come to killing them. With the amount of magic wielded, there should have been significant Drain. Right now he felt... nothing. He cast a Full Heal over his companions.

"Think he meant to do that?" Elwood asked Hobbs.

"Yeah, he did," Dajah said.

"Dajah, what the fuck happened?" Elwood asked. "You *you* again?"

"For now. The cells..." Searching inward, Dajah appreciated Queen's mutated, lingering cells. They thrived off the energy provided by the *Sa'Nar*. The Drain couldn't touch him, but it was only a matter of time before he lost control again.

"Forget about the cells," Hobbs said. "We got a job to do. I can give you another shot, but we don't have much left and I'd rather save it for Queen."

"What the hell'd you inject me with?"

"A risk," Hobbs admitted.

"Xant had Hobbs studying both the formula Caerus uses to block your connection to her and the anti-anomaly compound since day two," Ron explained.

"Part hobby, part necessity," Hobbs said, shrugging. He pulled the katana out of Olivera's body and offered it handle first to Dajah. "Get your ass off the ground. The others went this way."

They couldn't access the lower cavern. Something heavy and organic blocked the tunnel, with quakes and gunfire erupting from the other side.

Ron pulled his sidesword, casting a spell that made the blade sparkle. He was ready to slice into the blockage.

Dajah held his hand up to stop him. "I've got a better idea."

❖

Kiera knew they were surviving more than they were harming Queen. The Irishwoman pointed out a spot on one of her primary tentacles that appeared necrotic. Closer inspection identified other changes in the alien's flesh, but the compound worked too slowly. Queen's amusement was fading by the second.

Tentacles and shockwaves effectively halted most advances, while crystal shards materializing around her core provided an additional challenge. Slivers flew with dangerous accuracy. It was thanks to the last-minute Shields Xant cast that none of them were fatally skewered.

Crystal shattered against Kiera's barrier. *Won't last much longer, and if Xant casts another spell it's gonna kill him.* A few collapsed boulders offered cover for her to shoot from.

The commander faltered then doubled his efforts, unloading rapid-fire projectiles. When his automatic rifle ran dry, he threw his sword like a javelin. The blade lodged into Queen's side where her human form joined that mutated weed-ball of a core.

"You'll pay for that!" she hissed, sending dozens of shards in Xant's direction.

His barrier shattered, several crystals piercing Xant's torso and limbs. Kiera unloaded her last magazine, but it wasn't enough to stop the appendage from enveloping Xant. His body disappeared in writhing loops. A muffled scream followed the snap-crack of bone.

"This is our chance, lass!" Ginny yelled.

They ran.

Casting an Ice spell over the surface of the lake, the Irishwoman created a solid, slippery path to Queen's core. She raced up it with Kiera close behind and slashed deep into the alien's human torso with both chakrams.

Kiera willed all excess energy out her hands, coating her weapon in electrified death. She thrust it between where she believed Queen's ribs were and ripped away. Gooey bits of organs leaked from the gash. The alien roared, blasting Ginny off the platform with a concentrated energy wave. A slew of tentacles headed Kiera's way.

The first three missed. The fourth swept her legs out from under her and she hit the ice, sliding to the edge. Others pinned her fast, slithering beneath and around her body, lifting her into the air. The muscular coils wrapped again and again, leaving only Kiera's head exposed.

Malice reflected in green eyes too similar to Dajah's. Breath fled Kiera's lungs as the alien tightened her hold. She couldn't breathe. She couldn't scream when ribs cracked and pain raced through her.

Use it!

The voice wasn't hers, but she understood. Every symbol flared. Every point of contact between her body and the foreign appendage became an energetic conduit. She fried Queen's tentacle so completely it disintegrated around her. Rancid, burnt flesh filled the air. Kiera fell, landing on Ginny's ice platform. Lightning bolts continued to spark off her. The alien hissed foreign curses.

Breathing hurt, but adrenaline kept Kiera on her feet. She remembered Ethan's use of stolen Anodorian abilities. *The discs! I need the discs!*

Again, voices spoke in her head: *You're not ready.*

I don't care! Kiera sheathed her sword and flung both hands out, palms directed at the human imitation. She concentrated, reflexively pulling energy from the world around her. Flat, spinning discs of light manifested in front of her hands. With a burst of willpower and determination that cost everything, the discs sailed towards their intended target.

Black oblivion consumed her.

CHAPTER 54

Dajah entered through the opening in the waterfall, trailed by colorful vapor tendrils that longed to feed the alien cells within him. Queen hadn't so much controlled him as the cells controlled themselves. Caerus's drugs, combined with Hobbs's modified compound, continued to obstruct the full bond.

A quick inspection of the scene told a story. So did Queen's frustrated litany of curses as she glared at the unconscious, symbol-glowing body on a platform someone created with Earth magic.

Ginny and Xant laid motionless on the beach.

"They're not dead ?" he asked, landing on the shoreline.

Silence fell upon the alien. Glowing green eyes narrowed in Dajah's direction, studying him. "The others?" she asked.

"Dead."

"That took you long enough, Dajah."

He snorted and walked to Xant, crouching down to check for a pulse. "He's alive." Ensuring his tone stayed neutral, he caught Ginny lifting her head several yards away. Dajah met her gaze and smirked. Then he ran his sword through Xant's chest.

"No!" Ginny cried, summoning the alien's attention.

Queen made no move to attack her, more curious about Dajah's actions. He felt her eyes burning into him, her presence saturating, trying to find an opening to repair their connection, to *know* she could control and not just command him.

Dajah pulled the katana out of Xant's body and headed over to Ginny. Her attempt to crawl away was pathetic. At least one of her legs had bone fragments twisting out through a mutilated calf. The rest of her body wasn't much better.

"You're really trying to reach that stupid weapon?" he asked.

Ginny dug her fingers into the sand, pulling herself inches at a time. Reaching the lone chakram first, Dajah stepped on it.

She tried prying it up regardless. "Don't be doin' this, Dajah!"

She'd get one last look at his sparkling blade and silver-white armor before his katana pierced her back. He pulled it free.

"Finish this one as well," Queen said, motioning to Kiera with her human hands. "She's a threat to both of us."

Dajah flicked the blood from his sword, starting towards the platform. He kept his observations subtle, noting numerous places on Queen's body where wounds healed slower than they should with her half-submerged in *Sa'Nar*. Her tentacles undulated with anticipated victory.

"Kill her, Dajah." It was a plea as much as a command.

"I can't do it here. If she falls off, the *Sa'Nar* might heal her. She's not fully human."

"I can see what she is!" Queen snapped. "Take her to the shore and finish her."

Grabbing Kiera by the ankle, Dajah took to the air and dropped her on the beach. She never flinched when his sword went through her chest, but her symbols dulled, going out one at a time.

"YES!" Queen roared.

Methodically, Dajah pulled the weapon free, flicked it, and sheathed it.

He kept Queen's attention. If she'd been more observant, she might notice that none of those bodies bled out. One of her thicker tentacles rose for him. Dajah landed on it and bowed deferentially, wings folded back. "What now, Quen'ethellia?"

"Now you'll go back to Caerus and destroy them."

"Shouldn't I stay here and protect you? Others wait in the temple."

"Annihilate them on your way out."

"As you wish." Dropping to one knee, he palmed the syringe strapped to the back of his thigh and offered his other hand out to her. When Queen extended hers in turn, he took it and stood, placing a delicate kiss on the back of her hand.

I'm not your puppet anymore.

They both knew she let her guard down. Dajah held tight and jerked her body towards him, stabbing Hobbs's syringe into her neck. This close to her brain, the effects should be immediate.

The alien screamed, sending out a shockwave that blasted Dajah into the air. He landed on the platform, drawing his sword.

"What is this, Dajah?!" She pulled out the syringe, crushing it in her hand. "How dare you!"

Queen bludgeoned his mind with wave after wave of forced control. Chemicals combined with Earth magic proved superior, and as soon as she realized he was mentally untouchable, her eyes darted past him. She wouldn't find bodies on the shore. By now, the others would have Kiera, Xant, and Ginny inside the passage, tending to whatever injuries his spell-charged sword left behind.

Dajah attacked. Queen's attempt to bat him aside resulted in the loss of two tentacles. A third destroyed the Ice platform, propelling him into the air. He was still inside her guard, driving another diagonal slice across her body. Queen manifested a crystal sword in time to block, and they exchanged blows in rapid succession.

Her crystal matched the durability of Heaven's Dust, and Dajah's wings complicated matters. If they stood on solid ground, the battle would have been over before it started. Queen limited his openings as he adapted his fighting style to air-combat. She threw everything she had at him: Shockwaves. Tentacles. Crystal. Magic.

Fear must be a new sensation. You're getting desperate. And you should be afraid of me.

He reinforced his barriers every third hit, dodging when attacking wasn't an option. Crystal shattered to Dajah's left. Sections of ceiling crumbled at random. He needed to be tactical. Coming at her again, one, two three different advances were parried. The alien fell for his next feint and he sliced deep into her side.

Queen threw up her tentacles, creating a thrashing, deadly hindrance to reaching her core again. Switching styles, he opted for a dive-and-retreat approach, swooping in at one angle, slashing or clipping whatever piece of her presented itself closest, and retreating.

The next shockwave threw his trajectory and a tentacle smashed him against the wall. His armor took as much of a beating as the cavern did. Neither would hold up forever. Throwing his hand out, Dajah blasted a hole through the tentacle and flew in, scoring lines of crimson through several appendages along the way.

They locked swords. He didn't need to win the power struggle, only get inside her guard again. Dajah twisted his body so the angle of his katana caused Queen's sword to slip off. She would have had an opening if she knew better. Instead, he ducked another tentacle and whipped his blade back around.

She was in time to block, but alien-enhanced crystal was ultimately no match for Heaven's Dust. He cleaved her sword in half, lodging his katana deep in her chest. The wound bled profusely when he pulled out. Necrotic discolorations spread. Queen's shriek pierced his eardrums and the cavern exploded with magic and crystal projectiles. Extremities flailed violently, smashing anything they could. *Sa'Nar* splashed and roiled, wisps coming off in short strands.

Dajah put distance between them as his last barrier failed. Before he could cast another, falling rock clipped one of his wings. A thicker appendage broke his fall. Then Queen ripped it out from under him. He dove towards the beach.

She caught him just as his feet brushed sand. Yanking his

sword up, he sliced into the tentacle without the leverage to severe it. Another slimmer, dexterous appendage trapped his arms by his sides and slammed him into stone.

Ammunition bombarded the alien.

Further down the beach, Ginny and Xant stood beside Ron and Elwood, each hale. They used every weapon they had left, and the color changes on Queen's flesh were unmistakable. She released Dajah from her tentacle, leaving three of his four wings broken. He didn't bother assessing the damage to the rest of his body.

Kiera and Hobbs rushed over when he landed.

"What do you need us to do?" Hobbs asked.

Dajah's eyes fell to Kiera. She was breathing, moving, alive... There wasn't time for explanation or apology, so she'd have to accept a genuine smile in exchange. "It's spreading. Keep damaging her as much as possible."

Bright hazel eyes met his and she nodded, drawing her sword. "Let's finish it then."

Dajah sprinted to the nearest tentacle, the others following his lead.

Queen's wounds didn't heal – they turned rancid. A single bullet ate away holes like caustic acid. Any laceration paralyzed entire tentacles. Her human half greyed, and the massive, disc-like structure forming her larger body rotted around the edges. Wings went limp. Vine-tentacles wilted. Her attacks came as manic, desperate attempts to bring the massif down on them.

Casting a targeted Heal on the wing opposite his functional one, Dajah returned to the air. Chunks of rock crashed into the *Sa'Nar*, turning its colors dark with Queen's blood.

"Kiera, make me a window!" he yelled, dodging collapsing pieces of cavern.

Using a heavier caliber rifle, Kiera took specific shots at the alien. It wasn't enough to get the raving creature's attention until everyone joined in. They blitzed her, giving Dajah the opening he needed. With a clear path, he dropped between flailing tentacles and shriveling wings to land on the bulk of her form.

He rammed his magic-charged sword straight into her body, and these weren't healing spells. Fractals of energy exploded in white-purple fireworks within and around the alien. The verbal response was deafening — screams and percussions erupted one after another. Dajah pulled his katana free and flew back to the beach.

Tentacles collapsed where they were, disintegrating from the tips inward. Queen's alien form fell apart, dissolving into the *Sa'Nar* as her humanoid body attempted to reach the shoreline. She crawled onto the black sands, dripping radiation. From the cloudy crystal beads of her gown to the diseased, necrotic skin, missing clumps of hair, and oozing wounds, there was no question the alien was dying. Caerus's drugs prevented even the *Sa'Nar* from healing her.

Dajah moved closer. Identical green eyes stared at one another.

"*Why?*" she asked, voice weak. Foamy saliva trickled out from cracked lips.

"Because this planet doesn't need you feeding off it, and I'm done being your slave."

He took her head with one clean, swift slice.

CHAPTER 55

Kiera kept a white-knuckled grip on her sword as Dajah approached the dying alien. His katana ended her with a single blow. The head lolled aside. The body deflated. Parts of the cavern crashed around them, splashing into the dark, muted lake.

She spared a glance for the others. Bleeding, bruised, hurting... alive. Queen bled out a thick, ink-swirled crimson and her body disintegrated. The final vestiges became indistinguishable from the black sands.

Dajah collapsed.

"No!" Rushing to his side, she skid to the sand on her knees and checked him. Pulses came too slow. Visible skin was pale and clammy. She peeled up one of his eyelids to find his iris dull, like the life had been sucked out. "Dajah, wake up!"

Hobbs appeared moments later, examining him with a medic's eye.

"What's happening?" she asked. Dajah failed to react to any of the reflex tests Hobbs administered. "Is it the Drain? Did he use too much magic fighting?" Slipping her hand into Dajah's cooler one, she squeezed. *He's dying, isn't he?*

"Best guess?" Hobbs said, lowering the penlight from Dajah's non-reactive pupils. "Something's happening to the QZ-5 cells in his body."

Queen's death was supposed to mean freedom for Dajah. Any

time Kiera questioned what would happen beyond this point, her answers came as foolish optimisms. Now she questioned everything.

Geodes crashed beside her, kicking dust and sand into the air. The entire massif was falling apart. All Kiera wanted was to look into those green eyes, see that smirk that made her want to kiss and smack him at the same time.

She did smack him, hard, with her free hand. "Dajah, get your ass up. Now!"

"We need to go," Xant said. "Laurence, grab Dajah."

Ron crouched beside Kiera, placing a firm, comforting hand on her back. He met her eyes and then scooped Dajah's limp body into his arms, positioning him over his shoulder. "We do need to go."

Another set of hands pulled Kiera to her feet. "Come on!" Ginny insisted. "Dunna be makin' me smack ya, Kiera. Ya know I'll do it."

Sense and reality registered. Dajah wasn't dead, but they'd all be soon if they lingered much longer. It was time to clear the cavern. Fast.

Queen's throne room was decimated. One of the last columns crumbled right in front of Kiera. Ear-splitting cracks echoed everywhere. The quick-draining pools meant the support wall containing the waterfall lost all integrity.

They squeezed through Dajah's magic wall into the temple, finding Carley in a puddle of cold blood, her throat sliced open. Paul's corpse rested propped against one of the crystal lamps. The entry wound in the side of his head suggested he never saw it coming. Cemond was nowhere to be found.

Elwood checked both bodies and shook his head. Magic had its limitations. "Monsters didn't do this, sir," he said to Xant, as if it wasn't obvious.

Kiera was too focused on the unconscious man draped over Ron's shoulder to care much for the argument that ensued. Cemond was one of Sasha's men, though easy to forget compared to the likes of Vance and Olivera.

"Why would he kill them? Carley and Paul posed no threat," Hobbs said.

"Doesn't matter," Ron said. "If we find that creepy bastard along the way, they'll see justice. Elwood, grab her mapping tablet. We need to move."

Dajah's critical, unresponsive state provided plenty of motivation for Kiera to keep going. So did the instability of the tunnels. Even after leaving the temple, flowstone and other formations broke and fragmented with each passing tremor. Fortunately, the more distance they put between themselves and Queen's grave, the labyrinthine structures stabilized.

It was a small comfort.

Elwood had taken point, leading with Carley's tablet. He paused at the next intersection, shortly after they passed the bodies of Charles Green and the others. The half-Fey stabbed the tablet with his index finger repeatedly.

"What's it now?" Ginny asked, stepping up beside him.

"Battery's dead," Elwood said.

"Whatcha mean 'battery's dead?'" Ginny took the device, going through similar motions. "Don't it have a backup charge?"

Kiera's heart threatened to burst out of her chest. She moved to Ron and checked the mess of black feathers and silver armor that was Dajah. He was still out cold.

"Let me see it," Hobbs said. The Irishwoman placed the tablet in his waiting hand and Hobbs did whatever Hobbs did. "The entire system's corrupted."

We shouldn't be standing here! Any minute Kiera expected mutated beasts to fall on them, or another tunnel to collapse.

Hobbs offered the tablet to their commander. "Sir, it's useless."

"Carley wouldn't have corrupted the damn thing," Ginny said.

"She might have," Ron said. "The anomaly affected her. For all we know, she's the reason none of our equipment functioned properly."

"Forget the tablet," Xant said. "We marked the route."

Any doubts that Cemond murdered Carley and Paul in cold blood evaporated the instant they entered the next batch of passageways.

"Seriously?!" Elwood ran his fingers over the etched markings they placed on the way in. Identical markings existed on every opening and rock.

"This took time," Ginny said. "He must'a left as soon as we entered that damn throne room. Why bother?"

Ron uttered some curse in a language Kiera never heard before.

Xant tried his radio. Static answered.

"Anyone remember which way we came?" Hobbs asked, pulling out a fluorescent pink paint stick.

They agreed on a route. Hobbs marked their path, but after circling to the same passage three times, the commander called a halt.

"Take five," he said. "Current section's stable enough."

Dajah knew which way to go. He made it seem so direct... Kiera didn't realize how many alternate routes dead-ended or spiraled back on themselves. They even stumbled on paths lacking markings, having to backtrack. It would have taken days for any team to chart a way to that temple without Dajah.

As things stood, it'd take a healthy dose of luck for them to find a way out any time soon. Xant was right to break. With the tunnels mostly stable and no immediate threats, they could all use the respite.

Ron laid Dajah out on the ground and Kiera sat beside him, pulling his head into her lap.

"Thank God," Ginny whispered, leaning against the nearest wall. She slid down it with an exhausted sigh and sat.

Hobbs and Elwood found outcroppings wide enough for their asses. Everyone's clothing was ripped or torn in some way. Despite healing, at least some of Kiera's ribs were still broken. Other injuries and aches manifested the longer she sat, and her team didn't look any better. Ginny was covered in bruises, with an angry welt on her left cheekbone. Xant put on a good show for the rest of them, but Kiera saw the way he winced or held his side when he thought no one was looking.

Then there was Dajah.

Combing her fingers through his matted, bloody hair, Kiera inspected his body. The unusual armor cracked in countless places, with missing sections exposing deep bruising or lacerated, raw flesh. Green veins previously running through the material were hollowed-out rivulets.

Ron removed a bottle from his FS watch and insisted everyone take a drink. Kiera sipped the bitter tonic and passed it on to Ginny. Food and beverage were foreign concepts. She couldn't recall the last time she ate anything or felt hungry.

The cave fell quiet. Exhaustion blurred five minutes into forty. Only Dajah's condition kept Kiera conscious. She checked his pulse routinely and stared at his chest until it completed a full rise and fall. When he started trembling, she wrapped him in a thermal blanket.

Hobbs broke the silence. "Anyone hear that?"

"Hear what?" Elwood asked drowsily. "You interrupting my peace and quiet?"

"There it is again," Hobbs said, sitting up. "*Listen.* Something's coming."

Kiera hoped it was Cemond. She'd break every bone in his body starting with his fingers. The president's last lackey killed two innocents and sabotaged their escape for what? Barring further catastrophes, they'd find their way out eventually. Their FS watches held enough rations and supplies to last a month. Cemond merely delayed the inevitable.

"Footsteps," Ron said, standing. The commander followed suit.

Kiera dropped her hand to the sword sheathed at her side. Eight men in full arctic gear rounded the curve, stepping into their light. They moved in disciplined, military formation, weapons ready.

"Sir!" one of them shouted. Lowering his rifle, he approached

Xant.

Cautious optimism washed over the commander. "Riggly, that you?"

The man removed his mask and pushed back his hood. His uniform was unlike the ones Caerus provided Special Tactics, but appeared adequate for the environment. Xant's expression softened as they shook hands.

Riggly asked, "This everyone?"

"Everyone that made it," Xant said. "We lost contact with the others after a collapse over twelve hours ago. No reason to believe they're still alive."

No reason to believe they're not. Kiera frowned.

The rest of Riggly's team spread out to check on them.

Kiera gripped her sword's handle, her other hand reaching protectively over Dajah's chest as two men approached. "He needs help," she warned. *We survived too much for Sasha to pull shit at the end.*

"I'm not gonna hurt him, Kiera." She questioned how he knew her name, then recognized the silver braid slipping free when he removed his head gear. He felt the side of Dajah's neck while removing his Earth Beads. "How long's he been like this?"

Kiera stared at Taron, trying to make sense of the impossible.

What'd Ron make us drink?

"Kiera?" the other man asked, only his voice was feminine and sounded exactly like Steffi's. That's when she knew she was hallucinating.

Taron used Dajah's Beads, casting a proper group healing. Kiera flinched as bones snapped back into place. The white-hot sear of accelerated healing closed tears in her flesh and rebuilt muscle in hyper-time.

Dajah's physical wounds mended in seconds, but he didn't wake.

"What happened to him?" Taron asked again.

Ron stepped in. Healed, the dark, muscular man was a force to be reckoned with. "He took off Queen's head and passed out. You should be in a cell seven thousand miles from here. Xant, who are these people?" It was the first time he questioned their commander outright.

"Taron? It's really you, isn't it?" Kiera asked, tears wetting her cheeks.

He nodded. The man beside him removed his mask, revealing himself to be Steffi. Behind her, Matt.

"How?" she asked. "How are you all here?"

"Your friends at Caerus put trackers inside both of you," Matt said. "Gary hacked the signal as soon as we got here."

"Gary's here?" she asked, scanning the remaining masked individuals.

"Well, not *here* here," Matt said.

"Hate to spoil this reunion," Xant interrupted, "but if we don't get out of this cave and off this hunk of ice in a hurry we're gonna have bigger problems."

"What are you talking about?" Elwood asked.

"Secondary Objective. With Paul and Carley dead, I can only assume Cemond left to give the president the confirmation she needs."

Ron's height grew as he straightened. "Confirmation for *what*?"

"Confirmation of the anomaly's location. President Bekarda will send a modified hydrogen tunneling missile with additional anti-anomaly compound to finish the job."

"That's why he did it," Ron said, more to himself.

"Why who did what?" Elwood asked.

"Cemond," Ron answered. "He needed to slow us down in case Queen corrupted us. To make sure no one else left the massif. Ten to one the orders came directly from the president."

"Maybe we should be discussing this *while* we're moving," Matt suggested. "We've got hovercrafts and a plane waiting outside. Shall we?"

CHAPTER 56

The hovercrafts pulled into the cargo bay and they took off the instant the loading ramp closed.

Kiera tried making sense of what happened. Xant arranged for Taron's escape. If Cemond's mission was real, there was no way for Taron to get off the island, arrive in Antarctica, and find them in the middle of a cave maze in time.

And Chase was nowhere to be found.

"Everyone grab on to something. This won't be pretty!" Gary's voice sounded over the speaker system. As the plane became airborne, a high-pitched whistle cruised past.

"That'll be the first blast," Xant said. "We might have ten minutes to get as far from here as possible."

Kiera's emotions were all over. *Sasha didn't trust us to stop Queen, only to find her. Now she's burying Antarctica. A missile like that will spread anti-anomaly compound everywhere in the fallout.*

The aircraft jerked. Crates broke open. Melons and cases of bamboo paper formed deadly projectiles. A rogue package bounced loose and collided with the side of Hobbs's head, knocking him out. One of Xant's buddies caught him before he went rolling.

Queen's getting the last laugh after all.

Xant counted the minutes out loud. At eight, the supersonic blast wave hit, followed by a high-velocity shockwave. Kiera's eardrums ruptured, buzzing a painful tone through her brain.

Gravity shifted and they plummeted through the skies. It was due to the skill of the pilots and the spells Ron and Taron cast that they didn't crash into the Weddell Sea.

Martin announced their attempt for an emergency landing on some unpopulated island off the coast of Argentina.

"We can glide," Gary added. "Still got wings, so we're taking this baby down. Hang on!"

Wings. Dajah's wings hung around him as limp as the rest of his body while he remained oblivious to the world. Kiera stayed close, with his brother on the other side.

Everyone braced.

The wheels snapped on impact, sending the plane into an uncontrollable skid. Two of Xant's friends went sailing into the air. One crashed into a wooden pallet. The other managed to grab some bindings and stabilize himself.

Dirt and trees rushed past the tiny windows, scraping. Kiera clung tightly to Dajah until friction brought them to a halt and smoke overtook everything. Flames followed. Instead of evacuating in a hurry, someone cast magical protections so they could all discuss what should happen next.

Given the fact that Caerus had monitoring satellites all over the southern hemisphere, Xant agreed with Matthias's suggestion to fake their deaths. Kiera stared absently at Gary and Martin, this being the first time she'd actually met them in person, and watched the hackers-turned-pilots rig a device to incinerate the interior of the plane.

Everyone left under cloaking spells.

They were deep into forest when the BOOM made Kiera recoil. Her hand dropped first to her empty thigh holster, then to her sword's handle. Black smoke curled up from the crash site, ensuring Caerus would spot it.

"Get to the easternmost side of this island," Matt instructed. "I'll meet you there in a little over an hour. Maybe two."

"Where are you going?" Riggly asked.

Matt grinned. "If you think for a second Caerus assumes you're dead without proof, you're wrong. I'm going to secure some bodies. Which reminds me. I'll need some skin and hair samples from each of you."

"Trust him," Steffi said. "He can get almost anything."

Several questioned how he'd procure bodies on a deserted island, but no one objected to losing a few strands of hair before Matt headed towards the smoke. Gary took over leading. Mars and Gunner carried Dajah now. The remaining survivors of Special Tactics fanned around them with Xant's personal crew, and Kiera put one foot in front of the next.

A mile in, Dajah started seizing.

"Hold up," Gunner said. The twins set Dajah down and Hobbs checked him.

"His condition's deteriorating."

"Let me see him," Steffi said, coming over. Peeling a piece of armor from his forearm, she sunk her fangs into Dajah's wrist. It took seconds for her to assess him before her eyes went to Taron. "The alien cells are out of control, killing off his human ones."

Kiera's heart was beating rapidly again.

Steffi's lips curved down in grim acknowledgement and Kiera saw a lifetime of sadness in their depths. "They're the only things keeping him alive. Too few human cells are left to sustain him."

She doesn't think he's gonna make it.

"I might be able to slow them down," Hobbs said. He clicked through his watch, scrambling for solutions. This wasn't Hobbs's usual, calculating focus. "How much time do you think he has?"

"Not enough to make it off this island," Steffi said.

Taron's brow furrowed as he studied his brother.

"Can we buy him more time with magic?" Ron asked.

No one's helping him! Kiera's eyes darted between those gathered. Dajah didn't need a committee; he needed action.

"No," Steffi said. "Earth magic can't selectively target cells within an individual. I don't know of any magic that can."

I do.

Kiera climbed on top of Dajah and laid her palms flat against his chest before she second-guessed herself. Energy leached into her from the surrounding landscape and she could name each drop – Yerba mate, water lily, dirt composed of dozens of unique essences, oxygen... The symbols on her skin surged with power.

Heal, heal, heal. She repeated the phrase silently, willing intention through her palms. Dajah's lifeforce opened to her. She saw every channel, every connection beyond the physical, and she understood. Queen's mutated cells were ravaging what was left of his body.

Ancestors, help me!

Multiple voices spoke in unison: *You cannot heal this. The connection is broken. A binding agent is required.*

Kiera poured energy into him, trying to stabilize what remained. "Hobbs, can you make something to reverse what Caerus's drugs did to him?" She didn't dare take her eyes off Dajah's pallid face.

"Probably. What good'll that do?"

"We have to restore the connection between his human body and his alien cells. We need a binding agent," she said, unsure if anyone would comprehend. She wasn't even sure *she* fully understood it.

"Turn him," Ron said.

Kiera peeled her eyes from Dajah to observe the pseudo-immortal.

"You're a pureblood," he said to Steffi. "The virus you carry binds cells."

"It doesn't just bind them," Steffi said, "it corrupts them. Infects them. My blood hasn't been pure for years."

Will it work? Kiera asked the voices.

It carries great risk.

"Do it, Steffi. *Please.* They said it'll work."

"Who said it will work?" Steffi asked.

"Just trust me. He's dying. I'll make it work!"

Dajah's essence slipped further from the world of the living.

"She can do it," Ron said, voice portentous.

"Fine, but I can't make a vampire instantaneously. Get a tarp and move him onto it. Remove as much armor as possible. The rest of you need to go. Wait for Matt at the coast."

A hand touched Kiera's shoulder. She looked up to see Ron standing there. "Release what you're holding onto. We need to prepare Dajah."

Kiera sat with Ginny while Taron and Ron removed Dajah's armor. They had him stripped down to his base Caerus layer in minutes. Each section of armor discolored the moment it was separated from Dajah's body, becoming brittle and fragile.

Hobbs and Mars stayed. Xant led the others away, wishing them luck.

"He needs to lose enough blood that his body's not going to fight this," Steffi said. "Once he's infected, if it takes, he'll need blood to replenish what he's lost."

"He can have mine," Taron said.

"No, he can't. You've got alien cells inside you, too. He doesn't need more right now."

"He'll have mine," Kiera said. "It'll help with the transition." Again, she knew the truth behind her words without understanding it.

"Are we talking about a transfusion?" Hobbs asked, pulling out a medical kit. "Do you need to worry about blood typing?"

Steffi shook her head. "Not for this."

"I'll place an IV to make this easier," Hobbs said, approaching Kiera.

"Now, Taron," Steffi said.

While Hobbs stuck a needle in her forearm, Kiera watched Taron slice both of Dajah's wrists down to the arteries. *He's so weak already. This is insane!*

Steffi sampled Dajah's blood periodically, anything but

reckless. "We're close. Taron, give me your knife. Kiera, whatever you're going to do, get ready." She placed her hand on Dajah's cheek. "I wouldn't do this for anyone else but you or your brother. I hope it saves your life."

Turning his head, Steffi bit into his neck. Kiera knelt beside them. She knew Steffi's virus wouldn't be able to corrupt Queen's cells. Somehow *she* had to forge the connection.

Her symbols flared.

Steffi pulled back and cut across her forearm. Lifeblood essence glowed in Kiera's mind, leaking out of Dajah's wrists, oozing from the wound in Steffi's flesh. She solidified her connection with Dajah as Steffi placed her wound to his lips. A thin bead of crimson ran from his mouth against a pale cheek.

Kiera saw double. On the outside, Dajah's response was non-existent. Inside, a war raged. Luminescent sparks multiplied, spreading rapidly through his system. They touched his human cells, infecting some but not all. His alien cells were enveloped in chromatic prisms, repelling any attempt the sparks made to gain access.

Kiera weaved Anodorian energy through Dajah's essence, strengthening his connection with the living while she felt her own lifeforce weaken. She pulled harder, transmuting energy from everything around her and channeling it.

Others whispered and gasped in the background, raising concern, but she wouldn't break her connection until the task was complete.

"Bandage him and start the transfusion," Steffi said.

Kiera's Lifeblood flowed into his arm, bathing the warring energies within. She glimpsed the connections, watching a delicate balance form between human and alien, sustained by the essence of ancient bloodlines.

His heart beat stronger. His color improved.

Steffi's voice grew distant. "Whatever Kiera's doing, we can't use any other magic on him for the next thirty-six hours. That's how long a full transformation takes, and we can't risk giving the alien cells an advantage."

Ron's voice sounded in Kiera's mind: *Push any harder and you'll upset the balance. You need to stop.* She realized his hand was pressed against her shoulder. Dajah was closer to the living than the dying, but not by much.

He's stronger than you realize, Ron prompted. *Let him be.*

Kiera pulled her hands back and every glowing symbol on her body extinguished. A wave of exhaustion passed over her. She faltered and nearly fainted, caught by Xant's Second.

"How?" she asked weakly.

"Rest," Ron said.

Kiera closed her eyes, hearing helicopters in the distance.

"We're cloaked, but all this isn't," Taron said. "We need to move them as soon as it's safe to do so."

"How's this friend of yours planning on getting us out of here without Caerus noticing?" Hobbs asked.

"And how's he plannin' on gettin' these bodies for the plane?" Ginny added. "Caerus'll go straight for the smoke first. Then they're gonna be right over us, tryin' to figure out what made this big patch of dead stuff."

Mars answered them. "Knowing Matt? He's got the bodies staged by now. Wouldn't worry about that."

"*How?*" Hobbs insisted.

"He's *donasdogma caosgo nax,*" Ron said. "A procurement demon."

"What language is that?" Steffi asked.

"Enochian. I'm assuming he'll use demon portals to extract us. There's a neo-vortex pull to the east."

"How do you know that? Are you demonkind, too?" Steffi asked.

"I was around long before their kind."

"Seriously?" Hobbs asked. "What the hell are you? We joke about your immortality, but I've never met anyone else like you before."

"And you probably never will," Ron said.

CHAPTER 57

Pain suffused every aspect of his being, unbuffered by adrenaline. Unshielded, nerves burned and frayed. It hurt to breathe. Hurt to move. Once the initial acuteness of reality faded, Dajah found himself weak. Moving a finger took more effort than it was worth. Pounds weighted down his eyelids. For moments he was unaware of who he was, or why he was... wherever he was. He was blind if he couldn't open his eyes, and none of his senses functioned correctly.

Someone breathed nearby, but context was relative. The noise could have been right beside him or miles away. Or in his head.

I'm hearing myself. I'm the one breathing.

The realization brought uneasiness when he couldn't pair it with other information. Defaulting to basics, Dajah willed himself to stillness and became more aware of his body. Lying flat on his back, his limbs were splayed out. Temperate air and soft lighting surrounded him.

Where am I supposed to be?

Antarctica, Special Tactics, Queen... He remembered taking her head and turning around to face Kiera. Then every cell in his body spasmed, and he couldn't recall a damn thing between then and now.

I'm not dead. Death isn't this uncomfortable.

Attempting to muster adrenaline failed and Dajah groaned. He settled for opening one eye. Then the other. A drab, beige flatness hovered before him.

Above me. I'm lying down. The ceiling's above me.

"Dajah?" someone asked. He couldn't place the voice, only identify its general direction.

"Kiera?"

"Don't tell me you hit your head *that* hard," a woman said. "We look nothing alike."

Turning his head used up additional energy, but it was worth it to see Steffi standing a few feet away. "...how?"

"Long story," she said. "First, how do you feel?"

Like shit. Dajah favored quick, snarky responses, but opted for truth. "Weak."

"You almost died. We had to take some drastic measures to save your life. I need you to drink something."

Certainly feels like Death breathing down my neck.

He wasted more energy failing to lift his arm. "Am I really this weak?"

"Partially. You're also tied down to the bed."

Snorting, he saved his muscles additional effort. *Because when am I not tied down after some incident with Queen?* The name triggered an immediate reflex – Dajah searched within for any trace of the alien's presence and found none. Focus shifted to the Styrofoam cup Steffi held near his face. She bent the straw for him.

"Drink this, Dajah."

The fastest way out of bed without creatively escaping his restraints required cooperation. Expecting some bad-tasting herbal tea, Dajah sipped thick liquid. He'd tasted enough of his own blood to recognize the metallic undertones, but this was more than blood. At least, it didn't taste as bad as blood did when pooling in his mouth, and it *did* make him feel better.

He finished the cup before Steffi took it away.

"How about now?" she asked.

"Better, I guess. Still shitty. Why am I drinking blood?"

A wry frown turned her lips. "We didn't have another option

at the time. Your alien cells raged out of control. There were more than I've ever tasted in your blood now that I understand their signature. They were killing off your human cells."

"So you turned me into a vampire? I don't... feel like one."

"We tried to. Honestly, I don't know what you are. Kiera did something to bridge the connection between your human and alien cells. My virus acted as the foundation for that bridge. The alien cells haven't taken over but they're still there. You're not a vampire in the classical sense. I'm not even convinced you're one by half. Still, your body didn't reject the blood. That tells me plenty."

"Kiera did something? Where is she?"

"Out walking with the redhead."

"Ginny? Why?"

"Because we have no idea what kind of side effects you'll experience. Right now your body's weak but stable. You need to feed the transformed cells. If you don't, the alien ones may attempt to gain the upper hand. Some of your cells remain human. Whether the virus will turn the rest of them in time..." She shrugged, offering a warm smile. "We had to make sure you wouldn't wake up, run off, and bite the first human you came across. If the blood lust had you, I wasn't going to let anyone else be the first person you saw."

"Way too many words, Steffi. Can you just untie me?"

"Are you feeling any urges to go around and sink your teeth into someone's neck?"

"No more than I want to run around and stab them with my sword." He managed a subtle smirk.

Steffi eyed him skeptically. Dajah narrowed his eyes right back.

She gave in, unlocking his restraints. "Don't make me regret this."

It took all his regained energy to fold his legs and sit up on the bed, feeling somehow lighter. Before he could ask, Steffi said, "Your wings disintegrated." Something about her tone was off, but he saved his strength for relevant questions.

"Where are we? How long was I out of it for?"

"We're in Iowa, and you've been unconscious for three days."

"What the hell are we doing in Iowa? ...and who's *we*?"

"Matt brought us here using a demon crossroad portal. Your commander arranged for Taron to be taken off Caerus's island by some people he trusted. Taron contacted us, and Matt diverted his closest plane, gathered everyone with the portals, and we flew down to Antarctica.

"The only reason we found you was because Caerus put tracking devices inside you and Kiera. Believe it or not, your commander had his own tracking device. One of his friends had the encryption keys. Gary hacked the code, boosted the signal..." She trailed off with a wave of her hand. "Don't worry. We removed the trackers."

"Everyone made it?" he asked.

"Everyone who survived Queen. Taron's in the other motel room with the rest of our crew. Your Caerus team left shortly after we arrived except Ginny. She and Kiera left for their walk an hour ago."

Dajah processed her words slowly, taking it all in. A *lot* happened since he passed out in Queen's cavern.

"I'm going to get Taron," Steffi said. "Stay on the bed."

Taron stood in the doorway, leaning against the frame. "You look like shit."

Dajah snorted.

"If it's any consolation, you've looked worse."

"What happened on the island? How'd you get out of that cell?"

"Xant came to talk to me when you were on lockdown. I made a few suggestions and we reached an understanding. All I had was the man's word. Fortunately, James Xant's honorable. His word's good. I *told* you not to worry about me."

Dajah stared at his brother. He was supposed to interpret *that* from Taron's departing words in the cell? "I've seen Xant stand up against Bekarda for us, but I don't understand why he'd go against her orders and release you. Was she in on it?"

"Doubtful," Taron said. "She planned on blowing up Antarctica as soon as she knew where to point her missile. Guess Xant didn't like the idea of dying unnecessarily. He had men loyal to him outside of Caerus, but none of them are Matt. We insisted on bringing our crew, evening the odds."

"So she blew up an entire continent?"

"Leveled a substantial chunk of it. Matt helped stage everyone's death. It's not over with Caerus, but we've bought ourselves time."

"Guess I owe you one."

"You owe me plenty," Taron said, the very hints of a smirk forming, "but Kiera and Steffi saved your life."

Dajah took a deep breath, meeting the green-eyed gaze of his brother. "Where do we go from here?"

EPILOGUE

en days later...
Kiera knew that bigger cities made it easier to disappear. Matt set them up in a condo owned by someone he trusted, and Steffi put them in contact with a woman who'd ensure a steady supply of Dajah's now-essential dietary supplement.

Steffi believed Dajah required blood to sustain balance within his cells, and that he'd have at least a few vampiric side effects from the infection. Beyond that, it was anyone's guess.

Kiera bent some cosmic law saving his life, and she still didn't understand all she had done. Ginny told her afterwards how the ground around them shriveled up and decayed. Living plants turned to ash. The air grew stagnant.

The voices Kiera heard, those she assumed belonged to ancestors past, wouldn't speak to her now, and any attempt to connect with her Anodorian abilities failed. But Dajah was alive. It was a small price to pay for an ancestry she knew nothing about.

Ginny and Taron stayed with them, helping to make sure Dajah didn't neglect his human side while he took his daily dose of crimson. He hated how slowly he healed – Kiera saw it every time he drank blood or grew fatigued with minimal effort. Whether he'd recover his full strength in time, they needed to be wary of blood frenzies and other warnings Steffi laid out in an extensive list of what Dajah should and shouldn't do.

So far he stayed in control.

When Ginny told her she was leaving, the news hit hard.

Can't blame her. Now that Dajah's stable, I'm sure she's anxious to go home.

The day was bittersweet.

"Are you going back to visit or stay?" Kiera asked.

"Visit for sure. Stay?" Ginny cocked her head and her pupils flickered for an instant. "Depends on what I'm findin' when I return. Kiera, if you need anythin,' call me. I'll be there. It's what friends do."

Kiera hugged her, fighting down tears. "You're the truest friend I've known in too long."

"Yer not too bad yourself," Ginny said, returning the hug. "When that lad of yours is back to normal, come visit."

"We will." Releasing the hug, Kiera memorized the woman before her. "Before you go, there's something I gotta ask. What's your real name?"

"You're askin' now?" Ginny laughed.

"Everyone calls you Ginny," Kiera said, shrugging. There was never any sense to who was called by a first name, a last name, or a nickname when it came to Special Tactics. "Never questioned it, but if I find myself in Ireland and want to look you up..."

"Einin Mac Giolla Mháirtín of Waterford," she said.

"That's... pretty. Where'd Ginny come from?"

"Long story, aye? Come to Ireland and you might find out. Anyway, Ginny's a lot easier for most of ya to say."

"That's true. I'll miss you, Einin Mac Giolla Mháirtín," Kiera said with perfect pronunciation.

The Irishwoman raised an eyebrow.

"My granma's English isn't flawless. It's made me master foreign vowels with a knack for accents."

Ginny hugged her once more. She said her goodbyes to Taron and Dajah, then climbed into the waiting taxi.

Alarms set the windows and doors to Dajah's rooms. He didn't blame anyone for the extra precautions, but so far he suffered none of the side effects Steffi warned about. The routine blood drinks probably helped. Being almost dead was an understatement. The real test would come when he felt whole again.

That night, much like the others, Kiera sat on the edge of his bed while he changed. He watched her contemplative reflection in the mirror as he pulled on a sleep shirt. Her head tilted, eyes distant and thoughtful. Without Queen or Caerus to ruin things, Dajah allowed a measure of hope that their relationship could last.

He wanted to take her into his arms and satisfy her in every way possible.

They refrained from intimacy for the same reasons Dajah slept alone – Steffi worried close emotional contact this soon after transformation might trigger some vampiric impulse. Unconvinced, Dajah respected the fact that Kiera and Taron cared about him. They remained cognizant, so he remained patient. Gave it time. Kiera wasn't going anywhere.

"Dajah," she said. "I've been thinking a lot about Antarctica since Ginny left. Haven't asked because... I don't want you to get upset with me."

He turned to face her. "Why would I do that?"

"Because I doubt it's something you wanna talk about."

Taking a breath in, Dajah joined her on the bed. "What do you need to know?"

"What really happened with Queen? Why'd you go off on your own? Turn into some asshole in crystal armor with four black wings. Do you remember any of it?"

Though Dajah learned more details about what happened after he almost died, no one asked him what led up to the confrontation. He assumed they figured he couldn't recall details, or that bringing it up might trigger the alien cells.

"I remember all of it," he said, releasing a sigh. "We were in a narrow tunnel when she attacked. Offshoots of her tentacles ran everywhere inside that mountain. She injected the others with her cells. Controlled them. She couldn't control me because of Caerus's drugs. I managed to knock Ginny out, but Queen didn't leave me a choice with the others." After a thoughtful pause, he said, "I was the only one able to get close to her."

"What happened when you found her?"

"We talked."

"You *talked*?"

"Can't explain it, Kiera. Been hearing the woman in my head ever since I can remember. I *had to* talk to her." He couldn't put what meeting Queen in the flesh meant in words.

"So what'd you talk about?"

Dajah spent the next few minutes describing what Queen told him about the *Sa'Nar*, her people... "She said she wasn't the real reason our planet was dying."

"Of course she'd say that to manipulate you."

"She told me answers existed within the *Sa'Nar*. That I could tap into it, understand the energies the way she did because her cells coexisted inside me."

"Didn't Caerus use that radiation to try and enhance the abilities of their test subjects?"

He cringed inwardly at her choice of wording but didn't take it personally. "Yeah, but I couldn't stop asking myself, 'What if she's right?' She had to go – she'd never stop trying to control me while she was alive – but what if she *wasn't* an immediate threat to the planet?" Dajah met her eyes. "I couldn't take the chance."

"So you touched it, and then tried to kill us."

All he could do was nod.

She leaned in, wrapping her arms around him, and kissed him on the cheek. "It's ok. You're a good person, Dajah. You wanted to make sure Queen was wrong."

This time Dajah forced his smile. *Not that good of a person.*

Queen implied the *Sa'Nar* had answers, but he stuck his hand in because it was a potent, intoxicating lure of power. *Can't promise I won't do it again if I get the opportunity.*

He'd never admit that to her.

"Get some rest. I'll make breakfast in the morning." Kiera left with a smile, pulling his door shut. At least one of them felt better.

With his brain in overdrive, obsessing over how many ways things should have gone wrong, it took hours to fall asleep.

The dream came.

*

Dajah crouched near the Sa'Nar, reaching his hand into inviting depths. A flood of information saturated his senses. Invaded his mind. Overwhelmed everything. No one could make sense of that much knowledge.

His alien cells thrived off the radiation, influencing his thoughts and mutating his body.

For an instant, the unfocused chaos of the Sa'Nar became crystal clear in the form of a voice:

"Hey, little brother."

Dajah couldn't see Zayan, but he felt him. Thriving, whole... at peace.

"Sorry for everything you've had to go through," Zayan said. "I'm so proud of you, though. And don't be too harsh on Queen. I begged her to help me end it. To not tell you or Taron. Couldn't handle any more of their tests. Selfish of me, but I worried if either of you knew ahead of time I wouldn't be able to go through with it. Sorry you had to be the one, but I'm eternally grateful. Don't worry about me, ok? Everything's gonna work out just fine, D."

Dajah's vision cleared and he found himself before an ancient stone door with red symbols. The markings reacted to his awareness badly. Negative, ominous foreboding pulsed out in waves, making him nauseous. The sensations were so potent and toxic, they annihilated his very existence.

*

Panting and drenched in sweat, Dajah immediately left his bed. He pulled the curtains wide open to bathe in the soft light of morning. The sun burned away what remained of the nightmare, but the feelings weren't quick to subside. Any bittersweet joy he felt in reconnecting with Zayan was consumed by a terrible reality. He couldn't escape it any more than he could deny his own nature. Like most dreams, this nightmare was a memory he'd forgotten until now. Something the *Sa'Nar* revealed to him.

In that instant, a truth manifested. He knew it with every fiber of his being:

Queen was right. She wasn't the biggest threat to the planet.

And she might have been the only thing keeping it at bay.

THE END

If you enjoyed *The Assassin's Weapon*, please consider leaving a review on Amazon.com, Barnes & Noble, Goodreads, or wherever you purchased the novel.

Dajah and Kiera's story continues in Book 2 of the Sa'Nar Chronicles: *The Three-Fold Door.*

ABOUT THE AUTHOR

Nic M DiSalvo believes she's really here to save the world in her own unique way. When she's not working with animals in her *other* professional career, Nic might be found devouring the newest mind adventure, replaying a favorite video game, cosplaying at a local convention, or driving into storms to get that perfect lightning shot. She lives in Philadelphia with her four-legged fur child, Apollo, and a few tanks of fish.

Keep in touch!
www.nicmdisalvo.com

The following pages represent a WORK IN PROGRESS for Book 2
of the Sa'Nar Chronicles: *The Three-Fold Door*. The final version
may differ slightly or significantly.

PROLOGUE

Balam waited for the old man to finish his tirade. Any common oracle or psychic could predict a future point in time. Orchestrating a specific outcome to manifestation required true mastery, and few appreciated all the nuances required to accomplish such a feat.

"The Breath comes," Carrigan stressed. "I delivered that Anodorian as requested *months* ago. What have you delivered besides empty promises?"

The Lord Commander epitomized zealotry at its finest, but Balam didn't fault him for it. They had a mutual interest. The problem was that the future wanted to veer from their goals and required Balam to take delicate steps. Play the long game.

His supporters grew restless.

"You've trusted me this far," Balam said. "The game's in play, but free will is a fickle thing."

"Your Door will never open without ours."

In that, Carrigan was correct. All the research over countless centuries confirmed the order – Novusia's Door *had* to be opened first. Due to their natures, Balam and Carrigan were bound to their respective realms, and that added layers of complication.

Leaning back, Balam admired the shimmering oval hovering above his summoning basin. Unlike the Sacred Portals that allowed physical passage to those Unbound, this merely facilitated communication.

"You've waited how many centuries for this?" Balam posed. "What's a handful of weeks?"

"All I have is your word. That's hardly reassuring."

"As I said, the game's in play. Small moves. She'll be yours soon enough."

"And you're positive she's the one?"

"I will be."

"That's entirely too cryptic, demon."

"Yet you'll have to make do with it. The future calls, Carrigan. Until next time." Balam ran his fingers through the magic-infused blood pool, scattering the shimmer and closing the connection before the Lord Commander got in a last complaint.

"Sir, they're here," his servant informed.

"I'll see them in the courtyard."

Four men and one woman ignored the refreshments set for their welcome. Instead, they paced and fidgeted, pretending to study the archways or the octagonal Moroccan fountain in the center of his courtyard.

Balam made his appearance, styled in modern nobleman's finest with his curved jeweled dagger sheathed to his left hip. More ceremonial than functional, he knew the dagger would draw the woman's eye – she'd acquired it for him after all.

"Veronica Mayfair," he said, greeting her with a dip of his head. "Good to see you again, though your condition concerns me."

Psychic malady cloaked Veronica's form like a personal raincloud, dampening her spirit's brightness. Those with Sight could see it clearly, even when she held her head high and appeared vibrant and thriving in the flesh.

"Peter Rameriz," she said, addressing him by his current name, "thank you for seeing us."

"I understand you've contracted a particular ailment and need my expertise."

"More like a piece in your collection, but yes."

"Let's not stand on ceremony. Be frank, woman. If I'm not too out of practice, I'd say your condition is time-sensitive."

Veronica nodded. "I've been told there are only two ways to

break this curse. One requires an artifact in your collection. The other requires you."

Balam laughed. "I haven't broken curses in a very long time. It's why I hire people like you – to do the work for me."

"But you do know how to counter what's wrong with me."

Veronica held her ground, confident in her statement. The dark-haired man standing behind her looked angry. If Balam studied him closer, concern for Veronica's well-being shone above everything else. This was a desperate man. A man who'd do anything for the woman he cared for, even betray his own flesh and blood.

"I do," Balam admitted. "I have the means to do so in this very estate, but it will cost you."

"What do you want?" the man asked. His companions shot him a glare in unison. He opted to study the floor in silence after that.

"The Abraxis Stone. Lift the curse, deliver it to me, and I'll remove the one plaguing you."

"Not an easy task," Veronica said. "The Stone's been lost for centuries."

"Actually, it's been found. I know the woman who has it. We have an arrangement in place."

"Peter, I'm short on time. What guarantees do I have?"

They always wanted guarantees. Reassurances. Veronica was no different from Carrigan. Neither truly understood how important a man's word was. Or at least, how important it used to be.

"I will work a temporary spell to stall the curse. It'll buy you the time required to secure the Abraxis Stone. Once delivered, curse-free, I'll solidify the spell for permanence. It's a fair trade." He knew she'd agree to it, and even if she didn't, her partner would do it behind her back.

Balam nudged the present towards his predestined future.

"You have a deal," Veronica said. She stepped forward and held out her hand.

<u>PART I</u>

CHAPTER 1

Julius Matthews and Sasha Bekarda watched Kiera sink into radioactive quicksand. The more she struggled, the faster rippling, translucent sands consumed her. Something writhed and churned beneath the surface. Intensifying pressure exceeded the ability of her lungs to expand. Tentacle-like appendages breached the surface. She screamed out all her remaining air and bolted upright in bed.

With one hand on her chest, her heart beat a frantic rhythm until controlled breaths slowed the flood of adrenaline.

The waning crescent moon revealed a quiet bedroom, save for the patter of a passing shower against the window. Kiera's enemies existed now only in nightmares, and it'd been weeks since she'd had one this vivid.

Dajah, on the other hand, woke drenched in sweat three nights out of seven. For him, the nightmare was the same – not Queen, not Caerus, not anything related to his questionable upbringing, but a door he claims he saw in the Stream pool beneath Queen's throne room.

Her heartbeat slowed to an acceptable rhythm. She turned to study the man beside her and was plunged right back into a nightmare. The bed was empty.

"Dajah?" she called, knowing there were plausible explanations. *It's too quiet.*

Kiera grabbed the SIG Sauer beneath her pillow and left the bed. Rain intensified as storm clouds moved in. Their front door was left ajar, the condo devoid of other occupants.

Where the hell are you, Dajah?

Gifted courtesy of Matthias and Taron, their unit was one of thirty in a ten-story high-rise. The door across from them was broken into. Worse, traces of blood led from one unit to the next, ending at the stairwell.

Kiera cocked back her P220 out of habit, ensuring the chamber was loaded. She approached the first unit and nudged the door open with her foot. "Hello? Anyone in here?"

Thunder struck in the distance. Traces of fresh blood led to the bedroom and a mutilated corpse.

A family lived in the second unit – two teenage boys and their mother. One of the boys was on his way to the kitchen when he was attacked. Overturned furniture told the story of the struggle.

"Your brother came out to see what all the noise was about. He didn't stand a chance," Kiera said to the next body. "And your mom?"

The woman was in the threshold of the bedroom with a charred hole through the center of her chest.

"Queen's dead. These bodies were bled out."

Cursing, Kiera sprinted back to their unit. She donned a pair of jeans beneath her oversized sleep shirt, swiped the cell from her dresser, and stepped into a pair of boots. The phone was ringing as soon as she reentered the hall.

Stefanie de'Llewellyn picked up. "Kiera? It's not even four a.m. What's wrong?"

"Dajah finally lost his shit," she growled, following the blood trail. "I woke up and he was gone. The other condos were broken into. Bodies attacked carelessly."

"Listen carefully," Steffi said.

She found him before long, pinning some homeless man to the concrete. The struggle ceased when clenched, gnarled fingers relaxed in death. Dajah had his face buried in the man's neck but froze with her next step. He twisted like some feral beast studying its victim, all recognition absent. Green irises glowed in the dim lighting, accenting bloodshot sclera. Crimson ran in rivets down his chin onto already-stained, rain-drenched sleepwear.

He shifted into a crouch.

Kiera raised an eyebrow, squeezing the grip of her handgun.

Dajah snarled and sprinted at her with inhuman speed.

He dropped face-first with a Drowse spell. Apparently, a blood-sick, half-vampire, alien Weapon forgot every ounce of training he once drilled into her. Neither of them ever took off their Earth Beads.

She shot him in the shoulder for good measure, watching the wound heal before her eyes. So she kicked him in the side. Twice. "Idiot!"

The last thing they needed was to draw unwanted attention. OPASA's influence was thirteen hundred miles away, but Caerus operated worldwide. Kiera knew Sasha Bekarda would send a team the instant she got word they survived Antarctica.

This little stunt's gonna cost us.

◈

It was an adrenaline-laced roller coaster. The stirrings had woken him with an intense, burning *thirst*. Dajah was careful not to disturb Kiera on his way to the kitchen. Somewhere between the bedroom and the hallway, he was standing in their neighbor's condo. Next thing he knew, the man beneath him went still.

Death had an unfortunate way of stopping the heart and collapsing the circulatory system. When that happened, blood no longer coursed freely through one's veins. Obtaining it became difficult. Patience waned. More than that, the blood of the living held a vitality that satisfied far beyond what bags of refrigerated crimson offered. Once Death claimed Dajah's meal, he was left wholly unsatisfied.

So he found his next victim.

And the next.

And the next.

Until everything stopped.

The sting across his cheek caused his own blood to heat. Breathing deep, he picked up the scent of another and expected the *need* to return, but his blood lust was sated.

"I know you're awake!" Kiera smacked him again.

Dajah opened his eyes and focused on the woman crouched before him. All blissful, intoxicated satisfaction fled and habitual training kicked in: Cool steal against his wrists. The dull soreness of arms twisted back behind something and held for too long. Motor oil and asphalt. Stale air.

"Look at me, Dajah." Her eyes fumed controlled anger. "How long?"

"How long *what*?" he countered.

An open hand met his cheek hard enough to jerk his head sideways. He took a slow breath to cool rising adrenaline, reminding himself that this was Kiera and not some enemy pressing her luck. Rage simmered beneath the surface at the insult.

"How long since the last time you drank?"

Dajah didn't look at her, opting to focus on a crack splintering the ground. Steffi's instructions encouraged him to drink a few ounces of bagged blood daily to minimize cravings and prevent 'unfortunate side effects.' No one really knew how his body would react to the transformation over time. He didn't experience anything he thought of as a disadvantage. If his senses were heightened permanently, it was only by subtle degrees. The same could be said for strength, speed, maybe even his ability to heal, but he had zero opportunities to test it.

He'd followed Steffi's instructions for weeks. After he and Kiera moved out on their own, and Taron's hawk eyes weren't watching his every move, Dajah figured he could lighten up on the crimson cocktails.

Kiera waited for an answer, open hand curling into a fist.

"Ten days," he said, bracing for the backhand. Instead, she stood up and started pacing. Static punctuated the air.

"Damn it, Dajah! I get it. You weren't given a choice. You don't like having to depend on anything, but this was the price for your life. Part of you can't survive without blood. When you try to go too long without it, shit like *this* happens!"

He didn't fully agree, but now wasn't the time to voice such things.

"Do you have any idea what you did? How many people you just killed, or the mess I had to contain?"

The disconcerting reality was that he didn't. He couldn't recall everything that happened, just snippets here and there. All he remembered was how it *felt*.

She stopped pacing and folded her arms across her chest. "You're trading one form of control for another when you don't feed your vampire cells routinely. You didn't like it when Queen controlled you. Are you going to let Steffi's virus do the same?"

Her words stung worse than anything she could have done with her hands. Dajah lifted his gaze, meeting her eyes. "It was stupid, but I can't keep living like this. Drink daily. Don't wander off too far. Did you eat food? How are you feeling?" He snorted. "It's like I'm right back on Caerus's island having to take those damn injections. I didn't have the cravings, Kiera. I wasn't even sure those little sips were doing anything."

"You didn't think you needed them," she said.

Frustration left his lips in a sigh. Kiera and the others meant well, but they were taking his recovery too far. He was *already* recovered from Antarctica.

Was this what Zayan felt like at the end? Like everyone else was just waiting around for him to fail?

It was a foolish thought. Dajah was never so weak or debilitated that he couldn't feed or dress himself. Still, he could imagine the toll it took on Taron to see him so close to death after Queen. Kiera never treated him like an invalid, but she did adhere to Steffi and Taron's warnings.

Giving in to whatever sympathy sparked her emotions this time, Kiera crouched in front of him and took his face in her hands. "We'll figure something out, ok? At least we know how long you can go without a drop. It gives me an idea that might help."

Dajah forced a smile, trying to convince himself that she didn't look at him the same way everyone used to look at Zayan. "What?"

"You'll just have to trust me. We're leaving this place for a while."

9798989073207